He reached out and gently traced his fingertip over the slant of her cheekbone. Her skin was as smooth as cream and he had no doubt it would taste just as rich.

His throat tightened as the urge to kiss her, make love to her, began to tie his muscles into knots. "No. That's not what I want to do, Bella. But then you already know what you're doing to me. I imagine that makes you feel pretty damn good, doesn't it? Knowing you can make a big man like me weak in the knees."

Her eyes narrowed and then her head shook back and forth. "Why would you think such a thing? I have no desire to wield power over you. Or anyone else, for that matter. That's one of the reasons I like being a lawyer. Because I believe everyone should be on equal ground."

"Well, in my case—"

"In your case, Noah, you're thinking too much. Worrying too much. Why can't you simply let yourself feel?"

"Because I'm feeling things that aren't good for me."

HOME ON THE RANCH:

A NEVADA COWBOY'S HONOR

———— �֎ ————

USA TODAY Bestselling Author
STELLA BAGWELL

New York Times Bestselling Author
CATHY McDAVID

Previously published as *Her Rugged Rancher* and
The Rancher's Homecoming

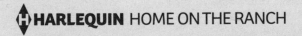

HARLEQUIN HOME ON THE RANCH

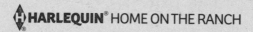

HARLEQUIN® HOME ON THE RANCH

ISBN-13: 978-1-335-00866-4

Recycling programs
for this product may
not exist in your area.

Home on the Ranch:
A Nevada Cowboy's Honor
Copyright © 2020 by Harlequin Books S.A.

Her Rugged Rancher
First published in 2016. This edition published in 2020.
Copyright © 2016 by Stella Bagwell

The Rancher's Homecoming
First published in 2013. This edition published in 2020.
Copyright © 2013 by Cathy McDavid

This edition published by arrangement with Harlequin Books S.A.

For questions and comments about the quality of this book, please contact us at CustomerService@Harlequin.com.

Harlequin Enterprises ULC
22 Adelaide St. West, 40th Floor
Toronto, Ontario M5H 4E3, Canada
www.Harlequin.com

Printed in U.S.A.

CONTENTS

After writing more than eighty books for Harlequin, **Stella Bagwell** still finds it exciting to create new stories and bring her characters to life. She loves all things Western and has been married to her own real cowboy for forty-four years. Living on the south Texas coast, she also enjoys being outdoors and helping her husband care for the horses, cats and dog that call their small ranch home. The couple has one son, who teaches high school mathematics and is also an athletic director. Stella loves hearing from readers. They can contact her at stellabagwell@gmail.com.

Books by Stella Bagwell

Harlequin Special Edition

Men of the West

Christmas on the Silver Horn Ranch
Her Rugged Rancher
His Badge, Her Baby...Their Family?
The Cowboy's Christmas Lullaby
Her Kind of Doctor
The Arizona Lawman
Her Man on Three Rivers Ranch
A Ranger for Christmas
His Texas Runaway
Home to Blue Stallion Ranch

The Fortunes of Texas: The Lost Fortunes

Guarding His Fortune

Montana Mavericks: The Lonelyhearts Ranch

The Little Maverick Matchmaker

Visit the Author Profile page at Harlequin.com for more titles.

HER RUGGED RANCHER

STELLA BAGWELL

To my editor, Gail Chasan, for letting me be me.
With much love and thanks!

Chapter 1

Of all the damned luck!

Noah Crawford muttered the words under his breath as he rounded a curve of the narrow dirt road and spotted a slender young woman with long dark hair walking in the same direction he was traveling. A saddled bay mare followed close on her heels.

He jammed on the brakes and dust billowed as the truck and trailer came to a jarring halt. Up ahead, the woman quickly took herself and the horse off to the side, then with a hand shading her eyes, turned to see who'd made the untimely stop behind her.

Bella Sundell.

Her name shivered through him like an unwanted blast of cold wind. Hell's bells, what was she doing out riding in the middle of the afternoon? Why wasn't she in Carson City, practicing law with her brother?

He'd worked on this Nevada ranch for seven years and during that time he'd never seen this woman on horseback. Nor had he spoken more than two dozen words to her. In fact, he often went out of his way to steer clear of her.

Too bad there wasn't some way to dodge her now, he thought, as he snatched up his gloves and climbed out of the truck. But she was his boss's sister. Besides, he wouldn't ignore anyone who needed help.

Striding across the hard packed dirt, he called out to her, "What's wrong?"

"Thanks for stopping, Noah." She pointed to the horse's front right foot. "She slipped on a rock and jerked a shoe loose when we were riding in the canyon. I thought I'd better lead her the rest of the way home. I didn't want to take the chance of damaging her hoof."

Trying to look anywhere other than her lovely, smiling face, he sidled up to the mare, then bent over to examine her foot.

"Riding in the canyon," he remarked. "That's a little risky for a woman alone, don't you think?"

Silence followed his question, but that hardly surprised Noah. She didn't have to answer to him. He was just the ranch foreman of the J Bar S, hardly her keeper.

Reaching into the front pocket of his jeans, he pulled out a Leatherman tool and quickly went to work jerking out the remaining nails of the loose shoe.

Behind him, he could hear Bella clearing her throat. "In case you hadn't noticed, it's the middle of May and the weather is already hot. It's shady and cooler down in the canyon. Especially along the creek bed."

"It might be cooler," he reasoned. "But it's rough

terrain and a fair distance from home. Anything could happen to you."

"Anything could happen to me right here on the road," she politely pointed out. "A cowboy not watching where he's driving could run over me and Mary Mae."

Like him? To argue the point with her would only end up making Noah look like a fool. A lawyer's job was to give advice, not take it. And this one was clearly no exception.

Turning his attention to the loose shoe, he levered off the piece of iron, then lowered the mare's foot back to the ground.

"Hang on, girl," he spoke softly to the horse. "We'll get you fixed."

After giving Mary Mae an affectionate pat on the shoulder, he forced himself to turn and look directly at Bella. The result was a familiar wham to his gut. The first time he'd met this woman, he'd been bowled over by her appearance. Creamy skin, long hair just shy of being black, warm brown eyes and soft expressive lips all came together to make one hell of a sexy woman. So much of a woman, in fact, that the passing years hadn't dimmed his reaction to her.

"When we get to your place I'll see about putting her shoe back on." He gestured to his truck and trailer. "Climb in. I'll get the mare loaded."

She hesitated and he realized she must have sensed his reluctance to become involved in her problem. Even though, to Noah, the loose shoe was a reasonably small problem. Bella was the big one.

"I'm sorry to put you out like this, Noah. If you're in the middle of doing something I can walk Mary Mae on home. It's not all that far."

"She doesn't need to keep walking on that bare foot. And I'm not in the middle of anything, except helping you," he said curtly.

Not waiting for her permission, he snatched up the mare's reins and led the animal to the back of the long stock trailer. Once he had the mare loaded, he returned to the cab to find Bella already seated on the passenger side.

Climbing behind the wheel, he fastened his seat belt and started the engine. "Better buckle your seat belt."

She rolled her eyes at him. "Are you kidding? Here on the ranch?"

He slanted a glance in her direction, but the brief look was enough to take in her lush curves hidden beneath a pair of tight-fitting jeans and a white shirt left unbuttoned to a tempting spot between her breasts.

He let out a long breath. "That's right. Anything—"

"Can happen," she finished for him. "You've already said that. Is that your motto or something?"

Noah shoved the truck into gear. "If we had a wreck before we got to your place, you might be inclined to sue me for damages. With you being a lawyer and all," he added dryly.

The sound she made was something between a laugh and a groan. "Jett's a lawyer, too. Are you worried he might sue you if you ruin a piece of equipment or lose a calf?"

"No. Just making a point. It's better to be safe than sorry."

When Noah had first come to work on the J Bar S, Bella had been living up in Reno with her husband. But the marriage had fallen apart and Jett had convinced her to move in with him here on the ranch. She'd been work-

ing as a paralegal, but that job apparently hadn't been
enough to suit her. In the past few years, she'd gone on
to finish her education and pass the bar exam. Now she
shared an office with her brother, Jett, in downtown
Carson City. He could say one thing for the woman,
she certainly didn't lack ambition.

"Okay. To make you happy." Shrugging, she stretched
the belt across her shoulder and locked it in place.

Noah let out a silent groan. He wouldn't be happy
until he was finished with this woman and out of her
sight. Just being this close to her bothered the hell right
out of him.

"You're probably wondering what I'm doing out riding instead of practicing law," she said.

Was he that transparent? "It's none of my business."

She went on as though she hadn't heard his curt
reply, "It's all Jett's doing. He urged me to take the day
off and go shopping." She let out a dreary little laugh.
"He thinks I've gone to Reno to buy dresses. I decided
I'd rather go riding."

She probably had five or six closets stuffed with
dresses and all the other fancy things a woman like
her considered necessary. Noah figured she spent more
money on one dress than his whole month's salary. But
that was none of his business, either.

"I see."

She turned a curious glance on him. "Do you? I
doubt it. Jett has this silly notion I'm sad because my
old boss got married last weekend. He thinks I need
to get out and get my mind off Curtis. Ridiculous. I'm
not sad. And I never had my mind on Curtis in the first
place. Not like that."

So what man do you have your mind on now, Bella?

The question was so heavy on Noah's tongue it was a struggle to bite it back. Hearing about her personal life was the last thing Noah needed or wanted. Of all the women he'd encountered since he'd left Arizona, she was the only one he'd ever given a second thought about. And though Jett sometimes casually mentioned his sister in conversation, Noah had never used the opportunity to ask his boss anything directly about Bella. No, Noah had learned the hard way that it was best to keep his distance from women and his thoughts to himself.

She said, "I suppose you never just ride for the fun of it. Your job forces you to spend a lot of time in the saddle."

His job was his fun, he thought. It was his whole life. With his eyes fixed on the narrow road, he asked, "Do you ride often?"

"Every chance I get. That's why I begged Jett to let me keep Mary Mae and Casper at my place instead of stalling them back at the ranch. Whenever I get the urge, I can saddle up and ride without having to drive back to the ranch yard."

Four years ago, Noah had been the only man working for Jett on the J Bar S. At that time his boss had owned only a small herd of cows, and a few using horses. But then Jett had met and married Sassy Calhoun and everything had changed. The couple had immediately started adding to the herd and purchasing adjoining land to support more livestock. In a matter of a few short months, the ranch had quickly grown to be too much for Noah and Jett to handle themselves. Especially with Jett still working as the Calhoun family lawyer and doing part-time private practice in town. Since then, five more ranch hands had been hired and Noah had been elevated to the position of ranch foreman.

"Yeah, Jett asked me about taking the two horses out of the working remuda. I told him we could manage without them."

From the corner of his eye, he could see her head turn to look at him and the smile on her lips struck a spot so deep inside Noah, he hardly knew what had hit him.

"Hmm. When I first came to live with Jett, he only owned two horses. My, how things have changed," she said with wry fondness. "Now he has a whole string of horses, herds of cattle, and a wife and three kids."

When Bella had moved into the J Bar S ranch house with Jett, her brother had been single and trying to recuperate from a failed marriage of his own. The situation had worked well for the siblings until Jett had married Sassy and started a family. After the third baby arrived last year, Bella had decided her brother and his family needed their privacy. She'd had her own house built about a half mile from the main ranch house and almost within shouting distance of Noah's place. A fact that he tried to forget, but couldn't.

"Things around here have been growing all right," he finally replied.

The road grew steeper as it wound up the side of the mesa. Noah shifted the truck into its lowest gear and the motor growled as it climbed the switchback curves. Behind them, the trailer gently rocked as the mare braced her legs for the rocky ride.

When the vehicle finally crested the last rise, the land flattened and they entered a deep forest of ponderosa pine. After traveling a hundred yards under the thick canopy of evergreens, they reached the turn off to Bella's house.

A graveled drive circled in front of a two-story structure made of rough cedar and native rock, shaded by more pines. Since she lived alone, Noah had often wondered why she'd wanted so much space. To fill it with a bunch of kids, or was the huge structure just to impress her friends?

Pushing away both annoying questions, Noah parked the truck and trailer in a favorable spot to unload the mare, then killed the engine. "I'll fix Mary Mae's shoe and unsaddle her for you. Do you keep her stalled at the barn?"

She pushed aside the seat belt and reached for the door handle. "No. I have a little paddock fenced off for her and Casper. I'll show you."

He opened his mouth to assure her that he could handle the task alone, but before he could utter a word, she was already climbing out of the cab.

Cursing to himself, he left the truck and quickly strode to the back of the trailer. Bella was already there, shoving up the latch on the trailer gate.

Instinctively, he stepped next to her and brushed her hands aside. "That thing is heavy. Let me do it."

Thankfully, she moved back a few steps and allowed him to finish the task. But even that wasn't enough space to give Noah normal breathing room. Something about Bella made him forget who he was and why he'd turned his back on having a woman in his life. That was reason enough for him to get Mary Mae fixed as fast as he could and get the hell out of here before he started staring at her like a moonstruck teenager.

She stood watching, her hands resting on her hips.

"Just because my job requires sitting at a desk doesn't mean I'm helpless and weak. I have muscles and I know how to use them, too."

"You can use them when I'm not around." He let the trailer gate swing open and immediately the mare backed up until she was standing safely on solid ground.

Bella immediately snatched a hold on Mary Mae's reins and Noah realized she had every intention of hanging around until this job was finished. So much for losing her company, he thought hopelessly.

"Do you have tools with you to deal with her shoe?" she asked.

"I have tools. Just not a big assortment of shoe sizes. This one I just took off still looks pretty straight. I can reset it," he told her.

"I didn't realize you were a blacksmith."

His gaze fixed safely on the mare, he said, "I'm not."

"What are you then, a farrier?"

"No. Just a guy who's taken care of horses for a long, long time. But if you'd feel better about waiting on a real farrier to fix Mary Mae, that's fine with me. He'll be coming by the ranch in a couple of weeks to deal with the remuda."

She didn't answer immediately and Noah glanced around to see she was looking at him with surprise. "Why would you think I'd want to wait?" she asked. "I don't want her going without a shoe for that long. Besides, I trust you."

She said the words so easily, as though she didn't have to think about them, as though she considered Noah worthy of handling any task she could throw his way. The idea caused a spot in the middle of his chest to go as soft as gooey chocolate.

"I'll get my things." He gestured to a flat piece of ground a few feet away. "If you'd like, you can take her over there in the shade of that pine."

Because he'd been helping the other ranch hands brand calves today, his shirt was still soaked with sweat while his caramel-colored chinks and blue jeans were marked with dirt and manure. No doubt he stunk to high heaven, but there was nothing he could do about sparing her the unpleasant odor. Except keep his distance. Something he'd do even if he smelled as fresh as a piece of sweet sage.

Beneath the cool shade of the pine, Bella stood near Mary Mae's head, keeping a steady hold on the reins, while her gaze remained fixed on Noah. With the mare's foot snug between his knees, he was bent over the up-turned hoof, carefully hammering nails into the iron shoe.

While he was totally absorbed with the task, Bella used the opportunity to study his big hands. The backs were browned by the sun and sprinkled with black hair. The fingers were long and strong. Just like him, she couldn't help thinking.

Six years ago when Bella had first come to live on the J Bar S, her brother had introduced her to Noah. At the time, he'd been the only man helping Jett take care of the sprawling ranch. In spite of her being numb from a fresh divorce, she'd found Noah's presence striking and unforgettable. But even then it had been obvious he wasn't a sociable man. He'd said little more than hello to her that day and since then she could count on one hand the times he'd spoken to her. Until today.

A few minutes ago, when he'd stopped along the road

to check on her, she'd been totally surprised. Not that he was the type of man who'd ever say no to a woman in need of a helping hand. But this morning Jett had told her the men would be branding calves on the far side of the ranch today. She'd not expected to see Noah or any of the ranch hands on this section of the property.

The fact that Noah had been the one to happen by secretly pleased her. Of all the men Bella had encountered since her divorce, he'd been the only one who'd intrigued her. And to be totally honest with herself, he was the only one who'd turned her thoughts to the bedroom. She realized part of the reason for having such a sensual reaction to the man was his strong, sexy appearance. Yet he was also elusive, full of secrets and determined to keep his distance from her. Just the sort of man a woman liked to undress.

Funny, she thought, how Jett had believed she was besotted with Curtis, the lawyer she'd worked with for a few years before she'd passed the bar exam. True, she'd liked Curtis and admired his skills in the courtroom. And more than likely she would've gone on a date with him, if he'd ever felt inclined to ask. But he'd not asked and in the end, she'd been okay with that.

As for Noah, she'd never tried to catch his attention. He clearly didn't want to be her friend, or anything else. And she wasn't one to push herself on anyone. Besides, Jett had told her long ago that Noah was a very private man, who enjoyed the company of a horse far more than that of a human. There'd been many times she'd felt like that herself.

Pulling her thoughts back to the moment, Bella saw he was working quickly to snip off the excess ends of the nails he'd driven through the shoe and were now protruding through the outer wall of the mare's hoof. Using a big steel file, he smoothed away the residual bumps, then placed Mary Mae's foot back on the ground.

"All finished." He straightened to his full height and turned to face her. "The shoe should stay in place for a couple more weeks or so. By then she'll need four new ones anyway."

Bella nodded that she understood. "I'll make sure Jett sends the farrier up here to take care of her and Casper." She gestured toward the barn located several yards beyond the house. "I don't think you've seen my barn. After we get Mary Mae unsaddled I'll show you around."

As she waited for him to make some sort of reply, she lowered her lashes and slowly studied his face. For years a black beard had been a trademark of his appearance, but last spring Jett had commented about Noah shaving off his beard. A few days later, as she'd driven by the ranch yard, she happened to spot him from a distance. The change in his appearance had been dramatic, to say the least. And now that Bella could see him up close, she could admit she was mesmerized.

Noah was not a handsome man. Not by conventional standards, anyway. His craggy features were set in a wide, square-jawed face with a nose that was too big, and sun-browned skin that resembled the texture of a graveled road. Yet there was something about his dark blue eyes and strong quiet presence that oozed sexuality. And right now it was seeping out of his tough work clothes and going straight to her brain. But he clearly wasn't getting the same vibe from her. The taut look of discomfiture on his features said he wanted to excuse himself and run for the hills.

After a long stretch of awkward silence, he finally said, "Let's go."

With the mare following close behind her, Bella started toward the barn. The evening sun was beginning to wane and the air had cooled somewhat. The breeze whistling through the branches of the pines felt good against her face, but it couldn't do anything about the heat that Noah's presence was stirring up inside her.

Bella, you're a fool for having erotic thoughts about Noah Crawford. He's a loner. For all these years he's been content to live in a line-shack. He doesn't want a conventional life. And he especially isn't looking for a woman who wants a family of her own.

Disgusted at the nagging voice sounding off in her head, she mentally swatted it away and glanced over at the object of her thoughts.

"I imagine Jett told you that he tried to talk me out of building the barn."

"He mentioned it."

"Hmm. I'll bet he's done more than mention it," she said with a short laugh. "But as you can see, I don't always take my brother's advice. I wanted a place to keep my horses or whatever animals I might take a notion to get."

"What other kind of animals would you want?"

The doubtful tone of his voice didn't surprise her. People had all sorts of strange ideas about lawyers. He was probably thinking she considered herself above doing barnyard chores. Or maybe he thought the only things she knew about were depositions and plea deals.

"Oh, I think I'd like to have a few goats. I love the

milk Sassy gets from her little herd. And I want to keep a few yearling colts around. Just for the fun of teaching them about being haltered and saddled—you know, basic training stuff."

"You know about dealing with yearlings?"

There was more disbelief in his voice and Bella refrained from shooting him an exasperated look. Except for what he probably heard through Jett, this man couldn't know much about her.

"Noah, I'm thirty-two years old. I know a little more than filing my nails and curling my hair. I've been around horses all my life. One of my best childhood friends lived on a horse ranch. We spent hours watching her father train and sometimes he allowed us to help. It was always fun. Now Sassy has the mustangs and I help her with them whenever my job allows me the free time."

She glanced over to see a stoic expression on his face. Which wasn't surprising. The few times Bella had been in his presence he'd not just kept his words to himself, he'd also hidden his emotions behind a set of stony features.

He said, "You might know the fundamentals, but exposing a yearling to a saddle and bridle is not for the faint of heart. It's dangerous."

"Dear Lord, Noah. The way you talk, simply living is a dangerous task."

"Maybe it is," he muttered.

She wondered what he meant by that, but knew better than to ask. Instead, she remained quiet and thoughtful as they walked the last few yards to the barn. Along the way, she listened to the jingle of his spurs and the faint flap of the leather chinks against his jeans. The sounds were those of a hardworking man and they comforted her in a way she'd never expected. She had no doubt that if he ever had a woman in his life, he'd certainly be able to take care of her, to protect her in all the ways a man could protect a woman.

When they reached the big red barn, Bella opened the double doors, then gestured for Noah to lead Mary Mae inside.

Once they were standing in the middle of a wide alleyway, Noah looked around him with interest. "You must've had the barn built of cinderblock for fire purposes."

"That's right. I'm sure that you know as well as I do that up here on the mesa, water is a scarce commodity. And we probably live at least twenty miles from town and the nearest fire department," she reasoned.

"I didn't realize the barn was this big," he remarked. "From the road it looks smaller."

"Jett says I went overboard. But I wanted plenty of room." She pointed to a hitching rail made of cedar posts. Beyond it was a room with a closed door. "There's the tack room. Let's take Mary Mae to the hitching post to unsaddle her."

At the hitching rail, he gave the mare's reins a wrap around the post and proceeded to loosen the back girth on the saddle. While he worked, Bella decided to talk more about the barn. Hopefully, the subject would distract her from the sight of Noah and the way his broad shoulders flexed beneath the blue chambray shirt.

"Besides the tack room, there's six horse stalls and a feed room," she said, while thinking she sounded more like a real estate agent than a woman trying to make

conversation with a sullen man. "The loft has plenty of
space for several tons of hay, too."

"Very nice," he said.

Did he really think so? Or did he think she was just a
girl with too much money to spend on things she knew
nothing about?

The answers to those questions hardly mattered, she
thought. She might have erotic fantasies about Noah, but
he'd never be anything more than a ranch employee to
her. After six years of ignoring her, he'd made it fairly
clear he wasn't interested.

"Thanks. I'm proud of it."

It took only a few moments for him to finish unsad-
dling the mare. While he stored the tack and saddle
away, Bella grabbed a lead rope and looped it around
Mary Mae's neck.

"There's no need to put a halter on her. She'll lead
like this," Bella explained. "Come along and after we
put her out to pasture you can join me for coffee."

Even though she didn't glance his way, she could
feel his eyes boring a hole in her back. As though she'd
invited him into her bedroom instead of her kitchen.

"Uh, thanks, Ms. Sundell, but I'd better be getting
on home."

Impatient now, she said, "My name isn't Ms. Sundell
to you. It's Bella and furthermore, you know it. As for
you getting home, you live not more than five minutes
away. And there's still an hour or more before sundown.
What's your hurry?"

Not waiting to see if he was going to follow, Bella
headed down the alleyway until she reached the opposite end of the barn. There, she opened a smaller side
door and urged the mare through it.

Once the three of them were outside, walking beneath the shade of the pines, he answered her question, "I have a busy day scheduled tomorrow. I need to rest."

A loud laugh burst out of her and from the corner of her eye, she could see the sound had put a tight grimace on his face.

"Rest? Right now I imagine you could wrestle a steer to the ground and not even lose your breath. You need to come up with a more believable excuse than that."

He moved forward so that he was on the right side of the mare's neck and a few steps away from Bella. "Okay," he said, "here's another reason for you. I'm nasty and sweaty. I don't need to be sitting on your furniture."

She laughed again. "It's all washable. Besides, I made a rhubarb pie before I went riding. I'll give you a piece."

"I've never eaten rhubarb."

"Good. You're in for a treat."

"I don't think—"

She interrupted, "It would be impolite for you to refuse my invitation. Besides, the pie and coffee will be my payment for the shoe job. Fair enough?"

"I wasn't expecting payment."

No. He seemed like the type of man who didn't expect anything from anybody and it was that cool sort of acceptance that completely frustrated her.

Holding back a sigh, she said, "I realize that."

Bella hardly thought of herself as a femme fatale, but she figured most any single, red-blooded man would be happy to accept her invitation. For the pie, if no other reason. But Noah wasn't like most men. She expected if there was such a thing as a loner, he was the perfect example of one.

A short distance away from the east side of the barn, the pines opened up to create a small meadow. After she turned Mary Mae in the pasture to join Casper, she fastened the gate safely behind her.

"How do you water the horses?" he asked curiously.

"In spite of what I just said about water being scarce, I found a small spring with a small pool not far from here on a ledge of the canyon wall. The horses can access it easily and the pasture fence includes it. I try to check it daily to make sure it hasn't dried up."

"You're fortunate."

Bella knew he was talking about the water supply, but she couldn't help thinking that he was right in so many ways. After her divorce from Marcus, she'd not been able to see much of a future. Oh, she'd not given up on life by any means, but she'd certainly been bitter and disillusioned. Coming to the J Bar S, and living with her brother, had helped her get past the failure of her marriage. She might not have the family she always wanted, but at least she had a home of her own and a blossoming career as a lawyer.

"Believe me, Noah. I realize that every day." She turned toward the house. "Come on. Let's go have a piece of pie and you can tell me whether I can cook or not."

A few moments later, Noah followed Bella across a stone patio filled with lawn furniture and equipped with a fire pit. For entertaining her many friends, he thought. Most of them would probably be business people or folks connected to her law practice. He doubted a simple cowboy like him, who spent his days in the saddle, would be sitting under the shade of the pines, sipping summer cocktails.

They entered a screened-in back porch filled with more furniture and potted plants and then she opened a door that took them directly into a spacious kitchen equipped with stainless-steel appliances and a work island topped with marbled tile.

"Sorry for bringing you in the back way," she said. "But it would've have been silly to walk all the way around to the front door."

It was silly of him to be in the house in the first place, Noah thought grimly. In fact, he felt like a deer tiptoeing into an open meadow. He was just asking for trouble.

"I'm used to entering back doors, Ms.—uh, Bella."

She laughed softly. "Maybe one of these days you'll tell me about some of those back doors you've walked through."

Only if he was drunk or had been injected with sodium pentothal, Noah thought.

"That kind of confession might incriminate me," he said.

Her eyes sparkling, she laughed again and Noah felt the pit of his stomach make a silly little flip. Without even trying, she was the sexiest woman he'd ever met. And her sultry beauty was only a part of the reason. The richness of her voice, the sensual way her body moved, the pleasure of her laugh and glint in her brown eyes all came together to create a walking, talking bombshell.

"You need to remember that information shared between a lawyer and his client is private," she joked, then pointed to a long pine table positioned near a bay window. "Have a seat."

He looked at the table and then down at his hands. "I think I'd better wash my hands first."

Pink color swept over her face. "Oh, I'm sorry, Noah. I haven't really lost my manners. I just wasn't thinking. Follow me and I'll show you where you can wash up."

They left the kitchen through a wide opening, then turned down a hallway. When they reached the second door on their right, she paused and pushed it open to reveal an opulent bathroom.

"There's soap and towels and whatever else you need. Make yourself at home," she told him. "When you're finished you can find me in the kitchen."

"Thanks."

She left him and Noah entered the bathroom. At the gray marble sink, he scrubbed his hands and face with soap and hot water, then reluctantly reached for one of the thick, fluffy hand towels draped over a silver rack. If his hands weren't clean enough, they'd leave traces of dirt and manure on the towel. It would be embarrassing to have Bella discover he'd messed up her fine things.

Hell, Noah, why are you worrying about a damned towel or tracking up the tile? And why should you be feeling like a stallion suddenly led into a fancy sitting room instead of a barn stall? Bella isn't a snob. In fact, she acts as if she likes you. Why don't you take advantage of the fact?

Disgusted by the voice sounding off in his head, Noah hurried out of the bathroom. The sooner he accepted this payment of hers, the sooner he could get out of here and forget all about her and her warm smile and sweet-smelling skin. He could go back to being a saddle tramp. A man without a family and a past he desperately wanted to forget.

Chapter 2

When Noah returned to the kitchen, Bella was standing at the cabinet counter. The moment she heard his footsteps, she glanced over her shoulder and smiled at him.

"I waited about pouring the coffee. It dawned on me that since the day is so warm you might prefer iced tea."

He removed his gray cowboy hat and Bella watched one big hand swipe over the thick waves. His hair was the blue-black color of a crow's wing and just as shiny and she suddenly wondered if a thatch of it grew in the middle of his chest or around his navel. And how it might feel to open his shirt and look for herself.

"The coffee would be good," he told her.

Clearing her throat in an effort to clear her mind, she said, "Great. Well, if you'd like, you can hang your hat over there by the door and I'll bring everything over to the table."

He waited politely until she'd put the refreshments on the table and taken a seat, before he sank onto a bench on the opposite side of the table from her.

Bella cut a generous portion of the pie and served him, then cut a much smaller piece for herself.

"I'd offer to put a dip of ice cream on top, but I'm all out," she told him.

"This is more than fine," he assured her.

Even though he began to consume the pie and drink the coffee, Bella could see he was as taut as a fiddle string. Apparently he was wishing he was anywhere, except here with her. Strangely, the notion intrigued her far more than it bothered her.

From what Jett had told her, he'd often encouraged Noah to find himself a woman, but the man had never made the effort. If Jett knew the reason why his foreman shied away from dating, her brother had never shared it with her. And she'd not asked.

It would look more than obvious if she suddenly started asking Jett personal questions about his foreman. Still, she'd often wished an opportunity would come along for her to get to know more about the rough and rugged cowboy.

Now, out of sheer coincidence, he happened to be sitting across from her, without anyone around to listen in on their conversation. She wanted to make the most of every moment. She wanted to ask him a thousand questions about himself. And yet, she couldn't bring herself to voice even one. She didn't want to come across as a lawyer digging for information, any more than she wanted to appear like a woman on the prowl for a man.

"So how do you like your new house?" he asked.

Encouraged that he was bothering to make conversation, she smiled. "I do like the house. It's comfortable and meets my needs. But I have to be honest, there are times the quietness presses in on me. After living with Jett and Sassy and three young children, the solitude is something that will take time for me to get used to."

"I don't think Jett expected or wanted you to move out of his home."

She shrugged with wry acceptance. "I didn't want to end up being one of those old-maid aunts who got in the way and made a nuisance of herself."

She felt his blue gaze wandering over her face and Bella wondered how it would be if his fingers followed suit. The rough skin of his hands sliding along her skin would stir her senses, all right. Just thinking about it made goose bumps erupt along the backs of her arms.

He said, "I doubt that would've ever happened."

She grunted with amusement. "Which part do you doubt? Me being an old maid? Or getting in the way?"

"Both."

"You're being kind."

"I'm never kind," he said gruffly. "Just realistic."

Yes, she could see that much about him. A practical man, who worried about the dangers of life rather than embracing the joys.

"Well, it's all for the best that I moved up here on the mesa. Sassy and Jett need their privacy. I wouldn't be surprised if they had another child or even two to go with the three they have now."

"Wouldn't surprise me, either."

A stretch of silence followed and while she sipped her coffee, she watched him scrape the last bite of pie from the saucer.

When he put down his fork, she decided she'd better

say something or he was going to jump to his feet and leave. And she didn't want him to do that just yet. Having him sitting here in her kitchen felt good. Too good to have it all end in less than fifteen minutes.

"Jett tells me the calf crop is turning out to be a big one this year," she commented.

"That's right. And Sassy has had some new foals born recently. Have you taken a look at them?"

"No. Unfortunately, I've been tied up with several demanding cases. But I plan to stop by the ranch house soon to see the kids. Maybe she'll drive me out to the west range to see them."

"You like being a lawyer?" he asked.

His question surprised her. She figured he wasn't really interested one way or the other about her personal life. But he'd taken the trouble to ask and that was enough to draw her to him even more.

"Yes, I do like it. That's not to say that I don't get exhausted and frustrated at times. But for the most part, I like helping people deal with their problems."

"Must be nice for you to get to work with your brother. Jett is easy to get along with. Me being here for seven years proves that," he added.

She smiled faintly. "Jett values your work, Noah. If it wasn't for you taking charge of everything I'm not sure he could even have this ranch. Aside from that, he cherishes your friendship."

"Yeah, well, I owe him a lot." Avoiding her gaze, he placed his cup on the table, then scooted the bench back far enough to allow him to rise to his feet. "The pie was delicious, Bella. Thanks. I can now say that I've eaten rhubarb."

Before she could stop herself, she blurted out, "Going already?"

He still didn't look at her. "I have chores at home to deal with."

"Then you probably don't have time for me to show you through the rest of the house?"

"Afraid not."

She tried to hide her disappointment when she spoke again, "We'll save that for next time."

He didn't reply to that and Bella figured he was probably telling himself there would be no next time. She'd never had a man make it so clear that he wanted nothing to do with her. But rather than put her off, it only made her more determined to spend time with him again.

As he gathered his hat from the rack on the wall and levered it onto his head, Bella stood and joined him at the door.

"I'll walk with you out to the truck," she told him.

"No need for that."

There wasn't any need, she thought. But she wasn't going to let him get away that easily. "Don't deny me. It's rare I have company of any kind."

They left the house the way they came in and as they walked toward his waiting truck, he said, "I imagine you have plenty of company, Bella."

She smiled faintly. "What makes you think that?"

"Jett does a lot of entertaining at home. And you two are brother and sister."

"Jett and I are siblings, but we think differently. Besides, most of his entertaining has to do with his law practice or ranching cronies. As for me, I don't normally mix business with my home. I have invited our mother over for a night or two, though. She thinks I need my head examined for building a house up here on the mesa, away from everyone. She'd go crazy from the solitude."

"And you haven't?"

That made her laugh. "Not yet. Of course, my sanity is subject to opinion," she joked.

He didn't smile. But then, she didn't expect him to. She'd never seen a genuine smile on his face.

By now they'd reached the driver's side of the truck. After he'd opened the door and climbed behind the wheel, he glanced at her briefly, then stared straight ahead at the windshield.

"You be careful when you ride in the canyon," he said.

She wanted to believe his warning was out of concern for her safety. Not because he was a bossy male. "I will. And thank you again for your help."

"No problem."

He closed the door and started the engine, leaving Bella with little choice but to step back and out of the way.

"Goodbye," she called to him. "And you don't have to be a stranger, you know. The sky won't fall in if you stop by once in a while and say hello."

He lifted a hand in acknowledgement, then put the truck into gear. Bella remained where she stood and watched the truck follow the circle drive until it disappeared into the dense pine forest.

So much for making an impression on the man, she thought. Noah hadn't even bothered to give her a proper goodbye. But then Noah Crawford wasn't like any man she'd ever met before. And that was darned well why she was determined to see him again.

* * *

Later that night, as Noah sat on the front step of his little cabin, he was still cursing his unfortunate luck of running across Bella. If he'd stayed with the men a half hour longer before heading home, he might have missed her. Or if she'd still been down in the canyon, he would've never known she was there or that her mare had thrown a shoe.

But for some reason, fate had aligned everything just right to put them on the road at the same time. No, fate had situated everything all wrong, he thought dismally. Now he was going to have a hell of a time getting Bella off his mind. After this evening, each time he passed her fancy house, he would think about too many things. How the kitchen had smelled of her baking, the way she'd talked and smiled as they'd sat at the pine table, and last, but hardly least, the way his heart had thudded like the beat of a war drum each time he'd looked at her.

Through the years Noah had worked for Jett, the man had never warned him to steer clear of his sister. Why would he bother? Both of them knew that Bella would never give Noah a serious look, anyway.

No, early on Noah had made his own decision to avoid Bella. Because he'd instinctively understood she was the sort of woman who could cause him plenty of trouble. Certainly not the devastating kind that Camilla had brought him, but enough to cause havoc in his life.

The sky won't fall in if you stop by once in a while and say hello.

Had she truly meant that as an invitation? he wondered. Or had she simply been mouthing a polite gesture?

What does it matter, Noah? Even if she meant it, you

can't strike up a friendship with Bella. Getting cozy with her would be pointless. She's an educated lady, a lawyer with enough smarts to figure out a loser like you.

Shutting his mind to the mocking voice trailing through his head, he watched a small shadow creeping along the edge of the underbrush growing near the left wall of the cabin.

"Jack, if that's you, come out of there."

His order was countered with a loud meow and then a yellow tomcat sauntered out of the shadows and over to Noah. As the cat rubbed against the side of his leg, Noah stroked a hand over his back.

"Ashamed to show your face, aren't you? You've been gone three days. Hanging out somewhere with a girl cat, letting me believe a coyote had gotten you. I ought to disown you," he scolded the animal.

In truth, Noah was happy to have his buddy back. A few years ago, he'd found the yellow kitten all alone, on the side of the highway near the turnoff to the ranch. And though Noah had never owned a small pet before, he'd rescued the kitten and brought him home. Later on, when Jack had grown old enough to be considered an adult, the cat had made it clear to Noah that he was going to be an independent rascal. Whenever he got the urge, Jack would take off, then come home days later, expecting Noah to fuss over him as though nothing had happened.

"But I won't disown you," Noah said to the cat. "And you damned well know it."

Rising from the step, he opened the heavy wooden door leading into the cabin and allowed Jack to rush in ahead of him. Inside, Noah went over to a small set of pine cabinets and retrieved a bowl.

After filling it with canned food, he set it on the floor in a spot Jack considered his dining area. With the cat satisfied, he walked over and sank into a stuffed armchair. To the left of it, a small table held a lamp and a stack of books and magazines. Noah didn't own a television. Something that Jett often nagged him about. But Noah had no desire to stare at a screen, watching things that would bore him silly. Instead, he'd rather use his small amount of time at home to read or listen to music.

Home. Most folks wouldn't call his cabin much of a home. Basically it was a two-room structure, with the back lean-to serving as a bedroom, while the larger front area functioned as a living room and kitchen. The log structure had been erected many years before, when Jett's maternal grandparents, the Whitfields, had owned the property. According to Jett, as the ranch had prospered, his grandfather, Melvin, had needed a line-shack and had built the cabin and its little native rock fireplace with his own hands. After a while, he'd upgraded the dirt floor to wooden planks and built on the extra room at the back. To Bella this cabin would be crude living, but to Noah, the simple space was all he needed. That and his privacy.

He was thumbing through a ranching magazine trying to get his mind on anything other than Bella, when his cell phone broke the silence. As he picked it up, he noted the caller was Jett.

"Did I wake you?" he asked Noah.

Noah rolled his eyes. "I'm not getting so old that I fall asleep in my chair before nine o'clock."

Jett chuckled. "I thought you might be tired after branding today. That's why I'm calling. Just checking to see how everything went."

Jett wasn't one of those bosses that called daily to line out the next day's work. Ever since Noah had taken this job, Jett had been content to let him run things his way and at his own pace. That was just one of the reasons Noah wouldn't want to be anywhere else.

"No problems," he told him. "One more small herd to go—the one over on the western slope and we'll have them all branded. Can't do it tomorrow, though."

"Why not?"

"Used up all the vaccine we had. Me or one of the boys will have to go into town tomorrow for more."

"After I sent Bella home, I ended up being swamped with work today, but I would've found a way to go by the feed store and picked up the vaccine for you," Jett insisted.

"I thought about calling you. But we need a roll of barbed wire and a few more things anyway. Better to get it all at one time."

Besides working on selected days at his law office in town, Jett also acted as the lawyer for the Silver Horn Ranch, a position he'd held for years. Since his wife Sassy was a member of the Calhoun family, who owned and operated the notable ranch, Noah figured Jett would keep the job from now on.

"Well, there's no urgency about the branding. Whenever you and the boys can get to it will be soon enough. I don't plan to sell any of the calf crop on the western slope, anyway. I've given them to Sassy."

It wasn't surprising to hear Jett had given the calves to his wife. The man was always giving or doing something for her. On the other hand, Sassy deserved her husband's generosity. She'd given him three beautiful children, worked hard to make the ranch a success, and most of all she adored him. Jett was a lucky man and he knew it.

"I—uh, ran across your sister today," Noah said as casually as he could. "She'd gone riding and her mare had thrown a shoe."

"Yes. I spoke with her earlier over the phone. She was very grateful for your help. Thanks for lending her a hand, Noah. You know, she's very independent. I'm surprised she didn't tell you she'd take care of the mare's shoe herself."

Noah rose from the chair and walked over to the open door. If he looked to the southwest, he could see the lights from Bella's house, twinkling faintly through the stand of pines. Now that he'd been inside her home, it was much too easy to picture her there.

"She didn't put up a fuss," he replied.

Had Bella told her brother that she'd invited him inside for pie and coffee? Noah wondered. The memory of his brief visit with her still had the power to redden his face. Looking back on it, Bella had probably thought he was a big lug without enough sense to paste two sentences together. Even now in the quiet of his cabin, he couldn't remember half of what he'd said to her.

"Speaking of fussy, I wish you'd stop being so damn hard to please and try to find yourself a woman," Jett said.

"That isn't going to happen," Noah muttered. "Not ever."

"Never say never, Noah. You don't know what the future holds for you."

"My future damned sure won't have a wife in it!"

His outburst was met with a moment of silence, then

Jett said, "Well, I'm glad to hear you're feeling like your old self tonight."

Noah swiped a hand over his face. When he'd first responded to Jett's ad for a ranch hand, he'd expected him to ply him with all sorts of questions. That was the nature of a lawyer, he figured. But the only facts Jett had seemed interested in was whether Noah had experience taking care of cattle and if he was wanted by the law. It wasn't until time had passed and a friendship had developed between the two men that Noah had confided he'd left a bad situation behind him and it had involved a woman. Jett had seemed to understand it was a matter that Noah wanted to keep to himself and he'd never asked him to elaborate. Still, that didn't stop his friend from urging him to find a wife.

A wife. The idea was laughable.

"Why wouldn't I be feeling like my old self?" Noah asked grumpily.

Jett said, "Oh, I don't know. One of these days you might soften up and be a nice guy for a change. Miracles do happen."

Before Noah could think of a retort, Jett went on, "I got to go help Sassy. She's trying to get the kids to bed. If you need me tomorrow, call me."

"Yeah. Good night, Jett."

Ending the conversation, Noah slipped the phone into the pocket of his shirt and stepped back outside. The night air had cooled and the clear sky was decorated with endless stars. A gentle breeze stirred the juniper growing at the corner of the cabin and somewhere in the canyon he could hear a pack of coyotes howling.

Normally he savored soft summer evenings like this.

But tonight he was restless. Being near Bella has stirred up dreams and plans that he'd pushed aside long ago.

This job was all that he wanted and his friendship with Jett was too important to let a woman ruin it, he thought grimly.

I wish you'd...try to find yourself a woman.

Noah's jaw tightened as Jett's remark echoed through his mind. Even if he wanted a wife, it would be impossible for him to find one. Ever since he'd first laid eyes on Bella, he'd not been able to see any other woman but her.

Feeling something move against his leg, he looked down to see Jack sitting on his haunches, peering up at him.

"Yeah, Jack, I know I'm a fool of the worst kind. But you're not in a position to be pointing fingers. You do enough womanizing for the both of us."

The remainder of the week was a busy one for Bella. Between two heated divorce cases, an adoption case, plus a custody trial, she'd hardly had time to eat or sleep. And it didn't help matters that Noah had continued to pop into her mind at her busiest moments, playing havoc with her ability to focus on her work.

Ever since he'd stopped on Tuesday afternoon to help her with Mary Mae, she'd not been able to push the man out of her mind. Now it was Sunday afternoon and as she sat on the back porch listening to the lonesome sound of the wind whistling through the pines, she could only wonder if he was at his cabin and what he might think if she showed up on his doorstep.

You're thinking about him because he's a mystery, Bella. Because he's lived alone in that line-shack for all this time and you don't understand why he's such a recluse. That's the only reason the man is dwelling in your thoughts. That's the only reason you want to see him. Just to satisfy your curiosity.

The mocking voice in her head caused her to sigh with frustration. Maybe Noah's solitary life did intrigue her, yet there was much more about him that played on her senses. If she'd been more like some of her daring girlfriends, she would've already made an effort to try to catch his attention. But she wasn't the type to pursue a man. Besides, how did a woman go about garnering the attention of a man as cool and distant as Noah? If she knew the answer to that she might have tried years ago.

The other day when he'd helped her with Mary Mae, she'd caught quick glimpses of what was hidden behind his blue eyes and rugged face. And those few peeks had been stuck in her mind, tempting her to see him again.

Tired of fighting a mental battle with herself, Bella rose to her feet and hurried into the house. Mr. Noah Crawford might as well get ready for company, she decided, as she stepped out of her skirt and into a pair of riding jeans. Because he was about to have a visitor, whether he wanted it or not.

Less than a half hour later, Bella reined Casper, her gray gelding, to a stop beneath the shade of a tall cottonwood and slipped from the saddle. After she'd secured the get-down rope to a strong limb, she approached the cabin.

Although there were no sounds coming from the log structure, the door was standing wide open, as were the two windows facing the front yard. Not that the space could actually be called a yard, she thought. It was mostly a thick carpet of pine needles with patches of bramble bush and Indian rice growing here and there.

At the doorstep, she shoved her cowboy hat off her head. A stampede string caught at the base of her throat, allowing the headgear to dangle against her back. After running a hand through her hair, she rapped her knuckles against the doorjamb.

"I'm here."

Jerking her head in the direction of his voice, she spotted Noah standing a few feet away at the corner of the cabin. One look at his tall, dark image was enough to push her heartbeat to a fast, erratic thump.

Unconsciously, her hand rested against the uncomfortable flutter in her chest. "Oh, hello, Noah! I didn't see you when I knocked," she said.

"I was at the back of the house," he explained. "I heard you ride up."

Heard her? Casper hadn't neighed or even kicked over a small stone. He must have superhuman hearing, she decided.

"I was out riding and thought I'd stop by to say hello." The explanation for showing up on his doorstep sounded lame, but it was the best she could do. She could hardly tell him she'd purposely invited herself.

His sober expression said he didn't believe a word she'd just said. Yet she found herself smiling at him anyway. Mostly because something about him made her feel good inside.

He said, "At least you're not riding down in the canyon."

She smiled again. "No. But that doesn't mean I've marked that riding trail off my list. It's too beautiful to resist."

He looked different today, Bella realized, as her gaze took in his faded jeans and gray T-shirt. The few times she'd been in Noah's presence, he'd always been dressed for work with long-sleeved shirts, spurs strapped to his high-heeled boots, and a gray felt on his head. She'd never seen his bare arms before and the sight had her practically gawking. She'd not expected them to be so thick and muscled, or his skin to be nut-brown.

"So you're riding the gelding today," he remarked. "Is the mare okay? Any problem with her foot?"

"No problem. I just thought it was Casper's turn to get out for a while."

He didn't say anything to that and Bella figured he was waiting for her to say she needed to mount up and finish her ride. Well, that was too bad. She wasn't going to let him off that easily.

"Uh, am I interrupting anything?" she asked politely.

He hesitated, then said, "I was just putting some meat on the grill. On Sunday I usually make myself an early supper."

"Mmm. I don't suppose you'd have enough for two, would you?"

His brows shot up, but Bella was determined not to feel embarrassed by her forward behavior. It wasn't as if she was asking him to kiss her.

"It's only hamburgers," he said.

"I love burgers. Especially when they're grilled. Are you a good cook?"

"I can't answer that. I'm the only one who ever eats my cooking."

She chuckled. "Then you really need for me to give it a try. I'll give you an honest review."

His attention lifted away from her to settle on Casper. Bella was glad to see the horse already understood he'd reached his destination. His head was bowed in a sleepy doze, his hind foot cocked in a relaxed stance.

Noah said, "Bella, I think "

Bella quickly interrupted, "If you don't have enough food to share, that's fine. A cup of coffee will do me."

He grimaced. "It's not the food. I—"

"Don't like my company?" she asked pointedly.

Dark color swept up his neck while the frown on his face deepened. And watching his reaction, Bella could only wonder if she'd gone crazy. The man clearly didn't want her around. Any sensible woman would proudly lift her chin and walk away. But there was something in his eyes that made her stand her ground. A bleak, desperate look that called to her heart.

He blew out a long breath. "I wasn't expecting you, that's all."

She stepped off the porch and walked over to him. "I apologize for showing up unannounced. But it's a lovely afternoon and I was getting very tired of my own company."

Then why didn't she drive down to her brother's house, where she could find plenty of company? Noah wanted to ask. Why didn't she get on her horse, ride off and leave him alone?

If Noah was smart, he'd do more than ask her those questions. He'd tell her outright that he didn't want her around here messing with his mind, making him feel things he didn't want to feel. But he couldn't bring himself to utter any of those things to her.

Just seeing her again was making his heart thump with foolish pleasure. Hearing her sweet voice was like the trickle of a cool stream to a man lost in the desert.

He couldn't forbid himself those pleasures. Even if they might eventually hurt him.

"Well, it just so happens I have enough food to share." He gestured toward the open door. "If you'd like to go in, I'll see about making another patty for the grill."

"Thanks. I would like."

Noah followed her inside the cabin and moved to one side as she stopped in the middle of the room to glance curiously around her. He could only wonder what she thought about the log walls, low-beamed ceiling and planked floor, much less the simple furnishings. But then, he'd not invited her up here for a visit, he thought. She'd invited herself.

"This is cozy. And so much cooler than outside," she commented, then glanced at the short row of cabinets built into the east wall of the room. "Those are nice. Did you help build them?"

Did she actually believe he might be that talented? The idea very nearly made him smile, but he stopped himself short. What the hell was he doing? He didn't smile at women. He didn't even like them. Not after the hell Camilla had put him through.

"I helped measure and hammer a few nails, but not much more than that. When it comes to carpenter work I can do a few repair jobs, but nothing major."

She said, "I made a little doghouse once with the help of my grandfather. It turned out pretty good, but the darned dog never would get in it. Probably because Grandmother kept letting him in the house."

The main ranch yard of the J Bar S sat just across from Jett's house. While Bella had lived there, Noah had often spotted her going to her car as she left for work in the mornings. And sometimes late in the evening as he'd dealt with barn chores, he'd seen her return. She would always be wearing dresses and high heels and carrying a leather briefcase. With that image fixed in his mind, it was hard enough to accept she was a competent horsewoman, much less imagine her using a hammer and nails.

"Sounds like your grandmother spoiled your project," he said.

"Not really. My cats used it."

He inclined his head in the direction of the windows. "I don't get much sunlight in here. I'll turn on a lamp."

"Don't bother on my account. I can see fine."

Noah wasn't having any trouble seeing, either. Yet he was having a problem deciding if the vision standing in his cabin was real or imagined. Other than Jett and a couple of the other ranch hands, he'd never had visitors up here. And bringing a woman home was definitely off-limits. How Bella had managed to be here was a different matter. But she was here just the same and for now he'd try to deal with the situation as best he could without being rude.

"Have a seat. The couch is a little hard. You might find the chair more comfortable."

"Thanks, but I'll sit later. Let me help you with the hamburger meat. I can make the patty."

She followed him over to the kitchen area and though she stood a few steps away from him, Noah felt completely smothered by her presence.

"I'll do it," he told her. "You're a guest."

Laughing softly, she leaned her hip against the cabinet counter. Noah tried not to notice how her jeans hugged the ample curve of her hips and thighs and the way her blouse draped the thrust of her breasts. And even when he looked away, the image was still so strong in his mind it practically choked him.

"I'm not a guest," she reasoned. "I'm just a neighbor who's intruded on your privacy. But thanks for letting me."

Why did she have to be so nice? Why couldn't she be one of those spoiled, abrasive women that got on everyone's nerves? Why couldn't she be a woman who considered herself too good to come near his cabin, much less enter it? Then he wouldn't be having this problem. He wouldn't be wanting to throw caution to the wind and let himself simply enjoy her company. Instead, she was warm and sweet. And just having her near filled him with a hollow ache.

"Well, I don't normally have company. Uninvited or otherwise," he told her. "So my manners are a little rusty. I'm afraid you'll have to overlook them."

He glanced her way to see she was smiling and for a moment his gaze focused on her dark pink lips and white teeth. That mouth would taste as good as her voice sounded, he imagined.

"Who's worried about manners? You and I are family," she said. "Well, practically. You've been here on the ranch longer than I have. We just never had the opportunity to talk much. When I was still living with Jett, you would stop by, but never say a word to me. I'm glad you're being much nicer today."

He laid a portion of ground meat onto a piece of wax paper and smashed it flat. "A guy like me doesn't have anything interesting to say to a lady like you."

From the corner of his eye he watched her move a

step closer. "Lady? I've not had a man call me that in a long time, Noah. Thank you."

Her voice had taken on a husky note and the sound slipped over him like a warm blanket in the middle of a cold night.

"That's hard to believe, Bella."

She shrugged. "Not really. Men aren't very chivalrous nowadays. At least, not the ones I cross paths with. Maybe that's because of my profession. In the courtroom they see me as an adversary. Not a lady."

"Jett says you worked hard to get your degree. He also says you're good at your job."

"Jett is obviously biased. But I can credit him for getting me in the law profession. When I was growing up, I never dreamed of being a lawyer. But after Marcus and I divorced the course of my life changed. Jett got me interested in being a paralegal and from there I guess you could say I caught the bug to be in the courtroom."

Her gaze fell awkwardly to the floor and it suddenly dawned on Noah that every aspect of this woman's life hadn't been filled with success. She'd endured her own troubles with the opposite sex. And though he'd heard Jett label his ex-brother-in-law as a liar and a cheat, Noah had never questioned the man about Bella's divorce or how it had affected her. It was none of his business. But that didn't stop him from wondering how much she'd really loved the guy.

Or whether she was finally over him.

Chapter 3

Clearing his throat, Noah said, "Excuse me, Bella, but I'd better take this out to the grill. It's probably hot enough to put the burgers on now."

"Sounds good," she told him. "I'll join you."

She followed him out of the cabin and around to the back. Although there were only a few clumps of grass growing here and there over the sloping ground, he kept it neatly mown. For a makeshift patio, he'd put together four flat rocks. On one corner of the space, he'd erected a small charcoal grill atop a folding table.

A few steps away sat a lawn chair made of bent willow limbs and cushioned with a folded horse blanket. Near it lay a huge pine trunk that had fallen long before Noah had ever moved into the cabin. The smooth, weathered log made a playground for squirrels and chipmunks and a seat where he often drank his morning coffee.

While he positioned the patties on the hot grill, Bella ambled a few feet away where the forest opened up to a view of bald desert mountains in the distance.

"Are those mountains on Jett's land?" she asked.

It surprised Noah to hear her call it Jett's land. He'd always suspected that she was a partial owner in the ranch, but apparently he'd supposed wrong.

"No. They look close, but they're at least ten miles away. Why do you ask?"

"Just curious. This is going to sound silly, but there are places on this ranch that I've never seen. Especially since Jett and Sassy bought the adjoining land a few years ago."

"You obviously knew your way to the cabin," he said.

"That's right. My grandparents built the cabin," she told him. "And when I was a little girl, my grandmother and I would come up here in the summer and pick wild berries."

"I met your grandparents back before Christmas, when they came up to see little Mason after he was born. Nice folks."

"Yes. I keep promising to drive down for a little visit with them, but it seems like I can never get that many free days in a row to make the trip to California." She turned and strode back to the shaded area where he was standing. "One of these days I'm going to clear my work schedule and go anyway. My grandparents aren't getting any younger and I want to enjoy them while they're still around."

"Melvin talked to me about the little ranch he owns

now. I'm glad he's still healthy enough to have horses and cattle."

Ignoring the chair, she sank onto the pine truck and crossed her ankles out in front of her. Noah closed the lid on the cooker and took a seat in the lawn chair a few feet away from her.

"Do you have grandparents, Noah?"

He said, "The only grandparents I ever really knew have passed on. Mom's parents were never around, so I have no idea if either of them are still alive or where they might live." The look of surprise in her eyes prompted him to add, "I don't know where she or my dad are, either. They divorced when I was thirteen. After that, Mom left and never came back. Dad stuck around for a few months, then left me to be raised by his parents."

Just as he'd expected, she looked stunned. And that was exactly why he'd revealed that part of his upbringing to her. He wanted to make sure she understood the sort of background he'd come from. That he'd been a child his own parents hadn't wanted and his grandfather had merely tolerated.

"Oh. I didn't know. Jett never mentioned the circumstances of your parents to me."

"That's because I've never talked to Jett about them. Your brother and I mostly talk about the present and the future."

"Yes. Well, Jett has some pretty awful memories of his own that he'd rather leave in the past. Most of us do."

She smiled at him and Noah was surprised to see she was still looking at him as though she liked him, as though he was someone she wanted to spend time with.

He could only think she was either a very bad judge of character, or a very special woman.

The scent of the cooking beef began to fill the air and Noah got up to check on the progress of the burgers.

While he flipped the meat, she asked, "Do you like living here in the cabin? Away from everyone?"

"I'm a simple guy, Bella. I have everything I need or want right here." At least that was what he'd been telling himself since he'd arrived in Nevada. But there were plenty of days Noah still felt the nagging need for a place of his own, and even more nights when he imagined himself with a wife and children to nurture and love. Yet once he'd left Arizona, he'd vowed to live a solitary life and so far, he'd had no trouble sticking to that sensible choice. Whenever he got to feeling like Jack, and the urge to go on the prowl for a woman hit him, all he had to do was think about Camilla. Remembering all the lies she'd told doused his urges even better than a cold shower.

"I guess the cabin seems pretty crude to you," he added.

"I wasn't thinking about the cabin," she told him. "I was wondering if you ever get lonely."

For most of his thirty-five years, Noah had been lonely. As a kid, he'd had buddies in school, but he'd never been able to invite them to his house for a meal or a simple game of catch in the backyard. Not that he would've been embarrassed by the Crawfords' modest home situated on the poor side of the tracks. Most of his friends had been just as impoverished as the Crawford family. No, it had been his parents' violent arguments that had ruined his chance to be a normal kid. And later, well, he'd let himself trust in another human being and ended up learning he couldn't depend on anyone to stick by him. Not even a good friend.

"I don't have time to get lonely," he lied. "Every morning I leave here before daylight and usually don't return until dark. That doesn't leave me much time to pine for company."

It wasn't until he'd put the lid back on the grill and risen to his feet that she said, "It must be nice to be that contented with your own company. I'll be the first to admit I get lonely."

He grimaced. "You should have stayed in your brother's house. With all those kids there's never a dull moment."

She shrugged. "I was getting in the way."

"Jett didn't want you to move out. I don't suspect Sassy did, either."

"Both are too nice to admit they were sick of Aunt Bella being underfoot—" she smiled wanly "—but I figure you probably understand how it feels to be, how should I say, standing on the outside looking in."

Noah had to choke back a mocking groan. She, or anyone else, couldn't possibly know how he'd felt as a child. His parents had barely acknowledged his existence. They'd been too busy trying to tear each other down. And later, his grandfather had only been interested in getting him raised to an age where he could kick him out into the world. Yeah, Noah knew all about being on the outside. But Bella didn't need to know everything about his broken childhood, or the years that had followed before he'd finally settled here on the J Bar S. She'd probably feel sorry for him, and he didn't want that from her, or anyone else.

He sank back into the lawn chair. "I understand, Bella. More than you think."

She sighed. "While I was married and living in Reno I never imagined I'd ever be calling the J Bar S my home. I expected to stay in the city and raise a family with Marcus. Now I've been here nearly six years and Jett is the one with the family. I'm not a mother, but at least I'm a lawyer," she added wryly. "Guess I should be thankful all these years haven't been totally wasted."

So in spite of her ex-husband deceiving and hurting her, she still she wanted a husband and family. He couldn't decide whether she was a glutton for punishment, or a very brave woman.

"Looks to me like you've had a pretty successful life so far," he replied. "A person has to learn to appreciate the blessings they have, instead of always wanting more."

From the corner of his eye he could see her frowning. The expression was much easier to deal with than her smiles. As long as she disapproved of him, the less likely he'd be to lose his senses around her.

"Hmm. You're saying I should be satisfied with what I have?"

He turned his head to look at her. "Well, you have a lot more than most, Bella."

She gazed thoughtfully toward the mountains in the distance. "Yes, probably so. But a woman likes to dream, Noah."

Oh yes, he thought bitterly. Noah knew, firsthand, how a woman could fantasize. Unfortunately, in Camilla's case, her dreams had been twisted and wrapped solely around him. It hadn't mattered to her that Noah and her husband, Ward, had been the best of friends and partners in Verde Canyon Ranch. No, she'd tried to make her dreams come true, no matter the consequences. As a result all three of them had been thrown into a nightmare, one that Noah still couldn't forget.

Giving himself a hard mental shake, he got to his feet. "I'd better check the meat," he told her.

Five minutes later, Noah was carrying a platter of sizzling patties into the cabin with Bella following close behind.

"Too bad you don't have a picnic table of some sort," she remarked. "It would be nice to eat outside."

"If you'd rather eat outside, we can. But it's a nuisance trying to balance everything on your lap."

Bella shook her head. "This is fine. It's just that the weather is almost perfect and I love eating outdoors. We'll do it some other time—at my house."

He didn't say anything to that and Bella figured hell would probably freeze over before she ever got him to visit her house again. But she wasn't going to think about that now. At least she was getting to spend time with the man and he was talking much more than she'd ever expected him to.

He placed the platter of meat on a small round table positioned beneath one of the open windows, then added a tray of prepared vegetables he'd taken from the refrigerator.

"I don't have any tea or soda," he told her, "but I can offer you a beer or water."

"Beer goes perfect with a burger," she told him. "Is there anything I can do to help? If you'll show me where you keep your dishes and silverware I'll set the table."

He slanted a look at her as though he wasn't sure he

wanted her to be milling about in his kitchen, but after a moment he motioned his head toward the cabinets.

"The plates are in the cabinet on the left. The silverware is in the drawer underneath."

While she set the tiny table, he fetched the drinks and a bag of potato chips. Once everything was ready, he surprised her by pulling out one of the scarred wooden chairs and helping her into it.

His nearness stirred her like nothing she could remember and though she told herself she was being foolish, she couldn't seem to slow the erratic beat of her heart or stop the excitement rushing through her.

"Thank you, Noah."

He took his seat across from her and as they began to put their burgers together, Bella asked, "Are you finished with all the branding now?"

"We wound it up yesterday. Now it's time to deal with a bunch of fencing. The men won't like it but that's okay. They can't have fun every day."

Bella smiled as she added salt and pepper to her burger, then pressed everything inside a bun covered with sesame seeds. "Does that mean they consider branding as fun?"

"The lucky ones who get to rope and drag calves to the fire think of it that way. The hands working on the ground might have different ideas. They have the hardest job. That's why after a few hours I make the men change places."

It wasn't surprising to hear Noah tried to keep things fair. As the foreman over a group of ranch hands, she expected he was always evenhanded. But how would he be as a lover or husband? Would he see her as his equal?

Or was he an old-fashioned man who would expect his woman to submit to his wants and wishes?

Oh, Lord, Bella, why would you be wondering about those sorts of things? It's clear he doesn't want a family. You need to snap out of these silly daydreams you're having about this cowboy. One of these days you'll cross paths with a guy who's meant to be your soul mate. And it's not elusive Noah.

Shutting her ears to the voice going off in her head, she bit into the hamburger and immediately groaned with pleasure.

"Mmm. You're a good cook, Noah. This is delicious."

He shrugged. "I've cooked my own meals ever since I was a kid. So I've had plenty of practice."

Had he fixed his own meals out of necessity, she wondered. Or simply because he'd wanted to? From what he'd said, his parents had more or less abandoned him. But surely his grandparents had been around to see to his needs. Or had they? She wanted to ask him, but reminded herself that Noah wasn't on the witness stand or even sitting across from her desk at the office.

Eventually, she decided to ask something a little less personal. "Did you grow up here in Nevada?"

For a moment she thought he wasn't going to answer and then he said, "No. I'm originally from Arizona. The southern part."

"I took a trip with my mother to Tucson once. It's beautiful down there."

"Yes."

His one-word reply disappointed her. She'd hoped her remark would lead him to open up about his former home or something about his past life. But he wasn't going for it.

She went on. "But I happen to think our little area of the world right here is very pretty. Do you ever drive over to the lake?"

His brows pulled together. "You mean Lake Tahoe?"

She nodded and his frown grew deeper.

"No. I don't have any business over there."

Impatient now, she could barely keep from groaning out loud. Exactly where did he have business, she wanted to ask him. Were his interests confined to riding the range or in a dusty round pen, breaking a horse to ride?

She swallowed another bite of burger before she said, "Put like that, I and thousands more like me, also don't have any reason to go to Tahoe, except to enjoy the scenery. Jett and I have fond memories of the lake. When we were kids our father would often take us there for picnics." She sighed. "But that was before he took a permanent walk out of our lives."

Glancing across the table, she saw his blue eyes thoughtfully studying her face and immediately she could feel a rush of heat fill her cheeks.

"I don't recall your father ever visiting the ranch. And Jett never mentions him."

"It's been years since our father has been near Carson City. Once in a while I get a phone call from him. Or Jett will receive a letter in the mail. The last he heard, Dad was promising to come see his grandkids. So far that hasn't happened."

He looked confused. "So you still speak with your father?"

She smiled faintly. "Why not? We understand he's a wandering musician. If we'd tried to hold him here, he would've been miserable. And that wouldn't have done our mother or us kids much good. As long as he's playing in a band somewhere, he's happy. I think it took Jett a lot longer than me to accept our father's indifference. But having Sassy to love has made my brother look at things from a more understanding perspective. Some people just march to a different drummer and our father is one of them."

He reached for the bag of chips and poured a pile onto his plate. "Must be nice not to resent the man."

She shook her head. "I could never resent him. He was always a very loving man. He still loves us—in his own way. And that's what matters the most to me."

"It's clear we see things in a different way, Bella. If I ever had the misfortune to run into my old man again, I'd take great pleasure in busting him in the mouth."

The hard bitter look on his face struck Bella far more than his words. The fact that he was harboring such anger and resentment toward anyone, much less his father, surprised her. Especially when she'd heard Jett describe how kindly and gently he treated every animal on the ranch. But she had to remember he'd not been as fortunate as she and Jett. They'd had a very loving mother, who'd worked hard to make sure her children had a normal home. From what Noah had told her, he'd not even had that much.

Not wanting to sound preachy, she simply said, "I'm sorry, Noah."

"Yeah. I'm sorry, too."

They finished the meal with only a few exchanges of small talk. Afterward, Bella helped him clear the table and wash what few dishes they'd used. As the two of them moved around the small space, an awkward tension began to build and she decided it was probably time for her to say goodbye.

With the last plate dried and put away in the cabinet, she folded the dish towel she'd been using and placed it on the end of the cabinet counter. "Thanks for the meal, Noah. I think I'd better be getting Casper back home before it gets dark."

She expected to see a look of relief cross his face. Instead, his expression remained stoic, making it impossible to discern his reaction to her announcement.

Who are you trying to kid, Bella? His reaction is as clear as a cloudless day. He could've offered you coffee or pointed out that the evening was still young, anything to invite you to stay longer. Face it, he's had all of your company he can stand.

Bella was trying to ignore the insulting voice going off in her head, when Noah said, "Right. It wouldn't do for you to meet up with a bear or mountain lion in the dark."

As far as Bella was concerned, he was much more dangerous to her well-being than any wild animal. Because she was drawn to him in ways she couldn't quite understand. She only knew that being in his presence quenched a need deep inside her.

She moved to the open doorway, then paused. "I keep a little bear bell tied to my saddle horn. The jingle helps ward away any predators." Now that she thought about it, the little tinkling bell was probably the sound that he'd heard when she'd first ridden up on Casper.

He hardly looked impressed by her safety measures, but he didn't say anything and Bella quickly stepped out of the cabin and walked over to Casper.

She was untying the get-down rope from the tree

limb when she sensed Noah walking up behind her. The fact that he'd followed her out of the cabin surprised her and as soon as the rope fell loose, she turned a questioning look at him.

A frown was on his face and his gaze connected with hers for only a brief moment before it dropped to the ground. He said, "Before you go there's something I need to say."

Her heart was suddenly pounding with foolish hope. Maybe he had enjoyed her company after all, she thought. Maybe he was going to tell her he'd like to see her again.

"Yes?" she asked.

His gaze returned to hers and she gave him an encouraging smile.

He cleared his throat. "I—uh, just wanted to say it was nice having you here."

She couldn't remember the last time a man's words had filled her with such warm pleasure. "I enjoyed it very much, too, Noah."

A frown pulled his brows together and as he swiped a hand through his thick hair, it became clear to Bella that he was carefully trying to choose what he was going to say next. Could it be he was trying to decide how best to ask her out on a date? It was crazy how much she wanted that to happen.

Finally he said, "Look, Bella, you're a nice lady. And I have to be honest with you. I—well, I would appreciate it if you wouldn't do this again."

Certain she must have heard him wrong, her head moved stiffly back and forth. "This? What are you talking about?"

The confusion in her voice only seemed to frustrate

him more and he raked a hand over his black hair as his eyes evaded meeting hers.

"Coming here to the cabin —my home."

The direct meaning of his words hit her so hard she felt like someone had whammed a fist to her stomach.

"Oh." Pain spread through her chest as she quickly turned back to Casper and began to tighten the saddle cinch. Oh, Lord, she'd made a giant fool of herself, but strangely that wasn't the reason for her pain. No, it was the fact that he was so callously rejecting her. "Guess I've made a pest of myself. Sorry."

She'd fastened the end of the latigo neatly in its holder and was backing the horse away from the tree in order to mount him, when Noah spoke again.

"It's not that, Bella. It's—just for the best. Can we leave it at that?"

She supposed she should have felt embarrassed. After all, she couldn't remember any time in her life when a man had so bluntly spurned her. Even Marcus with all his cheating and lies had vowed he loved her and had desperately tried to hang on to her. Even her old boss, who'd recently gotten married, had liked Bella as a person. But for some reason, Noah just flat-out wanted no part of her. The realization made her want to cry, or scream. She didn't know which. In the end she chose to do neither.

"Sure, Noah. You don't have to explain. I apologize for making a nuisance of myself and ruining your evening. Don't worry. It won't happen again."

Not daring to look at him, she crossed the split reins over Casper's neck and started to lift the toe of her boot to the stirrup when Noah's hand suddenly wrapped around her elbow.

Insulted even more, she shrugged his hold away. "Thank you," she said stiffly, "but I don't need help getting into the saddle."

To her surprise, he wrapped his hand around her upper arm and she twisted her head to look at him. His blue eyes were partially hidden beneath the scowl of his brows, but there was a fire, a glint of life in them that she'd not seen before.

"I know I'm not the sort of gentleman that you rub shoulders with, but I do have manners, Bella."

She'd never been a mean-spirited person, but she did have her pride, even though he was trying his best to crush it.

"Really?" she asked, her voice etched with sarcasm. "Well, if you had, good manners would have been telling me that you enjoyed my company—even though you didn't."

She expected him to drop his hold on her arm and move aside, but he clearly had other ideas. He tugged her around to face him and Bella's knees went weak as his steely blue gaze grabbed on to hers.

"Don't twist my words, Bella. I didn't say anything about not enjoying your company."

"But you just said—"

"I don't want you back up here. I know what I said. And I meant it."

No man had ever shaken Bella as much as Noah had at this very moment. There was something about his dark, brooding presence that reminded her of a stormy night, when shutters slammed and every shadow seemed to lurk with hidden dangers. And yet just to have him touch her was wildly exciting.

"Why?" she asked quietly.

"You little fool," he muttered. "Don't you have it figured out by now?"

"No. I—"

Before she could finish, he yanked her forward and straight into his arms. The shock caused her to drop her hold on Casper's rein and the horse moved a few steps away.

"Then I need to make it clear. I can't have you around me. Not when I want to do this."

She watched in fascination as his face dipped toward hers. Then his lips made contact with hers and instantly her eyes squeezed shut, her breath caught in her throat.

Noah was kissing her!

For a split second the fact was so shocking she couldn't think or react. Then just as quickly pleasure exploded inside her, causing her arms to wrap around his neck, the front of her body to press tightly against his.

Ever since he'd stopped on the side of the road to help her, she'd been dreaming of kissing him, tasting his lips and having his strong arms wrapped around her. Now, reality was proving to be a thousand times more potent and far more delicious than anything she could've conjured up in her mind.

As the kiss went on, Bella could feel herself sinking into a pool of liquid pleasure and it didn't matter that she was in danger of losing her breath. She didn't want the bliss to end.

But just as suddenly as the kiss had started, it ended with Noah tearing his lips from hers. The break did little to stop her reeling senses and she was forced to hang on to his shoulders to steady herself.

"You see now why I can't have you near me?"

The gruff rasp of his voice caused her eyelids to

flutter open and she found herself staring directly into his eyes. At the moment the blue orbs were dark and stormy, but whether that was a result of anger or passion, she couldn't tell.

"Oh, Noah," she whispered. "I—"

Before she could say anything else, he turned and moved a few steps from her. Bella wiped a shaky hand over her face, then walked over to stand at his side.

"I don't understand," she finally managed to say.

He let out a short, caustic laugh. "You think I do? Ever since I first laid eyes on you I've been wanting to do that. Stupid of me, huh?"

The trembling that had started on the inside of her during their kiss had now pushed its way to the outside, making her hands shake and her voice quaver. "I've been wanting to do that ever since I laid eyes on you, too. Does that make me stupid, too?"

A tight grimace twisted his features. "No. It makes you a liar."

Bella stepped in front of him and stabbed him with an angry look. "You can call me bold or forward or unladylike, but don't call me a liar. That's one thing I'm not."

"Then you must be a hypocrite. Jett says you had a crush on your old boss—that you still do. He's the one you've had ideas about kissing. Not me!"

Doing her best to hang on to her temper, she said, "Jett doesn't know what he's talking about. I never had a crush on Curtis. Not while I worked as a paralegal in his law office or after I left it. I admired him for many reasons and even thought he'd make a good husband— but I could see he wasn't meant for me."

Bella couldn't go on to explain that being around

Curtis had never filled her head with erotic images. She'd never pictured herself making wild, passionate love to the man, the way she had with Noah. But those secret fantasies were far too intimate to share with this man.

Shaking his head, he glanced toward Casper, and Bella followed the direction of his attention. Thankfully the horse had been trained not to run away. At the moment he was happily tearing at the tufts of grass growing in scattered patches over the rocky ground.

"Forget I mentioned anything about the man," Noah muttered gruffly. "Who you have your eye set on is none of my business. Unless you try to make me your target. So before you make your play, you need to know that I'm not about to let anything develop between us. Not now. Not ever."

Bella proudly lifted her chin. "Then why did you kiss me?"

"That was my way of explaining the situation."

She refrained from rolling her eyes toward the tree-tops. "It sure didn't feel like a demonstration, explanation, or anything of the sort. It felt like an old-fashioned kiss—the kind two people with mutual attraction share. And if you could be totally honest with me, you'd admit that you want to do it again. I do."

His jaws clamped so tight Bella figured his back teeth were probably in danger of crumbling beneath the pressure.

Turning his gaze back to her, he said, "Bella, I'm sorry, but I don't have the luxury of playing games with the opposite sex. Especially when the games could become dangerous."

"I would've never guessed you could be such an ass,

Noah Crawford," she said in a low, angry voice. "But I should've known. It's no wonder you live such a solitary life. There's no one around here worthy of your presence!"

With tears threatening to fall, she hurried over to Casper and swung herself into the saddle. Yet before she could kick the horse into a gallop, Noah was there, reaching up and dragging her out of the saddle.

Bella practically fell into his arms and she was forced to grab hold of his shoulders to keep from sliding down the front of his body.

She gasped with shock. "Noah! What—are you—doing?"

"I'm doing what both of us want!"

The words came out on a fierce growl and then he was kissing her again. Only this time the meeting of their mouths instantly turned into a frenetic search that lasted so long Bella was certain she was going to faint.

The rushing noise in her ears grew so loud she couldn't hear the wind or the birds or even the moans in her own throat. Then, just as her knees were about to buckle, he lifted his head, allowing her to suck in a reviving breath of oxygen. Yet before she could gather herself completely, he stepped back, removing the anchoring support of his shoulders.

Forced to grab on to the fender of Casper's saddle to keep from falling, she stared in shocked wonder at him.

"Noah, I—"

"Don't say anything else, Bella," he said in a husky growl. "Just go home. Before I say to hell with everything and carry you inside the cabin."

Shaking almost violently now, she followed his order and quickly swung herself onto Casper's back. The horse instantly sensed her turmoil and began to dance and shake his head against the bit. Without sparing a glance at Noah, she urged the animal into a gallop and didn't ease the pace until she was long gone from the cowboy's view.

Chapter 4

Three days later on a late Wednesday evening, Noah was in the barn, taking an inventory of the ranch's saddles and tack when a footstep behind him had him glancing over his shoulder.

The instant he spotted Jett striding toward him, he inwardly winced. This was the first time this week that he'd seen his boss. Any information they'd needed to share about ranch work had been done over the phone and Noah had been hoping by the time he faced Jett again, he would've forgotten all about his afternoon with Bella.

But so far Noah had found it impossible to get Bella, or the kisses they'd shared, out of his mind. From the moment she'd galloped Casper away from the cabin, his thoughts had been obsessed with the woman. Now he didn't know what to do to shake the misery he was carrying around inside him.

"Hey, Noah. I saw your truck and wondered what you were still doing here. It's getting late."

The tall, dark-haired man dressed in worn jeans, cowboy boots and a gray battered hat looked nothing like a lawyer, but Jett Sundell was a damned good one and an equally good rancher. Along with those attributes, he was a devoted husband and father and one of the best friends Noah had.

"Hello, Jett." He gestured toward a group of saddles the men used on a daily basis. "I was just going over our saddles. I'm afraid Reggie broke the tree in his today. He roped a bull and it jerked him and his horse over. The horn was literally buried in the ground. Now the whole damned thing is wiggling."

A look of concern crossed Jett's face. "Don't worry about replacing the saddle. I want to know about Reggie and the horse."

"They were lucky. I don't know how, but both came out of the spill unscathed. Reg got a lot of ribbing from the men, but he took it all with a laugh. I called Denver over at the Silver Horn to see if they had any used saddles for sale. He tells me they have a few. Most are pretty worn, but at least it would be a hell of a lot better than spending a couple of thousand for a new one."

Jett nodded. "I'll be working the Horn tomorrow. While I'm there I'll have a look at them. Rafe has all the using saddles for his men handmade, so whatever they have for sale will be good ones." He walked over and took a seat on an overturned feed bucket. "Sassy's been trying to locate some hay. I realize it's only the first part of May and we should have grass for a while, but what with the drought, she's concerned that by the time winter rolls around hay will be as scarce as hen's teeth. The alfalfa crops over in Churchill County are already sold and they're not even ready to cut yet."

"She's probably right. I figure the sooner we fill the barns, the better," Noah agreed.

Bending forward, Jett rested his forearms against his knees and looked over at Noah. "She found some timothy for sale, but the stuff is way up in Idaho and baled from last year's crop. I told her to keep searching. I don't want the cost of shipping that far. Especially when it's not fresh-cut."

"Don't worry," Noah told him. "It's early yet. Has she talked to Finn? The last I heard, her brother had his hay meadows producing. If he has surplus, he might sell what he doesn't need."

"You're right. I'll talk to Sassy about it tonight." Chuckling, he added, "That is, we'll talk after bath time, story reading and rocking Mason to sleep."

Of Jett and Sassy's three children, Mason was the baby of the bunch, born just before Thanksgiving last year. Noah was very fond of all three kids, but he couldn't deny he was particularly attached to little Mason. The dark-haired baby rarely uttered a cry and whenever he saw Noah, he always reached for him.

Mason would probably be the closest thing he ever had to having a son. The hollow thought had Noah moving restlessly over to a wall where a slew of bridles neatly hung on rows of nails. Automatically, he picked up a shiny pair of bits and worked the moving parts back and forth.

"You didn't see Bella around this afternoon, did you?" Jett asked.

Just hearing her name was like a punch in the gut

and for a moment he gripped the bit so hard he very nearly bent the silver shank. "No. Why?"

"Just wondering," Jett replied. "She wrapped up her work early this afternoon and said she was coming home. I was hoping you might have seen her out riding. She hasn't been herself at all this week. I've been a bit worried about her."

Noah stared unseeingly at the wall of bridles as the last few minutes of Bella's visit to the cabin played over in his mind. Try as he might, he still didn't know what had prompted him to kiss her. Then like a crazy man, he'd pulled her off Casper and once his mouth had landed on hers, he'd lost all control. But then so had she. The memory of her soft, eager lips moving against his, the way her body had practically wrapped itself around his, still had the power to make his groin ache with need.

"—riding the canyon. Noah? Hello? Are you with me?"

Jett's voice finally penetrated his deep thoughts and with a mental curse at himself, he looked over at his friend.

"Sorry, Jett. I was thinking about something. What were you saying?"

Frowning at him, Jett rose from the makeshift seat. "There must be something in the air that's causing late spring fever or some sort of mild dementia. Bella's been going around the office in a fog. Now I can't even keep your attention. Are you all right?"

No. There was nothing right about him, Noah wanted to say. But he couldn't. How could he explain to Jett that he was overwhelmed with the need to make love to his sister? That every moment of the day, she was on his mind like a wide-awake dream? Not only that, his encounter with Bella was the very thing he'd desperately tried to avoid all these years he'd been on the J Bar S. It was crazy. And he had to put a stop to it before his job, his whole life here on the ranch, came to an end.

"Hell, yes, I'm all right. Why wouldn't I be?" he asked gruffly.

Jett shrugged as he passed a keen gaze over Noah's face. "You tell me. You're not acting like your usual self. Have any of the guys been slacking or giving you a problem?"

"No. They're all working hard and no tempers have flared. I'm just tired, that's all. In fact, if there's nothing else we need to talk over, I'm going to head home."

"Go ahead. I figure Sassy's probably waiting dinner for me anyway." He moved closer and gave Noah an affectionate slap on the shoulder. "Don't pay any mind to me, Noah. It's just that I worry about you."

Noah was momentarily taken aback. It was true that Jett considered him more of a close friend than an employee, but he'd never expressed this kind of concern before. "Worry? Why would you do that?"

A wry expression crossed Jett's face. "Because I want you to be happy. And it's obvious that you aren't."

Ignoring the hollow pain in the pit of his stomach, Noah let out a mocking snort. "Since when did you become a psychiatrist?"

"I don't need a doctor's degree to figure out that much."

Noah hung the leather headstall back on its hook. "I guess the next thing you're going to do is tell me I need to get out more. Find myself a woman and have a passel of kids."

"Well, it wouldn't be the first time I've told you that."

"I wish to hell it would be your last."

"A family would change your life—for the better," Jett argued.

"Over my dead body," Noah muttered, then giving his hat an unnecessary tug onto his forehead, he started toward the door. "I'm going home."

"Noah, wait a minute."

Reluctantly, Noah paused and turned to face the other man. "Jett, I really don't want to get into this."

Jett shook his head. "I'm not about to give you a lecture, Noah, or anything like that. I just wanted to say that we've been good friends for years now. And I've never tried to stick my nose in your private life. Past or present. But it's always been clear to me that you're running and hiding from something. I just hope that one of these days you'll turn and face whatever it is that's haunting you. Because until then you'll just be going through the motions of living."

His jaw tight, Noah muttered, "If that isn't one of your lectures, I'd sure hate to hear one."

Grinning now, Jett made a backhanded wave at the door. "Go on. That's all I have to say about the matter. I'll call you from the Horn tomorrow and let you know about the saddles."

The sudden change of subject had Noah heaving out a breath of relief. "Fine. I'll see you tomorrow."

"Yeah. Have a good night, buddy."

Outside, Noah crossed the ranch yard to where his truck was parked near the saddling pen. By now darkness was fast approaching, shrouding the barns and connecting corrals with deep shadows. The rest of the ranch hands had left more than an hour ago and, other than a handful of goats eating from a trough, the work area was quiet.

At any other time Noah would have lingered to relish the peacefulness, but not tonight. He wanted to get away from Jett and the sight of his happy home lit with warm lights. In a few minutes, when Jett walked through the door, the kids would fling themselves at him and Sassy would no doubt greet him with a kiss.

Noah didn't know what that might feel like. To have a family shower him with such love. And he'd probably never know. Because he wasn't ever going to put his trust, or his well-being, in the hands of a woman. No matter how sweet her kisses were.

The drive to Noah's cabin took fifteen minutes, not because there were several miles between the two places, but rather the road was rough, making it slow traveling. As Noah maneuvered the truck over the rub-board surface, he tried once again to clear his mind of Bella, but she remained stubbornly fixed in his thoughts.

Jett had said he was worried about his sister and Noah couldn't help but wonder if her behavior had anything to do with last Sunday and her visit to the cabin. Or was he putting too much importance on those hot kisses they'd shared?

Damn it, he'd not wanted to insult her or hurt her. God help him, she was the only woman he'd ever felt the need to cherish and protect. That's why he'd said those cutting things to her, because she deserved much better than him. He'd thought his bluntness would show her he wasn't a man who was worthy of her. She needed to understand that he was only a cowboy with nothing to offer her. Nothing at all. And yet, these past few days, he'd been overwhelmed with the longing to see her face again, to hear her voice and feel her soft lips yielding to his.

As he neared the turnoff to Bella's place, he told himself he wasn't even going to look in her direction. But that all changed when he spotted a light flickering through the pines and realized it was coming from Bella's barn.

If she was having trouble with one of the horses and needed help, she could call Jett. But he had a feeling she wouldn't want to disturb her brother's evening, unless it was absolutely necessary. No, she'd try to deal with the problem herself before she asked for help.

With a groan of self-disgust, he wrenched the wheel at the last moment and steered the truck onto her driveway.

Bella was walking up the alleyway of the barn when she spotted the headlights sweeping in front of the open doorway. At this time of evening Jett was usually having dinner with his family and none of her friends in town had mentioned they might drive out for a visit. She couldn't imagine who the unexpected caller might be.

She quickened her stride, while dusting bits of alfalfa hay from the front of her shirt and jeans. By the time she reached the front entrance, she spotted a man walking toward her. His hat was sitting low on his forehead, making it impossible to see his face, but there was no mistaking the tall, muscled body or that long easy walk.

Noah!

Without even realizing it, her heels dug into the soft earth, bringing her to an abrupt halt just inside the doorway.

He quickly closed the last few steps between them

and all at once a familiar trembling began to consume her entire body.

"What are you doing here?" she asked bluntly. "Has something happened to Jett or his family?"

"Nothing is wrong. I saw your light in the barn and thought something might be wrong with one of the horses."

If she had any backbone at all, she would tell him to get lost. That she would rather crawl on her belly before she asked for his help. But she'd never been a vindictive person. Besides, how could she send him away when everything inside of her was jumping with crazy joy at the sight of him?

"You have a cell phone," she said flatly. "Why didn't you call Jett and ask him to check on me?"

His lips thinned to a straight line and as Bella studied his rigid features, she wondered why his kiss had tasted so incredibly good. And why, after days of fighting with herself, she couldn't get it or him out of her mind.

"He doesn't need the bother."

Her boots planted in a wide stance, she folded her arms over her breasts. "You think I'm just a bother, period. Don't you?"

His nostrils flared. "Do you need any help?"

She relaxed her stance. "I'm not having any sort of problem. I was simply down here visiting."

The annoyance on his face turned to one of confusion and he glanced over her shoulder, toward the back of the barn. "Visiting? Is someone else down here with you?"

She laughed. "No. Just the horses. I was grooming them and giving them a few treats. They're very good listeners. Did you know that?"

"I try to listen to mine. Not the other way around."

She smiled faintly. "No. I don't expect you ever need to talk to anyone. Not even your horse."

"You don't know what I need," he muttered.

Even though the overhead lighting in the barn was dim, she could see his brooding gaze traveling over her and Bella wondered if he still had the urge to kiss her. Or had he gotten that weakness out of his system?

"Apparently, you don't either," she retorted.

"I need to be left alone," he said stiffly. "I know that much."

Shaking her head, she stepped toward him. "Seems to me that you've had that for seven years. After that length of time you ought to be the happiest man on the planet."

"Maybe I am, Bella. So if you don't need my help, I'll be on my way."

He turned to go, but she quickly caught his arm. "Noah, wait."

His gaze scanned her face, then dropped pointedly down to the hand she'd curled around his forearm. "Why?" he asked simply.

Once again she could feel herself trembling, her heart pounding. He was like a drug, she decided. One that entered her bloodstream the moment she laid eyes on him. "I—because I wanted to thank you for stopping. I'm grateful that you cared enough to offer your help."

He glanced away from her. "It was stupid of me. You don't need a man's help. Especially mine."

Even though his remark was cutting, at least it gave her a glimpse of how he actually viewed her.

"What gave you that idea?" she asked.

He didn't answer immediately and about the time

she'd decided he was going to ignore her question completely he turned his attention back to her.

"You're a successful career woman, Bella."

Reluctant to remove her hand from his arm, she left it there, relishing the warmth of the hard muscle beneath her fingers. "I see. So that makes everything easy for me."

"Something like that."

Her short laugh was full of disbelief, but she didn't expand on the matter. This chance meeting with him was too precious to have an argument cut it short.

"I have supper on the stove," she told him. "If you've not eaten yet, I'd like for you to join me."

He started to pull his arm away, but she tightened her hold on him.

"I can't. My clothes and boots are nasty."

"I like you just the way you are. Tells me you've been working. Besides, I owe you a meal." She dropped his arm and stepped over to where a light switch was situated on the wall. After flipping it off, she said, "I've already put the horses back in the pasture. So if you'll help me shut the doors, we'll be on our way."

To her relief he didn't put up any more argument and after the double doors on the barn were secured, they walked side by side along a path outlined with solar footlights.

At the back of the house, they entered the kitchen, where Bella went straight to the sink and began to wash her hands.

"Hang your hat and make yourself at home," she tossed over her shoulder. "You know where the bathroom is."

When she heard no movement behind her, she looked over her shoulder to see him standing in the middle of the room. His hat was clutched in both hands and from the look on his face, bolting was the main thing on his mind.

"Is anything wrong?" she asked.

He raked fingers through his flattened hair and two pieces fell onto a black eyebrow. "Bella, didn't you hear anything I said the other evening?"

With her back to him, she dried her hands on a paper towel. "Yes. I heard everything you said. But that doesn't mean I'm going to follow your orders."

"I said some nasty things to you."

"Yes, you did," she agreed. "But I've already forgiven you. Besides, you were only trying to make me dislike you."

She heard his footsteps come up behind her and it was all she could do to keep from turning and sliding her arms around his waist. She wanted to rest her cheek upon his chest, to smell his skin, feel his breath upon her hair and the warmth of his body seeping into hers.

"Bella, why are you making this so hard for me?"

His voice was soft and the sound caressed her like gentle fingers on her skin.

She turned to face him and the anguish and need she saw churning in the blue depths of his eyes touched her as nothing had before.

Swallowing at the tightness in her throat, she said gently, "Noah, I'm not trying to make you miserable. I enjoy your company and I think you enjoy mine. I'm not asking you for anything. Just a bit of your time. What can be wrong with that?"

"All right," he surrendered. "As long as you know there can be nothing between us—nothing serious, that is. I guess it won't hurt for us to be friends."

Joyous relief poured through her and she gave him a wide smile. "Friends, yes! Now you go on and wash up while I get our meal ready. I hope you like beef stew."

He gave her a half smile, yet Bella felt as though he'd just given her the moon.

"Sure. I like it just fine."

She watched him leave the room, then sped over to the stove and switched a flame on under the pot of stew.

Noah was staying! Her heart kept singing the words over and over as she set the table, fetched crackers from the pantry and heated cornbread muffins in the microwave.

Have you lost your mind, Bella? Just because Noah is going to eat a bowl of stew with you doesn't mean it's time to get all dreamy-eyed and sappy in the head. The man said he'd be friends. And you can bet your bottom dollar that's all he'll ever be to you. So why bother? Why are you feeling all this silly romantic joy? It's only going to hurt you later on.

The voice going off in her head was something she'd been fighting ever since she'd discovered Marcus had been having affairs. Each time she'd let herself look at a man or dream of having a family, it reminded her how he'd shattered her trust, her whole future. But time had helped heal the hurt she'd endured from her cheating ex-husband. Oh, she still had scars from the ordeal, but she was determined not to let Marcus ruin any more of her life. It was time to let herself hope and love and plan again.

By the time Noah returned to the kitchen, she had everything set out on the table except for their drinks.

"I have a pitcher of iced tea, but if you'd rather have beer, I think I have one in the refrigerator," she told him.

"The tea will be fine."

She poured their drinks. "Everything is ready. Let's eat."

He helped her into the long bench, then took a seat at the other place setting. All the while, Bella could hardly keep her eyes off him. This evening he was wearing a white Western shirt made of heavy cotton. Since his trip from the bathroom, he'd rolled the long sleeves back on his forearms and his dark skin made a vivid contrast next to the shirt. His damp hair was smoothed back from his forehead and lay in curling tendrils at the back of his neck. Just looking at his rough, rugged exterior practically took her breath away.

"So how did your day go?" she asked as she ladled thick stew into a bowl and passed it over to him.

"Busy. We moved cattle from Sage Meadow over to Salt Lick Flats. Reggie took a spill on his horse but thankfully he and the horse are okay."

"That's good. I'm sure you know that Reggie and his wife have a new baby girl. It would be especially awful for him to be hurt now."

"Yeah. His wife has been pretty fragile ever since the baby was born, so I think Reg has been having to shoulder a lot of the household chores at home, along with his work on the ranch."

"Oh, I wasn't aware Evita was having problems. I should pay her a visit and see if I can help in some way."

He looked at her. "You'd do that?"

His surprise put a frown on her face. "Why wouldn't I? Reg is a part of our ranch family. And I know Evita well. I'll make a point to go by their place tomorrow."

He didn't say anything as he began to eat and Bella wondered why it surprised him that she'd want to help a friend. True, he didn't really know her, but surely he could see she wasn't a snob or self-absorbed person.

You're a successful career woman.

He'd stated the fact as though that set her above other women and made men an unnecessary part of her life. She could only hope he'd give her the chance to show him how wrong his thinking was.

"Jett told me you left work early today."

Her spoon paused halfway to her mouth. "Jett was talking to you about me?"

He didn't look across the table at her. Instead, he focused on the bowl of stew and the muffin in his hand. "He's a little concerned about you. That's all."

Before she'd left the office this afternoon, Jett had asked her why she'd been moping about all week. Bella hadn't been able to tell him the truth of the matter. That she'd been miserable over her argument with Noah. Unless Noah had mentioned their little Sunday dinner to Jett, then her brother didn't even know she'd been with the ranch foreman, much less that she'd been kissing him.

She broke off a piece of muffin and slathered it with butter. "I'm fine. I wrapped up a trial case this morning and the rest of the work on my desk can wait until Monday, so I decided to close up shop and come home."

"To go riding?" he asked.

Bella shook her head. "I considered it. But I ended up staying here in the kitchen instead."

A few moments of silence passed as they continued to eat. Finally, he said, "This is good. Where did you learn to cook? From your mother? Or do you watch all those cooking shows on television?"

She chuckled. "How do you know about cooking shows? You don't have a television."

"So you noticed You must think I'm really eccentric."

She could have told him that she'd noticed everything about him and his modest home. Moreover, she'd spent these past few days thinking of little else.

"Not really. Actually, I'm a little envious. Sometimes I wish I could do away with every technical gadget I own. The contraptions intrude not only on our privacy, but also upon a person's life."

"But the convenience is nice," he reasoned. "When I'm out somewhere on the ranch and need to make a call to Jett or someone, I don't have to ride all the way into the ranch yard to reach a phone. That is, if the signal is strong enough for my cell phone to work."

She nodded. "When Jett first got the ranch from our grandparents, there wasn't even a phone in the house. Now he has a little office inside the barn, complete with a landline and internet access. The ranch has changed so much these past few years. And mostly because Sassy became a part of Jett's life."

"Hmm. I've not forgotten the first day Jett went to pick her up at the airport. Instead of taking her to the hotel room she'd already reserved, he brought her here to the ranch."

Bella chuckled. "That's right. And she's been here ever since. At that time none of us knew she was actually Orin Calhoun's daughter. I think it still shocks her to think she's part of such a wealthy family."

He grunted mockingly. "There's no chance of that happening to me. I know for a fact which side of the track I came from."

She thoughtfully stirred her stew. "Sassy came from very humble beginnings. You know, her adoptive parents perished in a fire when she was just a young teenager. Being wealthy was never her plan. All she ever wanted was a family. And I have a feeling you wouldn't ever want to be that wealthy—I mean the Calhoun kind of wealth."

He shook his head. "I don't need to be rich. Not that way."

"Lucky for Jett you feel that way or you wouldn't be content to work here. You'd have a ranch somewhere of your own."

A shuttered look came over his face as he reached to dip himself another helping of stew from the iron pot sitting in the middle of the table.

"I'd never want a place of my own," he said.

The sudden sharpness to his voice told her she'd somehow stepped onto sensitive territory.

"Oh. Well, Jett has said he gives you a part of the calf crop every year as a bonus and you've never sold a one of them. That gave me the idea you might be saving them to put on your own land."

The corners of his lips tightened. "You believe that's what defines a man? What he owns?"

Confused by the abrupt change in his attitude, she frowned. "Not what he owns, Noah, but rather what he does."

He said nothing and Bella could see he wasn't at all convinced she was expressing how she really felt on the subject.

Holding back a sigh, she picked up her glass and leaned back in her chair. "When Marcus and I first got married he and his two brothers worked for their father's asphalt company. Marcus located jobs and arranged the contracts. The position paid well and he never had to dirty his hands."

"Some men are just lucky."

She sipped the sweet tea, while wondering where she'd found the courage to talk about Marcus. He was a subject she didn't care to share with anyone. After all, he was a constant reminder that she'd not used good judgment. But something about Noah seemed to open doors inside of her and everything came rushing out.

"Marcus certainly didn't see it that way. He was constantly harping to me that his family wasn't giving him the respect or appreciation he deserved. Eventually, he quit and tried to cobble together his own highway construction business."

A cynical groove marked his cheek. "You can't blame a guy for wanting to be independent."

"I understood that part of it. But Marcus was too young and inexperienced to jump into such an endeavor. He borrowed a lot of money, lost it and somehow managed to borrow more. But by that point our marriage was on the rocks."

His lips slanted with disapproval. "So is that why you divorced him? Because his business failed?"

She shook her head. "His business didn't fail. After the shaky beginning it started making money. Quite a lot, in fact. But the money, or the fact that he was his own boss, wasn't important to me. I would've much rather had a husband who considered honesty and fidelity more important than his ego."

He looked at her. "So you divorced him because he was a cheater?"

Blowing out a heavy breath, she placed her glass

back on the table and picked up her spoon. "That's right. I've spent a lot of sleepless nights wondering what it was about me that was missing and what Marcus had been searching for in all those other women. The only answer I could ever come up with was that I wasn't woman enough to keep him faithful." Smiling faintly, she glanced across the table at him. "But that's all over with."

His blue gaze made a long survey of her face and Bella realized that ever since they'd entered the house, she'd not even bothered to glance in the mirror. No doubt her hair was mussed and her makeup had faded away hours ago. But she liked to think that Noah was a man who looked beyond the surface. She only hoped he couldn't see all the scars and doubts she carried. More than anything she wanted him to think she was brave and strong and worthy of his attention.

"Is it really?" he asked.

Did he actually care? Or was she reading too much into the simple question?

"Truly."

"That's good," he said softly, "because you should never think of yourself as lacking."

Coming from any other man, she would take those words with a grain of salt. But coming from Noah made them mean something.

"Thank you, Noah," she said huskily, then feeling a bit like a blushing teenager, she quickly rose from the table and crossed over to the cabinet counter. "Please keep eating. I'm just going to put some coffee on to brew. It will go good with dessert."

"You have dessert?"

The faint surprise in his voice caused her to chuckle.

"Unfortunately, I have an insatiable sweet tooth, so I'm baking all the time. Even when I'm swamped with work, I somehow manage to throw something in the oven. Tonight I have peach cobbler. Made with fresh California peaches. So you might want to save a little room for a dish of it."

"I'll try to make room for it," he said.

But would he ever make room in his heart for her?

Is that what you want, Bella? For Noah to love you? The man is carrying a load of baggage. If he ever knew about loving anyone, somewhere along the way, he's forgotten it all. Is that the kind of man you want to hang your feelings and hopes on?

Prompted by the questions going on in her head, Bella glanced over her shoulder at him. From where she stood, she couldn't see his face. But the sight of his proud dark head and the strength of his broad shoulders was all it took to convince her that she wanted him in her life.

He insisted they could only be friends. But she had to believe that sooner rather than later, she could prove to him that they could be much, much more.

Chapter 5

Minutes later, after they'd finished the stew and Noah had helped her clear the table, Bella suggested they take dessert to the living room.

"My jeans and boots are too grimy for that," he told her. "Let's go out on the back porch. The night has probably cooled by now."

"Sounds good to me," she agreed. "I'll put everything on a tray."

Noah stood to one side, watching her dish up bowls of cobbler and fill two cups with coffee.

She did everything with a simple grace that was both charming and sexy and Noah couldn't deny that being near her was like sitting in front of a warm fire on a cold night. It not only filled him with pleasure, it soothed the empty holes inside him. He'd never thought any woman could affect him that much. And especially not a woman like Bella, who was clearly cut from a better piece of cloth.

Noah figured he should be feeling guilty or stupid for accepting her invitation for supper. But he couldn't. For the first time in years, he actually felt like smiling.

Seeing she was about to pick up the tray, he moved in and pushed her hands aside. The moment his fingers brushed against hers, she paused to look up at him and Noah's gaze instantly dropped to her lips.

From the moment he'd walked up to her at the barn this evening, he'd been aching to kiss her, to find out for himself if all that passion he remembered had been real or exaggerated. But he couldn't kiss her. He'd sworn they could only be friends. And for his sake and hers, he had to stick to his promise.

Clearing his throat, he said, "I'll carry it. You get the door."

With a faint nod, she stepped around him and headed to the door. Noah followed her onto the porch where she switched on a lamp near a long wicker couch.

A low coffee table was positioned in front of the couch so Noah placed the tray on it. A few steps away, Bella rubbed both hands up and down her upper arms. "It has gotten rather cool. I think I'd better go grab a sweater. Make yourself comfortable and I'll be right back."

She went into the house and Noah sat down on the far end of the couch. While he waited for her to return, he glanced around the long porch and suddenly found himself thinking back to another time when he'd sat on a ground level porch made of rock and gazed out at the rough, ragged hills of southern Arizona. He and Ward, the owner of the Verde Canyon Ranch, had often sat together in the late evenings, sipping coffee and talking over the day's work.

The two men had always had plenty to talk about. With Verde Canyon covering several thousand acres, there'd always been something to be done, cattle to be tended, horses to be trained and fences to be mended. *Verde Canyon*. It was the only place he'd ever truly called home and he'd expected to live there until the day he died. But even the best-laid plans could be torn apart. Now he was just grateful that he'd found Jett and could make his home, such as it was, here on the J Bar S. At least here, his head wasn't filled with dreams and hopes and plans. No, those had all died on the Verde. And that's where they were buried.

"Sorry about that, Noah. You should've started without me."

Bella's voice interrupted his deep thoughts and he looked around to see her taking a seat on the opposite end of the couch. She'd wrapped a lacy shawl around her shoulders and loosened her ponytail. Now the dark waves settled around her shoulders like a silky cloud. His fingers itched to touch it, to lift it to his nose and breathe in the scent that was uniquely hers.

"I needed the extra time to let all that stew settle," he said. "I honestly don't know how I can hold another bite."

With a soft laugh, she said, "Well, you don't have to eat all the cobbler just to prove you like it."

She handed him one of the dessert bowls, then placed a coffee mug where he could easily reach it.

"Thanks."

He settled back and began to eat and Bella did the same.

After a long stretch of silence, she said, "The moon

looks beautiful shining through the pines. The coyotes must like it. I can hear them howling down in the canyon."

"I hear them, too. Another reason why you shouldn't ride down there alone. You never know when you might run into a hungry pack of them."

She shook her head as though she considered his warning far-fetched. "Have you always been so overly protective?"

Only about you, Bella. Even though the words whispered through his head, he managed to bite them back before they could pass his lips. "No. I was an adventurous kid, always picking up snakes and lizards. I'd roam the hills outside the little town where we lived. I was always hoping I'd find a herd of javelina or a mountain lion."

"Did you go alone?"

He'd always been alone. At least, it had always felt that way to him. "Most of the time. My friends were too afraid of getting into trouble with their parents to go with me."

Even though he wasn't looking at her directly, he could feel her thoughtfully studying him. That was something different for Noah. The rare times he was with a woman she might look at him with amusement or even lust. But none ever studied him as though she was interested in the man beneath the surface. The notion that Bella saw him differently left him feeling restless and very vulnerable.

"Did your parents know where you were or what you were doing?" she asked.

His short laugh was a brittle, hollow sound. "They

didn't care. They were more concerned about fighting over money or booze, or the one junky car they owned."

"I'm sorry. That must've been tough."

Sometimes in the quiet of the night, Noah could still hear the yelling and banging, the threats and tears. Back then, no matter where he'd tried to hide in the house, the violent sounds would reach him. Now after all these years, he still couldn't outrun the memories.

"It could've been worse. They never laid a mean hand on me." He stared out at the pines and the patches of silvery moonlight on the ground. "As a very small boy, I can remember my mother being very loving to me. She made me feel wanted and protected. But something changed, I didn't know what. Except that my parents had started fighting. After that, she began to push me away. Finally, she left and never came back."

"Hmm. That's odd that she didn't take you with her when she left."

Surprised by Bella's comment, he looked over at her. "Why do you say that? It was obvious she didn't want me around."

She shook her head. "You don't know that for sure. She clearly loved you once and a mother just doesn't stop loving her child. And she sure doesn't abandon it. She might have had emotional issues and figured you'd be better off without her. Or she could've been afraid. Your dad might have used you as a threat against her."

"No. Mom wasn't afraid for herself," he reasoned. "She stood up to him like a bulldog terrier."

She leaned forward and returned her bowl to the tray. "You don't understand, Noah. I didn't mean she was afraid for her own safety. I have the feeling she was trying to protect you. Believe me, in my line of work I see it all the time. Women make bad choices and then they become so afraid they make even worse choices. Your mother probably ran off because she didn't know any other way to handle the situation."

Noah had never thought in those terms. As a teenager he'd carried around the bitter hurt of being abandoned and that feeling had never left. Now Bella expected him to see things in a different light.

A sardonic smile twisted his lips. "Do you always look at things through rosy glasses? I thought you had to be a hard-nosed cynic to be a lawyer."

Chuckling, she touched a fingertip to her nose. "Oh, it doesn't feel that hard to me," she joked, then her expression turned serious. "Have you ever tried to locate your mother?"

A spot deep inside him squeezed so hard it caused his fingers to curl into his palms. "No. I don't even know if she's still alive."

"I have connections," she said. "I could make a search for you. No charge, of course."

"Bella, think about what you're asking," he said gently. "I've been doing fine like I am. What would it accomplish if you found her?"

"Have you ever thought she might need you?"

Her question should've had him bursting out with laughter. The notion that Margo Crawford might need her son was certainly absurd. And yet Noah couldn't feel any humor.

"No. I've never thought about it. And I don't intend to."

She seemed to accept his response because she didn't say anything else on the matter. In fact, she didn't say anything for a long time and Noah decided he didn't like her silence. Even when she was saying things that provoked him into thinking and feeling things he'd rather forget, he still enjoyed the sound of her voice and the idea that she wanted to connect herself with him through conversation.

After several more moments stretched in silence, he said, "Your parents obviously had their differences. Did they do a lot of loud arguing—fighting?"

She shook her head. "Not at all. I know that sounds odd, but you have to understand that my dad was, and I'm sure still is, one of those gentle souls that wouldn't raise his voice to anyone. Mom always said it was impossible to have an argument with Dad because he was always so kind and loving with her and us kids. I guess what I'm trying to say is that the memories of when our family was whole are very happy ones."

"You're lucky."

"I know that, Noah. In my work, I see far too many torn families."

Releasing a heavy breath, he looked away from her. "Yeah. I imagine you do."

He finished the last of his coffee, then before he could talk himself into remaining with her for a few minutes longer, he rose to his feet.

"Thanks for the meal, Bella. It's getting late, so I'll say good-night."

She quickly got to her feet. "Just a minute and I'll get your hat for you."

Noah knew better than to follow her back into the kitchen. Not when he wanted to find any excuse to pull her into his arms.

He waited at the door of the screened-in porch, until she emerged from the kitchen, carrying his hat. With a quick thank-you, he took it from her and levered it low on his forehead.

"I'll walk you to your truck," she said as she tied the shawl she was wearing into a knot between her breasts.

"That isn't necessary."

"I never said it was."

She moved past him, through the porch door and down the steps to leave Noah with no other choice but to follow.

As they walked along the footpath toward the barn, neither of them said anything and Noah could only wonder what she was thinking, wanting, feeling, and why any of that should matter to him.

Once they reached his truck, she stood no more than a step away and her flowery scent mingled with that of the nearby pines.

She said, "I'm glad you stopped to check on me, Noah. And I'm especially glad you decided to stay."

His hand rested on the door handle, but he couldn't bring himself to trip the latch. "I hadn't planned on it," he admitted.

"Why did you stay?" she asked.

His gaze left the shadows beyond her, to focus on her face. "I'm not exactly sure," he muttered, then shook his head. "That's not the truth. I stayed because I wanted to. Because I'm a glutton for punishment, I suppose."

She frowned. "So you consider spending time with me punishment?"

"If I let myself get involved with you it will be. We both know nothing good could come of it. Our worlds don't fit. We'd only end up hurting each other."

She moved closer and he drew in a sharp breath as her palm came to rest against the middle of his chest.

"Why wouldn't we fit together?" she asked softly. "I know what you are and you know what I am. There wouldn't be any surprises."

She made it sound so simple and tempting.

"Look, Bella, I'm not a family man," he said huskily. "Hell, I wouldn't know how to be. And that's what you need. Not someone like me."

She brought the other hand up to join the one already lying on his chest and Noah wondered how so much heat could radiate from her palms. Fire was flashing from his face all the way down to his groin.

"I need a man in my life before I can ever think about having a family," she reasoned.

"I'm not that man. And I can't ever be."

She opened her mouth to contradict him, but he didn't give her the chance.

He said, "All that stuff I told you tonight about my childhood, that's only a part of my past."

"Most everyone has things in their past they're not proud of, Noah. Me included. It's your future that I'm interested in."

He grimaced. "God willing, my future life won't look any different than it does right now."

"So you always want to live alone? You don't want a wife or children?"

"No. A wife and kids deserve someone who can give them love and devotion and make them happy. I can't even make myself happy."

She moved closer and Noah swallowed hard as the front of her body nestled itself against his.

"Perhaps that's because you haven't tried," she said, her voice barely above a whisper.

Like a single mound of sand trying to hold back an

angry sea, the will to keep his hands off her suddenly crumbled. He wrapped them around her shoulders and pressed his fingers into her soft flesh.

"I've been trying to tell you, Bella, that we can only be friends. I've been trying to—"

"Reject me. Yes, that's obvious." She slid her hands upward until her fingers were touching the exposed flesh between the parted folds of his shirt. "But I don't think you really want to do that."

He reached out and gently traced his fingertip over the slant of her cheekbone. Her skin was as smooth as cream and he had no doubt it would taste just as rich.

His throat tightened as the urge to kiss her, make love to her began to tie his muscles into knots. "No. That's not what I want to do, Bella. But then you already know what you're doing to me. I imagine that makes you feel pretty damn good, doesn't it? Knowing you can make a big man like me weak in the knees."

Her eyes narrowed and then her head shook back and forth. "Why would you think such a thing? I have no desire to wield power over you. Or anyone else for that matter. That's one of the reasons I like being a lawyer. Because I believe everyone should be on equal ground."

"Well, in my case—"

"In your case, Noah, you're thinking too much. Worrying too much. Why can't you simply let yourself feel?"

"Because I'm feeling things that aren't good for me."

Slipping her arms around him, she nestled her cheek against the middle of his chest. The gesture of trust melted the cold chunk of reasoning inside him and without thinking, he stroked a hand over her dark hair.

A soft sigh slipped past her lips to mingle with the

sound of the whispering pines. "After Marcus upended my world, I didn't think I'd ever want another man. Instead of thinking forward, I kept thinking in the past and all that I'd lost." She lifted her head and looked up at him. "But I'm beginning to see how that mindset was cowardly and stupid. I want more for myself than just wishing and hoping that things could be different."

"I'm not afraid, Bella. I'm practical." And that sensible side of him had kept him very cautious around any woman he met. If by some miracle he ever decided to take a wife, she needed to be cut from the same tough rawhide as himself. Not delicate lace, like Bella.

She said, "Being practical has no connection to falling in love. I might get hurt all over again. But so be it. I have to try to reach for my hopes and dreams."

Her words were like a battering ram, pounding at the door to his heart. Inch by inch he could feel the protective barrier caving and the fear that she might actually break through had him thrusting her gently away from him.

"Then you'd better go try to find all those dreams with another man," he said roughly.

A crushed expression momentarily froze her features and then her jaw went firm and resolute.

"Yes, I think I should do just that."

She turned and began walking back to the house. Noah stared after her, while telling himself he was doing the right thing. She would eventually find a good man to love. Yet even as he was struggling to convince himself, the image of some other man kissing her, holding her, making passionate love to her hit him like an avalanche.

Jealousy, or something much deeper, pushed him to

go after her and in three long strides, his hand was on her shoulder, halting her steps.

"Noah, what—"

Whatever she was going to ask halted as he yanked her into his arms and brought his mouth down on hers. At first there was no response in her, but after one long second her lips parted and with a low groan, she flung her arms around his neck. Her reaction fueled the desperation and hunger that had gripped him from the moment she'd placed her hands on his chest and he crushed her body tight against his, while his tongue thrust past her teeth and into the warm cavern beyond.

Like a leaf sucked into a whirlwind, his senses spun in a vicious circle until he lost all thought. Nothing mattered but the pleasure that was pouring from his head to his toes, filling up every empty spot with soft, warm emotions he'd never felt before.

But the need for air finally forced him to lift his head and he opened his eyes to see she was gazing up at him, her expression dazed and confused.

"What does this mean, Noah?" she asked in a soft, husky voice. "You just told me to go find some other man."

"Damn it, I don't know what anything means anymore! But I'm certain about one thing—I don't want you with another man." His hands slipped down her back until his palms were cupping the fullness of her bottom. "Not like this."

"Noah."

His name came out on a soft breath and when her hands gently cradled his face, the notion that she could consider him as something precious was all it took for unbridled emotions to swell his chest and tighten his throat.

"I can't make you promises, Bella."

"I don't expect any. I'm just asking you not to put a wall between us."

Sighing, he lifted his gaze from her face to the dark shadows surrounding them. "You have your sights set on the wrong man, Bella. But you'll figure that out sooner rather than later."

Her warm body stirred against him and heat burned like red hot coals in the pit of his belly. If he listened to his body instead of his head, he'd lead her straight into the house and make love to her. But he wasn't brave enough to take that reckless leap. He understood that once he took Bella to his bed, there would be no turning back. No chance to catch himself before the fall.

"I think I should warn you that I'm rarely wrong."

Her smile was a light in the darkness and Noah could resist it no more than a drink of cool water on a hot day.

"We'll see," was all he could manage to say before he bent his head and sought her mouth again.

This time he kept the kiss brief. Even so, just having her lips next to his was enough to leave him shaken and wanting more.

"I have to go, Bella."

"Are you sure?"

Her whispered question made it clear she was inviting him into her bedroom and into her life. The idea was beyond tempting, but thankfully it was also just scary enough to give him the strength to ease her out of his arms.

He let out a long breath. "Yeah. Sure."

"When will I see you again?"

"I can't say. We'll be busy moving cattle all next week. I'll try to stop by one evening on my way home."

She smiled again. "Okay. Unless something keeps me late at the office, I'll be here."

"Good night, Bella."

Before his resolve could crumble, he walked straight to his truck. But once he started the engine and turned the vehicle toward his cabin, the headlights swept across the backyard to illuminate Bella's silhouette. She was standing where he'd left her and now as she watched him pull away, she lifted a hand in farewell.

Pain squeezed the middle of his chest and as he drove the short distance to his place, he wondered how this thing with Bella had happened and exactly what he was going to do about it.

Chapter 6

By the time the middle of the work week rolled around, Bella had acquired three more cases to her already busy schedule. Two involved women seeking divorces, both from very wealthy husbands. The third was a young man accused of stealing valuable jewelry from a home where he was employed as a gardener.

Normally, Bella didn't deal in criminal cases. Nor did her brother, Jett. Both siblings usually focused on family law. But in this instance, the accused was the brother of an old schoolmate of Bella's and she'd not been able to turn away from her friend's plea for help.

Rising from her desk, she left the small room that made up her office and into an area where a young Hispanic woman sat typing at her desk.

Pepita Alvarez, better known as Peta to all her friends, acted as secretary to both Jett and Bella, which made the woman's workload enormous. Yet each time Bella or Jett made noises about hiring more help for her, the young woman insisted she could handle the job on her own. Bella marveled at her efficiency.

As her shadow crossed Peta's desk, the black-haired beauty looked up. "Oh, Ms. Sundell, I didn't hear you. Do you need something?"

Bella smiled. "I was just wondering if Jett has anyone with him right now."

"No. I think Mr. Taylor left a few minutes ago. That was his last appointment for the day."

Bella chuckled. Mr. Taylor was an eccentric old man, who gave Jett fits by wanting to make changes in his will nearly every week. Her brother had finally given up on reasoning with the man. Instead, he merely followed Mr. Taylor's wishes and sent him a bill for services rendered.

"I wonder what changes he wanted made to his will today?" Bella mused out loud. "Bet the five thousand to his cat won't change."

Pepita shook her head. "Last week he wanted to make sure his twelve chickens went to his granddaughter. Poor old man. He's a hypochondriac. He believes he's going to die any minute."

"If that were to happen, Jett would really miss him. Not to mention the old man is contributing to the college funds for Jett's kids." She gave the secretary a conspiring wink. "I'll go see if he survived the meeting."

Her brother's office was located on the left side of the building and, like Bella's, had a picture window overlooking a busy street of Carson City. Up until a few years ago, Jett had worked exclusively as the Silver Horn's attorney, but after marrying Sassy, he'd made the decision to cut down the hours he put in at the ranch and start a practice for himself.

Jett appeared to juggle both jobs without any problems—although Bella didn't know how he kept up with the workload, especially when he had his own ranch to deal with, too. But Sassy had taken on a large responsibility of handling the day-to-day running of the J Bar S, while Noah made sure everything that needed to be done got done.

"I see you lived through another visit from Mr. Taylor," she said to her brother as she entered his office. "Or would you like two aspirin and the shades lowered?"

Chuckling, he tossed aside a manila folder and looked up at her. "If that little man was all I had to deal with my job would be easy. So what's up with you? We've not talked all day."

She took a seat in one of the polished wooden chairs in front of his desk. "I've been busy. And I took on a case earlier today that has me a bit worried."

Surprise arched his dark brows. "Worried? That's not like you, sis. You're always confident."

She closed her eyes and massaged the burning lids. Jett understood that Marcus's infidelity had hurt her terribly, but no one, not even her brother, realized how much the experience had trampled her self-worth. Even now, after acquiring a law degree and proving herself competent in the courtroom, she still had moments when she doubted herself. And her effort to get close to Noah wasn't helping matters. He was the only man she'd ever tried to pursue and his reluctance to have anything to do with her was making her feel like a pathetic kitten trying to catch a fierce bald eagle.

Trying to shake the image of Noah from her mind,

she looked at Jett. "Remember Valerie Stanhope? She was a friend of mine in high school."

"Short girl with mousy brown hair and glasses?"

"That was her. Although the years have turned her into a very pretty woman. Anyway, her brother, Brent, was arrested on theft charges and I agreed to represent him. I've only handled one other criminal case in my life, Jett. What if I bungle this thing and he ends up serving time in prison? I'm not sure I could deal with that on my conscience."

Thoughtful now, he picked up an insulated coffee mug and took a long sip. "What sort of theft? If it's petty, just make a plea deal and forget it. He'll probably be right back in trouble again."

Bella shook her head. "Not petty, thousands. Jewels from the home where he worked as a gardener. Brent swears he never knew about the jewels and Valerie believes the whole thing is a case of insurance fraud."

That caught Jett's attention and he whistled under his breath. "You better have someone do some deep investigating, sis. And that won't be easy or cheap. Did you warn Valerie about the cost?"

"No. I told her not to worry about it. I'll do the digging myself."

Jett groaned. "Oh, Bella, how do you ever expect to make money if you're going to work pro bono?"

"There are more important things to me than padding my bank account."

"Where money is concerned, you've always been more like Dad. It's never ranked very high on your wish list." Shaking his head, he said, "Well, you do only have yourself to support, so I guess it doesn't matter."

Cutting him an annoyed glance, Bella rose from

the chair. "Thanks, brother, for reminding me that I'm thirty-two and still have no family."

"Sis, I'm not trying to rub salt in the wound. I happen to believe you're going to find the man of your dreams. In the meantime, you have a new house. That's something to feel good about."

Her house was beautiful. But without a husband to share the place with, the rooms were nothing more than hollow spaces. She'd give up every square foot, every last stick of furniture if Noah would invite her to live with him in the line-cabin. Did that mean he was the man she wanted to spend the rest of her life with? With each day that passed she was beginning to think so. But was she chasing a fool's dream?

"Yes, my house talks to me every night," she said with bitter humor, then turned to leave the office. "I think I'll call the sheriff's department and see if Evan can give me anything on the Stanhope case."

Jett snorted. "Just because Evan is Sassy's brother doesn't mean he can share department info with you."

Pausing, Bella twisted her head around and frowned at him. "As the guy's lawyer I already have the police report. I want to know what's been written between the lines."

"Good luck. You're going to need it." Jett's mocking chuckles were suddenly interrupted by the telephone. "Just a minute, Bella, it's the ranch calling."

Expecting the caller to be Sassy, who always kept her conversations brief, Bella decided to stick around for another minute, just in case her brother had something better to offer than sarcasm.

After a short moment passed with the phone jammed

to his ear, Bella watched his features grow tight. Something was wrong. She could feel it.

"Barbed wire," Jett repeated. "How did that happen?"

Moving back to his desk, she waited anxiously for him to wrap up the call.

After another long stretch of listening, Jett said, "Yeah. Sounds just like Noah. I'll make sure he gets a tetanus shot. Don't worry. You tried and he's stubborn. Thanks for letting me know, honey. I'm closing shop now, so I'll see you in a few minutes."

As Jett hung up the phone, Bella realized her heart was hammering with fear. "Noah has been hurt?"

Although she'd made an effort to keep any note of panic from her voice, the concern she was feeling must have shown on her features because Jett shot her an odd look.

"Sassy tells me the men were mending fence and a piece of barbed wire popped loose of the stretcher. It whacked Noah across the back before finally wrapping around his arm. She says some of the gashes were pretty deep. He refused to go to the doctor, so she stitched up three of the worst wounds and ordered him to go home."

Sassy would be able to do that, Bella thought. The woman was a tough-as-nails ranch hand. She could pull a calf or stitch up a wounded animal as well, or better, than Jett. Still, Noah needed professional medical attention and the urge to race to him was like a storm building inside her.

Telling herself to remain calm, she said, "I thought the guys were moving cattle this week. What were they doing mending fence?"

Jett's eyes narrowed shrewdly. "How did you know

the men were moving cattle? You been talking to Sassy?"

Bella quickly turned her gaze to the window and the busy traffic beyond. "Uh—that's right. We talked a couple of nights ago. She must've told me. Or maybe you mentioned it."

Bella actually had spoken with her sister-in-law, but nothing had been said about cattle or horses. The two women had discussed the children and the celebration Sassy was planning for little Skyler's upcoming birthday. It wasn't that Bella cared if Jett knew about Noah having supper with her a few nights ago. She and her brother had always been very close and they shared their thoughts and feelings about things with each other. But she instinctively knew that Noah wouldn't appreciate her saying anything about their encounters to Jett. Noah was a deeply private man and until he gave her a signal otherwise, she wasn't going to let on to Jett, or anyone, that the two of them had spent time together.

Besides, she thought dismally, five days had passed since Noah had kissed her good-night and she'd not seen or heard from him. Twice she'd heard his truck rumbling by her place as he drove to his cabin, but he'd not stopped either time.

Because he didn't want to get involved with her, she thought glumly. Not on a meaningful level. He seemed to have enjoyed kissing her and if she really tried, she might seduce him into her bed. But that would be as far as he'd let his feelings toward her go. That's why she needed to face facts and move her attention to a man who might really love her.

You'd better go try to find all those dreams with another man.

If she'd use some common sense, she'd follow those cutting words Noah had thrown at her, Bella thought sadly. But the memory of his kiss and the way her heart melted at the mere touch of his fingers were enough to convince her to not give up on the man.

While thoughts of Noah had been churning inside her head, Jett had shut down his computer and was now gathering a slew of papers he'd strung across his desk.

"Well, the hands have been moving cattle, but a fence got torn down in the process and that's where the barbed wire came in." He glanced over at her. "I'm finished here. I'm going to head on home so I can check on Noah. The stubborn mule-head. If I didn't care about the guy so much, I'd kick him in the rear."

"I realize you stay in shape, brother, but you might have a little trouble doing that. Noah's not exactly puny."

Laughing, Jett stuffed a few papers in a briefcase and jammed the worn leather holder beneath his arm. "That's why I'm not going to try it, dear sister." On his way to the door, he pecked a kiss on her cheek. "Are you working late this evening?"

"I have another appointment in thirty minutes. I'll see you tomorrow."

He left through a back entryway and locked the door behind him. Once he was gone, Bella realized her legs were wobbly and she sank into one of the chairs in front of Jett's desk.

Noah had been injured. She'd not expected the news to affect her this much. Especially when it wasn't a life-threatening issue. But it could have been, she thought sickly. If the wire had hit his eye he could have been blinded. Or if it had slashed an artery he could have easily bled to death before reaching a medical facility in town.

A light tapping noise had her looking around to see Peta's face peering around the edge of the door. "Is anything wrong, Bella? I heard Jett leaving and he didn't say a word."

"There was a little accident at the ranch. He's left to make sure everything is okay."

The secretary walked into the room. "Oh, I hope it wasn't serious."

"Don't worry. Everything is under control."

Except her emotions, Bella thought.

Moving closer, Peta carefully scanned Bella's face. "I'm glad to hear that. But are you sure you're okay? You look pale and, well, tense."

Forcing a smile, Bella waved her hand in a dismissive way. "Oh, that's just because I'm dieting. The more I think about not eating, the more it wears on my nerves."

The secretary laughed. "I know the feeling. But Bella, you have a fabulous figure. You don't need to diet."

Rising to her feet, Bella attempted to put a cheery look on her face. "You're too kind, Peta. Now, let's get back to work. The Morrison divorce case is on the court docket tomorrow. I need to make certain my paperwork is in order before I face the judge. Would you get that file for me?"

"I'll have it for you in just a minute."

Bella returned to her office and, as promised, Peta appeared almost instantly with the file in hand. She thanked the secretary and after Peta left the room, Bella opened the file and tried to focus on the legal documents. But all she could see was Noah, his flesh ripped and bleeding.

Everything inside her was screaming to go to him. But Jett was already on his way to Noah's cabin. It would look ridiculous for her to follow. And since Noah had never offered to share his cell phone number with her, she couldn't even call him.

Something between a disgusted groan and a helpless sob slipped past her throat and she dropped her head in her hands. She was either turning into the biggest fool of the century or a woman in love. Either way, Bella had a feeling she was tumbling straight toward a heartache.

Later that evening, dusk was spreading shadows around the cabin as Noah sat on the front step. Between his legs, Jack rubbed back and forth and emitted a string of coarse meows.

"You're not fooling me, you old codger. This isn't a display of sympathy for my wounds. You want me to get up and get you something else to eat. Like a can of tuna. But that's too bad. I'm all out of tuna."

Instead of meowing another loud protest, Jack went on sudden alert, his unblinking green eyes staring out at the road that dead-ended in front of the cabin.

Knowing the cat could hear sounds he never could, Noah followed Jack's frozen gaze, but saw nothing except a few tufts of grass bending to the breeze.

"There's nothing there, boy. No bear or coyote. But maybe a little field mouse you've been terrorizing has found out where you live and he's come for revenge. Huh?"

The cat moved off the step at the same time Noah heard the faint tinkle of a bell and the crunch of footsteps on gravel.

"What the hell is she doing?" he muttered the question more to himself than the curious cat.

Noah had already risen to his feet, when he spotted Bella rounding a curve in the road. The sight of her caused his stomach to clench, his jaw to tighten. These past few days, he'd purposely avoided stopping at her house. Mainly because he knew that each minute he spent with the woman brought him closer to making love to her.

Moving off the step, he stood on the rough ground and waited for her to get within earshot. Then, not bothering with a greeting, he asked, "What are you doing walking? Is your car on the blink?"

"The road from my house to here is too rough for my little car," she explained. "So I walked."

Since he'd left her house a few nights ago, he'd halfway convinced himself that Bella wasn't really as pretty or sexy as the image he carried in his mind. But he'd only been fooling himself. Just looking at her made him ache with longing.

"You shouldn't have. Dusk is when the predators go on the prowl."

She lifted her wrist to show him she was wearing a bear bell, then quickly slipped it off her wrist and jammed it down in the pocket of her jeans. "It's not even a quarter of a mile from here to my place and I'm the only one prowling about this evening," she said, then gestured toward the yellow tom, who'd sidled up to Noah's leg. "Who's that? I didn't see him the day I was up here."

"Jack isn't always around. He comes and goes whenever he gets the notion."

A smile tilted her lips as she eyed the cat. "He's a

handsome guy. I'm surprised he doesn't go back to the barn and stay with his furry friends."

"Jack isn't a barn cat. When he was just a baby, I found him alone on the edge of the highway."

"And you've had him ever since. He's lucky that you rescued him." She bent down to pet the feline, but before she could put a hand on him, Jack quickly dashed off into the shadows. "Well, I can tell he definitely belongs to you."

Noah couldn't help but smile. "I've taught him to be cautious."

"No doubt," she said with a laugh, then her expression grew serious as she gestured toward his bandaged forearm. "I was in Jett's office when Sassy called him about your accident. I wanted to come see for myself how you're doing."

Did she really care that much? The notion tore at him. He couldn't deny he wanted her love and attention. Yet the scarred, cynical part of him didn't want to risk having everything, including his heart, torn away. Enduring that sort of loss once in a man's life was more than enough.

"Well, I can tell you that my arm is stiff and sore and my back ouches if I move a certain way, but otherwise I'm fine. Didn't Jett tell you?"

"I had to work late this evening," she said. "I haven't seen Jett since he left the office to come up here."

He mouthed a curse word under his breath. "Jett shouldn't have bothered on my account. Jack gives me worse scratches than this whenever I try to give him a dose of wormer."

She rolled her eyes. "Jett cares about you. So do I. That's why we bothered to check on you."

Besides the Sundell family, only one other person had ever really cared about Noah and that had been Ward Stevens. Yet even his old partner had eventually turned his back on Noah. But not before he'd sworn to forget the very name of Noah Crawford. Sooner or later, Jett and Bella would do the same. That's what happened with people he let himself get close to.

"Come on," he said gruffly. "I'll make us some coffee."

She followed him into the house and he shut the door against the cooling night air. A lamp was already on in the living area of the small room. Noah walked over to the kitchen and switched on a light above the sink.

"Let me make the coffee," she insisted. "You don't need to be moving your arm. You might tear the cuts open."

He grunted with amusement. "Not hardly. Sassy has me trussed up tighter than a stuffed turkey."

Bella moved over to the short span of cabinets and he stood to one side watching the subtle movements of her body as she gathered the makings for the coffee. Tonight she was wearing black jeans and a thin white blouse tucked inside the waistband. Her dark hair hung loose against her back and swung against the fabric like a curtain pushed and pulled by a gentle breeze.

Unable to ignore the desire rising up in him, he walked up behind her and slipped his good arm around her waist. She dropped the spoon of coffee grounds onto the cabinet and then with a little moan, fell back against him.

Noah bent his head and buried his face in the side of her fragrant hair. "You shouldn't be here," he murmured. "But I'm glad you are, Bella."

She twisted around to look anxiously up at him. "When I heard you'd had an accident it scared me. An incident like that can be deadly." She touched a hand to his cheek. "Are you sure you're okay?"

"What I'm feeling right now is a lot more dangerous than a few cuts on my arm," he said huskily.

"Noah—"

The soft invitation in her eyes was almost his undoing. Before he caved in to temptation, he quickly stepped back and sucked in a deep breath.

"You'd better fix the coffee, Bella."

A look of frustration stole over her face, but she didn't argue or reach to touch him. Instead, she turned back to the cabinet and began cleaning up the spilled coffee grounds.

Moving to the other side of the room where the couch faced the small fireplace, he started to take a seat, then decided he was too restless to sit. Especially with her up and moving about the kitchen.

He ended up standing by the open window, watching the distant mountains being swallowed up by a darkening sky, and wondering why he was such a coward. Why couldn't he simply take what Bella was offering and be thankful she wanted to be near him?

Because she's not just any woman, Noah. She's beautiful, classy and a successful lawyer to boot. She's not the sort to have an empty affair. She's looking for a man to love. A man to be her husband. And she's looking straight at you. That's why you're scared.

Annoyed at the voice in his head, he looked over at Bella. "If you'd like I can turn on the radio or CD player. I have a stack of old standards. Jo Stafford,

Dinah Washington, that sort of music. And I have a collection of Western swing and cowboy trail songs."

"That's a strange combination," she said. "I figured you for the modern country stuff—dancing on a barroom floor dusted with sawdust."

He let out a short laugh. "Me, dance? I have two left feet. Besides, that was my father's thing and it triggered many fights with my parents. I think that's why that sort of entertainment never appealed to me."

She said, "Our father spent a lot of time in nightclubs. But he was there to play in a band. Not to drink or pick up women. He wasn't that kind of guy."

She poured water into a fast-drip coffee machine and closed the lid. "But back to your question. I think I could use the quiet tonight, if you don't mind. Peta, our secretary at work, always keeps music going in the background, which is good. It keeps our offices from feeling like tombs. But sometimes it's nice not to hear anything, especially after a hectic day like today."

The weariness in her voice prompted him to return to her side. "I hope you didn't let my little run-in with a piece of barbed wire ruin your day."

Sighing, she shoved a hand through her hair and for the first time tonight Noah noticed her eyes looked tired. The fact struck him hard. For some reason, he'd never imagined Bella putting in an exhausting day of work, or agonizing over her job. The times he'd seen her, she always looked fresh and full of energy. He'd assumed her finances were so secure she could make her workday as light or as busy as she wanted. Apparently her world wasn't that easy.

"I was worried about you," she admitted. "But it all started this morning. I took on a criminal case. That's something I don't normally do. Now I'm afraid I've made a mistake."

"If you feel that uncertain, why did you take the case in the first place?" Two weeks ago, he would've never asked Bella such a question. Before that day he'd stopped to help her with Mary Mae, he hadn't wanted to know what went on in her day-to-day life. He had no desire to hear about her hopes and fears or anything in between. Distance. That was the safe way to treat a provocative woman like Bella. But somehow she'd closed the distance between them and now, damn it, he wanted to know her every thought.

Sighing, she turned back to the coffeepot. As she filled two cups with the steaming brown liquid, she said, "An old friend asked for my help and I couldn't refuse her."

"That's admirable. Helping out a friend."

She handed him one of the coffees and they moved over to the couch. Thinking he'd put as much space as possible between them, Noah sat on one end. But Bella eased onto the middle cushion to leave only inches separating their knees.

After she took a careful sip of coffee, she said, "That's just it. I don't know if I can handle this case. All afternoon I've been wondering if I should tell her to find a more experienced lawyer. You see, this is about her brother. He's been arrested on theft charges. And from what she tells me it sounds like a frame job."

Noah felt like cold water had been thrown straight at his face. He knew exactly what it meant to be set up for a fall. He'd not forgotten how the lies and suspicions had eaten at his insides until there'd been nothing left but the shell of a man.

He stared blindly at the floor as his past rushed at him from all directions. "What about the brother?" he asked stiffly. "What's his story?"

"I've not talked to him yet. I'm planning to do that tomorrow. Along with a request to get his bail lowered."

He sipped his coffee in hopes the warm, rich brew would ease the frozen muscles in his throat. "So you think he deserves a chance to tell his side of things?"

Noah could feel her brown gaze boring into the side of his face and from the corner of his eye he could see the space between her brows pucker with confusion. "Well, naturally. Why wouldn't he deserve a chance? Everyone should be considered innocent until proven guilty."

"That's only in a fairy-tale world, Bella. In real life things don't work that way."

"You say that like—have you ever been in trouble with the law?"

He cut her a skeptical glance. "And if I said yes, would that make you get up and leave?"

"No. Everyone makes mistakes of one kind or another. If you have, I figure you've already paid for them."

"I've paid for them all right," he said cynically. "But if it will ease your mind I've never had any run-ins with the law."

She placed her cup on a small table where he kept a stack of reading material, then scooted across the cushion until her thigh was pressed alongside his. Noah watched with a mixture of fear and fascination as she brought her hands up to frame his face.

"Noah," she said softly, "there's so much about you that I don't know or understand. I wish you'd share your thoughts with me. Even a little would make me happy."

The gentle way her hands were cradling his cheeks was unlike anything he'd experienced before. The affection flowing from her fingertips left him feeling cornered and vulnerable and far too weak to pull away.

"You're asking a lot from me, Bella." His voice sounded oddly thick, as though he'd just woken from a deep sleep.

An enticing little smile curved her lips as she murmured, "That's because I want to give you a lot."

Her mouth moved toward his and Noah couldn't deny her or the need inside him. He closed the fraction of distance between their lips and the sweet taste of her instantly flooded his senses, and sent desire throbbing through his body.

He started to draw her closer, then realized he was still holding onto his coffee. Without breaking the contact of their lips, he somehow managed to lower the cup over the arm of the couch and set it safely on the floor. Once he was rid of the hindrance, he wrapped his arms around her and pulled her upper body onto his.

Her breasts flattened against his chest, while her mouth parted, inviting him to take more. Desire shot straight to his brain and sent a torrential rain of heat pouring through his body.

Like a starved man, his tongue thrust past her lips and began a slow, seductive exploration of the ribbed roof of her mouth, the sharp edges of her teeth. Immediately her tongue tangled with his, causing an erotic dance to ensue and all the while he could hear her soft whimpers, feel her fingers digging into his upper shoulders.

The urgency of her kiss drove him onward and he couldn't touch her enough, kiss her enough. As his lips feasted on hers, his hands roamed her shoulders and back before finally slipping low enough to cup around her bottom.

Bella was the first to finally tear her mouth away and as she sucked in long, raspy breaths, she pulled apart the snaps on his shirt.

Once the fabric fell away to expose his bare skin, she said, "I wondered if the rest of you was as brown as your face. Now I can see for myself that you are."

Helpless with need, Noah couldn't do anything to stop the reckless path they were taking. And when she lowered her head and touched her tongue to the center of his chest, his last exhausted attempt to resist collapsed. Like a dam trying to hold back churning flood waters, it burst wide and suddenly it was far too late to push her aside and walk away from the danger.

Slowly, the tip of her tongue made a swathe of moist circles upon his skin until the throbbing need inside him built to an unbearable pressure. Finally, he thrust his hands in her hair and gently lifted her head. And when his gaze connected with her smoky brown gaze, he was too overwhelmed to speak.

"Am I hurting your arm? Your back?" she whispered.

"You're making me hurt all right. But not in those places," he told her in a voice rough with desire.

The corners of her lips tilted upward as she slipped her warm hands down over his rib cage and farther downward to the button on the waistband of his jeans.

"I don't have nursing skills," she said impishly, "but I can try to ease the pain."

He quickly moved them to a sitting position, but even then, she kept her hands on him, as though she feared he still might try to slip away from her grasp. The idea that he could make an escape now was laughable. Except that there was nothing funny about surrendering to this woman's arms. Mistake or not, he was tired of always denying himself the pleasures a man dreamed about, the love he needed to make himself whole.

"Bella." He breathed her name as he nuzzled his nose against her cheek. "I don't want this to happen and then you have regrets."

She eased her head back far enough to look into his eyes and in that moment Noah felt like a very young man, one who'd never been intimate with a woman before. Just touching Bella, looking into her eyes and having her hands move over him felt different and new. And so wonderful it nearly sucked his breath away.

"I don't want you to have regrets either, Noah. That would hurt me more than anything."

"Bella, I—

Before he could finish, she gently placed a finger upon his lips. "You don't have to say it. Neither of us can predict the future. You've already told me no promises. I can live with that for now."

She could live with it at this very moment, Noah thought, but how would she feel later? How long would it be before she wanted more from him? Things that he could never give her? Like marriage, a home and children?

He wasn't going to dwell on those questions tonight, Noah decided. No, for now he was going to simply enjoy the fact that a beautiful woman wanted to be in his bed. Tomorrow would be soon enough to deal with the consequences.

Chapter 7

Noah rose from the couch and pulled her along with him. Once she was standing beside him, Bella's legs began to tremble as if she'd just jogged a fast five miles.

With a breathless little laugh, she snatched a hold on his arm to steady herself. "I think you've knocked my legs out from under me, cowboy."

"I can fix that." Bending forward, he put an arm around her back and the other beneath her legs, then lifted her easily off the floor. "Just hang on."

"Noah! Your arm—the cuts!"

"Shh. A little flyweight like you isn't going to hurt my arm."

Past the tiny kitchen, a door led into a shadowy bedroom. As he carried her into the small space, she caught a glimpse of a standard-sized bed with an iron slatted head and footboard and covered with a light-colored patchwork quilt. Along the outside wall, a window stood open, allowing the pine-scented breeze to drift into the quiet haven.

At the side of the mattress, Noah set her down on a braided rug, but kept his arms planted firmly around her. Their strength and warmth enveloped her with a sense of homecoming and she wondered if he had any clue as to how much he was affecting her. How much he was coming to mean to her.

Her heart was thumping wildly and the more she breathed, the more light-headed she felt. It seemed as if she'd wanted to make love to Noah forever. From the first moment she'd ever laid eyes on him, a feeling of wild, wicked desire had popped into her mind. It hadn't made sense then. But it did now. And as she slipped her arms around him, she felt as though her life was just beginning.

Tilting her head back, she met his gaze and a swell of emotions caused tears to sting her eyes. "Noah, it's been a long time since I—well, have been with a man. Please forgive me if I'm awkward."

His hands gently cradled the back of her head. "Oh, Bella. You could never be anything but perfect. And anyway, I'm not exactly Mr. Romeo."

She splayed her hands against his bare chest and curled her fingers into the patch of curly black hair. "You are to me, Noah," she whispered. "And I want you just as you are."

"You don't know what you're saying. But right now I don't care. All I care about is you. And this."

His head dipped to hers and then his lips were on hers, creating a magic that caused her head to buzz. Excitement hummed along her veins and the glow deep within her ignited into a scorching flame that took away her breath and her ability to think. All she could do was react to the urgings of her body.

Tearing her lips from his, she began to shove his shirt down over his shoulders. In her haste, she forgot about the bandages on his forearm, until he winced and jerked his arm free of the sleeve.

"Oh, Noah, I'm sorry!"

"Forget it." He tossed the denim shirt to the floor. "Just let me do it. It'll be faster."

She stood to one side, watching as he stripped out of his jeans, then sat on the edge of the bed to remove his boots. Once he was down to nothing but a pair of plain white boxers, he reached out and pulled her between his legs. But not before she'd caught an eyeful of broad shoulders and a wide chest dusted with curly black hair. A corded abdomen narrowed down to a trim waist, while the long legs pressed on either side of her were all hard, sinewy muscle.

Being this close to his naked body, with the masculine scent of his bare skin wafting all around her was all it took to send ripples of excitement rushing through her. When his fingers began to clumsily deal with the buttons on her shirt, her nipples tightened with anticipation, her body ached to be connected to his.

Curving her hands over both of his shoulders, she leaned closer, while mentally willing his hands to move faster.

"I thought you said you could do this faster," she said in a breathless rush.

He groaned with frustration. "I thought I could. But these damned buttons are too little for my big fingers."

"Let me do it this way." Brushing his hands aside,

she grabbed the hem of the shirt and quickly tugged it over her head.

After she'd tossed the garment to the heap of clothing he'd already made on the floor, he stood and lifted her onto the bed.

"Be still," he ordered as he reached for the closure on her jeans. "I can handle a pair of jeans."

While he dealt with the button and zipper, Bella focused on the black waves of hair falling over his forehead. She'd never been this close to such a rugged, sexy man and the idea of making love to him was more potent than a shot of whiskey.

By the time he'd stripped her down to nothing but a set of pale pink lacy underwear and joined her on the bed, she was trembling with need, her breaths coming and going in jerky spurts.

He rolled her toward him and she wrapped her arms around his neck and aligned the front of her body next to his. With one arm, he pressed even closer and the sensation of his heated skin sliding against her breasts caused a shiver to ripple through her and a moan to find its way past her lips.

"You feel like a piece of hot satin against me."

His voice was rough with desire and the sound was just as provocative as the touch of his hands moving against her back and down to the lace covering her hips.

"And you feel like everything I've ever wanted," she whispered. "Make love to me, Noah."

He tilted her chin to an angle where his lips could reach hers. His kiss swallowed up her sigh and then he broke the contact between their lips to begin a slow, sweet caress along the side of her throat.

Eventually the tempting kisses reached her collarbone and his hand found its way to the middle of her back to unfasten her bra. Once the flimsy garment slipped away from her breasts, his hands cupped their fullness while his gaze devoured the plump flesh.

When his head lowered and he drew a puckered nipple into his mouth, she cried out with pleasure and thrust her hands into his thick hair. His tongue laved the sensitive bud until she was writhing against him, desperate for even the tiniest form of relief.

Eventually, the hot throbbing in her nipple spread downward until it pooled in the intimate spot between her thighs. The unbearable ache caused her to tug on his hair and lift his head away from her breast.

"Noah—I—can't—wait! I need to feel you inside me! Now!"

Her frantic urgings pushed Noah's desire to the boiling point and it was all he could do to stay in control as he peeled off his shorts and rolled her onto her back.

Once he'd positioned himself over her, he took a moment to look down and as he gazed at her partially closed eyes and swollen lips, her dark hair lying in tangled strands upon the worn quilt, he was quite certain he'd never seen anything more lovely or precious.

"Bella. Oh, Bella, I wanted this to be slow and sure and perfect. But I—"

He didn't finish the rest as she suddenly snatched a hold on his hips and jerked him downward.

"It will be all those things next time," she whispered.

With her hand on his manhood, she guided him into her soft, warm folds. After that Noah wasn't aware of anything except the movement of her body rising up to his, her hands skimming over his back and buttocks, the hot trail of her lips against his skin and the feel of her teeth sinking gently into his shoulder.

The need she was building in him far outweighed anything he'd ever felt before and the realization rocked the ground beneath him. As he frantically drove himself into her, flashes of the room spun wildly around him, while outside the window, the sound of calling night birds faintly registered through the hazy fog.

Tiny particles in his brain were questioning whether he'd gone crazy. If he had, then crazy was a place he didn't want to leave. For the first time in his life he wanted to give the deepest part of himself to a woman, and the feeling was so euphoric he wondered if he must be dying. No living man could feel like this and still be alive.

Time ceased to matter as over and over their bodies crashed together in a perfect rhythm that grew faster and faster until Noah's breath was gone and his heart pounded as if something wild had suddenly inhabited his chest.

Beneath him, Bella was groaning, her hands gripping his buttocks. And then suddenly she was arching and straining against him.

"Noah. My Noah!"

She was slipping over the edge and taking him with her. The frantic fall had him snatching her upper body close to his and with his mouth on hers, he made one final thrust. The release was so great he was certain he'd been catapulted to heaven. Every cell in his body felt like a glowing star and for one brief instant he felt immense happiness.

Rolling away from her, he lay on his back and fixed his gaze on the open window. His breathing was still coming in rapid gulps and though his heartbeat had slowed, it continued to throb loudly in his ears.

He'd never felt more weak and vulnerable in his life. Yet there was a sense of contentment in him that contradicted each doubt that swirled through his mind. In the end, he didn't know which feeling would win out, but for the moment it didn't matter. All that mattered was the fact that Bella was lying next to him. His bed was no longer empty. And neither was his heart.

Sighing, she turned onto her side so that she was facing him. Noah looked over at her and winced with longing as he scanned the soft light in her eyes and the tender smile curving her lips.

"I don't know what to say, Noah. Except that nothing like this has ever happened to me. Not like this."

Her hand reached over and came to rest in the middle of his chest. Noah lifted it to his lips and kissed the tips of her fingers.

"It shouldn't have happened here in this old cabin. You deserve much better."

She scooted close enough to press a kiss against his damp shoulder. "This old cabin, as you call it, was built by my grandfather. I happen to like it. Besides, what just happened between us would have been just as great if we'd been on the ground underneath a pine tree."

The fact that she looked at everything so simply and logically made it impossible for Noah to express his feelings. She couldn't understand his thoughts or fears. He'd be wasting his time to try to explain them.

"Yeah. I expect it would," was all he could manage to say.

Propping herself up on one elbow, she gave him a long, pointed look. "I told you I would have no regrets,

Noah. And I don't. But I'm not so sure you can say the same for yourself."

With a groan of frustration, he pulled her head down to his and cupped his hand against her damp cheek. "If you're thinking I regret what just happened, you're wrong. I feel blessed and honored to have you here with me."

Her soft brown eyes swept over his face. "And what about happy? That's how I want you to be, Noah. Happy."

He tried to smile and the effort made him realize the expression was one he'd rarely displayed in his lifetime. "I'm not sure I know what that is, Bella. If I was ever happy, the feeling didn't stick around. Maybe because I'm not capable of holding on to it. Or maybe I just didn't know what it was when I had it. Either way, you don't need to be worrying yourself about pleasing me. You've given me more than I ever expected to have."

Her hand moved gently over his chest and Noah wondered if this might be how it felt to be touched by an angel. Bella was making him feel wanted and needed and that was a heavenly thing.

The need to put an end to his soft thoughts made him ease away from her and rise from the bed. After fishing his shorts from the pile of clothing, he tugged them on and walked over to the window.

As he breathed in the cool night air, he hoped the sharp, tangy scent of the pines would help to clear his mind. Yet he knew that nothing on earth would be able to erase the passion he'd just experienced with Bella.

So what was he going to do now? How would he be able to keep his hands off her? And if he couldn't, what would it do to his job, his friendship with Jett?

He'd worked so hard to start his life over here on the J Bar S. If everything ended, he wasn't sure he'd have the will to start over again.

The deep thoughts were churning around in his head when Bella came to stand next to him.

"The night is beautiful," she said quietly. "The crescent moon looks like it's pouring silver dust over the mountains."

"It would be prettier if a band of clouds were pouring rain."

She chuckled. "Spoken like a true Nevada rancher," she said, then looked up at him. "Tell me how you came to be a cowboy and rancher, Noah. Was it something you always wanted to do?"

Noah had never talked much about his past. Sometimes with the ranch hands, he'd bring up a story or two about an ornery horse he'd ridden, or a particularly bad spell of weather he'd worked in. But that was as far as his reminiscing went. Bella deserved more than that, though.

"When I was just a little kid, I'd see cowboys on television and a few around the small town where we lived. But all I knew about them was that they rode horses and chased cows."

A knowing smile tilted her lips. "And that seemed exciting to you."

"Well, not any more than a fireman or policeman or some job like that." He slanted her a wry glance. "My parents weren't exactly the sort to encourage education. Being a lawyer like you was as far out of reach as becoming president of the United States."

"In other words, your parents never asked you if you wanted to be a doctor or lawyer."

He let out a caustic laugh. "Hell, my parents couldn't even figure out where their own lives were going. They weren't concerned about what their little snot-nosed boy might grow up to be."

Her hand rested on his arm. "I wish—well, that things had been different—better for you."

He shook his head. "I'm not telling you this for sympathy, Bella. I made out okay. I had a roof over my head and food to eat. And when I went to live with my grandparents some things got better. They had a fairly nice house, plenty to eat, and the utilities were never turned off. But Granddad was a rigid, narrow-minded man, who believed everyone should see things his way. Even if I'd wanted to go to college, he wouldn't have helped. For one thing he was a miser. Secondly, he was a retired copper miner. The job had made him a decent living and he thought I was stupid for not wanting to do the same."

Shivering slightly, she hugged her arms to her chest. "So what happened? How did you go from your grandfather demanding you become a miner, to working as a cowboy?"

Noah shut the window, then took her by the shoulder. "You're cold. Let's go back to bed."

Once they were under the covers and Bella's head was pillowed on his shoulder, he asked, "Warm now?"

"Mmm. Just right." She hugged her arm around his chest. "Now finish telling me about your grandfather."

She wasn't going to let the story of his young life die. Not until he'd finished the whole thing. But oddly enough, now that Noah had started talking, it was far easier than he'd expected.

"There's not a whole lot more to tell, Bella. I learned

early on that it was useless to argue my point. So I kept quiet and stayed out of his way as much as I could. When I was fourteen a friend found us a job on a nearby ranch mucking out horse stalls. We were too young to drive, so every day we had to walk five miles out from town and back. But we didn't mind. I fell in love with the livestock and the land and decided I wanted to become a rancher. The foreman was a nice guy and could see I wanted to learn. He and the hands took me under their wings, taught me how to rope and ride and deal with livestock."

"So how long did you work there?"

"For the next four summers. That was long enough to learn about the work involved in keeping a ranch going."

"From living on the J Bar S, I've learned it's never-ending work," she replied, then asked, "How did your grandfather feel about all this? Was he proud you were learning a trade?"

He snorted. "Proud? Oh, Bella. He didn't see me as a grandson. He saw me as a nuisance. As soon as I turned eighteen and graduated high school, I went off on my own and I've been taking care of myself ever since."

"Did you ever go back to visit your grandparents?"

He sighed. "I've gone back to Benson once and that was to attend my grandmother's funeral. She'd been a good woman and deserved more than what she'd gotten from her husband. Then three years later I learned Granddad had died. But by the time I'd heard about him passing, he'd already been buried. Which was just as well. I don't think I would have gone to say goodbye to him."

When several moments passed and she didn't say anything Noah decided he'd finally managed to break

through to her. The account of his childhood had succeeded in bursting the fairy-tale bubble she'd built
around him. They weren't from the same stock. In a
few minutes she'd find some excuse to get dressed and
make a beeline back to her fancy house. He should be
feeling relief; instead he felt dead inside.

Finally, she said, "When you first told me how your
father dumped you onto your grandparents, I wondered
how a man could do such a thing. How he could turn
out to be such a callous and, frankly, worthless human
being? But it's easy to understand now. He didn't know
how to love you or be a father. How could he? He'd
never had a loving father to teach him."

"I didn't have one, either, Bella. It's a defect in my
family that's been passed on and on. That's why it has
to stop with me. That's why I'm not about to father a
child or take a wife."

She lifted her head to look at him. "Cycles can be
broken, Noah. And you're strong enough to break it.
That is, if you want to."

Did he want to break the cycle and be everything
his father and grandfather hadn't been? There'd been
plenty of times Noah had watched Jett interacting with
his children and he'd wondered how it would be to have
a little person of his own to look to him for love and
guidance and security. To have a part of him live on
through his children was something most every man
wanted. But Noah could see that being a father was a
job that was far too complex for him to handle. Still,
the idea that she believed in him, even after all that he'd
revealed about himself, was enough to warm his heart.

Beneath the covers his hand slipped up and down

her arm. "This guy you're going to defend. I'm glad you're taking his case."

Her head stirred against his shoulder and he knew she was studying his face in the darkness.

"You are? Why?"

"Because sometimes a guy just needs someone to believe in him."

Shifting so that her upper body was lying across his chest, she brought her lips next to his. "We all need that, my dear Noah."

Like a soppy fool, emotions filled his throat and made it impossible to speak. But Noah figured he'd already said more than enough tonight.

With a groan of fresh desire, he deepened the kiss and when her arms fastened tightly around him, he pushed everything from his mind, except making love to Bella.

On Thursday of the following week, on her way home from work, Bella stopped by Jett and Sassy's to spend a few minutes with her nephews and niece.

When she entered the house, she found Sassy in the kitchen dicing vegetables and cutting strips of beef to make fajitas. Skyler, her three-year-old daughter, was sitting on the floor with a coloring book and a small box of crayons. The girl was dressed in jeans and boots, while the flowered headband holding back her strawberry curls gave her a sweet, girly look.

The minute she spotted Bella entering the room, she raced over and hugged her little arms tightly around her legs.

"Auntie Bella! Look, Mommy! Auntie Bella is here!"

The tall woman with a thick red French braid hanging against her back, turned away from her task at the cabinet to greet Bella.

"Well, hello, stranger," she said with a wide smile. "I was beginning to wonder if you'd disowned us or something. You haven't stopped by in days."

Bella reached down and lifted Skyler into her arms, then cuddling the girl close to her, she walked over to Sassy.

"I've been extra busy this week," she told her sister-in-law.

"Jett tells me the office is getting busier and busier."

Work wasn't the only thing that had kept Bella busy this past week. Each evening she'd been racing home, hoping that Noah would stop by to spend time with her.

The night she'd spent with Noah at his cabin had been magical and the next morning she'd emerged into a different world. Everything around her had seemed bright and vividly alive. Each minute of every day was special because it brought her that much closer to being in Noah's arms again.

Crazy or not, she'd given more to him that night than just her body. She'd given him her heart and everything that went with it. Her hopes and dreams and plans were all wrapped up in one tall, rugged rancher—even though she still had no idea what he was really thinking about her or the future.

Since then he had relented and stayed one night at her house. On another occasion, he'd eaten supper with her, but before the evening had progressed to the bedroom, he'd been called away on an emergency with a downed fence and loose cattle. That was three nights ago and she'd not heard from him since. The time apart was not only making her ache to see him, it was also making her wonder if something had caused him to change his mind about her and the two of them being together.

"Very busy. Peta doesn't want help, but we're going to have to hire another secretary soon. Are you sure you don't want the job?" Bella asked teasingly.

Sassy laughed. "Oh sure, why not? Between being a wife, mother, cook, housekeeper and ranch hand, I might as well add secretary."

Bella chuckled. "I know I've said this a thousand times, Sassy, but you're incredible. Jett is a lucky man."

A look of deep affection came over Sassy's lovely face. "No. You got it wrong, Bella. I'm the lucky one to have Jett."

"And Gypsy, don't forget her," Bella tacked on. Gypsy was a young Shoshone woman who worked during the day as the children's nanny. At night she went home to live with her grandparents in nearby Silver City.

"Yes, thank God for Gypsy," Sassy replied. "I couldn't do half of what I do without her help. I just hope she waits a few years before she finds a man and starts having babies of her own."

"Auntie Bella, we have a new baby!"

Skyler's announcement had her glancing down at the child, then tossing a questioning look at Sassy.

She let out a hearty laugh. "No. She doesn't mean that. Not yet."

"Yet? So you and Jett are thinking about another baby soon?"

"Why stop at three?"

Why indeed, Bella thought. Her brother and sister-in-law were deeply in love and they cherished their children. At one time, Bella had expected to have her own family by this stage of her life. But a cheating husband and a bitter divorce had gotten in the way.

Before Bella could give Sassy a reply, Skyler's little hand was patting her cheek in an attempt to get her attention.

"The new baby has spots on his rump. And his legs go like this." She made a wobbly gesture with her arms. "Mommy says he has to learn how to walk. Just like Mason."

"Mason isn't walking now, is he?" Bella asked with dismay. "He's not old enough to pull that off."

Smiling, Sassy turned back to her cutting board. "Skyler thinks her little brother is Superman. She believes Mason should be able to walk at seven months old. The baby she's talking about is our new colt. One of the mustang mares I got from Finn delivered her baby yesterday."

"You wanna see him, Auntie Bella? He's pretty! And he's gonna be mine. Not J.J.'s!"

Laughing at Skyler's emphatic statement, she kissed her niece on the cheek and sat her back on the floor. "I'll have to look at this new baby when I have more time. I have to be heading home soon. By the way, where are your brothers?"

"Daddy took J.J. to the barn," she answered in a sulky tone. "'Cause he's big. I'm big, too, see?"

Bella hid a smile as she watched her niece attempt to make a muscle in her arm.

Sassy groaned. "See," she said to Bella. "Our daughter needs a little sister to have tea parties with and play dolls."

"I don't wanna play with dolls," Skyler argued. "I wanna play with the calves and the new baby horse."

Bella laughed while Sassy shook her head with amused surrender.

"You go finish your coloring," she said to Skyler, "and let me and Auntie Bella finish our talk."

When the child finally made a move to do her mother's bidding, Sassy leveled a pointed look at Bella. "So tell me what's been going on," Sassy urged. "Anything new?"

Only that I've fallen in love with the man I want to spend the rest of my life with. But he doesn't want to make anything permanent with me. That's all, Bella silently answered her question. Aloud she said, "I've taken on a criminal case."

"Yes, Jett mentioned that to me. I think he's a little concerned that you're stressing yourself over the case."

She was stressing herself over Noah, but she couldn't tell Sassy such a thing. Her relationship with Noah was still something private between just the two of them.

Grimacing, Bella asked, "So my brother thinks I'm not experienced enough to handle it?"

"He didn't say that at all. He only said there's a lot of footwork and digging that goes with criminal cases. That's all."

Bella sighed. "Sorry. I didn't mean to sound defensive. It's just that I've been trying all week to gather useful information that might prove my client's innocence. But so far I've not gotten a break. This afternoon, I met with his accuser and that didn't go well." Pausing, she shook her head. "Actually the woman isn't the accuser, even though it was her jewelry that turned up missing. Her husband is the one who filed the charges."

"You say it didn't go well. What happened? She wouldn't talk?"

"Frankly, something has the woman terrified and I believe it's her husband. Though she didn't tell me that outright. Anyway, I have to find a way to make her open up. Because I'm quite certain she knows far more than she's admitting."

"Well, good luck there." Glancing over her shoulder, she gave Bella a clever smile. "What about your love life? Met anyone new?"

Noah had been here on the J Bar S for more years than Bella. But it wasn't until a few weeks ago that she'd been handed the opportunity to say more than five words to him, see him without anyone else around to distract either one of them. No, he could hardly be considered a newcomer here, she thought, but everything she felt for the man was certainly fresh and new.

"No. Not exactly."

Sassy whirled around, her expression eager. "Not exactly? Does that mean you've found someone you're getting interested in? Finally?"

Bella tiredly pushed a hand through her tumbled hair. "I guess you could say that."

"Oh! Who is he? Do I know him?"

You see him every day in the ranch yard, Bella wanted to say. Instead, she merely gave her sister-in-law a faint smile. "It's too early to talk about right now, Sassy."

Clearly disappointed, Sassy asked, "Why? Is he married and trying to get a divorce or something?"

"No. Nothing like that. He's just not ready for a relationship."

"Oh, I see." Groaning, Sassy rolled her eyes. "A man finally comes along and turns your head, but he has cold feet. Maybe you ought to look elsewhere, Bella. If you have to drag a man to the altar, he's not worth having."

Even Casper wouldn't be strong enough to pull Noah anywhere near a marriage altar, Bella thought ruefully. But it was too late for her to look at another man. Noah had already taken up a permanent position in her heart.

"You're right, Sassy. If you have to pull love out of a man like a tooth or a splinter, then you're not getting the real thing," she said, then desperately needing to change the subject, she asked, "Is Mason asleep? I'd like to peek in on him before I go."

"Gypsy took him to the nursery more than an hour ago to rock him to sleep. Another tooth is trying to come in so he's been fussy." She motioned Bella out of the kitchen. "Go check on them. It's time he woke up anyway. Otherwise, he'll keep his parents awake all night."

Bella laughed. "Good reason for me to go fetch him."

A half hour later, as Bella drove away from the main house, Sassy's questions continued to nag at her. Her sister-in-law had wanted to know if the man who'd caught Bella's eye was married or in the process of getting a divorce. Well, Noah wasn't married. That much was evident. But what did Bella really know about Noah's past? Had he ever been in love or engaged? Maybe he'd tried marriage before and it hadn't worked? That could be the reason he was so against the idea of becoming a husband or father.

Other than what he'd told her that night at the cabin about his childhood, he'd said next to nothing about his past. She understood that he wanted to forget the way his family had treated him. But what about the ten years after he'd left Benson and come here to the J Bar S? A lot could happen to a person in that length of time.

Short of robbery or murder, nothing about Noah's past would change the deep feelings she had for him. But something must have happened during those years. Something so heartbreaking it had made him retreat from any desire for love and family. And until she knew what it was, there was no hope in the two of them ever having a future together.

Chapter 8

Sex. That's all he wanted from Bella. That's all he needed.

For the past several days Noah had been repeating the mantra over and over to himself. But try as he might, he couldn't quite convince himself that the only thing he felt for Bella was physical. Maybe that had something to do with the way his heart swelled every time he thought of her tender smile, the sparkle in her eyes when she looked at him. She was a beautiful angel who believed in him. That was enough to make him love her.

Love? Oh, Lord, no! He didn't love Bella. He wasn't ever going to love anyone again. And nothing she could say or do could change his mind about that.

So what are you going to do, Noah? Just continue to use her because she's so willing and intent on having a relationship with you? What kind of man would that make you? A user like your father and grandfather? If

*you were any kind of man at all, you'll end things with
her. You'll set her free to find a loving husband and a
good father for the children she wants.*

The accusing voice in his head continued to haunt
him as he drove away from the ranch yard and headed
east toward Bella's house. But the moment he turned
onto her drive and spotted her walking toward the barn,
the hopeless thoughts flew out of his mind. Sooner or
later, he would have to end this insanity. But for right
now, he couldn't ignore this ache he had to be near her.

She must have heard the approach of his truck because she turned and glanced toward the road. The moment she spotted him, she waved and started walking
in his direction.

Noah parked the truck and quickly strode down the
shady path toward the barn. When he got within reach,
she didn't say a word. Instead, she wrapped her arms
around his waist and held on tight for long, long moments.

"My, my. I feel like a lost teddy bear that's just been
found."

Laughing softly, she tilted her head back and smiled
up at him. "I thought you were lost for good. It's been
three days since I've seen you."

Because of his work, Noah was forced to carry a cell
phone. And he used it when necessary. Especially when
he needed to speak with Jett about a ranching matter.
Otherwise, he didn't send text messages or talk on the
phone and he'd warned Bella of the fact when she'd
given him her phone number a few days ago.

"I guess you're thinking I should've taken the time
to call," he said ruefully.

"It would have been nice," she agreed, her smile forgiving. "But now that you're here it doesn't matter."

"These past few days I've had to work late for one reason or another," he explained. "I thought I was going to get to see you last night, but one of the horses got colic. I ended up staying over on the Horn until two o'clock this morning while Doc Simmons treated him."

"Oh no! Is he going to be okay?"

He shot her a wry grin. "Yeah. And in case you're interested, so am I."

Chuckling, she took him by the hand and urged him toward the barn. "I'm glad to hear you're going to survive, too. You can help me feed the horses. And then if you talk to me nicely, I might feed you, too."

He slanted her a clever look. "I'll try to think up a few sweet words. I'm hungry."

The sight of her smile warmed him as much as the feel of her small hand wrapped firmly around his. By the time they carried the feed out to the horses' trough and returned to the barn to put away the buckets, Noah couldn't keep his hands off her.

In the cool, dim interior of the feed room, he gathered her into his arms.

"I've been dying to do this." He kissed her. "And this," he added, his hands cupping around her breasts.

She dotted rapid-fire kisses on his lips and face, while her hands tugged the tails of his shirt out of his jeans. Her urgent response fed the desire that was already consuming him and he wondered how he could get them both back to the house before he lost all control.

"I've missed you so much, Noah. Make love to me. Now!"

He lifted his head, his gaze desperately searching her face. "Here?"

"Why not?"

The eagerness in her husky voice turned him inside out and before he recognized what was happening, their lips were locked together and he was easing her blouse off her shoulders.

Once the garment fell to the floor, he dropped his head and tasted the creamy skin. "Someone might come down here looking for you."

Her hands shoved at his shirt until her palms were sliding against his bare torso. Three days without her had seemed like an eternity and now that she was touching him, he was certain her fingers had turned to flames, scorching his skin and making him ache for relief.

"They'd call first. No one but you shows up unannounced," she said, her low, husky voice full of amusement.

His lips tracked a moist trail up the side of her neck and along her jawbone. "Want me to stop and give you a call first?"

"You devil. You're not stopping—anything," she finished with a needy groan.

His mouth returned to hers and while they kissed, she guided him backward until they were deep into the room and his legs bumped into a stack of hay bales.

Recognizing her intentions, he allowed her to push him down upon the shelf of hay. With his upper body resting on the makeshift bed and his feet planted firmly on the floor, the pungent scent of alfalfa filled his head. But the smell or the hard stems poking into his back was hardly a detraction from Bella.

Helpless with need, he watched her strip out of her clothing, then waited, his teeth gritted while she opened his fly and freed his throbbing manhood. To have her touching him there was almost too much to bear.

Intent on pulling her beneath him and driving himself into her, Noah jerked upward. But she had other ideas. She shoved him back down and pinned his shoulders against the hay.

"You just lie back and let me do this, cowboy."

Two weeks ago, her boldness would've shocked him. But not now. The few times they'd been together had been enough for familiarity between them to grow. In the beginning he'd fought hard to prevent the closeness from happening. But he'd failed miserably. Now making love to her was as natural as breathing.

"Bella."

Her name was the only word he managed to utter before she moved astride him, then quickly enveloped him into her welcoming body.

The pleasure was so intense he felt sure the hair on his head lifted from his scalp. From his waist down he was on fire and the need to douse it had him grabbing her hips and yanking her downward until their bodies were completely locked together.

"If you're trying to torture me you're succeeding," he said in a choked voice.

"I'm trying to love you," she whispered, then bent her head downward until she could press her lips to his chest. "That's what I want. What I need."

There was something very possessive in her voice. It warned Noah that she had no plans of letting him go now, or in the future. But at the moment he wasn't concerned about the grip she had on him. He'd worry about escaping a heartache later, when his mind was clear and she wasn't using her hands and lips and body to intoxicate him.

What started out fast and frantic ended the same way, but much later, after they'd eaten dinner and retired to Bella's bedroom, they made love again. This time with slow, meticulous pleasure. Once it was over, Noah found it difficult to set his world back on its axis.

Lying on his back, he stared into the darkness and wondered how much longer he could allow this thing with him and Bella to go on. He was falling deeper and deeper into a helpless pit of need. If he didn't climb his way out soon, he doubted he'd ever find the strength. And then what? Just lie back and watch himself ruin Bella's life? And his own?

A long stretch of silence passed before Bella rolled toward him and rested a hand on his arm.

"Are you asleep?"

"No. I thought you were," he answered.

"Mmm. My time with you is too precious to waste sleeping."

His throat thickened, making his voice gruff. "One of these days you're going to look back and wonder why you wasted all this time on me."

Sighing, she scooted off the opposite side of the bed and Noah watched her pull on an emerald-green robe and patter barefoot over to a set of French doors. Once she'd opened them wide and the cool night breeze was wafting into the room, she returned to the bed and sat down on the edge of the mattress.

"So you think I won't always want you here with me?" she asked.

Releasing a heavy breath, he shifted onto his side so

that he could see her. Now that she'd opened the doors, silvery moonlight was illuminating the room and bathing her profile with a soft glow. Never in his life had he ever dreamed he'd be this close to a woman like her.

"I know you won't," he answered.

"Why not?"

"Because pretty soon the sex will cool and then I won't have anything to offer you."

"That kind of talk is insulting to both of us."

"Sorry, Bella. I'm a realist. Not a romantic." He gestured to their surroundings. "Look at this room and compare it to my bedroom in the cabin."

Shaking her head, she traced her fingers alongside his cheek. "That room will always be special to me. Because it was where we first made love."

No, where we first had sex, he wanted to correct her. But he couldn't. In her mind it was love and he didn't want to hurt her any more than he had to.

"Besides," she went on, "what does this damned room have anything to do with us?"

He groaned. "Bella, I'm not a pauper. I have money saved and a small herd of cattle to build on. But I could never provide you with a home like this."

"Why would you want to? We don't need two houses," she reasoned. "And I don't need money or things from you, Noah. I thought by now you understood that."

He fixed his gaze on the open doors and watched the leaves on a cottonwood tremble beneath the night breeze. The idea of loving Bella, of making a life with her, made him tremble the same way. Only his quaking was caused by fear, not by a cooling wind.

"A man wants to give to his woman, Bella. Not take."

"I don't consider myself wealthy, Noah. And I won't until I have a family of my own. That's wealth. Not houses or land or anything money can get you."

If she stuck with him, she'd remain a poor woman, Noah thought ruefully.

She reached over and placed a hand over his. "I've not pressed you to talk about your past, Noah. But I think—well, I get the feeling you're still living there."

Everything inside him recoiled. "What makes you think that?"

"Because you're certainly not living for the future." The tips of her finger traced over his knuckles then down his wrist and onto his forearm. The cuts from the barbed wire were still stitched and covered with Band-Aids but she could have whacked the wounds with a rolling pin and the pain wouldn't come near to matching the empty feeling in his chest.

"I've already told you about my past."

"You've never told me about the years after you left your grandfather's place, before you came here. Was there a special woman in your life?"

"Why the hell would you want to know that?" he barked the question at her. Then before she could answer, he sat up on the side of the bed and pulled on his shorts.

"Because I care about you. Because I want to know the real reason you've hidden your heart behind a barrier of barbed wire."

"What if I don't want to tell you?" he asked bluntly.

She snorted. "If? It's already obvious you don't want to tell me anything. But I think I deserve a few answers, don't you?"

A feeling of inevitability came over him and he

looked at her. "What do you want to hear? The good stuff? The part about where I finally found a family that I put my faith in and cared about? Or would you rather hear the bad? The part about people I trusted turning their backs on me?"

The bitterness in his voice should have been enough to put her off, but it wasn't. Instead, she scooted closer and rested her hand on his bare knee.

"Why don't you tell me about all of it?" she suggested.

With a heavy sigh, he shook his head. "All right. Maybe you do need to hear this. Maybe then you'll see that I'm way too warped to give you the kind of love you deserve."

"Look, Noah, you can't get much worse than what Marcus did to me. Besides, nothing you can tell me is going to make me change my mind about you. You're a good man."

He swiped a hand over his face. "There's a few people down in Arizona who don't think so. And I figure the seven years I've been here hasn't changed their opinion."

"Why? Who are these people?"

"When I left the ranch near Benson I went to work on another ranch not far from Tombstone. A man named Ward Stevens owned Verde Canyon Ranch and almost from the first moment I met him I felt a kinship with the man. He didn't just own the ranch, but he also worked right along with the hands. He had more knowledge of horses and cattle in one finger than most of us will ever acquire in a lifetime."

"So you liked working for him?"

"It was like living a dream, Bella. The ranch covered

an enormous area and though much of it was stark and wild, there were parts when the rains came that would turn beautiful and green. Ward liked my work and dedication and after a few years, he gave me the opportunity to buy into the ranch. My part was small, but it was a partnership nonetheless."

"That must have been very special for you."

"A moment ago when you talked about money not buying the important things, well, that's how I felt about Ward. He treated me like a son and I would've done anything for the man."

She squared around so that she was facing him. "So what happened? If everything was so good, why did you leave?"

"I had no choice," he said flatly. "Ward believed I was sleeping with his wife."

"And you couldn't reason with him?"

He made a cynical grunt. "Aren't you going to ask whether I was having an affair with the woman?"

"Why would I bother with a ridiculous question? I know you wouldn't do something like that. To a friend or an enemy."

Dropping his head in his hands, he wondered why she had to have so much faith in him. Where did all that trust come from? Especially after she'd had a cheating husband.

"Well, it wasn't true. Oh, Camilla had pursued me all right. She'd tried every trick in the book to seduce me, but I wasn't about to stab my friend in the back. Besides, at that time I had met a woman I was beginning to care about. I was even thinking of asking her to marry me. That's how much Ward's love and friendship had boosted my confidence. But that all went to hell."

"So what happened? How did it all end?"

He lifted his head and looked at her. "I made one last effort to reason with Camilla. I even threatened to go to Ward and tell him what she'd been up to. After that she became, I guess you'd call it, a scorned woman To get back at me, she goes to Ward and tells him that I'd been after her. That for weeks I'd been trying to seduce her, but she'd resisted."

"And he believed her?"

"Every word. The more I tried to reason with the man, the angrier he got. He threatened to kill me if I didn't get off the ranch. By then I didn't have much choice in the matter. There wasn't any way to prove my innocence. So I sold my interest in the ranch back to Ward and left Verde Canyon."

"What about the woman you were planning to marry?"

The laugh that erupted from his throat tasted like bitter gall. "When she found out why Ward had run me off the ranch, she turned against me, too. She believed Camilla's story. Not mine."

Bella's head swung back and forth. "So you lost her, too," she said softly.

"I lost everything. Even my reputation. And that was the thing that bothered me the most. People around Tombstone had come to like and respect me. The ranch hands on the Verde had all treated me as their equal. I had finally lifted myself up and out of the broken life I'd had as a kid. But Camilla's lies wiped all of that away."

"I don't understand, Noah. Did Ward's wife seem like that sort of woman when you first went to work on the ranch?"

He shook his head. "Not at all. I never saw her so much as bat an eyelash at any man, other than her husband. She adored Ward, and he did her. He was quite a bit older than Camilla, but that didn't seem to be a problem. They both wanted children and she was having trouble conceiving. When she finally became pregnant they were so happy. Everybody was happy for them. And then when it was nearly time for the baby to be born something went wrong and she miscarried. For a long time afterward it was like a tomb around the house. The grief must have twisted something in her mind. I don't know. But she changed and for some reason looked at me as an escape from her problems."

"I suppose that's why everyone believed her. Because up until the tragedy with the baby, she'd always been a loving wife," Bella said thoughtfully. "So you left Verde Canyon and came here?"

"That's right. And I've never spoken to Ward or Camilla or anyone connected to Verde Canyon since." His expression grim, he looked at her. "See, Bella, I tried to love. I tried to be a part of a real family. It didn't work. I came away from the Verde more broken than I'd ever been before. I'm not about to let myself get into that vulnerable position again. It's not worth the pain."

She stared at him in stunned fascination. "Surely you can't equate all that happened in Arizona with me and you! There's no comparison!"

"Isn't there?" he asked caustically. "No, you're not Jett's wife, but you're his sister. One that he loves very dearly. What do you think he'd say or do if he discovered I'd been sleeping in your bed?"

Rising to her feet, she stood, her hands anchored on either side of her hips as she faced him. "Who I choose to sleep with is none of Jett's business. He'd tell you that himself. Furthermore, he respects you. I figure he'd probably shout, *Hallelujah, Bella finally has a man in her life.*"

With a grunt of disbelief, he reached for his jeans. "You're looking at life through rose-colored glasses."

Her lips pressed to a thin, angry line. "Why? Because I let myself believe in someone? Love someone? You're the one who's looking through distorted lenses, Noah. You see everything in a dark and twisted way! I'm sure a few minutes ago after we made love, you were lying there wondering how long it would be before I stuck a knife in your back."

Standing, he stepped into his jeans and after zipping them up, snatched his shirt from the floor. "Can you blame me?"

She stared at him as though he'd slapped her. "Oh, Noah," she said softly, "don't you think it's time to put all that behind you?"

"That's easy for you to say, Bella. You didn't live through it."

Her jaw tight, she watched him snap his shirt and stuff the tails into his jeans. "You think I lived in a rose garden all my life? You think I didn't go through hell with Marcus? Oh, poor pitiful me. Oh, poor pitiful Noah. Life has been bad to both of us. So let's just give up and go cry in our beer. Is that what you want?"

He jerked on his boots, amazed that he'd been so hot to be with her, he'd not even taken the time to remove his spurs. That was a sure sign he was in deep trouble.

"I want you to leave me alone," he snapped. "Go find someone else to psychoanalyze."

"If I thought you meant that, I—"

"I do mean it!" he interrupted.

He stalked out of the bedroom, but she raced on his

heels. "Where are you going? I thought you were plan-ning on staying the night?"

"That isn't going to happen. Not tonight. Not again."

By now he was striding through the kitchen, intent on escaping through the back door.

As he snatched his hat from a wall peg and tugged it low on his forehead, she hurried up to his side.

"So you're going to run away," she accused. "Run-ning and hiding from your feelings isn't going to fix anything. Besides that, I'm not going to let you take the coward's way out."

He couldn't believe that after all he'd said, after hear-ing the nasty story of Verde Canyon, she still refused to give up on him. A part of him wanted to call her a little fool. But the other part wanted to jerk her into his arms and never let her go.

"Don't waste your time on me, Bella. I don't want that. I want you to be happy."

Before she could try to stop him, he slipped out the door and hurried to the truck. But as he pulled away and headed toward the cabin, he wondered how much lon-ger he could stay here on the J Bar S. How long would it be before Bella's pursuit forced him to quit the ranch and move on?

Two days later, on Saturday afternoon, Noah and Jett rode their horses through a large herd of steers located on the far west range of the ranch. Signs of the continu-ing drought were everywhere. Grass was scarce and in some instances even the sagebrush had succumbed to the lack of water.

Noah was studying a motley-colored steer standing near a patch of prickly pear when Jett reined his horse to a stop. Propping his forearm over the saddle horn, he looked toward the valley floor.

"I remember when that part of the ranch used to be green. Now it looks like someone has set a match to it," he said grimly. "Sassy doesn't want to sell anything with a hide or hooves and I've tried to keep that from happening. But I'm afraid there's not much left to do. Any chance of rain won't come until early winter and even then there's no guarantees."

"Yeah. It's a bad situation," Noah agreed. "But Sassy's a sensible woman. If you decide to sell off half the steers, she'll understand you have no choice."

Jett sighed. "Yeah. But I hate to disappoint her. She thinks I'm some sort of miracle worker." With a wry smile slanting his lips, he looked over at Noah. "It's nice to have a woman put that much faith in you. But sometimes it awfully hard to live up to, you know?"

Noah lifted his hat from his head and swiped a hand through his damp hair. "I wouldn't know too much about that."

What are you lying for, Noah? Bella has put all kinds of misguided faith in you and you've done your best to let her down. When are you going to own up to the truth? When are you going to admit to yourself that you are a coward?

Noah could feel Jett's thoughtful gaze traveling over him and the scrutiny left him cold and sick. The same way he'd felt when he'd driven away from Bella's last Thursday night.

"Something is wrong with you," he said. "Spit it out."

Noah groaned. "Nothing is wrong. It's been damned hot today and I've been in the saddle for most of it."

"If there was ever a man that loves being atop a

horse, no matter the weather, it's you. So try again. That one doesn't fly."

Noah drew in a bracing breath and blew it out. "I might as well talk to you about this now. I've been planning on it, anyway."

Jett's horse made a restless side step and he steered the animal back so that he was facing Noah. "You're having problems with the men," he said before Noah could begin. "I had a feeling Parker was going to cause trouble. He's got an attitude of sorts. But I thought you could deal with it."

Noah shook his head. "There's nothing wrong with Parker. He's a good worker. The men are fine. This is something else…a woman."

Jett's expression looked like a man who'd just been shot. "A woman! Are you kidding me?"

"I wish," he said glumly.

"Why? I think it's great! A woman is just what you've been needing."

The sick feeling boiling in the pit of Noah's stomach grew worse. "You won't think so, when I tell you who the woman is," he muttered.

"I doubt it. I can't imagine you getting hooked up with some floozy. You're too cautious for something like that. Tell me about her," Jett urged.

Deciding he couldn't put it off any longer, Noah glanced away from his friend and fixed his gaze back on the motley steer. The animal was now grazing on the prickly pear, chewing the green pads, spines and all. At the moment Noah felt as if he'd eaten a few cactus thorns himself.

"It's Bella."

Jett stared at him for long moments before a wide

grin finally settled across his face. "You and Bella. I don't know why I hadn't thought of the two of you getting together, but I should have. You're perfect for each other. Damn, Noah, you've made me happy."

He'd expected Jett to be civil about the news, but not anything close to happy. "Hell, Jett, how long have you known me?"

"Close to seven years or something like that. Why?"

Frowning now, he stepped down from the saddle and stood next to his horse's head. The sorrel nudged him on the shoulder and Noah automatically pulled a peppermint candy from his pocket and gave it to the horse.

To Jett, he said, "You know what kind of man I am. I don't have much. And I don't want much. Give me a horse, a few cows to look after and a sky over my head and I'm satisfied. Is that the kind of man you think Bella needs in her life?"

"You're exactly the kind she needs."

"Damn, Jett, you need a vacation from your law office. You're not thinking straight. Bella doesn't need a man like me. I can't give her anything."

"If you're thinking my sister needs a man with money, then you're the one who's messed up. You can take away her loneliness. You can give her love and children and meaning to her life."

"And that's supposed to be easier than giving her financial security?" He shook his head. "No matter. I've already made it clear to Bella that I can't give her any of those things. I—don't plan on seeing her anymore."

The creak of Jett's saddle told Noah the man was dismounting long before he came to stand next to him.

"I hope you don't mean that," he said.

"I made it clear to Bella a few nights ago. But I don't

think— Well, she believes she can change my mind. I won't."

Jett thoughtfully stroked his chin. "I'm getting the picture now. I thought she was upset over a case she's been working on. Instead, it's you that has her all down and out."

If possible, Noah felt even worse. "I'm sorry about that, Jett. I never wanted to hurt her. It's just that she—" He shook his head. "She's put me up on some damned pedestal where I don't belong."

"That's the special thing about having a woman love you, Noah. She'll look past your faults and see the good. I thank God that each and every day Sassy does it with me."

At one time, back on the Verde, Noah had believed there was good in him. He'd worked hard to show everyone that he wasn't like his worthless father, or indifferent, petty, narrow-minded grandfather. But Ward's betrayal had cut Noah down. Now he told himself he didn't give a damn what people thought of him. Not even Bella.

"We better ride on to the windmill," Noah said, abruptly changing the subject. "If it breaks down we'll have some dying cattle on our hands."

Jett gave him an affectionate slap on the shoulder. "Yeah. Let's mount up."

Chapter 9

The next evening was Skyler's birthday party and though Bella wasn't in the mood for merrymaking, she couldn't miss her little niece's celebration.

Dressed in a red-and-white sundress, with her hair pulled into a messy bun, she drove to Jett and Sassy's to join the outdoor festivities.

She'd not been surprised to find a big crowd gathered at the back of the house, partaking of barbecued beef and all the trimmings, but she'd been a little put off by the handful of men who'd been trying to strike up a conversation with her from the moment she'd arrived.

"All right, dear brother," she said to Jett, once she had him cornered away from the crowd. "What do think you're trying to do? I'm not looking for a date or anything like it."

He glanced over his shoulder before giving her a

sheepish look. "Bella, I'm not responsible for those guys. Sassy invited them over from the Horn. I didn't tell her that inviting Noah would be enough to make you happy."

Surprised, Bella stared at her brother. "How did you—"

"Noah brought it up. I think he had some sort of crazy idea that I wouldn't approve of the two of you together."

Rather than letting Jett see the sadness in her eyes, Bella looked down at the cup of punch she was holding. "I'm afraid Noah has some mixed-up notions about a lot of things."

"I thought he'd be here this evening. He adores Skyler."

"But he hates crowds." *And he doesn't want to be anywhere near me,* Bella could have told him. "I wouldn't look for him to show up."

"I think you might be wrong about that."

She looked up to see her brother's attention had turned toward a group of people standing beneath the covered portion of the patio. And then she caught sight of Noah among them. The sight of him dressed in a white Western shirt and dark jeans caused her heart to lurch with surprise and an immense sense of despair.

Before she could tear her gaze away from him, she spotted Skyler running up to him. He reacted to the child by scooping her up and balancing her in the crook of one arm. Bella's heart winced with bittersweet longing as she watched the little girl wrap her arms around Noah's neck.

He would be a wonderful father, Bella thought. Mainly because he knew all the things not to do.

"Looks like I was wrong about him coming to the party," she murmured.

Jett tossed her a knowing grin. "Obviously. I'd better go say hello. I don't imagine he'll stick around for very long."

"Uh, Jett, please don't bring up my name to him. Okay?"

"Why would I bother doing that? You're already on the guy's mind. Besides, you're here and he's here. It's an opportune time for you two to get together."

Noah didn't want to get together with her. That was the whole issue, she wanted to tell her brother. Instead, she simply nodded and said, "I see Reggie's wife and she has the baby with her. Maybe she'll let me hold him."

Before Jett could say more, Bella quickly headed across the yard to where Evita was sitting in a lawn chair holding her new son. She visited with the young woman and baby for several minutes before she eventually walked over to the refreshment table.

After ladling more punch into her plastic cup, she stepped back from the table and was scanning the crowd for a glimpse of Sassy when one of the Silver Horn ranch hands walked up to her.

In his late thirties and single, Denver was undeniably handsome with darkly tanned features and brown hair that was naturally streaked with gold. She'd often heard Jett speak of the man before and knew he was one of the huge ranch's top employees.

"Don't you need some cake to go along with your punch?" he asked with a lazy smile.

Not wanting to appear rude, she smiled back at him. "No thanks. I've already had a giant piece. I'd better stop with it."

He picked up a foam saucer and piled several pieces

of pecans and candied mints on it, then stood beside Bella and began to eat the snack.

"It's a nice evening for a party," he remarked. "Not a cloud in the sky. But I imagine Jett wouldn't have minded to see a few rain clouds gathering."

"Rain would be a blessed relief for everyone." She glanced at him and wondered why she couldn't feel a spark of interest. Why did her heart have to be hung up on a dark, brooding cowboy who wanted to keep pushing her away? "What do you do on the Horn?" she asked politely.

"I oversee the cow/calf operation. I work closely with Rafe, the foreman. I expect you know him."

She smiled faintly. "Jett has been the Horn's lawyer for years and he's married to a Calhoun, so I'm fairly familiar with the entire family."

He said, "I hear you're a lawyer, too."

Bella wondered if Sassy had been discussing her with this man. The notion should've irked her, but it didn't. Sassy was a romantic and she wanted Bella's life to be rich with love and children. Bella supposed she was going to have to confide in Sassy soon. Her sister-in-law needed to know that Bella was locked in a one-sided love affair and that dangling a bunch of bachelors in front of her was pointless.

"That's right. But it will be a long time before I gain the experience Jett has."

"I'm—" Denver's next words suddenly faltered as something behind her caught his attention.

In the next instant, a familiar hand wrapped around her upper arm and Bella realized Noah was the cause of the interruption.

"Sorry, Denver," he said bluntly. "I need to speak with Bella privately."

Her mouth fell open as he quickly led her away from Denver and didn't stop until they were in the front yard, hidden from view by a thick stand of aspen trees.

"What are you—"

Before she could finish the question, her back was pressed against a tree trunk and his lips were devouring hers in a kiss that was spinning her head in a drunken whirl.

"What do you think you're doing?" he asked when he finally lifted his head away from hers.

She sucked in a ragged breath and blew it out. "I was about to ask you the very same thing!"

His nostrils were pinched, the corners of his mouth tight as his blue gaze sliced over her face. And then, just as suddenly his grip on her shoulders eased and he was shaking his head with self-contempt. "Dear God, I've gone crazy! Seeing you with Denver—something snapped in me."

Amazed, she stared at him. "You haven't so much as spoken to me this evening," she said in a voice that was both angry and hurt. "This display of jealousy seems out of place, don't you think? Especially when you told me the other night to go find some other man. Or have you forgotten?"

He took a step back and in spite of being annoyed with him, Bella wanted to grab the front of his shirt and tug him back to her. Which made her thinking just as crazy as his.

"I've not forgotten anything, Bella." He turned aside and stared across the ranch yard, to the barns and corrals where he started and ended his workdays. "And

I'm sorry. Again. Hell, that's all I seem to be able to do, isn't it? Apologize for being a jerk."

He looked so tall and strong, so achingly handsome standing there in his white shirt and black hat pulled low on his forehead. Moments earlier, when she'd been crushed in the circle of his arms, she'd caught a faint whiff of masculine cologne. Before this evening, her Noah had never smelled of anything more than horses and hay and leather. The added scent of sandalwood and sweet grasses made her realize she'd never seen him dressed to go out. The two of them had never been off the ranch together.

The fact might have annoyed another woman, but not Bella. It filled her with excitement to think there was still so much she had yet to learn about this man, so much the two of them could do together. If he'd only give them a chance.

Finally, she said, "I don't want your apology, Noah. I just want you."

He swallowed, then slowly turned back to her. "I'm beginning to see that my days here are numbered."

"What does that mean?"

"It means the only way I can end this obsession I have for you is to leave here."

His answer whammed her like a slap in the face. He thought of her as an obsession while she considered him her love, her life. He was intent on building a canyon between them. Just like the one he'd warned her about riding down.

With tears stinging the back of her eyes, she wrapped her hand around his forearm. "I'm not going to let that happen."

His features were as rigid as a rock mask. "How are you going to stop me? Threaten me, like Camilla did?"

God help her to keep from slapping his face, she prayed. "That chip on your shoulder is growing bigger and uglier. And frankly, I'm getting sick of looking at it. Somebody needs to knock the damned thing off. And I figure Denver could get the job done."

His gray eyes turned to twin blazes. "Like hell!"

Goading him in this way might be wrong of her, Bella thought, but if he wanted to play dirty, then she could, too. "Oh, I don't know, he looks pretty strong to me."

"Strong," he repeated, his soft voice full of danger. "Is that what you want from me?"

Just as she started to answer, he hooked an arm around her waist and jerked her forward. She toppled against him and he used the close proximity to cover her mouth with his.

The contact created an instant combustion and with a groan of sweet surrender, Bella's arms circled tightly around him, and her tongue invited his to join hers in a slow, sensual dance. The words they'd flung at each other no longer mattered. Noah was kissing her, holding her, and for the moment that was enough.

If not for the sound of a nearby vehicle firing to life, the hot embrace might have gone on and on. Instead, they broke apart and Noah quickly stepped back.

Bella gulped for air and tried to stem the shaking in her legs. "Some of the guests must be leaving the party," she voiced the obvious.

"Yeah. And as soon as I say goodbye to Jett and Sassy, I'll be leaving, too. You go on back to Denver. He's the kind of man you need. Not me."

When he walked away, Bella didn't try to stop him. In his present state of mind, it would be useless to try to reason with him. One second he was jealously jerking her away from Denver and the next he was telling her to go back to him. Even if she was a psychiatrist, she couldn't figure his hot and cold behavior. But one thing she did know. She had to use everything in her power to keep him on the J Bar S. Otherwise, her chance for a life with him would be over.

Late Monday afternoon, at an outdoor restaurant not far from Bella and Jett's office building, she sat at a small wrought-iron table, sipping on a cup of Columbian coffee and nibbling at a chocolate biscotti. Aaron Potter, the man sitting across from her, had graying dark hair and a wide affable face. His blue summer-weight suit was rumpled and the knot of his tie slightly askew, but as he talked she got the feeling he was good at his job and that gave her a measure of confidence as she headed closer to Brent Stanhope's trial.

"I'm very grateful to you for meeting me like this," she told him. "Frankly, I had reached a point where I didn't know what direction to take next. My gut feeling is that the husband has hidden the missing jewelry somewhere and plans to collect the insurance on it. The other jewelry is what he used to plant in Brent's car."

"And what was the husband's motive for framing his gardener? From what he tells me, he likes Brent. They've even gone to sporting events together."

This little café was normally one of Bella's favorites. And at this time of the evening, she was usually craving a dose of caffeine and sugar, but since her exchange with Noah at the party yesterday, she'd not wanted to eat or drink anything. And focusing on her work had become a major effort. She had to think of some way to make him see reason, but so far her jumbled thoughts had reached a blank.

"When I spoke with the wife, I got the feeling her husband had warned her not to talk. I also got the impression he controls her with physical threats—if you know what I mean. Brent's a nice-looking young guy. I got the feeling jealousy was the motive in this case."

"Hmm. Sounds reasonable. But a jury would argue that the husband could have simply fired the guy to get rid of him. He didn't need to go to the trouble of framing him with theft."

Bella nodded. "That's true. But the husband saw an opportunity to kill two birds with one stone. Get rid of Brent completely and make some money to boot."

A look of disgust came over the investigator's face. "About three years ago, this guy collected on an expensive vehicle. The insurance company couldn't prove he'd set the fire that turned the car into a piece of tinfoil, but I'd bet my savings account he was guilty then and he's guilty now."

"But how do you get evidence against him?"

"I have my ways, Ms. Sundell. One being to put a tail on the wife and husband and see what turns up. In the meantime, if your client can think of anything that might shed some light on where the jewelry might be stashed, then let me know." He pulled a card from his wallet and pushed it across the table to her. "In case you need to contact me after hours here's my home phone and address."

"Thank you, Mr. Potter."

After she tucked the card away in her handbag, the

two of them continued to discuss the case for a few more minutes before they departed the café.

Bella walked slowly back to the Sundell law office, her thoughts vacillating from the Stanhope case to Noah. When she entered the waiting area, Peta looked up from her work.

"Glad you're back," she said. "Jett wants to see you. I don't know what it's about, but he looked concerned."

"Thanks, Peta. I'll go right in."

After putting her handbag and briefcase in her office, she quickly headed over to Jett's office. She found her brother standing over his desk, gathering papers to take home with him.

"I just now got back from my meeting with the insurance investigator," she told him. "Peta said you wanted to see me."

Nodding, he pointed to a short couch positioned along the back wall of the room. "Let's sit down. I have something to show you."

Suddenly her heart was hammering with heavy dread. Had Noah made good on his threat and told Jett he was quitting his job as foreman of the J Bar S? She couldn't let him leave! Not without her!

Feeling dizzy with fear, Bella headed to the couch. A moment later, Jett joined her. A long business-sized envelope was in his hand.

"This came in my mail today."

Without any more explanation, he handed the envelope to her and as Bella read the address, she could feel the blood draining from her face.

"Jett, this is addressed to Noah in care of you. Why are you showing it to me?"

A clever smile slanted his lips. "Noah talked to me

about the two of you. So I figured you should be the one to give him the letter. It will give you a good excuse to see him."

Ignoring the envelope in her hand, she squeezed her eyes shut. "I guess he told you that he—doesn't want us to be together anymore."

Jett sighed. "Noah is a little misguided. But he'll come around."

"I'm not so certain," she said in a strained voice, then opening her eyes, she looked hopelessly at her brother. "Jett, he's talking about leaving. And all because of me. If that happened you'd be losing the best ranch hand you've ever had. And I—well, I can't even bear to think about him being gone."

Seeing her anguish, Jett put a reassuring hand on her shoulder. "Look, Bella, don't worry about me losing my foreman. From the day I hired Noah, I could see he was way overqualified for the job. He should be running a ranch of his own. He knows it and I know it. Something, I don't know what, is keeping him in limbo. But I don't push the matter with him, frankly because he's not the kind of man you can push. And in the end, I guess I'm selfish. I like having him here."

He pointed to the letter in her hand. "Do you have any idea of what this might be about?"

Bella's gaze dropped from her brother to the return address on the envelope. Camilla Ward, Tombstone, Arizona. "Oh! Oh, no!"

"Bella, what's wrong? Do you know the person who sent this letter?"

Completely stunned, she stared blindly at floor. "No. Not exactly. I mean, he's talked to me about this person before. But I have no idea why he'd be getting a letter from her."

Jett sighed. "Well, Noah has worked for me for seven years and he's never received mail through my office. Apparently this person wanted to make sure he received it."

"I'm wondering how she found him?" Bella voiced the question out loud. "He broke ties with her years ago."

Frowning, Jett asked, "Is she an ex-wife or some-thing?"

The clenched knot in Bella's stomach worked its way up to lodge in her throat. "No. She's— I guess you could call her one of Noah's worst nightmares."

Long seconds ticked away as Jett thoughtfully stud-ied the envelope in Bella's hand. Finally, he said, "If you want to tear that thing up, I'll pretend I didn't see it."

"Is that advice coming from a brother or a lawyer?" she asked dubiously.

"That wasn't advice. Just a brotherly suggestion."

Tearing up the letter and pretending she'd never seen it was tempting. After all of the loss and pain Camilla Ward had caused Noah, it would be an act of mercy to keep her from inflicting more. But Bella wasn't a de-ceitful or manipulating person. If she ever hoped to have a future with Noah, it had to be built on honesty.

"Thanks, Jett, but I couldn't live with that. And the more I think about this, the more I believe he needs to see it."

"So he can stick a match to it and put it all behind him once and for all? That kind of thing?"

She swallowed as apprehension coiled her nerves even tighter. "Exactly."

Jett glanced at his watch. "If you hurry, you might catch Noah before he leaves the ranch yard."

Noah didn't want to see her for any reason. How was he going to react when she showed him this letter? She couldn't worry about that now, she thought, as she hurried out of Jett's office. She could only hope that whatever Camilla Ward had to say would finally put an end to Noah's bitter memories.

Back at the J Bar S ranch yard, Noah was squatted at the front of a chestnut horse, running both hands gently over the animal's left cannon bone. There was a small amount of swelling in the tendon, but no obvious bump.

"I don't like the heat I'm feeling. Lead him down the alleyway, Lew," he told the young ranch hand, "so I can see how he's tracking."

He was intent on watching the horse's movements for any sign of lameness when he heard a light step behind him. Expecting it to be Sassy returning from her check on the mustangs, he didn't bother to look over his shoulder. Instead, he kept his focus on the horse's gait until Lew led the horse in a wide arc, then brought him back to where Noah was standing at the entrance of the horse barn.

"He's out of the remuda for now," Noah told cowboy. "Tie him to the hitching post out front and I'll bring the trailer around. Maybe Doc can make a quick diagnosis. In the meantime, put Coco in the catch pen with the rest of the herd. You can ride him tomorrow."

"Will do," Lew said, then added, "If you have something else you need to do I can take Sweet Potato over to the Horn."

"Thanks, Lew, but I can manage. You have a long drive home."

Lew darted a glance at something behind Noah, then with a shrug led the horse past him. "Whatever you say."

Noah turned with intentions of going to fetch the truck and trailer to van Sweet Potato over to the Horn. But two steps in that direction were as far as he got.

Bella was standing just inside the wide-open doorway of the barn. A close-fitting blue dress hugged her luscious curves and stopped just at the top of her knees. Her dark hair was pulled into a neat coil at the back of her head, while a pair of red high heels covered her feet.

She looked beautiful and sexy, but very unlike herself. Not because she was dressed as a career woman, but because a smile was missing from her face. And suddenly he was wondering if she'd stopped by the ranch to finally end things with him. Maybe his unreasonable behavior at the party yesterday had finally opened her eyes and she'd decided he was someone she didn't want in her life. The idea made him sick to his stomach. Yet it was inevitable and for the best.

"Hello, Noah," she greeted him. "Do you have a minute or two?"

"I was just headed over to the Horn," he told her, glad that he had a legitimate excuse to keep their conversation brief.

"This is very important. I have something to give you."

Her unexpected words had him moving closer. "Give me," he repeated inanely. "What—"

She inclined her head toward the open door of the feed room. "Let's go in there. This is rather private."

Being cooped up with her in a small space was the last thing Noah needed, but she didn't give him time to argue the point. She'd already turned away from him and headed into the feed room. That's when Noah noticed she was holding a white envelope behind her back.

Totally confused, Noah strode after her and followed her into the dimly lit room filled with sacks of grain, alfalfa hay and tubs of supplements.

When she came to a stop in the middle of the room, Noah stood a few steps away, his back resting against a stack of sacked bran.

"What is this all about?" Noah asked.

"You'll have to answer that," she said. "This letter came for you today at the office. It was sent in care of Jett."

Noah didn't get letters. Not the personal kind. His rural mailbox, erected at the main entrance to the ranch, was usually full of junk mail, or a random bill.

"Must be a mistake. I don't correspond with anyone."

She came to stand directly in front of him and Noah couldn't help but notice the piece of paper was trembling as she handed it over.

"Maybe not. But someone is trying to correspond with you."

He flipped the envelope around and immediately felt like someone had kicked him in the teeth. Camilla!

His first instinct was to throw the piece of mail to the floor and grind his heel into it. But shock kept him from making any sort of move.

Finally, he managed to ask, "Why didn't Jett give this to me? He's usually home before I leave the ranch yard."

"My brother thought I should be the one to give it to

you. He doesn't understand that you view me as a contagious disease," she added cynically.

Biting back a curse, he thrust the envelope back at her. "You wasted your time delivering this piece of garbage. Take it. Throw it away."

Her eyes widened with disbelief. "You don't intend to open it?"

"Why the hell should I? That woman ruined my life. Seven years have passed since I left Tombstone. What could she possibly be saying now that could mean a damned thing to me?"

Bella shook her head. "It must've been important to her. She obviously went to a lot of trouble to track you down."

"Like I should care," he sneered.

She studied him with dark expectant eyes and he realized she was expecting him to face this thing like a man. Not a coward.

Running and hiding from your feelings isn't going to fix anything.

Bella's words continued to roll through his mind, taunting and daring him to face the painful memories that had haunted him for all these years.

With a groan of surrender, he ripped the mail open, then handed the contents to her. "Please read it to me, would you?"

Uncertainty crossed her face as she glanced from the letter to him. "Are you sure? Maybe you should read this privately," she suggested.

"No. Whatever the woman has to say I want you to hear, too."

Nodding solemnly, she unfolded the stationery and began to read.

Dear Noah,
This letter is to sadly inform you of Ward's re-cent death. For the past two years his health had steadily declined, and heartbreaking as it was for me, he welcomed the end.

I understand I have no right to ask you for any-thing, but I need for you to come to Verde Can-yon as soon as possible. There's much we need to discuss.
Camilla.

Ward, dead!

Completely stunned, Noah moved a few steps over and sat down on a low stack of hay. "I can't believe it, Bella. Ward would've only been in his late fifties!"

She stepped over and placed a comforting hand on his shoulder. "I'm so sorry, Noah. I think—well, in spite of everything that happened with the two of you, I know how this must hurt."

Amazed that she could understand something that was only beginning to register with him, he looked up at her. "Why does it hurt, Bella?" he asked hoarsely. "I thought I hated the man."

"He wounded you deeply and that was your way of coping. Believing you hated him took some of the pain away."

An utter sense of loss welled up in him and before she could see the sting of tears in his eyes, he dropped his head and swallowed hard. "I just wish he hadn't gone to his grave believing I'd wronged him."

"Maybe he didn't."

Frowning now, he lifted his head. "Isn't it obvious? Camilla didn't write until after he was gone."

"There could be all sorts of reasons why you're hearing from her now instead of before the man died. That's why you have to go to Verde Canyon and see her. To find out exactly why she wants to see you."

He shot to his feet and began to pace around the dusty room. "Are you crazy? That woman caused me nothing but misery. She not only ripped apart a friendship, she tore down everything good I had built to that point in my life. Face her again? Hell no!"

He didn't realize Bella had caught up to him until she wrapped a hand around his forearm. "What are you afraid of? She can't hurt you now. Or are you worried you might run into your old girlfriend? The one you were thinking of marrying? Maybe her desertion bothered you much more than the debacle with Camilla and Ward."

He frowned with disbelief. "Do you honestly think that?"

She shrugged one shoulder. "I don't know what to think. The way I see it, neither one of these women should be striking a chord of fear in you, but it looks like they are. You're afraid to travel down to Arizona."

Groaning with frustration, he shook his head. "Kelsey was just a girlfriend. It's true I was considering asking her to marry me. But now that I've had years to think about it, I can see that notion wasn't prompted by love. It was because she was the first woman with any class to show me some respect and I was grateful more than anything. The fact that she lost faith in me probably turned out to be a good thing. Even if I had gotten around to proposing to her, I doubt a marriage between us would've lasted a year."

"Then if it's not her that's keeping you from going, it has to be Camilla."

"Damn it, Bella, it's not her! Not exactly. She was never anything more to me than a friend. And after she went crazy, I didn't even consider her to be that much It's just that the whole place—the Verde—I loved it with all my heart. I don't know that I can bear seeing the ranch again."

She squeezed his arm. "I'll go with you, Noah. We'll go together."

"Why would you want to do that? This is my baggage. My problem."

A tender expression came over her features as she slid her arms around his waist and snuggled the front of her body to his. "Oh, Noah," she said softly, "you should know by now that I love you. I don't want to share only good times with you. I want to share the troubled times, too."

Noah's heart was aching to put his arms around her, to hold on tight and never let go. But he couldn't let pain sway him. "No. You have some misguided notion that I'm a good man. Good enough for you, that is. And you're wrong."

"And you have the foolish notion that you can control what my heart feels for you. But you can't, Noah. No more than you can control what your heart is trying to say to you."

His jaw clamped tight, he moved away from her tempting body and turned his back to her. "I'm not going to Tombstone, Bella. We're not going. Ward is dead. Everything is dead. Over. Why can't you get that through your head?"

"Nothing is over, Noah. It's just now beginning.

Pretty soon you're going to wake up and see that for yourself. When you do, you know where to find me."

He was trying to think of some way to shoot down her comments when he heard her high heels clicking past him and out the door of the feed room.

Glancing around, he spotted the letter still lying where Bella had laid it on the hay bale. He walked over and stuffed it and the envelope in his shirt pocket, then strode quickly out of the feed room.

Sweet Potato was waiting at the hitching rail. He couldn't stop to think about Ward's death or Camilla's request for him to return to the Verde. And he especially couldn't let himself dwell on thoughts of Bella.

But as he jumped the lame horse into the trailer and headed toward the Silver Horn, three little words continued to revolve around and around in his head until they settled smack in the middle of his heart.

I love you.

What was he going to do now? Leave for Tombstone with Bella in tow? Or leave the J Bar S and Bella behind?

Chapter 10

By the time Friday rolled around Bella still hadn't heard a word from Noah, although she'd learned through Jett that Noah had shared the contents of the letter with him and explained what had transpired seven years ago on Verde Canyon Ranch.

For the past few days since they'd talked in the feed room, she'd been hoping and praying that he would come to the conclusion that traveling to Arizona and facing Camilla was the best way to start his life over and begin a new one with Bella.

She'd told him that she loved him and maybe that had been a mistake. He'd just learned that his old friend was dead and that Camilla wanted to see him. No doubt he'd been too shocked for his mind to register much. But he'd had days to think about it now, she reasoned as she shut down the computer on her desk.

You might as well face it, Bella. Noah doesn't want to start his life over with you. He doesn't care whether you love him or not. The only thing he ever wanted from you was sex and now even that is over. So move on and forget the man.

Bella was trying to shut down the voice in her head, when Jett suddenly walked into her office carrying a bouquet of red tulips.

Trying her best to give him a cheerful smile, she asked, "You're giving Sassy flowers tonight? What's the occasion?"

"These aren't for Sassy, though God knows she deserves to get flowers every day," he said. "These are for you, dear sis. I know you like red so I picked these."

"Picked them yourself, huh? Right from the flower shop?" she teased, then shook her head. "Why am I getting flowers? Do I look like I need something to perk me up?"

He placed the flowers on the corner of her desk, then leaned down to brush a kiss on her pale cheek. "Frankly, you've been looking awful."

Sighing, she switched off the lamp on her desk. "Thanks. Every girl wants to hear that."

He regarded her with a keen eye and Bella knew he was thinking about bringing up the subject of Noah. But thankfully, he didn't. Instead, he said, "The flowers are to say congratulations for getting Brent Stanhope exonerated of all charges."

Smiling wanly she rose to her feet and gathered a stack of case folders for Peta to file away. "I can't take the credit for that, Jett. Mr. Potter figured it out."

"Not without your help," he said knowingly. "You're the one who pulled the truth out of the wife."

Yesterday Bella had decided to talk with the woman again and her persistence had paid off. Rather than making threats, she'd appealed to the woman's fears and pointed out that her penalty for aiding her husband in a crime would be much less if she would confess. Thankfully, the woman had finally relented and admitted her husband had planned the whole scheme. As a result, the insurance investigator had caught him trying to sell the missing jewelry at a pawn shop in Las Vegas.

"Well, I'm just glad Brent is free and his record is cleared." She pointed to a gold-colored box on the corner of her desk. "Valerie sent me a card and chocolates. Along with a promise to take me out to dinner. Needless to say, she's happy."

Jett curled his arm around her shoulders and hugged her to his side. "I'm proud of you, sis. I only wish I could see a happy smile on your face. A real one."

"Don't worry about me, Jett. I'm not going to fall apart." Not yet, at least. But her heart was definitely close to cracking right down the middle.

"Noah is going to come around, sis. I don't have to tell you he's a man who holds things inside. He's needs time to digest everything that's happened."

Sighing, she said, "I'm beginning to think it's just not meant for me to have a husband and family. What am I doing wrong, Jett? After Marcus I waited so long to even let myself think of getting into another relationship. Now I've fallen in love with a man who's determined to be a bachelor for the rest of his life."

Before Jett could make a reply, she crossed the room and plucked the sweater she'd worn to work this morning from its hanger and tossed it over her arm.

When she returned to the desk and picked up the

bouquet of tulips, Jett said, "Right now Noah doesn't believe he's good enough to be your husband."

Frustration boiled over, making her glare at her brother. "What is it with you men and your egos?" She waved her hand in dismissive fashion. "Don't bother trying to answer that. It doesn't matter. I'm damned tired of trying to stroke Noah's, to try to pump him up and make him believe in himself! If he can't believe in himself, then why the hell am I wasting my time with him?"

She started toward the door, then realizing she'd forgotten her handbag, returned to her desk and collected it from the kneehole.

"Where are you going?" Jett asked.

She slung the strap of her handbag over her shoulder. "Home. Do you mind?" she asked sharply.

"I'm not your boss, Bella. You can do whatever you please. But don't you think Noah is the one you should be yelling this stuff at? Instead of me?"

Jett's questions brought her up short and with a rueful groan she shook her head. "I'm sorry, Jett. I shouldn't have gone off on you like that. I'm behaving like a shrew. And none of this is your fault. It's all mine."

"Forget it, sis. I already have."

With a grateful little smile, she kissed his cheek. "I'm going home and saddling up Casper. I've not given him any exercise in a while. Maybe the fresh air will help clear my head."

"Good idea. Just be sure and take a raincoat with you. The weatherman predicted a shower today."

Laughing now, Bella headed to the door. "Now, that is funny. Rain in June? After months of drought? You were listening to a fantasy, dear brother. Not a weather report."

"Just humor me and tie a slicker on your saddle. Okay?"

"Okay. Whatever you say."

Later that evening, Noah and two other ranch hands were standing just inside the door of the barn, waiting for the downpour of rain to slack enough to finish the barn chores.

"I don't think it's going to slow down," Reggie spoke above the roar of the rain pelting against the tin roof.

"I'm with you on that," Lew agreed. "And I don't want to stand here for hours. Let's drag out the slickers and finish the feeding."

"Don't complain, guys," Noah said, "this means more grass and less time spreading hay."

With good-natured grumbling, the two men left to fetch the slickers from the tack room. Noah remained standing at the door's edge, watching the rivulets of water creating tiny creeks across the packed ground in front of the barn. Lightning continued to crackle close by and Noah thought about the horses they'd turned out to pasture earlier that morning. Instinct would have them running straight for the shelter of the trees. Hopefully, the lightning would spare them.

Just as Reggie and Lew were returning with the slickers, Jett caught the faint sound of his cell phone ringing. As he pulled it from his pocket to answer, he stepped backward, hoping to lessen the din of the rain.

"Yes, Jett, it's raining here," he said before the other man had a chance to say anything. "We're going to have grass now, buddy!"

"The rain is a welcome sight," Jett agreed, "except that it has me worried."

"Can't do anything about the lightning, Jett. Just pray the cattle and horses don't get hit."

"It's not the livestock I'm worried about. It's Bella. She left work early with intentions of riding Casper. I warned her to take a slicker, but I never expected a storm like this. Otherwise I would've told her not to go!"

Noah felt like an icy north wind just whammed him in the face. "She probably has her cell phone with her. Have you tried calling?"

Jett blew out an impatient breath. "For the past thirty minutes. My calls are going straight to her voice mail. I've been ringing her landline, too, but no answer there, either. Are you still at the ranch yard?"

"Yeah. We still have a few chores here."

"Oh, I thought maybe with the rain you'd already headed home and spotted her along the way."

"Don't worry, Jett. I'm going to go look for her."

"Noah, that would be like searching for a rabbit in a field of rose hedge! When Bella goes riding it's not just a little five-minute jaunt from the house and five back. She might go for miles. Especially considering the mood she was in!"

Jett's last remark caught Noah's attention, but he didn't press the other man to explain. There wasn't time for that. Besides, Noah had been in a hell of a mood himself for the past few days.

"I said don't worry," Noah clipped. "I have an idea where she might've gone. I'll call you as soon as I find her."

He abruptly ended the call and turned to see Lew and

Reggie walking up the alleyway of the barn. He hurried to meet them and snatched one of the oiled dusters thrown over Lew's shoulder.

As he jammed his arms into the sleeves, he said, "Sorry, guys. An emergency has come up and I have to leave. You two handle things here."

Reggie asked, "Don't you need our help?"

Already in a run out of the barn, Noah yelled, "I'll call you if I do."

Once the dirt road passed the main ranch house, it was rough and rocky, but today with water already washing out ruts and dislodging boulders, the track was downright treacherous. Noah tried to go as fast as possible, but every few feet he was forced to downshift and jerk the steering wheel one way and then the other.

All the while he negotiated the truck over the rough terrain, icy fear continued to grow inside him. If Bella had ridden down the canyon, a flash flood could have swept her and Casper away. But even if she wasn't in the canyon, lightning was cracking all across the mesa. Even if it didn't strike her and the horse directly, it could definitely cause a tree to crash down on them.

What are you getting all panicky about, Noah? Other than being your boss's sister, she's nothing special to you. If she'd been that special, you would've already told her so. You would've confessed to her that she was the very beat of your heart. And you certainly wouldn't keep pushing her away.

Cursing at the mocking voice in his head, Noah twisted the windshield wipers to the fastest speed and hunched forward in an effort to see through the downpour. If Bella was out there, he'd have hell seeing her like this, he thought grimly.

Nothing is over, Noah. It's just now beginning. Pretty soon you're going to wake up and see that for yourself. When you do, you know where to find me.

These past few days Bella's words had been haunting him, making him wonder if he was a selfish bastard, a complete fool, or both. Now he was getting the uneasy feeling that she was right. His eyes were opening, but at the moment he didn't know where to find her.

By the time he reached Bella's house, Noah had failed to spot her or any sign of Casper's hoofprints in the muddy road. After a quick glance around, he headed to a garage built on the far end of the house. Her car was parked inside, so she'd clearly made it all the way home.

At the back door, he pounded loudly. "Bella? Are you in there?"

After a few moments passed with no response, he hurried to the barn. Mary Mae was dry and safe in one of the stalls, while Casper was nowhere to be seen. Noah was certain Bella would never stall one horse and leave the other in the pasture, so that meant she was still out in the storm somewhere. And the only way to find her was to saddle up and start searching.

A few minutes later, he reined the bay mare away from the barn and down a dim trail leading south. With heavy rain falling for more than an hour, there was no chance of spotting the tracks Casper had made when Bella rode away from the barn. Noah could merely guess and hope he was on the right path. But something deep in his gut told him she'd ridden to the canyon.

He'd warned her not to ride there alone. Besides the terrain being extremely rough, flash flooding could occur in a matter of minutes. But Bella didn't exactly follow his advice, he thought ruefully. In her opinion, he was overly cautious and too worried about something going wrong to let himself enjoy the pleasures of life. And perhaps he did approach everything with caution. Even loving her.

We've gone through this before, Noah, you don't love Bella. You love taking her to bed, that's all.

Then why the hell was he out here, in the middle of a violent thunderstorm, searching for her? Streaks of lightning were exploding over his head. Rain was pelting his face and turning the brim of his hat into a waterfall. He wasn't out here just because he enjoyed her warm, giving body, he thought desperately. No, Bella had become precious to him. So precious that if anything happened to her, his world would be nothing more than a black abyss.

After what seemed like an eternity, he reached the rim of the canyon and continued to travel along the edge until he found a spot he considered safe enough to descend the steep wall. But Mary Mae had other ideas and refused to take the path he'd chosen. Deciding she probably had more sense than he did about such things, he gave the mare her head and before long she found a crevice in the canyon rim wide enough for the two of them to pass through.

Patting her neck, he encouraged the courageous mare forward. "Good girl! Now see if you can get us to the bottom safely."

A half mile on down the canyon, Bella and Casper were perched on a narrow shelf of earth. Less than three feet beneath them, churning, muddy water raced over the canyon floor, carrying tumbleweeds, broken limbs and old logs. Small willow trees and bushes of sage bent beneath the force of the current and Bella realized if the rain continued to fall at this rate, the water would rise quickly and become even more dangerous.

Earlier this afternoon, when the rain had first started, she'd donned her slicker and turned around to head for home. But the storm had intensified very quickly. She'd tried to shelter beneath a small copse of evergreens and call Jett to give him her location and assure him she was on her way home. But the weather had knocked out the signal, making her phone useless.

Now the narrow shelf where she stood hunched next to Casper was only a temporary refuge. She needed to get herself and the horse out of the canyon. But even if she led the horse, rather than ride him, the bank behind them was far too steep and muddy for either of them to make the climb. That meant her only choice was to try to ford the water until she could find a place to climb to safety.

Oh God, she should've listened to Jett's prediction of rain. And she definitely should've heeded Noah's warning not to ride alone in the canyon. But for the past few days the constant ache in her chest had worn her down and the wild beauty of the canyon had started to call her. It was the one place where she could stop her mind from spinning long enough to really contemplate what was important in her life and what baggage she needed to throw away.

Before the storm had hit, she'd been thinking how much she loved Noah and how much he'd brought to her life. Earlier today, when she'd been talking to Jett, she'd lost her patience and her temper. But now, with rain streaming into her eyes and bolts of electricity dancing around her, she realized that no matter what

Noah said, or if he went so far as to leave the J Bar S, she wasn't going to give up on him or the hope of them being together.

God willing she made it out of this flash flood, she was going straight to his cabin and she wasn't going to leave until he agreed to go with her to Arizona. He'd left his wounded heart there. And until he got it back, there was no hope he'd ever give her a piece of it.

Suddenly there was a flash directly across the span of rushing water and she looked up just in time to see a huge pine splitting down the middle. Fire blazed along the trunk, while ear-deafening thunder echoed through the canyon.

Terrified, Casper jumped backward. Bella screamed and stared in horror as the horse's back feet teetered on the edge of the solid ground.

"Whoa, boy! Whoa!" Knowing she had to appear strong and reassuring to the horse, she firmly pulled him forward until he was safely back to the center of the ledge. Then gently stroking his neck, she pressed her cheek against his. "It's okay, big guy. We're going to get out of this."

Casper nickered as though he understood what she was saying and then she realized his ears had gone on point, telling her he'd spotted something out there in the storm.

Turning, she stared through the white wall of rain, blinking at the rivulets running into her eyes. She could see nothing. But then she heard the faint sound of another horse answering Casper's call.

Could it be coming from a wild herd of mustangs seeking shelter from the storm, or had someone actually come looking for her?

By the time the horses exchanged another whinny, Bella spotted a horse and rider slowly making their way along the side of the north canyon wall. The muddy water churned all the way to the horse's knees and not far from the rider's stirrups.

Oh, God! It was Noah on Mary Mae!

More terrified than she'd ever been in her life, she watched the two of them slowly making their way toward her and Casper. There was no way of predicting if the mare's next step might take them into a deep hole or if she might walk straight into a boulder. Either way, Noah would probably be jolted from the saddle and into the churning water. The mare would bolt and end up in even more danger.

Why was he risking himself like this? Why hadn't he called the county rescue unit and let them take care of her? Could she dare hope it was because he might actually love her?

"Casper, the storm has made me delirious," she said to the horse. "I'm not thinking straight!"

Long, tense minutes passed before Noah finally got close enough to call out to her. By then it was all Bella could do to keep her tears at bay.

"Bella, are you okay?"

"I'm fine," she called back to him. "Just wet. I don't know how Casper and I are going to get out of here."

"You're going to have to ride out. The way Mary Mae and I came in."

Bella had always thought of herself as brave, but when she looked at the swirling water below her, she could feel her knees begin to quake.

"I'm not sure I can. The ground was barely covered with water when I jumped Casper onto the ledge. I don't think he'll be too happy to leap off dry ground and into a raging creek."

"Happy or not, you have to make him do it," he yelled above the roar of the rain and thunder. "Mount up and I'll throw you a rope."

Seeing no other way, Bella followed his instructions and climbed into the saddle. Noah rode closer and tossed her the end of a lariat.

"Tie that around the horn. If Casper stumbles or falls it might help keep him upright."

Nodding, she looped the rope around the saddle horn and tied it as tight as her cold, wet fingers could manage.

"It's tied. Now what?"

"Make him jump toward me. Once he gets his feet under him we'll head back in that direction." He pointed to the east and Bella nodded that she understood his instructions, but following them through was going to be another matter.

Bella didn't have time to sit there worrying or trying to gather her courage. With each passing minute the water was rising. If they didn't get out of the canyon soon they were going to be swept away completely.

Fighting the urge to close her eyes, she kicked Casper forward. When he halted at the edge, she smooched to him and gave him a tap on the rump. He leaped and as they hit the water, it splashed all around her, momentarily blinding her. Beneath her, she could feel the horse stumbling, falling to his knees. Water filled her boots and soaked her jeans all the way to her waist, but she hardly noticed the discomfort. Instead her entire focus was on lifting the reins in an effort to help the animal stay upright.

"Hang on, Bella! Don't let him fall."

Somehow the horse found stable footing and with great relief, she slumped weakly forward in the saddle, but there was hardly time to catch her breath before the tug of the lariat reminded her that they had to keep moving.

It took them more than a half hour to navigate their way back to the point from where they could climb the canyon wall and finally reach safety. There were several times Bella wondered if she could go on. Between her heart racing with fear and the struggle to ride over such rough terrain, she was exhausted.

When they finally finished the climb and arrived on top of the mesa, Noah suggested they dismount and allow the horses to rest. Bella wholly agreed, but she was trembling so badly she couldn't move. Noah had to literally pull her boots from the stirrups and lift her out of the saddle.

Once she was in his arms, they both sank to the ground where Noah tucked her head to the middle of his chest and buried his face in her wet hair.

"Oh, Lord, Bella, I thought I was going to find you drowned or dead from a lightning strike!"

Her arms barely found the strength to wrap around his neck. "Noah! When I saw you riding toward me, I—you were an answered prayer."

Clutching her tightly against him, he stroked his fingers through the soppy clumps of her hair. "I couldn't believe it when I saw you and Casper on that ledge! You crazy little fool! I told you not to ride in the canyon alone! I told you it was dangerous!"

Rearing her head back, she looked at him. "That's right. You've told me just about everything, except what

I want to hear. Please, don't scold me, Noah. Not after what we've just gone through. You can do that later. Just tell me—"

He stopped her next words with a kiss that was both desperate and exhilarating. Then leaning his head back, he looked straight into her eyes. "All right, Bella. We'll go to Arizona. Together. Is that what you want to hear?"

With a cry of joy, she hugged him tightly. "It's a start."

On late Saturday evening, Bella and Noah's flight touched down at Tucson International Airport. From there they took a rental car to a downtown hotel where Bella had already reserved their rooms for the night.

While she dealt with the task of checking in, Noah waited in the lobby with their luggage. Since it was the weekend, the hotel was bustling with guests and hotel staff, but Noah hardly noticed the comings and goings around him. Beyond the wall of plate glass, a view of Tucson spread out beneath a blazing summer sun. Yet the buildings with their Spanish architecture and desert landscaping barely caught his attention. It was the wilderness beyond that grabbed his thoughts and hurled them back to the time when he had ridden over similar jagged hills and through stands of ancient saguaros, their arms lifted toward the blue heaven.

"All set," Bella suddenly spoke behind him. "We're on the seventh floor."

Pulling himself out of his memories, he turned to her and was immediately whammed all over again. A turquoise sundress hugged her slender waist while intricately designed cowboy boots covered her feet. Silver set with green malachite hung from her ears and adorned her wrist. But as always, it was the soft, tender smile on her face that made her incredibly beautiful.

Throughout the flight, he'd struggled to keep his eyes off her, but now that they were on solid ground, it was clear that keeping his hands to himself was going to be even more of a problem. More than two weeks had passed since the two of them had been intimate and the memory still continued to haunt him. For reasons he didn't want to examine, being in her arms that night had left him feeling particularly vulnerable and when she'd pushed him to talk about his past, everything about Ward and Camilla had come tumbling out of him.

He'd behaved like a jackass and stormed out, but that had been the only thing left for him to do. Except stay and admit to Bella that he'd fallen in love with her. And he'd not been ready for that. He didn't think he'd ever be ready to surrender that much of himself to anyone.

Picking up the bags, he said, "Fine with me. Let's go."

They walked to the nearest elevator and took a quick ride to the seventh floor. When they stepped off, Noah asked, "Which way to our rooms?"

"This way," she answered, pointing to their right. "But before we get there I—uh—should tell you we only have one room."

He dropped one of the bags in order to clasp his hand around her upper arm. "What do you mean, one room? I told you to book two?"

As Noah watched a soft pink color sweep across her cheeks, he knew he was in even more trouble than he thought. It was bad enough that he hadn't touched her in days, but now he was going to be sequestered in the same bedroom with her.

Her brown eyes glinted. "That would've only been a waste of money. Besides, you don't have to sleep with me unless you want to. The room is equipped with two queen-sized beds."

Unless he wanted to? Hell, for the past two weeks that's all he'd been wanting. But he'd been fighting the urge, just as he'd been fighting his feelings. Ever since he'd found her in the canyon looking half-drowned, huddling next to her horse, his emotions for the woman had been growing like a tumbleweed in a stiff wind. Yeah, he could admit that to himself, but he couldn't let Bella in on his secret. Not now or ever.

He dropped his hold on her arm and picked up the bag. "And we're damned well going to use them," he promised.

She rolled her eyes at him. "Whatever you say, Noah. I wouldn't want to make you do anything against your will."

The absurdity of her remark pulled a short laugh from him and the sound must have shocked Bella because she stared at him in comical disbelief.

"Noah, I think that's the first time I've ever heard you laugh." Smiling happily, she looped her arm through his and urged him down the corridor. "Come on, let's go find our room and get comfortable."

Although, Bella would've preferred to order their evening meal through room service, Noah insisted they go down and eat in one of the restaurants inside the huge hotel.

She didn't argue the point. After all, just getting Noah to this point was a miracle in itself and for the past two days she'd been wondering what had finally pushed him to decide to make this trip to Arizona.

Clearly the trauma of the storm had done something to him. Even so, she still didn't know what he was actually thinking or feeling. That evening, when the two of them had finally returned to her house, Jett had been there, anxiously waiting to make sure the two of them were unharmed. With her brother there, she'd expected Noah to make a quick exit. Instead he'd hung around to care for the horses and the sopping wet saddles and blankets. Later, he'd even made coffee for the three of them and once Jett had finally departed, she'd decided Noah would stay with her. At least long enough for them to make love. Instead, he'd asked her to make travel arrangements for the two of them, then given her an abrupt goodbye. Now she was beginning to doubt he'd ever want to take her to bed again.

"Thank you for dinner, Noah. It was delicious," she told him, once they'd had their meal and returned to their room. "You know what I was thinking while we were eating?"

He loosened the bolo tie around his neck and Bella allowed her hungry gaze to travel over his tall, muscular body. Other than the day at Skylar's birthday party, she'd never seen him in anything other than jeans or cowboy gear. He looked exceptionally handsome dressed in dark, Western-cut trousers, expensive alligator boots and a tailored white shirt. Yet she had to admit that she loved seeing him best in his chinks and spurs, his dusty felt pulled down on his forehead. That was her Noah. Her rugged rancher.

"That you shouldn't have ordered green sauce on your enchiladas?"

Laughing, she sank onto a small couch near the window and began to tug off her boots. "The sauce was scorching," she admitted, "but it was delicious. No, I was thinking how this is the first time you and I have ever been anywhere together—off the J Bar S, that is."

He shot her a wry glance. "There for a while during the storm, I thought I'd be attending your funeral about now."

"You probably imagined burying Casper, too," she added thoughtfully, then shook her head. "God, if I had caused that horse to be hurt, I would've never forgiven myself."

"I'm glad to know you care that much about Casper."

A knowing smile tilted her lips. "Well, I wouldn't have wanted you to be hurt, either."

Without making a reply, he walked over to the window and for long moments Bella sat there watching him stare out at the darkening sky. Whatever was on his mind, she wanted him to share it with her. But would he ever want to share that deeper part of him, she wondered. Would this meeting with Camilla finally open his heart? Or would seeing Verde Canyon make him even more disenchanted?

Rising from the couch, she went to stand by his side. "I don't believe I've thanked you for saving my life."

"You're being melodramatic. You're a smart, strong girl. You would have eventually gotten out of the canyon on your own."

She didn't bother to argue that point, instead, she said, "I realize you don't want to be here with me. And you certainly don't want to meet with Camilla tomorrow. But I'm very glad that you are."

His blue eyes were dark with doubtful shadows as

he glanced at her. "You have a misguided notion that seeing Verde Canyon is going to be cathartic for me—that suddenly I'll be liberated from all the hell Camilla and Ward put me through. Bella, nothing will ever wipe that from my mind."

She rested her hand on his arm. "You're right. Nothing ever will. But once you face this woman, I believe you can look past all the wrong. You'll be able to see the future and maybe then you can see me sharing it with you."

With a groan of misgiving, Noah turned and reached for her hands. "Where do you find this faith in me, Bella? You should've tossed in your chips long ago and told me to get lost. I'm not the sort of man a woman can understand, much less cozy up to."

Slipping her arms around his waist, she pressed her body next to his. "I find it oh, so easy to cozy up to you, Noah."

Desire stirred low in his belly, prompting him to close his eyes and push his fingers into her dark, silky hair. "Taking you to bed isn't going to fix anything," he murmured thickly.

"It will fix this ache I have to be in your arms," she whispered. "That's all I'm asking for tonight. Tomorrow—well, we can talk about promises then."

Aching. Longing. That's all he'd been doing since that Sunday afternoon so long ago when she'd shown up at his cabin.

"There might not be any promises tomorrow," he hedged.

Her arms tightened around him as her cheek came

to rest against the middle of his chest. "I'm willing to take my chances."

He didn't deserve this woman. And he was fairly certain that after they met with Camilla tomorrow, Bella would realize it, too. But for tonight he wanted to hold her, love her and pretend that she would always belong to him.

Groaning with a need that was blurring his senses, he lowered his mouth to hers.

Chapter 11

The next morning the sun had just begun to climb above the stark, jagged mountains rimming the city, when Bella and Noah sat down at the little table in their room to eat a breakfast of chorizo omelets and warm tortillas.

Waking up next to Noah had been bittersweet for Bella. For long minutes she'd lain there listening to the even sound of his breathing and savoring the warmth of his hard body nestled close against hers. Last night she'd sensed an urgency to his lovemaking. As though it might be the last time they would be together. It was a thought Bella refused to contemplate.

Now, as she forced each bite of food down her throat, she wondered what the day was going to bring to him and to her. This morning, he looked incredibly handsome with his black hair slicked back from his rugged face and a pale blue shirt covering his broad shoulders. Yet the tense lines etched around his mouth and eyes told her he was dreading the forthcoming meeting with Camilla.

Bella was dreading it, too. From what he'd told her, the woman had tried every way possible to seduce him. The idea made her cringe and yet she had to believe that this whole trip would be a turning point for Noah. Because no matter what happened with the two of them in the future, she wanted him to be happy.

She sipped her coffee and hoped it would push the food past her tight throat. "There's something I've been wondering about, Noah."

With a wry grunt, he looked up from his food. "Just something? I've been wondering about a million things. Like what the hell am I doing here? Jett and Sassy were going to a horse sale up at Reno today. I should've been there to handle the barn chores. Instead, I'm nearly a thousand miles away about to meet with a woman who not only stabbed me in the back but also deceived and manipulated her own husband. Even a psychiatrist couldn't figure out what I'm doing—that's how stupid this whole thing feels to me."

She let out a long breath. "I'll be honest, Noah. Half the time I'm thinking exactly like you are. But then I keep thinking about the short letter she sent you. Instead of her phone number, she gave you her lawyer's number. What exactly did he say when you called to let him know you'd be coming to the ranch today?"

He shrugged, but Bella knew he was feeling anything but casual. "Only that Camilla would be pleased. And that she didn't want to talk with me over the phone.

That everything she wanted to say needed to be said in person."

"Well, it won't be long now until we find out what's on her mind," Bella said. "How long will it take us to drive from here to the ranch?"

"About an hour and a half. Was there anything you wanted to see or do before we leave the city this morning? I told the lawyer, if all went as planned, we'd be at the ranch by ten-thirty. We're ahead of schedule."

He glanced at the silver watch on his wrist and it dawned on Bella that this was the first time she'd seen him wearing a timepiece. Which only pointed out that he was a free-spirited cowboy who only conformed to the norm whenever he was forced to.

"Thanks for asking, but I'd rather we go on," she told him. "That way you can point out some of the landmarks along the way."

"Fine. The sooner we get this over with, the better," he said.

Two hours later, Noah slowed the car as it passed over a wide cattle guard. Above it, a wooden sign hung from a simple arch made of rough cedar post.

Verde Canyon. In Noah's wildest dreams he'd never imagined he'd be back on this desert ranch. He'd never expected to ever see the house where he and Ward had shared meals and laughter and good times. He'd been a different man then. One that he no longer recognized. Would Bella have loved that Noah? The question was moot, he realized. If not for the break between him and Ward, he and Bella would've never met. That was something he'd never thought about until now. And suddenly the ache in his chest wasn't quite as hard to bear.

"This is beautiful, Noah," Bella commented as he drove slowly over the narrow dirt road. "It's so stark and wild. The mountains are very different than the ones around the J Bar S."

He glanced over at her. "Not a damned thing on them except mesquite bosque, creosote bush and a little desert grass. But there's something pretty about them. Especially after the rain comes and it all turns green. I'm surprised you like it."

Smiling faintly, she reached for his hand and he gave it to her.

"You still think of this area as your home, don't you?"

"Doesn't make sense, does it? I went through hell here, but yes, this was my home. I'd planned to stay here for the rest of my life. Guess it's hard to get something that deep out of your head."

"And your heart," she added knowingly.

He let out a long breath. "Yeah, I used to have one of those. For your sake, Bella, I wish I could get it back."

Ten minutes later they arrived at the ranch house, a rambling one-story hacienda with a beautiful tiled roof and a ground-level porch with arched supports. Red blooming bougainvillea grew up the walls, while huge terracotta pots filled with cactus and succulents lined the edge of the porch and the walkway. One lone mesquite tree cast a flimsy shade across the east end of the small yard.

Except for the mesquite tree being a bit larger, everything looked the same as he remembered. Noah wasn't sure that was a good thing or bad. One thing was certain, though—without Ward around, the ranch wasn't the same.

"Where is the ranch yard?" Bella asked as he parked in front of a low fence made of cedar rails.

"About a quarter mile on down the road," he answered. "You can see it from the back of the house."

He looked over at her. "Ready for this?"

"I'm ready. But before we go in, Noah, I think—well, maybe it would be better if you talked with Camilla alone. Whatever she has to say to you is personal and I—"

He interrupted her words with a shake of his head. "If what she has to say can't be said in front of you, then I don't want to hear it. Okay?"

"Okay."

They walked side by side to the front door. Noah's short knock was quickly answered by a young Hispanic maid with a wide smile and black hair twisted into a ballerina bun. She ushered them through a short foyer and into a long, casually furnished living room.

"Please have a seat and make yourself comfortable," she said warmly. "I'll tell Ms. Stevens that you've arrived."

The maid disappeared through an arched doorway at the far end of the room. Noah and Bella sat down close together on a green leather couch to wait.

"This is quite a house," Bella said as she glanced up at the cathedral ceiling supported by dark wooden beams.

Strategically placed skylights sent shafts of light spreading across a floor of Spanish tile, while here and there huge pots, filled with more cactus, gave the impression that the room was an extension of the outdoors. Except for changes in the furniture, it looked the same to Noah. And everywhere his gaze landed, he was reminded of Ward. The reality of the man's death was still hard for him to absorb.

"Ward didn't hold back when he had this house built. He wanted Camilla to have the best," he added stiffly. "Poor bastard. I hope he never knew what really happened—that Camilla lied and deceived him."

"Noah, you can't mean that," Bella said in a hushed voice. "I thought you wanted your friend to know the truth."

He shook his head. "Back then, I did. Now, I realize it would have hurt him even more. And he didn't deserve that."

She rested her hand on his arm. "You didn't deserve it either, Noah."

Her brown eyes were full of empathy, but Noah could also see courage and strength radiating from her and in that moment he realized that she was all he'd ever needed or wanted. If today he lost his job, the money and cattle he'd accumulated, every possession he owned, he could survive. But losing Bella would be like losing the air he breathed. Dear God, why had it taken him so long to realize the truth?

The sound of footsteps interrupted the self-directed question and he looked around to see the maid reentering the room. Camilla Stevens followed a few steps behind her.

Like the house and the land, Ward's wife hadn't changed all that much. At thirty-eight, the woman was still slender and attractive. Her blond hair was long and coiled into a neat twist at the back of her head, while her white dress and black heels implied she was planning to go out later.

Bella's fingers suddenly tightened on his arm and he

knew that no matter what transpired with this woman, she was counting on him to remain a gentleman. He couldn't let her down. Now or ever.

Barely conscious of what he was doing, Noah rose to his feet and Bella quickly joined him.

"Hello, Noah. Thank you for coming," Camilla said and reached to shake his hand.

Though it pained him, Noah complied. Mercifully, the handshake was brief and then Camilla turned her attention to Bella.

"This is Bella Sundell," Noah quickly introduced. "She made the trip with me."

The two women exchanged greetings and then Camilla gestured toward the couch. "Please sit," she said, "and Lolita will bring refreshments. Since it's still early you might prefer coffee or hot tea?"

"Coffee would be nice," Bella spoke up.

Noah merely nodded. It was hard to look at Camilla without thinking of Ward and as she took a seat in an armchair across from them, memories of his old friend rushed at him from every direction.

Camilla instructed the maid, then settled back in the chair.

Noah said, "I'm sorry about Ward. It's hard for me to believe he's gone."

"It's still hard for me to believe it, too," she said quietly, then suddenly looked away.

As Noah watched her eyes blink rapidly, he reminded himself that the woman was one of the biggest liars he'd ever met. Yet watching her now, he got the feeling that her husband's death had affected her deeply. Which didn't make sense. Seven years ago, when Noah left this ranch, she seemed to have forgotten she had a husband at all.

"I'm sorry," she said. "Ward wouldn't like me choking up like this. He wanted me to be brave."

"What happened?" Noah asked. "Your letter said his health had been declining. What was wrong?"

Camilla nodded. "For the past year and a half. He developed a lung disease—some long name I can't pronounce or even remember. In the beginning the doctors assured us it was a controllable condition. But Ward didn't respond to the treatments. We went to the best specialist, but nothing seemed to help. It was hell watching him die a little each day."

Noah let out a long breath and looked over at Bella to see she'd been touched by Camilla's recounting. Surprisingly, he'd been affected by it, too. He'd not expected Ward's wife to express any grief over his passing. The Camilla he remembered had turned cold and callous. This woman sitting in front of them acted as though she'd loved Ward deeply. It didn't make sense.

Just as an awkward silence settled over the room, Lolita returned with a tray. After the young woman had passed around cups of coffee, Camilla spoke again.

"Noah, before I get into the reason I asked you here, I want to say how sorry I am for everything that happened all those years ago. I realize that doesn't mean much. But I—well, all I can say is that I was having deep emotional problems at the time. When I lost the baby it was like I'd lost everything. I felt guilty because I couldn't give Ward the one thing he wanted. Especially after he'd given me so much. I don't know—something snapped in me. I was jealous of you, Noah. I believed Ward cared more about you than he did me."

"Camilla, that's crazy," Noah told her. "He loved you more than anything."

"Yes, it took a long time, plus a doctor's care, for me to finally realize the truth and come to my senses. But by then the harm had already been done."

Noah gripped his coffee cup as strange emotions suddenly surged inside him. This wasn't the way he'd expected Camilla to sound or behave. He'd not imagined her being apologetic or grieving.

"If you don't mind my asking," Bella spoke up, "did you ever talk to your husband about Noah? Explain what really happened?"

Sighing heavily, Camilla placed her cup on a nearby table, then folded her hands in her lap. As Noah waited for her answer, he noticed she was still wearing her wedding rings.

"Yes. But not until recently. For years I tried to find the courage to confess the truth to him. I recognized it was wrong to let him keep thinking Noah had betrayed him. Ward had loved Noah like a son. I believed if he ever found out I'd deliberately torn them apart, he would never forgive me. But once I accepted the fact that he didn't have long to live, I couldn't hold it inside any longer. About three weeks ago, I told him the whole sordid story."

Noah and Bella exchanged pointed looks.

Noah instinctively reached for Bella's hand. "How did he react?"

Camilla dabbed a tissue beneath her eyes and though Noah would have liked to think she was shedding crocodile tears, he recognized they were real.

"Naturally he was devastated. He was ashamed of the way he'd treated you. And mercifully he forgave me. Thank God he understood that the woman I was then wasn't the same woman he'd been married to for all these years." She rose from the armchair and began to walk restlessly around the room. "After that, he hired a private investigator to locate you. He wanted to see you—to ask for your forgiveness. We'd just discovered you were working on the J Bar S and I was in the process of contacting you when Ward suddenly took a turn for the worse and died."

"Too late," Noah muttered regretfully.

Camilla paused in the middle of the room, her rueful gaze passing from Noah to Bella, then back to him. "Yes. Too late. I was a coward. I should have confessed to him years before. Instead I lived with the lies. It hasn't been easy."

A few weeks ago, Noah would have been consumed with anger for this woman. The urge to jump to his feet and choke her would've been his first instinct. But he was feeling none of that and the realization stunned him. Why wasn't he angry? Where were all those bitter emotions he'd been harboring for all these years? It didn't make sense.

Once you face this woman, I believe you can look past all the wrong. You'll be able to see the future and maybe then you can see me sharing it with you.

He turned his gaze on Bella as her words whispered through his jumbled thoughts. Oh God, how had she known? How had she guessed that revisiting a nightmare would actually jolt him awake?

Bella's fingers tightened around his. "Noah? Are you okay?" she asked softly.

"I'm fine. Really," he assured her and he couldn't have meant it more. He inclined his head to Camilla, who was now standing on the opposite side of the room, staring sadly out the window. "I need to say some things to her."

Smiling gently, she nodded. "I'll wait here."

Rising from the couch, Noah went to stand next to the other woman. She looked around at him, her expression one of fatal acceptance.

"Camilla, you need to quit torturing yourself. You're not the only one who's been a coward all these years. I've been a bigger one. I should've found the guts to come back to Verde Canyon and face Ward again. Instead, I thought running away was the answer. I was wrong. We've both been wrong. I think it's time we let our mistakes go. Don't you?"

The anguish on Camilla's face slowly dissolved and a hopeful smile replaced it. "Thank you, Noah. Coming from you—well, it's the best medicine I could ever get. And now I'd like for you and Ms. Sundell to meet someone. He's waiting in the study with something to tell you."

Expecting Camilla was going to introduce them to the ranch manager, Noah collected Bella from the couch and the two of them followed her down a long tiled hallway until they reached a pair of closed wooden doors.

Noah had been in this very room many times. He and Ward had often talked over the business dealings of the ranch within these same walls. Now as the three of them stepped into the quiet space, he spotted a gray-haired man in a charcoal-colored suit sitting behind a large mahogany desk.

As soon as the elderly gentleman spotted their entrance, he politely rose to his feet.

"This is Harrison Grimes," Camilla quickly introduced. "He's been our family lawyer for several years."

With his arm wrapped tightly against the back of Bella's waist, Noah stepped forward.

"Nice to meet you, Mr. Grimes," Noah said, then gestured to Bella. "This is Bella Sundell. She's also a family lawyer."

"Oh!" Camilla exclaimed, then studied the both of them with confusion. "I thought she—Ms. Sundell came as your—friend. Did you think you were going to need a lawyer?"

Noah shook his head, then cast Bella a pointed look. "No. Bella is here because I—wanted her to be with me. Because we—we're together."

Camilla smiled with relief. "That's good," she said, then turned her attention to the lawyer. "So why don't you explain to them what's going on, Harrison."

"Certainly," he said, then tapped a legal document lying on the center of the desk. "Camilla has asked me to be here this morning so that I can answer any questions you might have concerning Ward's will."

"Will. What does Ward's will have to do with me?" Noah questioned.

The lawyer arched an inquisitive brow at Camilla. "You haven't told him yet?"

The woman shook her head. "No. I thought you could do a better job of it."

Harrison Grimes pointed to a pair of wing-back chairs sitting at an angle to the desk. "Perhaps you two better sit down."

"Yes," Camilla quickly added. "I'm sorry. With everything going on, I've forgotten my manners. Please sit."

Once Bella and Noah had made themselves comfortable, the lawyer eased down into the desk chair, then leveled a benevolent look on Noah.

"No matter how I say it, this is probably going to come as quite a shock," the lawyer said. "So I won't beat around the bush. You see, before Ward died, he instructed me to change his will in order to make sure that Verde Canyon and all of its holdings would go to you."

Noah was so stunned he was certain the breath had been knocked out of him. Shaking his head, he squinted at the lawyer. "Me? You're saying the Verde is mine?"

"That's right. The land, the house and other buildings, along with all the cattle and horses. Basically everything is yours now." He picked up the legal document and handed it to Bella. "Since you're a lawyer, Ms. Sundell, you might want to look through this. I'm sure you can explain anything Mr. Crawford doesn't understand."

Completely dazed, Noah shook his head once again. "I don't need legal explanations. I just—why did Ward do this? The illness must have affected his sanity!"

"I assure you that Ward had all his mental faculties before he died. This was his last wish. That you become the sole owner of Verde Canyon Ranch."

Bella appeared to be just as stunned as Noah and she looked inquiringly at Camilla. "What about you, Mrs. Stevens? Surely you can't be happy about this?"

Camilla merely smiled. "I couldn't be happier. If our child had lived, the ranch certainly would have gone to him or her. As it is, Noah is the closest thing Ward had to a son. He truly wanted to make up for the past. Plus, he died with the assurance that the ranch would remain in capable hands."

"And if you're thinking that Camilla has been left out in the cold, don't," the lawyer interjected. "Over the years Ward made some excellent investments. Camilla is getting more than enough to make sure her future is financially secure."

"But this is your home, Camilla," Noah pointed out. "What—"

"Don't worry," she said with a wry little laugh. "I'll be moving out next week. I'm going to live near my parents down in southern California."

She glanced at the dainty gold watch on her wrist. "Now if you two won't mind, I need to be going or I'll be late for church services. Please make yourself at home and look around all you want. I'm sure there's plenty you'll want to look over and talk about. If you need anything, Harrison will be here, as well as Lolita."

A few minutes later, after Camilla had departed, Bella and Noah walked across the backyard until they reached the split-rail fence. From where they stood in the hot sun, they could see the working ranch yard in the distance. Dust was boiling up from a network of cattle pens and the faint yips and yells from a group of cowboys could be heard on the desert wind. Nearby, the hills were covered with patches of cacti, creosote and blooming yucca.

Bella took in the beautiful sight and tried to imagine what Noah was thinking and feeling at this moment. He'd just become a rich man and she could only wonder what this might do to their fragile relationship.

"I thought coming down here and meeting with Camilla would be good for you," Bella said thoughtfully. "But I never imagined anything like this was going to happen."

He lifted his hat from his head and raked a hand

through the black waves. "It's still hard for me to take in, Bella. I thought Ward hated me. To think he's given me everything he worked for—I feel pretty damned humble right now. Not to mention feeling like a bastard," he tacked on, his voice gruff.

She frowned at him. "I don't understand."

He tugged the hat back onto his head. "All these years I've been simmering with resentment. Like a bulldog I hung on to the fact that I'd been wronged. I should've forgiven Camilla and Ward a long time ago." His arm slipped around her shoulders and drew her to his side. "That chip you talked about on my shoulder—I wore it like a badge. I've been such a fool!"

"All of that is over now," she said gently. "Truly over."

He made a sweeping gesture with his arm. "What am I going to do with all of this, Bella?"

She glanced up at him, her heart pounding with uncertainty. "You're going to keep it, of course. Verde Canyon is your ranch now—the place you call home."

With his hands on her shoulders, he pulled her around so that she was facing him.

"Home is where you are, Bella. It's taken me a long time to realize that. And as much as I love Verde Canyon, I love you even more. I want you to be my wife. But I can't ask you to make your home here with me."

I love you even more.

His words poured into her heart, healing every ache, and pushing out the last vestige of loneliness.

Resting her palms against his chest, she tilted her head back to meet his gaze. "Why can't you ask me?"

His eyes widened. "Why? Because it wouldn't be right. You have your own beautiful home on the J Bar S."

"And it's empty without you in it."

"You have your law practice in Carson City."

"I can practice law anywhere," she reasoned.

His head swung back and forth as though he couldn't believe what he was hearing. "You're very close to your brother and his family. You wouldn't want to live far away from them."

"Jett and Sassy are building their own lives together," she pointed out. "It's time I quit being just a sister and an aunt. I want to be a wife and a mother. Besides, whenever we get the urge to see them, we can always fly up for visits."

His arms formed a tight circle around her. "You make it all sound so easy."

"Loving you is very easy, my darling."

Bending his head, he brought his lips next to hers. "Today I've become a very rich man, Bella. Not because I inherited the Verde, but because I have you and your love. I hope you'll always remember that."

Happiness glowed in her eyes as she smiled up at him. "Don't worry. I'll never let you forget it."

Chuckling, he covered her mouth with a long, tender kiss that melted her bones even more than the hot Arizona sun.

When he finally lifted his head, she grabbed his hand and urged him toward an opening in the fence. "Come on, I want you to show me around the ranch. I need to pick out a perfect spot to pasture Mary Mae and Casper. Are there any canyons around here I can ride down?"

Laughing now, Noah slipped his arm around the back of her waist and urged her toward the ranch yard. "A few. But from now on I'll be riding right beside you."

Her heart brimming with happiness, she laughed along with him. "I'm going to hold you to that promise."

Epilogue

Six months later, on a cool November afternoon, Bella had just gotten home from a short shopping trip and was putting away the last of her grocery purchases when Noah entered the kitchen and announced he had a surprise to show her.

Now, as he led her into a big barn where most of the hay for Verde Canyon was stored, she looked curiously around the cavernous interior. "Noah, if you've bought me a piece of jewelry and hidden it somewhere in all this hay, you're going to have to dig it out," she warned teasingly. "And I could've told you I'd rather have a pair of cowboy boots than a diamond."

He laughed, something he did quite often these days. Bella had come to love the sound just as much as she loved her new home in the Arizona desert. With ranch hands that liked and respected him and a cow/calf operation that continued to produce, she could safely say that Noah was happily living out his dream of managing Verde Canyon.

After that memorable day they'd learned Noah had inherited the Verde, they'd flown back to Nevada. A few days later, they'd been married in the same small church Bella and Jett had attended since their childhood. Sassy had helped her find a beautiful dress in champagne-colored lace and Peta had taken over the task of decorating the church with candles and flowers. With only family and a few close friends in attendance it had been a simple, yet beautiful ceremony.

Jett and Sassy had been totally shocked by the news of Ward's will. Although they were extremely happy for both Noah and Bella, it was obvious Jett hated to see his new brother-in-law leave his position on the J Bar S. And he was especially emotional to see his sister move away.

Not about to leave Jett shorthanded, Noah had hung on as foreman for three more weeks in order to give Jett time to find a man to replace him. Bella had used that length of time to pack her belongings for shipping and close all her cases at the law office. As for her house, she'd turned it over to Jett to use however he chose.

With so much to do regarding the move to Arizona, Bella and Noah had forgone a honeymoon. But their lives had quickly settled into a comfortable groove and since then Noah kept offering to take Bella on a short trip to some exotic island. But as far as she was concerned, spending each day with her husband was a honeymoon for her.

As for Bella practicing law, a couple of months ago, she'd opened a little office in Tombstone in a building that had originally been used for a saloon. So far her work was sporadic, but it kept her busy for three days a week and that was more than enough to keep her content.

"Christmas is only a month away. If you're good, Santa might bring you a new pair of boots."

Noah's reminder pulled her away from her pleasant thoughts and she shot him an impish grin. "Hmm. If that's the case, these next few weeks I'll try to be on my best behavior."

"Yeah, I know what you consider good behavior," he said with a hungry growl, then pulled her into his arms and kissed her. "Like taking me to bed in the middle of the day."

Her lips tilted provocatively against his. "A cowboy needs a little rest now and then."

He kissed her one more time, then took her by the hand and led her over to a deep crevice in the hay.

"Take a look in there."

Bella did as he instructed and immediately let out a delighted yelp. A gray momma cat was curled around three little yellow fur balls. "Baby kittens! How precious! When did this happen?"

"Yesterday afternoon, I saw mother cat still looking like she'd swallowed a watermelon crossing the ranch yard, heading this way. But I didn't hear the faint meows until this morning."

Tapping a thoughtful finger against her chin, she asked sagely, "So do I need to ask who the father is?"

Chuckling, Noah pointed to the top of the haystack where a big yellow tom sat preening his fur.

"Jack!" Bella called up to the cat. "You naughty guy!"

"Yep, Jack has a family now," Noah said. "I think we can safely say he's made himself a permanent home on the Verde."

She gave her husband a shrewd smile. "I hope you look as proud as Jack does whenever our baby is born."

An odd look came over his features, then suddenly a wondrous light filled his eyes. "Bella—are you—does this mean what I'm thinking?"

Her heart overflowing with love, she stepped into the circle of his arms. "It means we're going to have a baby. The doctor is predicting it will arrive sometime in mid-May."

"Doctor? You've already been to see a doctor?" he asked, excitement filling his voice.

"I saw him this morning—that's why I drove in to Tucson."

"And you told me you were going grocery shopping for Thanksgiving dinner!" He scolded. "Sneaky! Sneaky!"

Her grin was completely guilty. "I wanted to surprise you. I did go grocery shopping. After I made a stop at the health clinic." Her hands reached up and cradled his face. "Are you happy?"

"I've got a bigger smile than Jack does right now. Why wouldn't I be happy?"

She traced her fingertips along his cheekbone and marveled at how much their love had filled their lives with happiness and meaning.

"There was a time when you said you didn't want to be a husband or father," she gently reminded him.

"I never thought I had the qualifications to be a dad. And I sure didn't want to make a mess of things, the way my old man had with me. But that was before I knew someone believed in me. Like you."

"And Ward," she added softly. "Wherever he is now, he's smiling because you're happy."

"I think so, too," he agreed. "And coming from me, this might sound crazy, but I'm actually glad things are working out for Camilla."

He'd learned the blessings of forgiveness and Bella couldn't be happier about the change it had made in him. "From the short letter she sent us, it sounds like she's making a fresh start to her life. I certainly wish her well." Pressing herself closer to his rugged body, she splayed her hands against his back. "And now that we're talking about fresh starts, I've been thinking it's time I made a search for your mother."

He looked stunned. "My mother? Why would you even be thinking of her?"

"Hmm. We're going to have a baby. The holidays are growing near and my mother is coming down for a visit, along with Jett and his family. It would be nice if you had someone in your family to share in our happiness."

"I've not seen my mother since I was a boy, Bella. I doubt you can find her."

"Does that mean you won't mind if I try?" she asked hopefully.

The radiance in his blue eyes warmed every corner of her heart.

"No. I won't mind," he said. "After all, I never could deny you anything, my sweet Bella."

"Not even a hamburger," she added slyly.

"Yeah, and look where that's gotten me," he joked, then his expression suddenly turned thoughtful as his hand rested on the lower part of her flat belly. "The middle of May, huh? The wildflowers will be gone by then. But the canyon will still be green. It'll be a beautiful time for our baby to come."

Verde Canyon. Yes, she thought, her heart overflowing with joy. They'd ride through the canyon together. Always.

* * * * *

Since 2006, *New York Times* bestselling author
Cathy McDavid has been happily penning
contemporary Westerns for Harlequin. Every day,
she gets to write about handsome cowboys riding
the range or busting a bronc. It's a tough job, but
she's willing to make the sacrifice. Cathy shares
her Arizona home with her own real-life sweetheart
and a trio of odd pets. Her grown twins have left to
embark on lives of their own, and she couldn't be
prouder of their accomplishments.

Books by Cathy McDavid

Harlequin Western Romance

Mustang Valley

Cowboy for Keeps
Her Holiday Rancher
Come Home, Cowboy
Having the Rancher's Baby
Rescuing the Cowboy
A Baby for the Deputy
The Cowboy's Twin Surprise
The Bull Rider's Valentine

Harlequin Heartwarming

The Sweetheart Ranch

A Cowboy's Christmas Proposal
The Cowboy's Perfect Match

Visit the Author Profile page at
Harlequin.com for more titles.

THE RANCHER'S
HOMECOMING

CATHY McDAVID

To my fellow brainstorming divas: Pam, Libby, Connie and Valerie. I'm always so inspired by our sessions and by the four of you. Thank you for asking the right questions and for forcing me to stretch as a writer. I wouldn't take the abuse from anyone else!

Chapter 1

Six weeks since the fire and the lingering smell of smoke still burned like acid in the back of her throat. Annie Hennessy covered her mouth and nose, remembering the days immediately following the fire when they were forced to wear face masks and hazmat suits as they waded through the waist-deep ruins of the inn that had been in her family for the past fifty years.

Like then, she bit back the sobs, afraid even letting one escape would cause her to break down entirely. Where would she and her daughter be then? Her mother and grandmother? Homeless, probably. Or living on the generosity of some relative.

Annie took a tentative step forward, wincing as something crunched beneath the sole of her hiking boot. She dreaded looking down but did anyway.

The charred remains of a picture frame lay in her

path, barely recognizable. Whichever room the painting had once hung in was anyone's guess. During the fire, the roof caved in on the second floor, which had then collapsed onto the first floor.

Only the foundation, parts of the exterior walls and a few blackened ceiling beams remained. All the precious heirlooms, antiques, furnishings and mementoes the Hennessy women had collected over the past half century had been reduced to a giant pile of rubble in a matter of minutes.

No, not everything. As Annie took another step forward, something metallic peeked out from beneath a plank of wood.

Squatting down, she shoved aside the plank, mindless of the grime smearing her hands. One by one, her fingers closed around the object, and her pulse quickened. Why hadn't she noticed this before today?

Like a miner discovering a diamond in a barren field, she unearthed the discolored desk bell and held it up to catch the late-afternoon sunlight streaming in from overhead. For as long as she could remember, this bell had sat atop the lobby desk. Hundreds, no, thousands of guests had rung it.

Another piece of Annie's shattered heart broke off.

She clutched the bell to her chest and waited for the strength to rise in her. She would add this to her collection of salvaged treasures. A metal comb, a silver teapot, an iron hinge to the storeroom door, to name a few.

Annie fought her way across the piles of crumbling debris covering the former lobby floor. Staying here another minute was impossible. Why did she insist on torturing herself by stopping every day on her drive home from work?

Because *this* was her home. Not the tiny two-bedroom apartment in town where she and her family currently resided.

Bracing her free hand on the front entrance door frame, she propelled herself through the opening and across the lawn, filling her lungs with much-needed clean air.

Her SUV stood where she'd left it, in what had been the inn's parking lot. The vehicle, a pea-green all-wheel-drive monstrosity, bore the logo of the Nevada Division of Forestry on its driver's side door.

Annie had started working for the NDF only last week and considered herself one of the lucky few. She'd gotten a job, low paying as it was. Too many of her friends and fellow residents were unable to find employment or even a place to live.

For the Hennessys' inn wasn't the only structure in Sweetheart, Nevada, that succumbed to the fire's insatiable hunger. Nine thousand acres of pristine mountain wilderness and two-thirds of the town's homes and businesses were destroyed—along with *all* of their livelihoods and very way of life.

Once behind the wheel, Annie didn't head to the apartment. Instead, she took the road out of town. Her mother wasn't expecting her for another hour. And as much as Annie wanted to see her beautiful daughter, she needed a few moments of solitude in a place that had escaped the fire. A place where her spirit could mend.

She slapped the visor down as she turned west. Before the fire, she hadn't needed to shade her eyes. The towering ponderosa pines on both sides of the road would have blocked the sun's glare. Now, a sea of scorched trunks and branches stretched for miles.

Every hundred feet or so, a single tree stood, lush and green and miraculously spared.

What Annie wouldn't give to have her family's inn be like those surviving trees.

This wasn't just the town where she'd grown up and the inn her place of work. Her roots ran deep. According to her grandmother, the Hennessy line went all the way back to the first settlers.

Shortly after the gold rush of 1849, a wagon train passed through the Sierra Nevada Mountains. On it, two young passengers met and fell in love. When the wagon train stopped in what was now Sweetheart, the man proposed to the woman. They married in California but returned to the spot where they'd become engaged to settle and raise a family. The next year, the man discovered gold. Word traveled and people arrived. The small town that sprang up was called Sweetheart after its first settlers and founders of the mine.

Many of the businesses in town, including Annie's family's, capitalized on the legend. To Annie, it was more than just a story, it was her heritage.

Ten minutes later, she stopped the SUV at the security gate blocking the entrance to the Gold Nugget Ranch and got out. Several years earlier, after the ranch had been closed to the public, the caretaker had entrusted Annie's family with a spare key. She was supposed to use it only for emergencies.

She considered mending her broken spirit as good an emergency as any.

To her surprise, she found the gate closed but padlock hanging open. Had Emmett been here and forgotten to secure the lock when he left? Doubtful. The caretaker was as dependable as ants at a picnic. But what other explanation could there be?

Returning to her SUV, she navigated the steep and winding mile-long dirt road to the ranch. Even before she got there, she spotted an unfamiliar Chevy dually pickup parked near the sprawling front porch.

The truck was empty. So was the porch. Whoever was here must be inside or out back. But why would they have a key to the gate?

Annie strode determinedly across the dirt and gravel yard to the porch steps. Every inch of the house and grounds was familiar to her. Not only had she visited on countless occasions, she'd seen it over and over while watching syndicated reruns of *The Forty-Niners* on TV.

The front door stood partially ajar and creaked loudly when she pushed it open. Her footsteps echoed ghostlike as she crossed the empty parlor.

"Hello? Anybody here?"

She should be nervous. The stranger prowling the house or grounds might be a vandal or a thief or even an ax murderer. Except what ax murderer drove a fire-engine-red pickup truck?

Maybe a real estate agent was here showing the ranch to a prospective buyer. It had been for sale the past several years, though there had been few lookers and no serious offers. Despite the ranch's claim to fame—a location used to film *The Forty-Niners* for eight years during the late '60s and early '70s—and a much reduced price, it was a bit of a white elephant.

Annie was secretly glad. For as long as she could remember, it had been her dream to buy the iconic ranch.

Since the fire, her only dream was to survive each day.

At a noise from above, she started toward the staircase. "Hello!" Taking hold of the dusty newel post, she let her gaze travel the steps to the second floor.

A figure emerged from the shadows. A man. He wore jeans and boots and a black cowboy hat was pulled low over his brow.

Even so, she instantly recognized him, and her damaged heart beat as though it was brand-new.

Sam! He was back. After nine years.

Why? And what was he doing at the Gold Nugget?

"Annie?" He started down the stairs, the confused expression on his face changing to one of recognition. "It's you!"

Suddenly nervous, she retreated. If he hadn't seen her, she'd have run.

No, that was a stupid reaction. She wasn't young and vulnerable anymore. She was thirty-four. The mother of a three-year-old child. Grown. Confident. Strong.

And yet, the door beckoned. He'd always had that effect on her, been able to strip away her defenses.

A rush of irritation, more at herself than him, galvanized her. "What are you doing here?"

Ignoring her question, he descended the stairs, his boots making contact with the wooden steps one at a time. Lord, it seemed to take forever.

This wasn't, she recalled, the first time he'd kept her waiting. Or the longest.

At last he stood before her, tall, handsome and every inch the rugged cowboy she remembered.

"Hey, girl, how are you? I wasn't sure you still lived in Sweetheart."

He spoke with an ease that gave no hint of those last angry words they'd exchanged. He even used his once familiar endearment for her and might have swept her into a hug if Annie didn't step to the side.

"Still here."

"I heard about the inn." Regret filled his voice. "I'm sorry."

"Me, too." She lifted her chin. "We're going to rebuild. As soon as we settle with the insurance company."

"You look good." His gaze never left her face, for which she was glad. He didn't seem to notice her rumpled and soiled khaki uniform. Her hair escaping her ponytail and hanging in limp tendrils. Her lack of makeup. "Th-thank you."

"Been a while."

"Quite a while."

His blue eyes transfixed her, as they always had, and she felt her bones melt.

Dammit! Her entire world had fallen apart the past six weeks. She didn't need Sam showing up, kicking at the pieces.

"What are you doing here?" she said, repeating her earlier question. "How did you get in?"

"The real estate agent gave me the keys." He held them up in an offering of proof, his potent grin disarming her. "I always liked this place."

He had. They'd come here often when they were dating. She'd show him the areas off-limits to tourists, all the while going on and on about her plans to buy the ranch and turn it into a bed-and-breakfast. Plans Sam had shared.

Now he was here, holding the keys.

He couldn't possibly be interested in purchasing the place. He lived in Northern California. Worked there. Had a wife and daughter there, the last she'd heard.

"How's your mom and grandmother?" he asked.

"Fine." She wouldn't admit the truth. None of them were fine after losing everything and they wore their scars each in their own way. "I have a daughter now. She's three."

His smile changed and became softer. "I'm happy for you. You always wanted kids. Your husband from Sweetheart?"

"Yes." She swallowed. "We're not married anymore." Good grief. What had possessed her to admit that?

"A shame." Emotions difficult to read flashed in his eyes. "Losing a spouse is hard."

He said it as if he had firsthand experience.

"I'm managing," she admitted. "*We're* managing."

"Maybe you can let me in on the secret."

"You're divorced?"

"Widowed. My wife died a year and a half ago."

"Oh, Sam." Her heart nearly stopped.

"A drunk driver ran the light."

She'd never known the woman but felt bad for the late Mrs. Wyler and for Sam. Having one's life implode was something she understood.

"That must have been awful for you."

He nodded and glanced toward the empty kitchen with its large picture window. "My daughter's here with me. She's out back. I should probably find her. I told the real estate agent I'd meet her in town at five to sign the papers."

Sign the papers! Even as Annie's mind formed the thought, he spoke it out loud.

"We're scheduled to close escrow tomorrow. I'm the new owner of the Gold Nugget."

Sam followed Annie out onto the porch, only to pause and watch her as she composed herself. He hadn't thought she'd take the news of him buying the Gold Nugget so hard. The sight of her features crumbling would stay with him always.

He leaned his back against one of the thick columns, giving her space. Like the ranch house and barn, the columns were constructed from indigenous pines harvested when the land was originally cleared. According to the plaque mounted by the entrance, that occurred more than two decades before ground was broken on the Sweetheart Inn.

He should, he realized much too late, have chosen his words more kindly. Annie loved the Gold Nugget almost as much as she did her family's inn. He'd been surprised to see the ranch listed for sale, assuming she and her mother would have purchased it years ago.

Annie had always been able to trip him up without even trying. A glance, a touch, a softly whispered response and his concentration went out the window.

Nine years, and she still had that effect on him.

Maybe buying the Gold Nugget wasn't such a good idea after all.

Sam instantly changed his mind. He'd returned to Sweetheart with a purpose, and unintentionally hurting Annie's feelings wouldn't stop him from fulfilling it.

"I'd like to see you while I'm here."

She halted midstep and sent him a look intended to cut him down to size.

"Not a date," he clarified. "To catch up. And to pick your brain."

"I have enough on my plate with rebuilding the inn," she answered tersely. "You can't expect me to be a part of whatever it is you've planned for the ranch."

"Not just the ranch. The entire town, too, and the people in it."

"I don't understand."

"I want to help, Annie."

Unaffected by his attempted sincerity, she narrowed her green eyes. "With what?"

"Rebuilding Sweetheart."

"Is this a joke?"

"I've hired a construction contractor to remodel the Gold Nugget."

"Remodel it!"

"Into a working cattle ranch. One where the guests can enjoy the full cowboy experience, not just go on rides."

"Full cowboy experience?"

"Yeah. Herd cattle, vaccinate calves, repair fences, clear trails, clean stalls if they want. I'm also planning monthly roping and team penning competitions for the adults and gymkhanas for the kids."

She shook her head in disbelief. "What person would want to clean horse stalls on their vacation?"

"You'd be surprised."

He understood her reservations. All of the local businesses had depended on the wedding trade. Florist shop, tuxedo rental, wedding boutique, caterers, photographers. Not to mention restaurants specializing in romantic candlelit dinners or those with large banquet rooms for receptions.

A guest ranch would have been a ridiculous idea and unnecessary if not for the fire. The same fire that Sam and his crew of Hotshot firefighters had fought and failed to prevent from ravaging the town.

Not his crew. He alone was responsible.

His stomach still clenched at the memory of that day. His anger at his commanding officer, his fear for the citizens' safety, the helplessness he'd felt when the wind changed direction and the fire leaped the ravine. The sorrow for all that was lost and could have been saved.

"There are only a handful of really great working guest ranches in this part of the country. Add to that the popularity of *The Forty-Niners,* and I think the ranch will be booked to capacity year-round."

"No, it won't. Sweetheart is where people come to get married. We perform a hundred wedding ceremonies every month."

"Where people *did* come. How many ceremonies have been performed since the fire?"

She clamped her mouth shut, saying nothing. No need for it; they both knew the answer. Zero. A measly six weeks had passed and already Sweetheart was dying on the vine. Without a miracle, it would wither away into nothing.

Sam wasn't about to let that happen and possessed the drive and the resources to prevent it.

"I can change that. Bring the tourists back. I'll also be able to provide jobs for some of the locals. From what the real estate agent tells me, there's plenty who need work." His gaze involuntarily strayed to her work shirt and the NDF badge sewn on to the sleeve.

She noticed, and her posture straightened. Pride wasn't something Annie or any of the Hennessy women had in short supply.

"Why do you care?"

"Sweetheart was once my home."

"For two years." Her voice broke. "Then you left."

All this time, and she was obviously still hurting. Sam would give anything to change that.

"I came back for you."

"Not soon enough."

True. And he'd paid the price. So, apparently, had she. "We were young."

"That sounds like an excuse."

"I take responsibility for what happened between us, Annie. I'd say I wish things were different but then we wouldn't have our children. Neither of us would change that."

"You're right." Her stiff posture had yet to relax. "If you'll excuse me, it's time for me to head home."

"You're angry I bought the ranch. I get that."

"For starters."

He placed a hand on her arm, and then removed it when she glared at him. "Please, Annie. Help me help Sweetheart."

"What about your job in California?"

"My foreman is covering for me the rest of the summer. Lyndsey and I will head home before school starts the first of September. After that, I'll fly here as often as needed. Lyndsey's grandfather will watch her."

Annie sucked in a sharp breath. Sam had hit a nerve.

After he'd left her that last time, he'd returned to California and within a matter of months wed his boss's daughter. Annie must have been devastated when the whole reason he'd accepted the job in the first place was because he wasn't ready for a commitment.

"I am sorry about your wife's death," she said.

"It was rough." Only Sam's father-in-law knew how rough. Sam would move heaven and earth to make sure Lyndsey never learned the entire circumstances of that terrible accident. "I'm in Sweetheart to start over and to get this town on its feet."

He couldn't tell her the real reason he was here, of his part in the fire or how often he'd thought of her during the past nine years. She'd never speak to him again.

"Why did you have to buy the Gold Nugget?" she asked.

"Ranching is my livelihood. What I know best." He intentionally omitted his volunteer firefighting. "And, honestly, I figured if you hadn't bought the Gold Nugget by now, you must have changed your mind."

"I didn't." Turning abruptly, she started toward her SUV.

"Annie, wait." He hurried after her.

She didn't stop until she was almost to the driver's door, and then not because of him. She'd spotted Lyndsey, who emerged from behind the house.

"Daddy," she called.

Sam could have kicked himself. He usually watched his daughter like a hawk. Today, he'd forgotten all about her. "Over here, sweetie."

"Look what I found in a hollow log behind the barn." She held the hem of her pink T-shirt out in front of her, the weight of whatever she carried making it dip in the middle.

Annie stood there frozen, observing Lyndsey's approach. He tried to imagine what she was thinking. Despite his daughter's girlish features, she resembled Sam, enough that most everyone who saw them together commented on it.

Not only had he married soon after that final parting with Annie, he'd fathered a child almost immediately. He wouldn't blame her if she hated him.

"What have you got?" Sam asked when Lyndsey neared.

The young girl eyed Annie with caution. Once outgoing and at ease with adults, she'd withdrawn since her mother's death. Leaving her home and friends and beloved grandfather behind for the summer hadn't helped, either. She'd been determined not to like Sweetheart from the moment Sam had announced they were going there.

"Lyndsey, this is Annie Hennessy," he said. "She's an old friend of mine from when I lived here."

Annie sent him a cool look, and he could almost hear her saying, *Old friend?*

When she focused her attention on his daughter, however, her expression melted. Annie did love children.

"Nice to meet you, Lyndsey."

Sam vowed in that moment he wouldn't leave Nevada until Annie looked at him with that same warmth.

Lyndsey responded with a shy "Hello."

"What have you got there?" Sam crossed the few steps separating them. When he saw what his daughter had cradled in her T-shirt, his heart sank. Lyndsey was going to be disappointed again, and he couldn't prevent it. "Oh, sweetie, I think they're dead."

"No, they're alive. See, they're moving." Gathering the hem of her shirt in a small fist, she tentatively touched one of the baby raccoons with her other hand. It moved slightly and gave a pitiful mew, rousing its littermate, which also mewed. "There were two other ones in the log, but they weren't…" She continued when she was more composed. "I left them there."

"I think you should put these two back in the log."

"But they'll die, too!"

"The mother can take care of them."

"The mother's gone." Lindsey's cheeks flushed the same pink shade as her T-shirt. "Something must have happened to her. Why else would she leave her babies?"

Sam wanted to drop to his knees and pull her into his arms. She was projecting her own unresolved emotions onto the situation. Wasn't that how the grief counselor had described her behavior during one of their sessions? It was hardly the first time and wouldn't be the last. They both had a lot of healing left to do.

"Daddy." Her voice warbled. "We can't let them die."

"What would we do with two baby raccoons?"

"We can raise them. Until they're big enough to live by themselves. We read a story in school about this family that rescued baby animals after Hurricane Katrina."

"They're so tiny. I doubt they can even walk yet. We don't know the first thing about raising—"

"Kitten formula."

Sam glanced over at Annie. While he'd been talking to his daughter, she'd edged closer.

"Dr. Murry in town can help you. He'll set you up with bottles and formula. You'll need a box and a blanket and a lamp to keep them warm. He'll tell you more about that, too." She gently stroked the head of one baby raccoon with her index finger. "They're severely dehydrated. If you don't get fluids in them soon, they won't last."

"Have you raised baby raccoons before?" Lyndsey asked.

"A few. Along with kittens, puppies, squirrels, rabbits, snakes, a crow, you name it. There was even a fox once."

Sam knew the fox hadn't survived from the stories Annie told him.

"Wow," Lyndsey gaped at Annie with awe.

"My guess is these little fellows are about eight or nine weeks old. And they would be walking if they weren't so weak. The mother might have had trouble finding food since the fire and wandered too far. If you're going to save them, you'd better get them to Doc Murry's right away. Anyone in town can direct you to his office."

"Lyndsey." Sam hated letting his daughter down, but he had to be realistic. "We're leaving in a month. Those raccoons won't be old enough to live on their own by then."

"Will you take care of them after that?" Lyndsey ignored Sam in favor of Annie.

"That's a lot to ask of Ms. Hennessy—"

"I'll figure something out," Annie assured Lindsey with a tender smile.

"You don't have to," Sam said.

"There's the wildlife refuge outside of Lake Tahoe. We're on a first-name basis. But you're going to have to save them first." She brushed Lyndsey's tousled hair from her face. "Better hurry. Keep them as quiet as possible during the ride."

"Come on, Daddy." Lyndsey started for the truck, wrapping an arm protectively around her precious cargo.

"Where are you staying?" Annie asked Sam.

"At the Mountainside Motel." The only one in Sweetheart open for business after the fire. "But we check out tomorrow. I have some furniture arriving. A few basics. Enough for Lyndsey and me to stay at the ranch."

"I'll try and stop by after work if I don't have to stay

late. Just to check on the raccoons," she clarified when
he raised his brows.

"Of course." He studied her closed-off expression.
"Thank you."

"I didn't do it for *you*." She walked away then.

Sam watched her go. Same proud, stubborn Annie.

"Daddy! Hurry."

"Coming."

As they traveled the winding drive to the main road,
a smile spread across his face. Annie might refuse his
assistance at every step, but together they were going
to rebuild her inn.

He owed her that much at least.

Chapter 2

Sam Wyler was back!

Annie still hadn't come to grips with that fact twenty minutes later when she pulled into the parking space beside the Hennessy half of the duplex they rented in town.

She'd kept one eye glued to her rearview mirror during the entire drive from the Gold Nugget, hoping he hadn't followed her. The last thing she wanted was for him to see where she lived.

Not that the two-bedroom apartment was exactly trashy. Just small and modest and nothing compared with the lovely and charming suite of rooms she'd occupied at the inn. The rooms Sam had seen when they'd sneak off to be alone and make love.

She'd assumed those nights spent together would last forever. Then, he'd left, returned, left again and married—because the daughter of the rancher who hired him was carrying his child—and become a father.

Annie stayed behind in Sweetheart, hoping for the same future every couple who eloped here did. Only that happy ending had eluded her.

Mostly. As Sam had pointed out, she did have her beautiful little girl. For now, at least.

Her ex-husband had recently started hinting that he and his new wife could provide a better environment for Nessa than an eight-hundred-and-fifty-square-foot apartment shared by four individuals. What next? Would he go so far as to sue Annie for primary custody? She didn't think so, but everyone and everything had changed of late.

It was true, now that the inn had burned, that Gary could provide better for their daughter. And, marital differences aside, he'd always been a good father.

That made no difference to Annie. If he tried to obtain primary custody of their daughter, he and his new wife—Annie would lay odds Linda Lee was behind this—were in for the fight of their lives.

If only Sam hadn't suddenly reappeared, knocking Annie for an emotional loop. She didn't need anything distracting her from what mattered the most: rebuilding the inn and safeguarding her family.

She swung open the apartment door and stepped inside.

"Mommy! You're home." Nessa ran at her from across the living room like a miniature missile, her face smeared with some unidentifiable food remains and a Barbie doll with chopped-off hair clutched in her hand.

Annie scooped up her daughter and let herself feel

truly good for the first time since leaving the apartment that morning.

"Hey, sweetums. How was your day?"

"Good. Grandma and I made biscuits. I ate two whole ones by myself. With jelly."

That explained the smeared food on Nessa's face. She tickled the girl's tummy. "How on earth did you put that much in there?"

"I'm big now."

"Yes, you are."

"You wanna play Barbies with me?"

"Maybe later. Mommy's a little tired."

"You're always tired," Nessa complained. "Ever since the fire. Grandma, too. And Great-granny Orla."

From the mouths of babes.

"I feel much better now that I'm home." She set Nessa down and kissed the tip of her nose, which was the only clean spot on her entire face.

"You want a biscuit and jelly? I can fix it for you."

"That'd be wonderful."

Annie sat on the couch and slowly removed her heavy hiking boots. By the end of the day, they felt as if they were lined with cement. She sighed when the first boot hit the floor, almost cried with relief when the second one followed.

Leaning back, she closed her eyes and relaxed for just a minute, listening to her mother patiently caution Nessa to be careful and not spill any jelly, in much the same way she'd cautioned Annie when she was growing up.

No one knew their way around the kitchen better than Fiona Hennessy. For almost her entire life, she'd overseen meals and housekeeping for the inn's twenty or thirty guests. Her small, compact stature belied the iron fist with which she'd ruled her domain.

These past six weeks, Fiona had continued the tradition of spending most of her time in the kitchen. Only now she was hiding from the world and desperately missing all that had been taken from her.

No more lion's claw bathtubs in the upstairs bedrooms, large enough to hold two. No more handmade, valentine-patterned quilts on which were strewn dried rose petals for arriving honeymooners. Or carved wooden trays that had held champagne breakfasts, discreetly delivered with a soft knock on the door. No more do-not-disturb signs, often hanging on doorknobs all the day long.

Annie hoped her mother's depression was temporary. More than that, she hoped her ex-husband, Gary, didn't notice Fiona's detachment when he picked up Nessa for "his days." That would only strengthen his argument that the apartment wasn't a good place to raise their daughter.

She would never wish him harm but often caught herself wondering why fate had chosen the inn to burn and left Gary's house and place of business intact.

"Here you go, Mommy."

Opening her eyes, Annie was greeted by Nessa holding a paper plate with two jelly-laden biscuit halves.

"That looks good." Annie pushed tiredly to her feet. "Maybe I should eat it in the kitchen." She took the plate from Nessa, amazed the biscuit halves hadn't already landed on the carpet. "What else is for dinner?"

"Nothing," Nessa singsonged. "Just biscuits."

Uh-oh. Annie walked to the kitchen, her steps slow and her stomach sinking. Nessa danced in circles beside her. Fiona stood at the sink, staring vacantly out the window. Definitely not good.

Her mother watched Nessa during the day while Annie worked for the NDF. Her paycheck and Granny Orla's social security, which she'd started collecting just this month, were their only sources of income. Without them, they wouldn't be able to afford even this lowly apartment.

Lately, Annie had begun to question if her mother was up to the task of caring for an active child. More and more often, Fiona would disappear into her own world. For minutes on end. Five, ten, twenty. Long enough for an unsupervised Nessa to find trouble.

What Fiona should be doing while Nessa played was dealing with the insurance company, finalizing their settlement and obtaining quotes from contractors for rebuilding the inn. That was their agreement.

Hard to do when she could barely drag herself out of bed in the mornings.

"Where's Granny Orla?" Annie asked Nessa, hoping her question would rouse her mother. "Taking a nap?"

"I dunno."

"At the Rutherfords," Fiona answered without looking away from the window. "They called."

"How long has she been there?"

"Most of the afternoon, I guess."

The Rutherfords and the Hennessys' other neighbors were a godsend. Annie's grandmother, sharp as a tack until the fire, had started taking walkabouts during the day, easily escaping Fiona's less-than-diligent guard. She mostly wound up on some neighbor's doorstep—one whose house hadn't been lost to the fire. The neighbor would invite her inside until Annie came by later to fetch her.

Last week, Annie had found Granny Orla at the inn ruins and was shocked she'd managed the two-mile trek alone.

Annie doubted Alzheimer's or senility was responsible for her grandmother's increasing confusion. Like all of them, she'd suffered a great loss. And, also like them, she'd chosen a means of coping. Fiona emotionally retreated, Annie buried herself in work and Granny Orla chose to forget.

"I'll go get her." Annie set her plate of biscuits on the table, the little appetite she'd had now gone. "You want to come with me, sweetums?"

"Yes, yes!" Nessa swung her Barbie in an arc.

"Okay. But you have to pick up your toys and finish your milk first." Annie cringed inwardly. Biscuits and milk wasn't the most nutritious meal. Then again, Nessa wouldn't starve.

Annie should eat, too, if only to keep up her strength. Seeing Sam had drained the last of it.

Why had he chosen now to return, and why buy the Gold Nugget? She still couldn't believe he'd asked for her help.

While Nessa gathered the many toys strewn throughout the house and returned them to the plastic crate stored in the bedroom she and Annie shared, Annie changed into more-comfortable clothes.

"We shouldn't be long," she said upon returning to the kitchen.

Fiona, who hadn't moved from the window, suddenly turned and stared at Annie with more intensity than she'd shown in weeks. "Sam Wyler's in town. He bought the Gold Nugget."

That took Annie by surprise. "I know," she said. "How did you hear?"

"Everyone's talking about it."

"I ran into him. On my way home. I stopped by the Gold Nugget, and he was there."

"I suppose if someone had to buy the ranch, I'd rather it be him."

"Mom! How can you say that?"

Fiona went slowly to the table, pulled a chair out for herself and dropped into it. "He's one of our own."

"Because he lived here two years?" Annie was aghast at her mother's calm acceptance. "He's going to turn it into a working guest ranch."

"I'm not sure that's such a good idea."

Finally! Reason had returned. "I agree. A bed-and-breakfast makes more sense." Like her own plans for the place.

"I like the idea of a working guest ranch. Not sure why someone didn't think of that before."

"But you said—"

"What I meant was the fire's discouraged people from coming to Sweetheart. Bed-and-breakfast or working guest ranch, both need customers."

"Fine with me. When he flops, we'll buy the ranch from him."

"Sam was always a hard worker. If anyone can pull it off, he can." Fiona talked as if she hadn't heard Annie.

"He'll be in competition with us. Once we rebuild."

"If we rebuild," Fiona said tiredly.

Annie didn't listen to her mother when she got this

way. "Did you have a chance to make Nessa's immunization appointment at the clinic?"

Fiona shook her head. "I was busy."

Biscuit making? Annie thought grouchily. Did that take all afternoon?

She tried to be patient and understanding with her mother. Really she did. Fiona's fragile emotional state made the task of rebuilding too overwhelming for her to bear. But once they broke ground, she and Annie's grandmother would be their old selves and life would return to normal.

Annie had to believe that. If not, she'd be overwhelmed herself, and she couldn't afford to let that happen.

Long before they finished rebuilding, however, Sam's working guest ranch would be up and running. Damn him! Annie wanted their inn and not Sam's ranch bringing the honeymooners and tourists back to Sweetheart.

"Mrs. Rutherford mentioned Sam has a little girl."

"He does." Annie made herself eat a biscuit half in case Nessa noticed.

Normally, her daughter would be pestering her to leave. Instead, she'd become interested in a puzzle she was supposed to be putting away.

"I heard she looks like him," Fiona said.

The food stuck in Annie's throat. "No need for DNA testing. She's Sam's child through and through."

Except for the sorrow in her eyes.

Annie was no psychiatrist, she didn't have to be. The girl was obviously troubled—which might not be Sam's fault. Her mother had died and, as Annie could attest, life-altering events changed a person.

"I bet he's a good dad."

She rose from the table, not wanting to talk about Sam or his daughter. "Come on, Nessa. Find your shoes so we can go get Granny Orla."

Nessa abandoned the puzzle and went on the hunt for her shoes.

"It was a shame things didn't work out for you and him," Fiona said from the table. "You must have really broken his heart."

"Let's not forget, he left me."

Fiona sighed. "Bound to happen. Can't fight the inevitable."

Her mother's words stayed with Annie as she and Nessa walked hand in hand to the Rutherfords'.

Ask anyone in town, and they'd say the Hennessy women were cursed. All of them, grandmother, mother and daughter, had loved their men, only to be abandoned by them. In Granny Orla and her mother's cases, they'd been left with a child to raise alone. Not Annie. Sam had simply taken off—which was practically unheard of in a town renowned for couples marrying.

Rather than be thought of as the third Hennessy woman to suffer unrequited love, Annie had rushed out and wed the first man to show an interest in her.

Can't fight the inevitable.

It hadn't made a difference. The Hennessy curse had continued with Annie. For here she was today, abandoned by not one but two men.

She squeezed Nessa's hand.

Please, please, she silently prayed, *don't let my baby be as unlucky in love as the rest of my family.*

Sam gazed over at Lyndsey and mentally kicked himself. She—and he by default—were now foster par-

ents to Porky Pig and Daffy Duck. Lyndsey had named
their new charges while in Dr. Murry's office, after he
informed her the pair were both males.

"Did you know baby raccoons are called kits?" Lyndsey struggled to buckle her seat belt while balancing
the cardboard boot box containing the kits on her lap.
Tube-fed, hydrated and vaccinated, they'd fallen into a
deep sleep atop an old towel. "And when they get older,
some people call them cubs."

"Is that so?"

Sam hadn't heard everything Dr. Murry told them
and listened intently as Lindsey repeated the instructions. He'd received not one but two phone calls while
at the vet's. The first from the moving company con-
firming the arrival of their furniture tomorrow. The
second call was from a cattle broker regarding a shipment of calves.

Sam added hiring a livestock manager and locating
a string of sound trail horses to his growing task list.

"Chicken's one of their favorite foods," Lyndsey said.
"And sunflower seeds."

"Well, we should get along just fine as chicken and
sunflower seeds are some of my favorite foods, too."

She giggled.

Giggled! Sam almost swerved off the road. He hadn't
seen his daughter this happy since before her mother's
accident.

Trisha Wyler had been pronounced dead upon arrival
at the hospital after a drunk driver ran a stop sign and
T-boned her Buick. Her passenger, on the other hand,
lived long enough to confess Trisha's secret.

Sam didn't just lose his wife that day—his entire be-
lief system was destroyed in one fell swoop.

His father-in-law was responsible for Sam keeping it together, reminding him daily of Lyndsey and the twenty employees at their three-thousand-acre cattle ranch who depended on him.

Sam went through the motions for six months, a huge, empty hole inside him that no amount of whiskey, angry rages, sympathy from friends and a seven-figure settlement could fill. Then, over a year ago, he returned to the Redding California Hotshots, a seasonal volunteer job he'd loved during the early years of his marriage. Within a few months, he was promoted to crew leader, then captain.

Long, grueling, sweat-filled days battling fires on the front line returned him to the world of the living.

Until the day the fire they were fighting in the Sierra Nevada Mountains jumped the ravine and bore down on the town of Sweetheart.

It was his fault. Had he disobeyed his commanding officer's orders like he wanted to, he might have saved the town. Saved Annie's family's inn. His superiors didn't hold him responsible but Sam did. Enough for ten people.

He quit the Hotshots a week later and found a real estate agent in Lake Tahoe who knew the Sweetheart area, his plan to return temporarily and assess how he could best help the town recover already in motion.

During one of their phone conversations, the agent mentioned the Gold Nugget Ranch. Sam made the offer the next day sight unseen and paid the full asking price without quibbling. As of tomorrow, he was officially in the hospitality business.

And, apparently, in the baby raccoon business, too.

He'd foster a hundred of them if Lyndsey would only giggle again.

While Sam had immersed himself in wilderness fire-fighting as a means to conquer his grief, his daughter grew further and further apart from him. He hoped their time together in Sweetheart would remedy that. Still, one summer of being an attentive father couldn't wipe out eighteen months of neglect.

"We need to buy canned cat food," Lyndsey insisted. Her hand lay protectively on Porky and Daffy. "Dr. Murry said they're old enough for solid food."

Did baby raccoons bite? Sam couldn't remember the vet's advice. "We will."

"Tomorrow?"

He thought of his lengthening task list. What was one more item?

"Tomorrow. After the furniture arrives." He eased onto the main road from the parking lot. It had grown dark outside while they were with the vet.

"How will we warm the milk?" Lyndsey asked.

"The stove works." If the propane tank was full and if he could locate a pan.

"Where will we get a cage?"

"The feed store might have one."

"What if they don't?"

"We'll figure something out. Don't worry." He could see his words had no effect. Worry lines creased his daughter's small brow.

Maybe he should call the grief counselor, get some advice on how to handle Lyndsey and her quickly form-ing attachment to the kits. Heaven knew he hadn't done well when left to his own devices.

"Ms. Hennessy might have a cage we can use." Was that still Annie's name or had she kept her ex-husband's?

Lyndsey's face lit up. "Do you think so?"

"Maybe."

Seriously? Who was he kidding? The inn had burned down to the ground. From what the real estate agent told him, Annie, her mother and grandmother were left with no more than a few hastily gathered personal possessions.

"Or, she might know someone who does," he suggested, thinking that possibility more likely.

"I want to take Porky and Daffy home to California with us," Lyndsey promptly announced.

"We already talked about this. You know it's not possible."

"Why not?"

"They're wild animals, not pets. Besides, you'll be busy with school."

"Benita will help me take care of them."

Their housekeeper barely tolerated dogs in the house. "Benita has enough to do."

"We can make a place for them in the backyard. Like at the zoo. With a swimming pool and everything. Dr. Murry said raccoons like water."

What answer could he give that would make her understand?

"Lyndsey, we can't take them home. They belong here. In Sweetheart. Living free in the wild."

"But the woods are all burned and the animals ran away."

"The trees will grow back and the animals didn't all run away."

"They'll die like their mother and brothers!" Her voice quavered with outrage.

"We'll turn them over to someone who will take good care of them. Like the wildlife refuge Ms. Hennessy mentioned."

"I want to see it first." There was no arguing with her.

Well, she came by it honestly. If Sam wasn't so bull-headed, he might have realized his marriage was falling apart long ago and taken action—he had no idea *what* action.

"Fine. I promise. Wherever the baby raccoons go, you'll see the place first."

"Kits."

"Kits," he corrected himself, aware that round had gone to Lyndsey. "In the meantime, until we leave Sweetheart, you can keep them." He proceeded slowly through one of the town's two stoplights.

"I wanna call Grandpa and tell him about Porky and Daffy."

"When we get back to the mo—" Sam hit the brakes, checking the rearview mirror to make sure no one was close behind him.

Annie, her grandmother and a little girl that had to be her daughter were walking along the sidewalk. Annie appeared to be struggling for control. Orla Hennessy, all of seventy-five, if not eighty, went in one direction and the little girl in the other. Neither paid attention to Annie, who'd momentarily stumbled in the confusion.

What in the world were the three of them doing out after dark?

Pulling onto the side of the road, he beeped the horn, thrust the transmission into Park and depressed the emergency brake. "Lyndsey, wait here. Don't get out, you hear me?"

She sat up in her seat. "Where are you going?"

"To help Ms. Hennessy. I'll be right back."

She clasped the box to her as if Annie and her family were going to reach in and swoop up her prize possession. "We have to get Porky and Daffy back to the motel and feed them."

"This won't take long."

"Ask her if she has a cage."

Did she ever run out of questions?

"Hey, there." Sam darted around the front of the truck to the sidewalk. "Out for an evening stroll?"

"Walking back from a friend's house," came Annie's tight-lipped reply.

"Hop in, and I'll give you a lift."

"No, thanks. We're fine."

He was surrounded by stubborn women.

"Sam Wyler! As I live and breathe, is that you?" Granny Orla broke away from Annie's grasp and propelled herself at Sam. "Aren't you a sight for sore eyes."

Sam returned the older woman's hug, his throat surprisingly tight. "How are you, Granny Orla?"

She held him at arm's length, giving him a thorough once-over, her eyes alight. "My, my. Handsome as ever. That granddaughter of mine should have never let you go."

"I'm right here, Granny." With both arms free, Annie had been able to secure a firm hold on her squirming daughter. "I can hear everything you're saying."

Granny winked at Sam. "I know that."

He flashed a broad grin in return. "I always did like you."

"That goes both ways, young man."

The older woman barely reached the middle of his chest. As Sam recalled, neither did Fiona Hennessy. Annie must have gotten her height from her father, whom she hadn't seen since starting first grade.

"You're a cowboy!"

Sam's attention was drawn downward to Annie's little girl, a tiny imp who more closely resembled her grandmother and great-grandmother than Annie. Except for her compelling green eyes, which were the same shape and color as her mother's.

"I am."

"Do you have a horse?" She studied him with suspicion, as if having a horse was the measure of a real cowboy.

"Lots of them, actually. At my ranch in California. And a pony. From when my daughter, Lyndsey, was your age."

"Can I ride him?"

"Nessa!" Annie gently chided the girl. "That's not polite."

"'Fraid California's too far away." Sam laughed, not the least offended. "But that's a good idea. I should have the pony shipped out here for the Gold Nugget. Then your mom can bring you over for a ride."

"What's the pony's name?"

He surveyed the traffic, which was light but a potential danger nonetheless. "Get in, and I'll tell you about her on the drive home."

"Can we, Mommy? Please?" Nessa yanked on Annie's arm, stretching it to its limit.

Granny Orla was one step ahead of her great-granddaughter. "Fine idea."

Outnumbered and clearly at her wits' end, Annie sighed resignedly.

Sam allowed himself a grin as he opened the rear passenger door and helped the three inside. Annie didn't avail herself of the hand he offered, but he didn't let that deter him.

He had the opportunity of sharing her company for the next several minutes and intended to make full use of it.

Chapter 3

Sam's daughter twisted around in the front seat the second Annie got into the truck.

"Did my dad ask you about a cage for the kits?"

"Just a minute ago." She tried not to be swayed by the blaze of hope shining in the girl's face. "I'll get one for you by tomorrow and drop it off."

"Really? Thank you!"

So much for not being swayed.

"What are kits?" Nessa asked, unable to sit still.

"Baby raccoons," Lyndsey answered.

"Where? Can I see?" She leaned forward.

"When we stop the truck, if you're good." Annie placed a restraining hand on her daughter.

"We'll be at the ranch tomorrow early," Sam said. "The furniture truck's due."

Great. She was now going to visit Sam a *second* time

at the Gold Nugget, *and* he was taking her home. What else could go wrong?

"Mind if I tag along?" her grandmother asked.

"You're welcome anytime."

"It won't be till later, Granny. I'll be coming straight from work, not stopping home first."

"Haven't seen the place in a while," her grandmother continued as if she hadn't heard Annie. "Not since last spring."

"I wanna go, too," Nessa chimed in.

Annie should have silenced her thoughts when she had the chance. At least Nessa seemed to have forgotten about the pony. For now.

"How are you getting along, Granny Orla?" Sam slowed, taking the turn leading to Annie's street. She'd given him directions when they first climbed into the truck.

"Terrible." Her grandmother went from animated to forlorn in the span of a single second. "We lost the inn."

"I heard. I'm sorry."

"Not half as sorry as I am. Don't know how we're going to make it. Much less rebuild."

"We'll find a way. Don't worry." Annie's assurance was as much for herself as everyone else in the truck. Especially Nessa. She might not understand everything they were going through, but she was astute and picked up on people's moods.

"I told Annie I'd like to help with rebuilding Sweetheart." Sam parked in front of the duplex. "Your inn and the entire town."

"We're fine." Annie noticed his gaze traveling to the modest duplex. Grabbing her daughter's hand, she wrenched open the door. "Come on, Nessa." They were out in a flash.

"I want to see the kits."

"Later, okay? It's getting late and the kits are sleeping."

"But we forgot Granny Orla."

Nessa was right. Annie's grandmother hadn't moved.

"Come on, Granny. Mom's waiting for us."

"She is?"

"Yes."

"Where?"

"In the apartment."

"The apartment?" her grandmother repeated slowly. "What's she doing there?"

Why now? Annie silently lamented. And why in front of Sam? She should have seen this coming. Any discussion about losing the inn brought on these… these…episodes.

"Please, Granny. It's getting late."

Sam came around the truck to the passenger side. "How 'bout I walk you to the door?"

The sympathy in his voice hit Annie hard. Half of her wanted to scream in frustration, the other half cry.

Nessa tugged on her hand. "Mommy, I have to go potty."

"Okay, just a second." Moving aside, Annie let Sam reach into the truck cab and coax her grandmother out.

Some of the older woman's animation returned. "Can't remember the last time a man walked me to my door."

"Wait here, Lyndsey," he instructed his daughter.

"The kits woke up. We have to feed them," she protested.

Annie could hear their soft mewing.

"I'll only be a minute," Sam said. "They won't starve."

Lyndsey slouched and hugged the box on her lap, her lower lip protruding.

Though it wasn't Annie's fault, she felt responsible for the delay. "I'll see you tomorrow, Lyndsey. When I bring the cage." She made a mental note to remember. "Will the kits be all right till then?"

"Dr. Murry showed me what I need to do." Her hand reached tenderly into the box.

Annie had no doubt Lyndsey would make the vet proud. If only her father had shown half that much tenderness when handling Annie's heart.

He did seem to be doing an admirable job with her grandmother, though. Was it possible he'd changed?

The front door swung open before Annie could dig her keys out of her pocket.

"There you are. I was getting worried." At the sight of Sam, Fiona's depression evaporated. "Sam Wyler!"

Annie's mother hugged him fiercely, much as her grandmother had. The gesture made Annie acutely aware that she and Sam had yet to touch since his return.

"How are you?" Fiona asked. "Come in, come in."

Annie ground her teeth. *Say no. Please.*

For once, her luck held.

"Thank you, Fiona, but I can't." He straightened his cowboy hat, which had been knocked askew during the hug. "My daughter's waiting in the truck."

"Bring her in, too. We'll have some ice cream."

"Ice cream!" Nessa jumped up and down.

"I appreciate the offer." Sam shot a look at the truck

parked on the curb. "But Lyndsey's babysitting a pair of abandoned raccoons she found earlier today in a log, and they need feeding."

"Raccoons?"

"Annie can explain."

"Then you'll have to come back another day. Your daughter, too."

"I'd like that."

"I'm gonna ride a pony," Nessa chimed in, forgetting all about her pressing need. "You said I could."

Sam patted her head. "I have to buy some horses first."

"High Country Outfitters are going out of business," Fiona said, "and selling off their entire stable of trail horses. With no customers, they can't afford the price of feed. You could probably pick up a few good head for a decent price."

"Who do I talk to?"

"Will Dessaro's their livestock manager. Anyone in town can tell you where to find him."

"I'll track him down first thing in the morning."

Annie almost did a double take. How was it her mother knew about High Country Outfitters going out of business and she'd heard nothing?

Because she'd been busy with work and caring for Nessa and holding her family together.

And she hadn't wanted to know. With each resident that was forced to move from Sweetheart, each business that shut its doors, she lost a small sliver of hope.

"I'd best get going, see to it those raccoons get fed." Sam touched the brim of his hat and grinned at all of them. Annie the longest.

Her heart might be damaged, but it could still flutter. Which, to her dismay, it did.

If only Sweetheart were bigger than three square miles and one thousand residents—a number dwindling daily. Then maybe she wouldn't be constantly running into Sam.

As she watched him stride confidently toward his truck, she wondered if that wasn't what she secretly wanted. She had, after all, made an excuse to see him tomorrow.

She spun on her heels to find her mother, grandmother and daughter all watching him, too.

Apparently she wasn't the only one susceptible to his charms.

The pickup and stock trailer looked out of place as it rumbled to a stop beside the old corral. So did the modern furniture that had been delivered hours earlier and set up in the ranch's three bedrooms, kitchen and parlor.

Sam's memories of the Gold Nugget were of a buggy sitting in front of the house, knotty pine rockers on the porch, blacksmith equipment hanging in the shed beside the barn and rooms filled with antiques and authentic reproductions used in filming *The Forty-Niners*. There had also been photographs of the stars and crew displayed on every wall in every room, along with articles on the actors' lives and trivia about the show.

For some unknown reason, those photos alone had survived when everything else in the house was auctioned off.

In the evenings, after the tourists had left, the ranch would become eerily quiet. He and Annie would sit in the rockers or at the long oak table in the kitchen or lie on the squeaky mattress and box spring in the master bedroom and dream about the future.

If old Mrs. Litey, the longtime curator of the Gold Nugget, had caught them, she'd have skinned them alive.

And now, the ranch was Sam's, thanks to the former owner deciding it was easier to sell the place than make the necessary repairs and upgrades.

A quick glance around revealed the ranch still needed a lot of work—starting with the corrals. The pine rails were broken and rotted in place and wouldn't contain the horses he'd purchased that morning for very long. Fortunately, the construction contractor and his crew were arriving on Monday.

Sam walked over to greet the young cowboy emerging from the cab of the truck, a large shepherd mix tumbling out after him. Sam and Will Dessaro had spent a good two hours together, during which Sam inspected each horse in the High Country Outfitters' string and negotiated the price. The deal was closed when he delivered the cashier's check he'd obtained at the neighboring town fifteen miles away.

"You made good time." He shook Will's hand. The man's grip was firm, his features strong and appealing. "Thought you might have some trouble loading all these horses by yourself."

"Not likely."

"Should we back the trailer up to the gate?" he asked.

"Don't need to."

This would be interesting, Sam thought as he watched Will open the rear of the trailer and lower the ramp. Only then did Sam realize all the horses stood loose, except for the first one. He alone was haltered and tied.

"Don't you think you should— "

Before Sam finished his thought, Will was leading the haltered horse down the ramp. The nine others followed out of the trailer, one by one, nose to tail. The dog trotted along beside them. To Sam's surprise, all ten horses stood quietly as Will opened the corral gate and then pushed inside, eagerly exploring their new home. Will swung the gate shut and latched it.

"I'm impressed," Sam said.

"Not a contrary one in the bunch."

Sam was a believer and convinced he'd made a good investment.

Together, he and Will unloaded bags of feed from the trailer's front compartment and stacked them under the lean-to. Next, they ran a hose and filled the water barrel.

"Be back in an hour with the rest of them." Will had promised he could deliver all nineteen horses in two trips, and it looked as though he was a man of his word.

"Any chance you can stick around afterward and maybe tomorrow? Help me with the horses?"

"Sure."

"I'm not interfering with your job?"

"High Country Outfitters is out of business. You just bought what was left of my job."

"Sorry about that."

Will shrugged. "I noticed some of the horses have loose shoes."

"Is there a farrier in town?"

"I did most of the shoeing for High Country."

"Any experience with cattle?"

"My grandmother raised me. She ran near a hundred head."

Will was looking better and better by the minute. He also knew the mountain trails.

"You're not by chance good at cross-country skiing?"

"Have all my own gear."

Well, well. "Anything you can't do?"

"Cook."

That made two of them. Lyndsey had already complained about breakfast and lunch.

Sam pushed his hat back and grinned. "You by chance in the market for a new job?"

"You offering me one?"

"I need a livestock foreman and someone to supervise the trail rides. Take guests on guided skiing excursions in the winter months. I'm thinking you have the experience."

"Okay." Will started toward his truck. His dog, resting in the shade of a bush, sprang instantly to its feet.

"Is that a yes?" Sam called after him.

"You need something in writing?"

He laughed. "We'll talk details when you get back."

"Fine by me."

Sam decided he liked the Gold Nugget Ranch's first official employee. The female guests were bound to like him, too, though Sam suspected Will would keep to himself.

Pressed for time, Sam went over to the corral and checked on the horses. Several bunched at the railing for a petting. The rest stared at him as if wondering why they hadn't been given any pellets.

"When your buddies arrive." He patted an overly eager black-and-white paint that could easily break through the railing if he weren't so docile. "And when I figure out what exactly I'm going to use for a feed trough."

By all accounts, there'd been no horses on the ranch since *The Forty-Niners* ceased production. He'd considered himself lucky to find that old water barrel in the barn.

There must be something else kicking around he could use. If not, he'd ask Will. The man struck Sam as being the resourceful type. And there was always the feed store.

He was halfway to the barn when a rusted-out sedan pulled into the ranch and stopped, the exhaust spewing a cloud of gray smoke when the engine was cut. Seconds later, a woman with an assortment of children spilled out of all four doors.

"Hi, can I help you?"

"Mr. Wyler? My name's Irma Swichtenberg. These here are my children."

The tallest, a teenager, tugged nervously on her hair while the shortest, a toddler, snuggled a stuffed toy.

"What can I do for you?" Sam asked.

"Miss Hennessy sent me your way."

"Annie?"

"No, sir. Fiona. I worked for her. At the inn. Housekeeping. She said you might be looking to hire someone." The woman swallowed nervously. "I'm a hard worker. Honest and dependable. Carrie watches the little ones for me so I won't ever miss a day." She placed a hand on the teenager's shoulder.

Sam could see Irma Swichtenberg was a proud woman and that asking for a job didn't come easy. For all he knew, she single-handedly supported her small family. Judging by the shape of their worn clothes, she was at the end of her resources.

"How good a cook are you?"

"Passable."

"The place needs a lot of cleaning. Been empty awhile. And I'm hardly the neatest person. My daughter's worse."

"Not much I can't handle or won't."

He believed her.

"I really need a job, Mr. Wyler. I'll work cheap."

Sam had made a promise to himself to help the people of Sweetheart and that included providing employment for as many of the locals as possible. That aside, he'd have hired Irma anyway. He liked and respected her that much.

"No need to work cheap. I'll pay you a decent wage."

When he named the rate, Irma's hands flew to her mouth. "You're not joshing me, are you?"

"Can you start in the morning? 8:00 a.m."

"I'll start now!"

"That's not necessary." He chuckled. "We'll decide on your schedule tomorrow. Might only be part-time until we're ready for guests."

"Thank you, Mr. Wyler." She rushed toward him, grabbed his hand and pumped it enthusiastically. "I'm grateful to you."

"My daughter and I are the ones who are grateful to you. Otherwise, we might starve or be buried alive in a mountain of dirty clothes."

She smiled shyly, displaying slightly crooked teeth. "I'll see you at eight sharp."

Something told him Irma would be here at seven forty-five. "Looking forward to it."

Gathering her brood, she hurried them to the car as if afraid Sam might change his mind.

Unlikely, he decided. So far, he was more than pleased with his staff. And he had Fiona Hennessy to thank.

If she and Annie weren't so determined to rebuild the inn, he'd hire Fiona to manage the Gold Nugget. He needed someone trustworthy, competent and with her vast hospitality experience. Someone whose skills would allow him to be a long-distance owner.

Sam made his way toward the barn in search of Lyndsey. She'd been in there the entire time with Porky and Daffy. A few good meals had made all the difference to the kits. They were active and curious and had already figured out their long, sharp claws were perfect tools for scaling the sides of a cardboard box.

They were also kind of cute, Sam had to admit, with their little button noses, whiskers and black face masks.

Lyndsey had moved them into an old wooden crate until the cage arrived. She couldn't be a more attentive and devoted caretaker. Sam was proud of her. And worried. He tried not to think about how she'd take losing the kits when the time came.

She was just where he'd left her, sitting cross-legged in the center of the barn floor. Sunlight poured in through cracks in the wooden walls, painting a pattern of stripes on her and the crate beside her.

"Hi, Dad." She cradled Daffy, the smaller of the kits, in her lap, his front paws balanced on her towel-covered forearm in the manner the vet had instructed. Daffy lustily drained a bottle of kitten formula.

"How're they doing?" Sam asked.

"They like the canned cat food!" Her face radiated delight.

"Dr. Murry says they'll eat almost anything."

"They licked it off a spoon."

Sam's earlier concern returned. "They didn't bite you, did they?"

"Oh, Dad."

He took that as a no and breathed easier.

"Grandpa said he can't wait to see them."

"Lyndsey, sweetie." He reached for her. "You—"

She stiffened and pulled away. "Don't say we can't take them home."

"Okay, I won't."

Withdrawing his hand, he squatted beside the crate and gave Daffy a little scratch. Porky was attempting to squeeze his apple-shaped head between the narrow openings in the crate.

"I can't believe how much difference one day makes."

"Porky purred and kneaded my arm when he ate."

"No fooling?" Sam attempted to pet Porky. The kit jerked instantly back and growled at him, his fur standing on end. He looked and sounded more comical than threatening.

"Dad! Be careful. You'll hurt him."

"Hurt him? What about me?" Sam inspected his hand. "I'm the one who almost lost a finger."

"It's instinctive. You have to move slowly."

He turned at the sound of Annie's voice.

She stood in the entrance to the barn, wearing her NDF uniform and holding an empty cage.

"Hey. Thanks for coming by." He pushed to his feet, noticing the exhaustion on her face. "You okay?"

"Just beat. We ran erosion and water repellency tests all day in the field."

Despite her busy schedule, she'd found time to locate a cage for Lyndsey and deliver it. If he could, he would take her in his arms and the hell with the consequences.

"Sounds grueling."

"It was."

She must have seen the urge reflected in his eyes because she retreated a step—just like she'd done yesterday when they first met and again last night when he picked her up on the way home.

Would she ever stop being wary of him? And if she did, what then?

Nothing, he thought. Even if they were able to move past their unhappy history, the timing was off, for both of them, and no amount of wishing would change that.

Chapter 4

Annie tried not to stare at Sam as she set the cage down and walked over to Lyndsey. He didn't make it easy. Levi's, a faded chambray shirt and a Stetson covering thick, dark hair in need of a cut was a look he wore well.

Standing straight, she reminded herself he'd left her high and dry. Not once, but twice. There would be no third time.

"Gosh, would you look at them!" She directed her smile at Lyndsey and the kits.

"They're eating canned cat food!" Lyndsey exclaimed. One kit scrambled up her chest toward her shoulder while the other one clawed at the crate.

"Already? I'm impressed."

"You think they're going to be all right?"

The kits were active, alert and responsive. All encouraging signs.

"It's a little too soon to say for certain, but my guess is they'll make it."

"Why did their mommy and brothers die? Was it because of the fire?"

"Not the fire itself." Annie started to say the entire eco-structure in the area had been profoundly altered, which, in turn, affected local wildlife, then decided the explanation was too complicated for an eight-year-old. "The land's changed, and the animals are have a harder time surviving than they once did."

"This one is Daffy." Lindsey lifted the kit from her lap into the air. "Want to hold him?"

"Sure." Annie took the kit and cradled it close. The warm feel and musky scent were familiar. How many baby raccoons had she rescued and raised? Six? Ten?

Now she was rescuing and raising her family. If only that were as easy as a pair of kits.

"You'd better take him." She returned Daffy to Lyndsey. "The fewer people who handle him and his brother, the better."

"Why?"

"They'll adjust easier to the animal sanctuary or the wild."

Lyndsey sucked in a gasp. "Won't they just die if you let them go?"

"At this age, yes. But the sanctuary will care for them until they're old enough to be safely released. And they'll teach them how to find food and to take care of themselves."

"That's what Ms. Hennessy did." The remark came from Sam. "With all the animals she took in."

"Some. Others weren't ever able to fend for themselves."

"What happened to them?" Lyndsey hugged Daffy closer.

"I kept them for the rest of their lives."

"You had quite a collection," Sam said. "I'd help you feed and clean the enclosures." He looked at Lyndsey. "Her mother used to call it the zoo."

Annie snuck a quick peek at him. The thrill she'd fended off earlier wound through her, proving she wasn't immune to him and the easy, sexy charm he exuded.

As if she'd ever been.

He was older now. Experience had left its mark on his face and made him even more handsome—and her more susceptible.

"Wow!" Lyndsey's eyes went wide. "That must have been cool."

"It was," Sam concurred. "And then, she'd treat my horses whenever they needed some minor medical attention. Cuts, colic, vaccinations. We were a good team." His gaze found hers and held it.

"Once, maybe." A rush of memories assailed Annie, and she forced herself to look away.

"You're like a vet!"

Thankfully, Lyndsey appeared unaware of the emotions flying between Annie and her father.

"Not hardly. But I thought I wanted to be one when I was your age."

"What stopped you?" Sam asked.

She turned and faced him. "The inn. I was needed there."

"Do you ever regret your choice?"

"Not for one second. Sweetheart Inn has been in my family for three generations. It will be for a fourth."

"What happened to the animals?" Lyndsey asked.

"I stopped collecting so many after your dad...after a while." Annie went over and retrieved the cage from where she'd left it. "Where are you keeping the kits?"

"In my bedroom," Lyndsey promptly answered.

"That was just for last night." Sam bent and stroked her hair. "We talked about this. The barn is the best place."

She pulled away, her mouth set in a firm line. "You always say no."

Annie sensed the friction between them wasn't due entirely to the kits. This battle had been waged before over something else.

"Your dad's right," she said gently. "The barn is better. For one thing, unless you clean their cage ten times a day, they'll smell. Really bad."

"I'll clean it."

"And they're noisy. Raccoons are mostly nocturnal."

"Nocturnal?"

"They sleep during the day and are awake at night. They'll keep you up and everyone else in the house."

"I'll sleep during the day." Lyndsey put the kit back into the crate. He and his brother immediately began play fighting, tussling and growling at each other.

"Sweetie," Sam said, his patience showing signs of wearing thin, "you can't."

Annie had anticipated Lyndsey's objection even before her father finished speaking.

"Why!" She sprang to her feet, fists clenched at her sides. "I'm not in school or summer camp." She wrenched away when he reached for her. "You won't let me do anything."

Annie should just shut up. She had more than enough

of her own problems to deal with without involving herself in Sam's. Yet, she couldn't stop herself.

"You could sleep out here with the kits."

Lyndsey stopped and gaped first at Annie, then Sam. "Can I, Daddy?"

"I don't think that's a good idea."

"Why not?"

"We don't have a cot, for one thing."

"Lay a tarp down next to the cage," Annie suggested. "Put a sleeping bag or some blankets on top of it."

"I don't want Lyndsey sleeping in the barn. It's not safe." His tone implied Annie might be interfering.

She should quit while she was ahead. Only, she didn't. "You could sleep out here with her."

Lyndsey jumped up. "Please, Daddy?"

"We'll see." He was clearly not enthused.

"Thank you, thank you." Lyndsey took his hedging as a yes and hugged him hard, pressing her face into his shirtfront.

He hugged her in return, his hand splayed protectively across her small back. The tender exchange charmed Annie.

Damn Sam. He was always getting to her. And now he'd added his cute, sweet and obviously wounded daughter to his arsenal.

"Come on, kiddo. Let's get the cage set up." Annie kept her voice matter-of-fact.

The three of them worked for the next twenty minutes, during which time Annie continued instructing Lyndsey on baby raccoon care. They covered such topics as water for drinking and bathing, diet—the kits would benefit from natural foods like fruit and nuts—and how best to clean the cage without them escaping.

Lyndsey was an apt student, but Annie was aware that Sam spent more time watching her than the kits, causing the back of her neck to heat uncomfortably beneath her uniform collar. Was he still annoyed at her for suggesting he and Lyndsey sleep in the barn?

"I have to run," she said when the cage was secured atop some wooden blocks and fully equipped with everything the kits would need, including an old stuffed toy of Nessa's that Annie found in the SUV.

Lyndsey flung herself at Annie, and she instinctively held the girl. Sam was a lucky man. She only hoped he realized it.

"Thanks for everything," he said. Without asking, he accompanied her outside.

"It's the least I can do. By some miracle those kits survived when few other animals in these woods have."

"You really think Lyndsey will be okay in the barn?"

"Look, I shouldn't have said anything earlier. It wasn't my place."

"I'm not angry."

"Honestly, I'll be surprised if she lasts the entire night. She'll probably wake you up about midnight, wanting to go inside."

"Don't tell me. You've spent the night with baby raccoons before." Amusement lit his eyes.

"Guilty. I was just like Lyndsey and didn't take my mother's advice." She paused at the SUV's door. "Can I make another suggestion without overstepping?"

"Sure." He leaned against the hood, crossing his arms and one boot over the other in a sexy stance that was very reminiscent of their younger days.

There'd been a time when she would have leaned

against the hood beside him, assuming her own sexy stance.

"Buy Lyndsey a book on raising kits," she said, focusing her attention on the barn. Anywhere but on Sam.

"Do they sell those in the feed store?"

"If not, order one online or print out articles from the internet."

"I don't know." His brow furrowed. "She's getting pretty attached to the critters as it is. Learning more about them might make it harder to give them up."

"Or easier. But that's not the point."

He gazed at her with interest. "What is?"

And here she was giving him credit for trying to be an attentive father. "If you have to ask, there's no use in me explaining."

"I'm a bit denser than most."

She huffed. "Spending time with your daughter. Supporting her interests."

"Like I used to do with yours."

His grin disarmed her for several seconds, during which a pickup truck and trailer pulled onto the grounds and made its way toward the corrals. Annie recognized the rig and the driver. She also noticed a group of horses she'd missed earlier, milling about in the corral.

"You bought High Country Outfitters' string."

Sam nodded, clearly pleased. "I'm also having Lyndsey's old pony and a few other seasoned work horses from California shipped out."

"That ought to get you started."

He didn't make a move to help Will unload the new arrivals. Then again, Will didn't require help.

"I hired Will, too. Oh, and Irma Swichtenberg."

"You hired our housekeeper?" Annie spun so fast the open SUV door caught her in the back.

"Your mother sent her by."

"My mother!" It couldn't be true. Sam was mistaken. "Why would she do that?"

"Irma needed a job."

"She has one with us."

"Even if you rebuild the inn, it'll take months. Irma can't wait that long."

Annie heard only one thing. "*If* I rebuild the inn?"

"All right, when. But in the meantime, you have to be realistic. Irma needs to work. She has a lot of kids depending on her."

"I am being realistic. I'm probably the most realistic person here."

His brows formed a deep V. "And I'm not?"

"A guest ranch? Seriously? This town is dying a slow death. No one wants to come here and they won't, not until the forest regrows. And that could take decades."

"So, why rebuild the inn?"

Anger rushed in, filling the gaping hole left by his careless remark. "The Sweetheart Inn has been in my family for over fifty years. It's the heart of Sweetheart."

"I understand that."

"I thought you did," she retorted. "Now I'm not sure."

"As soon as you've finished construction, you can hire her back."

His conciliatory tone didn't assuage her. "She'll come, too. She's loyal to us."

"Nothing I'd like more than for you to rehire all your former employees."

That threw her for a loop. "Aren't you afraid of the competition?"

"No."

His lack of concern only made Annie angrier. "Because you think we can't do it."

"Because there's room in Sweetheart for two hospitality establishments. Besides—" his grin widened "—there isn't anyone I'd rather be in competition with than you."

He was absolutely infuriating.

She climbed in the SUV and drove away before he could disarm her yet again and undermine the really good mad she'd worked up.

"When was the deductible raised?"

"Last year, on your renewal."

Annie stared at the policy summary page, the renewal date in the corner and the deductible amount referenced in bold. Everything the insurance adjuster said was true.

"Mom?"

Fiona didn't reply. As usual, she was standing at the kitchen sink, gazing out the window—and had been during most of the meeting with the insurance adjuster. Sometimes, when asked a question, she'd answer. Sometimes not.

Annie's frustration reached a new level, outweighed only by her discouragement. Insurance wasn't her area of expertise—her mother handled it. Added to that, Annie had taken the afternoon off work, without pay, in order to participate in the meeting. The least her mother could do was cooperate.

"Mom!" she repeated.

Silence.

It had been like this for the past three days, since

Annie came home from seeing Sam and questioned her mother's disloyalty.

Granted, *disloyalty* was too strong of a word, and she'd apologized for it later. But she'd been hurt and blindsided. Irma needed a job, and her mother was right to refer her to a prospective employer. That Sam was the employer stung.

"A five-thousand-dollar deductible isn't uncommon." The adjuster, a portly middle-aged man, sat next to Annie at the kitchen table. He was kind and understanding and patient when it came to explaining the policy. Still, that didn't change the fact the Hennessys would have considerably more out-of-pocket expenses than Annie had anticipated.

"Most of the furnishings and household items were antiques. I don't understand why we're only getting fifty thousand dollars when they're worth more like a hundred thousand."

"That's how the policy was written."

Annie glanced at her mother. If Fiona noticed, she gave no indication.

Before the adjuster had arrived, and while Nessa was napping, they'd scratched out a rough estimation of what it would cost to rebuild, restock and refurnish the inn. The final number had staggered them both.

According to the adjuster, the insurance company would only compensate them for a little more than half that amount. Even more discouraging, according to the adjuster, their previous policy limits would have resulted in a considerably larger payout. But Annie's mother, in an effort to curb expenses in a recessed economy, had kept their premium payment affordable by raising the deductible and lowering the limits of their coverage.

She should have paid more attention when her mother mentioned her plan, making this partially her own fault. Instead, she'd gone about managing the inn's daily operations, leaving the business end and food service to Fiona.

It was an arrangement that had worked successfully for the past decade and would have continued working if not for a fire ravaging the town and turning the inn into a giant cinder box.

"I'm sorry," Fiona muttered, finally breaking the silence.

"It's all right, Mom. You did what you thought was right." Annie vowed that when they rebuilt, she'd insist they not skimp where insurance was concerned. "We'll figure out something."

What that something was, Annie didn't know yet. She'd drained a large part of their rainy-day fund for the cleaning and security deposits on their apartment and putting food on the table.

"There are some federal programs out there for people who qualify," the adjuster said.

Her mother was supposed to be looking into those. Annie didn't think there had been any progress, though. "That's our next step."

"It's a paperwork nightmare," Fiona added.

"But possibly well worth it." The adjuster removed his glasses and rubbed his eyes. He was obviously tiring and wanted Annie and her mother to sign off on the settlement agreement. "Maybe there are some areas you can trim."

Trimming is what had landed them in this jam to

begin with. "We haven't actually received any quotes yet." Annie kneaded a crick in her neck. She was also growing tried—of the meeting and her mother's procrastination.

"What about your architect? He can design the inn with your budget in mind. Perhaps make it smaller."

"That's probably what we'll end up doing. When we hire an architect."

They could always add onto the inn later. As the town and the forests came back, so would the Sweetheart Inn. Annie preferred that to happen much faster, but they could take their time if needed. Just not too much time, she hoped.

"I understand there's a man in town," the adjuster said. "A Sam Wyler."

"What does he have to do with anything?"

"He brought in a construction contractor to remodel the Gold Nugget Ranch."

"So I heard," Annie said. Her mother's grapevine had reported that Sam's construction contractor and his crew had arrived yesterday.

"He's offering the services of the contracting crew to anyone in town who wants to use them and agreed to pick up a portion of the fee."

"Is that true?" Annie directed the question at her mother.

"So Hilda says."

Mayor Dempsey was a reliable source.

"It's true," the adjustor confirmed. "I have several other customers in town, and they've all told me the same. Haven't met the man, but it seems legit."

"Why would he agree to cover some of the contractor's costs?"

"Apparently he wants to help the town rebuild."

Exactly what he'd told Annie. "Where would he get that kind of money?"

She assumed Sam had done well for himself, given the new truck he drove and his ability to purchase the Gold Nugget, even at a reduced price. But money of the quantity they were talking about seemed vast even for him.

"I have no idea." The adjuster gathered the papers spread across the kitchen table and arranged them into a tidy stack.

"He was awarded a large settlement," Fiona said. "After his wife's accident."

More gossip from Mayor Dempsey. She made a point of keeping Annie's mother informed by calling regularly.

"Why would he spend the settlement money on Sweetheart?" It made no sense to Annie. "What about his daughter?"

"You might talk to him." The adjuster paused. "Seeing as you and he are acquainted."

Annie held her tongue, though it wasn't easy. The adjuster's other customers were probably delighted to spill the torrid details of Annie and Sam's former romance. The man probably knew everything there was about all three Hennessy women.

She shoved the insurance papers aside. Hell would freeze over before she approached Sam with a plea for assistance.

The insurance adjuster slid the settlement agreement back toward her. "This is probably the best you're going to get from the carrier. I recommend you—"

"I'm not ready to settle yet." She had been, until the man mentioned Sam.

"Ms. Hennessy—"

"No." Annie rose from the table. "I want more time. You said we have a few weeks."

"That you do." The adjuster stuffed the papers into his briefcase, minus the set for her. "Call me anytime."

Annie closed the front door after seeing the man off, a headache making its presence known. What she really wanted was to find her daughter and hold her. Kissing Nessa's sweet button nose and dimpled cheeks would restore her sagging spirits.

In the kitchen, Fiona had moved from the window. "Annie. Maybe we should reconsider. Accept the settlement."

Her mother had a point. "Moving ahead with the construction would do us all good."

"We don't have to rebuild."

That had to be the depression talking. Fiona wanted the inn as much as Annie and Granny Orla. "Of course we're going to rebuild. What else would we do?"

Fiona nodded. "I guess you're right." She started washing dishes.

Annie, more determined than ever, went in search of Nessa. There would be a new Sweetheart Inn. Maybe smaller to start with, but it would still be the heart of the town.

There had to be a new inn. If not, she and her family might never return to normal, and Annie couldn't let that happen.

Chapter 5

Nessa was in the bedroom she and Annie shared, sitting on the double bed beside Granny Orla. They had been more or less watching each other while Annie and her mother met with the insurance adjuster.

"What are you two doing?" She went over to Nessa, seeking the touch she needed and feeling restored.

"Playing." Nessa giggled giddily and uncovered what lay hidden beneath her collection of stuffed toys and Barbie dolls.

Laid out on the quilt were the different items Annie had salvaged from the ruins of the inn, including the recently acquired desk bell.

"Granny," Annie asked, concerned the game would trigger another episode, "how are you doing?"

"Peachy."

"Really?"

"Don't be silly." She looked up at Annie with clear, bright eyes. "Why wouldn't I be?"

"No reason." Annie breathed easier. Her grandmother was her usual self.

"We're just looking for my book. Thought it might be in here."

"What book?"

"You know, my book. The one I kept on a shelf in the sitting room."

Uh-oh. So much for being her usual self. Whatever book her grandmother had kept was surely lost.

"I don't think it's here, Granny," she said gently.

"Well, we'll have to go to the inn and find it."

"Maybe later." Annie had no intention of taking her grandmother there. It had been bad enough finding her at the inn ruins after one of her walkabouts. The place was far too dangerous for an old woman.

"Tomorrow?"

"We'll see."

The ringing of Annie's cell phone was the perfect excuse to end the conversation, until she glanced at the display and read the general store's number. She stepped out into the hall before answering the call.

"Hello, Gary. You on your way to pick up Nessa?" He was scheduled to take their daughter for a long weekend.

"Annie, hi. Actually, I'm still at work. My clerk for the evening shift is running late."

Gary frequently encountered staff problems. As the store's manager, it was his job to cover all shifts. Annie understood, but she was irritated nonetheless. Dempsey General Store and Trading Post had taken priority during the seven years of their marriage. It shouldn't take priority over their daughter.

"You're not coming?"

"I was hoping you could bring Nessa by the house. Linda Lee will meet you there."

Leave Nessa with his new wife? In their house, which, like the store, had escaped the fire? No way.

"What time will you be off work?"

"Not for several hours."

"You can pick her up then."

There was a long moment of silence before he replied. "Don't be difficult."

"Better yet, I'll drop her off at the store." Then Gary wouldn't have to see the apartment and remark, yet again, how small and cramped it was and how much extra room he and Linda Lee had.

"See you when you get here."

For whatever reason, he chose not to argue. Hurray for small favors.

"Nessa, honey, that was your dad."

Reentering the bedroom, Annie stopped in her tracks. While Nessa played with her favorite doll, Granny Orla sat on the bed cradling a pewter candlestick, tears streaming from her eyes.

Annie went over and kissed her grandmother's crinkly cheek. "Don't cry, Granny. We're going to be okay."

"I know that." She sniffed and patted Annie's arm. "It's just hard getting there."

After another kiss, Annie straightened and said, "Nessa, I'm going to drop you off at your dad's."

"When?"

"In a couple hours."

"After I go pony riding," she announced, moving

her Barbie through the air as if it sat astride a galloping horse.

"What pony ride?"

"At the ranch. Where the cowboy lives. He promised."

Annie vaguely remembered Sam mentioning something last week when he dropped them off at the apartment. "Nessa, honey, he doesn't have a pony."

"He does. He told Grandma."

"Yes, the other night—"

"No, today."

"He called." Granny Orla sat up, showing signs of recovery. "After lunch. He talked to Fiona. Invited Nessa out for a pony ride."

Nessa jumped up from the bed and grabbed Annie's hand. "Can I go, Mommy? Please."

"Honey, you can't." She used her most coaxing tone. "I'm taking you to your dad's."

"Nooo!" Nessa dropped Annie's hand and threw herself onto the bed in typical three-year-old-not-getting-her-way fashion.

"Nessa, that's enough."

Annie's mother must have heard the noise. "What's all the fuss?" she asked from the doorway.

"Mom, did Sam invite Nessa over for a pony ride?"

"He mentioned the pony arrived today with a few other head from his ranch in California."

Nessa promptly launched herself off the bed and hugged Annie's waist. "Mommy, Mommy, I really wanna go."

"I wish you'd spoken with me first," Annie said to her mother.

"Nessa was there when Sam called. What was I supposed to do?" Fiona huffed, the most emotion she'd shown in a long time. "If you don't want to see Sam, just say so. I'll take Nessa and swing by her dad's after the pony ride."

"Yay!" Nessa danced in a circle. "Pony ride!"

"It's not that I don't want to see Sam," Annie protested.

Fiona's elevated eyebrows indicated differently.

Annie rubbed her throbbing temples. When had the world and everyone in it started conspiring against her? The insurance company. Gary. Her mother. Nessa. Sam.

She sighed. "One short pony ride. Now, where's your suitcase?"

If Nessa was going to the Golden Nugget, Annie would be the one taking her.

"Lovely. Have a good time," her mother said with rather suspicious-sounding satisfaction.

Sam didn't expect to see Annie's SUV driving in to the ranch, not after the way they'd parted the other night.

His day, which had gone poorly so far, significantly improved. More so when Granny Orla emerged from the passenger side, looking alert and cognizant of her surroundings. A huge improvement from the last time he'd seen her.

Fiona must have decided to stay home.

"Where's the pony?" Nessa skipped beside her mother, reminding Sam of Lyndsey when she was that age.

The happy days. At least, the happier days, when his and Trisha's marriage was working. Over the next few years, without really realizing it, they transformed into strangers who happened to cohabit.

"Welcome." He flashed Granny Orla, Nessa and Annie a big smile. Only Granny Orla and Nessa returned it. "The pony's in the barn. Come on."

"Mind if I have a look at the house?" Granny Orla didn't wait for a reply and started up the freshly raked gravel walkway.

"Not at all. Irma's in there. She's just finishing for the day."

"Wait!" Annie headed after Granny.

"I'll be fine." She shooed Annie away. "You and Nessa go on, have yourselves some fun."

Sam thought Nessa was probably going to have a lot more fun than her mother, judging by Annie's worried frown.

Conversation came to a complete halt on the way to the barn. Sam refused to be deterred and asked Annie, "How's work? Done with the erosion tests?"

"We'll be conducting different ones for weeks. Months, probably. Assessing the degree of burn and the land's ability to recover."

"Why isn't the pony with the other horses?" Nessa was evidently disinterested in any talk about her mother's work.

"She's too little to be in the corral. The other horses will bully her and steal all her food."

Lyndsey scrambled to her feet the moment they entered the barn. Except to eat and sleep, she kept a constant vigil on the kits. Annie had been right about her abandoning the idea of sleeping in the barn. One night on the hard floor and the kits' constant ruckus had been enough. Sam was not-so-secretly overjoyed.

"Hi." Lyndsey greeted Annie enthusiastically. "Are you here to see the kits?"

"I am," she answered as if that had been her plan all along. "Lyndsey, you remember Nessa."

Not at all shy, Nessa skipped over to the cage and knelt down beside it, her eyes enormous. "Mommy, look! Baby raccoons."

Delighted at having an audience other than her father, Lyndsey launched into a detailed report of the kits' progress during the last week. The baby raccoons obliged by acting adorable. Standing on their hind legs and vocalizing, they reached their small handlike paws through the cage wire.

"They don't need much kitten formula anymore," Lyndsey said. "They're mostly eating solid food."

She sounded a lot like Dr. Murry, who'd dropped by recently to examine the kits and pronounce them "thriving."

"I'm gonna ride a pony," Nessa said, the kits failing to keep her interest long.

Lyndsey rose after making sure the cage latch was secure. "I'll go with you."

And here Sam thought he'd have to coax his normally antisocial daughter.

He and Annie exchanged looks, their most intimate communication since his return to Sweetheart. To his relief, her frown was replaced with a smile.

It unbalanced him. For a second, she was the young woman from nine years ago. The one he'd loved—and left.

Must be the barn. They'd escaped here often. The loft, with its stacks of sweet-smelling hay, was one of their favorite places. Sam had liked picking pieces of hay out of Annie's hair and remembering how they'd gotten there. He never quite found them all and someone inevitably noticed.

Lyndsey took Nessa's hand and led her to the stalls.

"She's big!" Nessa came to an abrupt halt and stared dumbfounded at a half-draft mare who'd stuck her head out to investigate.

Sam chuckled. "That's not the pony."

Annie approached the mare, her hand extended. "Is she sick?"

Leave it to her to notice.

"The pony and another horse I had shipped here managed the trip just fine. This old girl, however, began showing signs of distress and refused to eat or drink. Will and I treated her for colic, just to be on the safe side."

"Did it help?" She brushed the mare's forelock as she studied her.

"At first she didn't respond. I was just getting ready to call Dr. Murry again when she suddenly began eating. I guess the ten-hour trailer ride must have upset her system."

"She still seems listless."

"I'm going to keep a close watch on her for the next day or two."

"What's the pony's name?" Nessa gripped the side of the stall door and perched on her tiptoes in an effort to see the equally short equine on the other side.

"Mooney." Lyndsey squeezed in beside her.

"Mooney? That's a silly name."

"It's a good name. She had a twin sister called Sunny."

"What's a twin?"

"That's when the mommy has two babies inside her tummy."

Nessa's small mouth fell open. "How do babies get inside the mommy's tummy?"

Annie stepped over to the girls, hastily running interference. "We'll talk about it later, sweetie, okay?"

"Okay." Nessa jumped up and down, her sneakers kicking the stall door. "I wanna ride the pony."

"Nessa, no. You'll break the door."

Without thinking, Sam lifted Nessa up by the waist so she could see into the stall. She let out a small, excited gasp.

"You don't have to—"

Sam cut off Annie's objection. "It's all right. I've got her."

She gave him another of those intimate looks. This one hit him square in the chest.

The pony, a pint-size dapple gray, came over to sniff the hand Nessa held out.

"Be careful she doesn't nip you. Pet her nose like this." Bracing Nessa with one arm, he showed her the correct way.

Nessa copied him and then squealed with delight when Mooney nuzzled her fingers.

"She likes me."

"What say we saddle her up so you can have a ride?"

Nessa's answer was to squirm excitedly until he set her on the ground.

"Have you ever ridden a horse before?" It was Lyndsey who posed the question, assuming the attitude of a more experienced rider.

Nessa shook her head, her expression solemn.

Sam got a kick out of the exchange.

"Actually, sweetie, you have ridden before. Sort of." Annie turned her attention to Sam. "Some friends of her dad have horses. We'd go riding with them once in a while. When we'd get back, Gary would put Nessa in the saddle with him and walk around a bit. I have some pictures—" She hesitated and drew a fortifying breath. "Had some pictures."

The loss of something precious and irreplaceable shone in her eyes. She must suffer that same emotion a dozen times a day.

"We'll take more pictures today." Sam held up his cell phone.

"Good idea."

Again, she aimed her glance directly at him. Again, the jolt hit him square in the chest.

They may not be ready for a relationship or ever be able to have one, given their rocky history, but that didn't stop Sam from devising reasons for inviting Annie to the ranch again.

Mooney hadn't been ridden much since Lyndsey decided she wanted a "real horse," but the pony remembered the drill perfectly. When Sam handed Nessa the lead rope, Mooney walked calmly beside her and stood patiently while Sam saddled and bridled her.

Lyndsey explained the entire process, instructing Nessa on how to sit in the saddle and hold the reins. All Nessa wanted to do was pet the pony.

Sam checked the girth and gave it one last tug, making sure the saddle wouldn't slip. "This used to belong to Lyndsey, until she grew too big. It's just right for you."

He made a mental note to purchase a few more child and youth saddles for the ranch's guests. Maybe another pony or two. While most of the horses were trustworthy enough to carry young riders, the children might feel safer on a smaller mount.

Lyndsey held the lead rope while Sam lifted Nessa onto Mooney's back. "I can take her," Lyndsey said.

"Are you sure?" Annie's anxious gaze darted from the pony to Lyndsey to Sam.

"Mooney's completely broke," he answered, placing the reins in Nessa's hands and adjusting her feet in the stirrups. "And Lyndsey's good with horses. Besides, Mooney's short and close to the ground. Nessa won't have far to fall."

"Sam!"

He grinned. Annie had always been gullible, and he'd enjoyed teasing her, refusing to stop until she gave him a kiss. And once they started kissing...

Sam reminded himself to stay focused on the girls.

Lyndsey took the lead, walking ahead of Nessa and the pony. Outside, the late-afternoon sun streamed through the pine trees, and Sam had them stop so he could snap several photos.

"Let's get one with you and Nessa."

Annie posed with her daughter, delight on both their faces, Annie's arm circling Nessa's waist. Sam thought he might keep a copy of this particular picture for himself.

"Thanks," she said when they were done, her tone warm with appreciation.

"I'll need your phone number or email address."

She recited the information without hesitation. A big difference from before.

Pleased with himself, Sam keyed the number and address into his phone contacts. If he kept this up, he'd eventually penetrate that invisible shield of armor she wore, one chink at a time.

"Lyndsey's really patient with Nessa," Annie observed.

Nessa had been riding the pony for about ten min-utes, Annie and Sam walking behind the girls. Annie had been trying hard to avoid slipping into their former comfortable camaraderie.

Not easy. Memories had assailed her from the second she drove onto the Gold Nugget, even more than her visit last week. He was getting to her, and she'd have to be careful or risk a new heartache when he left.

"She's kind of bossy, if you ask me." Sam pushed back his cowboy hat then pulled it down again, a gesture she'd always found endearing. "To be honest, she doesn't have much experience with little kids. Her friends are mostly her own age." Deep furrows creased his brow. "I should've thought more about her missing her friends when I brought her here. Maybe that's why she's become so attached to the raccoons."

"You really think so?"

"Naw." He had to chuckle. "She's an animal lover. Like you."

"More like her dad, I'd say." Annie smiled and thought, *There, that wasn't so hard.*

"Dogs and horses are my kind of pets," he said. "Not wild animals."

"You were pretty tolerant of the ones I dragged home. Remember that magpie with the broken wing? You taught it to whistle 'Mary Had a Little Lamb.'"

"Then the darn thing wouldn't shut up."

"I was never so glad to release an animal back into the wild."

"Is that why you moped for three straight days?" He flashed her a grin, the heart-stopping kind.

Good grief, she should have known better than to bring up old times.

"You miss the animals?" he asked.

"I did. Do. Gary was never fond of animals, and

my house was too small for pets anyway. When we divorced, and I moved back to the inn, I limited myself to the occasional stray dog and cat."

"Did you lose any pets in the fire?"

"Not in the fire. But our landlord doesn't allow animals. We had to find temporary homes for ours with friends in Reno."

"That must have been hard."

"Yeah." The sympathy in Sam's voice touched her. "Nessa really loves dogs."

"You two can visit the kits and pony anytime."

His hint to come back was as subtle as a sandbag dropped from a second-story window. Annie didn't mind as much as she should.

"We'd better head back." She glanced over her shoulder at the ranch house. They'd been walking the footpath that circled it and the barn, a remnant from the days of *The Forty-Niners*. According to the curator, Mrs. Litey, the film crew had created the path over years of filming scenes from different angles. "I have to drop Nessa off at her dad's in about an hour."

"You have time."

Annie did. She was using her ex as an excuse. Sam's charms were far too potent.

"Can I ask why you married him?"

She resisted answering the point-blank question. Too many unresolved feelings. She settled on "The usual reasons."

"Do you want my opinion?"

"Do I have a choice?" Thank goodness the girls were out of earshot.

"I think you weren't over me and he was handy."

Annie burst out laughing. "That's some ego you have."

"Seemed kind of quick to me. We'd hardly broken up when you and he started dating."

Her laughter died. "You were gone a year. Breaking up was a technicality."

"I was gone eleven months."

"Same difference. And, really, who are you to accuse me of jumping the gun? You married Trisha four months later, as I recall, and she was pregnant."

"I won't disagree, I probably should have waited. But I was miserable and susceptible after losing you. I called you every week during those eleven months."

"You started out calling me every week," she corrected him. "It didn't last."

"I came back for you. Like I promised I would."

"Only to tell me it was over!" She stopped and took a restoring breath. This wasn't the time to lose her temper.

"Not how I remember it."

"You think *I* ended things?"

"That's what happened."

Un-freaking-believable. "No, it's not. You said we were through."

"Because you said you were tired of waiting. That read *breakup* to me."

"I thought…hoped…you were coming back for good. And you didn't. Wouldn't." She bit her lower lip. All these years it still hurt. "Which you made crystal clear."

"You were angry at me for taking the job in California."

Anger had hardly begun to describe her emotions. She'd wanted to marry Sam. For the two of them to have the kind of life she'd always dreamed of. Cozy cabin, white picket fence, two beautiful children. She was determined to be the first Hennessy woman in three generations to hold on to her man.

Then Sam appeared at her door one evening, telling her he'd found a job at a cattle ranch north of Sacramento. One that paid better and offered more opportunity.

She should have realized he wasn't ready for marriage, that she'd been pushing him too hard. Their young ages weren't the only reason for his reluctance. And it wasn't true that Sam hadn't loved her.

He'd needed to establish himself before he settled down. Make his mark on the world, like his father and brother in Ohio. But Annie had been impatient, and look what that got her.

"I wanted you to come with me."

His words tugged at her heart. "I couldn't leave. This is my home, the inn was my family's business."

"You could have left for a year. Hell, for a visit even. I needed experience, enough to land a foreman's job."

"Which you got when you married Trisha."

He shook his head. "My father-in-law cut no one slack, including me. I wasn't promoted for four years. Not until I'd earned it. And I'll thank him for that always. He's a great man and a good judge of character. He saw potential in me I didn't know I had."

She was wrong. Sam hadn't been handed the job as a wedding gift.

"I'm glad for you."

"But you're still hurt I started seeing Trisha right away."

"Okay. You win. I'm hurt and carrying a grudge. Can we not argue anymore? What's the point?"

For several moments, humming insects and their footsteps on the dirt path were the only sounds.

Sam spoke first. "There are a lot of things in my life I'd change if I could, including that."

"I really am sorry Trisha died." Annie's residual pain over their breakup was nothing compared to losing a spouse.

"Me, too." His gaze followed the girls' progress as they disappeared behind the barn.

Annie might be more concerned about Nessa if Lyndsey weren't such a competent riding instructor and the pony as docile as she was cute.

"It was never my intention to hurt you. Or Trisha," he added softly.

His sincerity didn't ease the lingering sorrow inside her. "What was it Granny used to say? Marry in haste, repent at leisure." Annie was silent a moment. "Guess I should have listened myself."

"Was your marriage to Gary that bad?"

"Not at first."

"What went wrong, if I can ask?"

She hadn't loved him. How could she when she'd been still in love with Sam? "We grew apart."

"Easy to do when you're not close to start with."

"We were close. Initially."

"I wasn't talking about you and Gary."

Sam and his wife had had problems? Despite his marriage being the result of an unplanned pregnancy, Annie had assumed he and Trisha were content, if not blissful.

"We made a go of it," he said. "For a while. Because of Lyndsey. I'm not sure exactly when we stopped trying."

"Gary and I stopped trying after the first year."

"Why did you stay married?"

"You really have to ask?" She gave a derisive snort. "I'm a Hennessy."

"It's just stupid gossip, Annie. Busybodies with too much time on their hands. Your family isn't cursed."

She smiled ruefully. "Funny thing is, dating Gary immediately after you left didn't lessen the gossip. If anything, we gave people more to talk about when our marriage started circling the drain. Gary was on the verge of leaving me when I got pregnant. I convinced him a child would change everything. It didn't."

Sam reached for her, his strong fingers curving around her neck and sliding into her hair. "We're quite the pair."

The sparks were instantaneous, like always with the two of them. They'd fight, then they'd make up. Lots of making up.

Annie steeled herself. She could not, would not, kiss him. In fact, she was marching ahead right this second and finding the girls. Except her feet didn't move.

Her body did. It leaned into him, the tug a familiar one. She could no more resist Sam today than she could years ago. He had only to look at her and she was in his arms, lifting her mouth to meet his hot, urgent kiss.

When, she dimly wondered, had she lost control? When had she ever really exercised it?

Annie might have pondered the questions longer if she wasn't entirely taken over by Sam and the electric sensation of his lips on hers. Sliding over them. Coaxing them apart. Making way for his tongue to enter and taste her completely.

Oh, heavens! This was insane. She'd let revisiting

their painful past erode her defenses. And now look. She and Sam were kissing.

He expertly applied the right amount of pressure with his mouth as his arms circled her waist and fitted her snug against him. Hard to soft. Taking and giving. Demanding and yielding.

Annie was forced to stand on her tiptoes or break off the kiss. To ensure that didn't happen, she anchored herself to him by gripping his shoulders. Then she released the tight hold on her emotions and let herself feel.

Only Sam. Only them. Only this moment.

This was how he used to kiss her, and kept kissing her until she didn't know where she was.

Where she was. The girls!

Annie pushed abruptly away from him, a groan escaping. She'd let Sam kiss her. She'd kissed him back. And their daughters were...

"Nessa! Lyndsey! Come back!" She frantically scanned the immediate area.

"They're just around the corner," Sam said.

Thank God. She shuddered to think of the explaining required if the girls had caught them.

"We shouldn't have done that," she stammered.

"Speak for yourself."

"Sam. We can't... I won't..."

He laughed. Laughed! "Still the same old Annie."

Before she could utter her first word of protest, the girls charged out from behind the barn, Lyndsey running and the pony, Nessa on its back, trotting beside her.

"Dad, Dad," Lyndsey hollered. "Look what we found." She carried something in her arms, grappling with it and the reins.

Annie used the three spare seconds afforded her to smooth her hair and straighten her shirt.

Sam, naturally, didn't have a single hair or piece of clothing out of place. With unflappable nonchalance, he asked, "What is it?"

"A cat." She held out a scrawny feline, which meowed plaintively. "It was hiding in a bush. Can we keep him? I'm calling him Sylvester."

Annie couldn't ever remember being so glad to see a cat in her life. Had it not distracted the girls...

What had she been thinking?

And that was the problem in a nutshell. When it came to Sam, all thinking, along with good judgment and common sense, went by the wayside.

Chapter 6

Annie shouldered open the door to the Dempsey General Store and Trading Post. Gary had worked here as a clerk when they started dating. During their marriage, he was promoted twice, taking over as manager when his predecessor retired two years ago last spring.

His new wife worked alongside him. Assistant manager or head salesclerk or whatever. She always wore the clothing the store sold: T-shirts with scenes of Sweetheart and quaint sayings about getting married, ball caps with deer or Conestoga wagons or linked gold rings on the front, thin rope necklaces holding a flask of liquid in which flecks of fool's gold floated, frilly blue garters. She liked to wear those on her arms.

Annie didn't know how long Gary and his wife would have to be married before she dropped the *new* and called Linda Lee by her name. Probably when Annie and the town stopped thinking of her as "Gary's ex."

Personally, she thought Linda Lee went overboard in her dress and attitude. The customers, however, seemed to appreciate—if not adore—her. At least, they used to. There weren't many customers in the store these days, adoring or otherwise.

"Daddy, Daddy!" Nessa charged ahead of Annie and Granny Orla. The little girl loved the store, especially the toy section.

Truthfully, Annie had loved the store, too—long before Gary went to work there. Some might say the shelves were loaded with cheap, touristy junk. After all, who really needed a fake bear hide or plastic talking fish? But the general store's log exterior and rustic decor had a charm that she found appealing.

As a child, her mother would let her ride her bike there to pick up some small necessity for the kitchen or one of the inn's guests. Even after Annie was old enough to drive, she still preferred to ride her bike.

That was how she and Sam had met. On the hill near Cohea Ridge where he and another wrangler were moving cows across the forest service road from one section of grazing range to another. She was training for a charity cycling event.

Her first glimpse of him was herding a recalcitrant calf through the gate. She'd stopped, watching till he was done, already falling for him.

He'd trotted over, tall and handsome in the saddle, and asked her out on the spot.

"Daddy, where are you?" Nessa called.

Annie blinked herself back to the present.

"Right here," Gary answered.

Nessa dashed down an aisle bulging with calendars, books, magazines and postcards, following the sound of her father's voice.

"I'm going to see if there are any of those chocolate mint cookies I like." Granny Orla also disappeared to scour the food section.

That left Annie on her own, not a place she wanted to be at this moment. Without any company, she had nothing to distract her from thoughts of Sam, the past and the kiss they'd just shared.

The kiss they'd just shared.

Such a mundane assessment describing an occurrence that had turned her already upside-down world on its side. Much like their first kiss soon after that meeting on Cohea Ridge eleven years ago.

He'd taken her to the ice cream parlor. She remembered thinking afterward that he'd tasted yummy. Like the hot fudge sundae she'd eaten.

He'd tasted yummy today, too, and his effect on her was no different.

She really was an idiot, learning nothing from the past.

It wouldn't happen again, of that she was certain. Sam Wyler wouldn't get to her, and she'd start by putting him far from her mind.

Holding on to Nessa's weekend bag, she strolled the same aisle her daughter had taken, only at a much slower pace. In the back of the store, Gary and his *new* wife were unpacking a shipment of mining equipment. Why bother? Amateur rock hounds and gold seekers were as scarce as honeymooners, what with most of the popular areas having been ravaged by the fire.

Annie hesitated, observing from behind a display.

Gary and Linda Lee were comfortable with each other, like an old married couple rather than a new one. The smiles they exchanged were sweet and intimate.

Had she and Gary ever been like that? A little perhaps. Once.

She and Sam had been like that. Right up to the evening he told her about the job in California.

"Hey, there!" Gary's new wife straightened from the open box on the floor and smiled brightly, greeting Annie as if they were on the best of terms.

Linda Lee. She really had to start calling her that. "Sorry I'm late."

"No worries. We've been hearing all about the pony ride. How exciting!"

"That was nice of Sam," Gary said.

It sounded strange, hearing him speak Sam's name. The two men had known each other casually back when Sam lived here, but they hadn't been friends. Later, Gary had hated being compared to Sam. Not by Annie. It was the gossips who couldn't keep quiet.

"He had some horses from the ranch in California shipped here," Annie explained. "One of them was a pony."

"And he bought the entire string from High Country Outfitters," Linda Lee added.

"News travels fast."

"Oh, no! He told us. When he was in here yesterday."

Sam had visited the general store and spent time talking to Gary and Linda Lee?

That shouldn't bother Annie, yet for some reason it did. Had they discussed her? She wouldn't put it past either man. They were probably curious about each other and her relationships with them. Past and present.

"We found a stray cat." Nessa's announcement was perfectly timed. "It's black-and-white and really skinny. Lyndsey named him Sylvester."

"Are you keeping it?" Gary's tone carried a hint of alarm. He only just tolerated cats.

"Can we, Mommy?" Nessa asked.

"No, honey. We aren't allowed to have any pets in the apartment."

Another reminder of their circumstances and the four-legged family members they'd had to find temporary homes for.

"I suppose we could take the cat," Gary said.

Linda Lee jumped on the bandwagon. "What a great idea. Then it would be yours whenever you stay with us."

"I'm gonna have a cat." Nessa bounced up and down with excitement.

Annie wanted to scream. This was so unfair. She was the cat lover, not Gary. He'd only agreed in order to look like the world's greatest dad in front of Nessa and Linda Lee.

"The cat belongs to Lyndsey," Annie said, proud of the control she exercised. "She's the one who found it."

"She might give it to us if we ask," Linda Lee suggested. "Sam mentioned they were returning to California in about a month."

Sam again? Annie's control wavered.

She shouldn't care. *Didn't* care. Sam was not some possession of hers. While he was in Sweetheart he was going to interact with people. People including her exhusband. And there was nothing she could do about it.

"Nessa," Annie began, "let's see what happens first."

"But I want a cat." She pouted. "And a pony."

Annie waited for either Gary or Linda Lee to promise a pony, too. "If you found a cat," she said, "you wouldn't want someone to take it from you."

"Your mother's right." Gary tweaked Nessa's ear.

Annie bit back her surprise. Before his marriage, he'd been supportive of her. Shortly after, he started siding with Nessa, often forcing Annie to be the tough mom. She hated it.

"We'll get you another cat," he said. "The pet warehouse store in Lake Tahoe is always sponsoring adoption events."

"Of course we will," Linda Lee confirmed.

"Yay!" Nessa threw her arms around her father's legs.

The scream Annie had suppressed earlier echoed inside her head. Having Gary undermine her in front of their daughter was bad enough. Now she had Linda Lee doing it, too.

"Annie." Granny Orla appeared, her arms laden with boxes of mint cookies and an assortment of other snacks. "There you are. I'm ready whenever you are. Oh, hi, Gary. And..." She scrutinized Linda Lee. "I'm sorry, dear, but your name has slipped my mind."

"Linda Lee."

"That's right." She turned and winked at Annie. "Don't know why I keep forgetting."

Though it was wrong on many levels, Annie took pleasure in her grandmother's faked memory loss.

"Annie, I forgot my purse." Granny Orla held out her purchases.

"I'll pay."

"On the house," Gary said, giving Granny Orla a friendly smile.

"Why, thank you!"

Something about the mischievous glint in her grandmother's eyes made Annie think this had been the plan all along. She felt even better.

"We should get going." She set the weekend bag by Gary's feet and gave Nessa a hug and kiss. "You be a good girl. I love you." This was the hardest part of her and Gary's shared custody agreement.

"I'll walk you out," he said when Annie straightened.

"That's not necessary."

"Be right back," he told Nessa and Linda Lee.

"No worries." Linda Lee unearthed a large round prospecting pan from the shipping box and handed it to Nessa, an isn't-she-darling expression on her face. "I've got my little helper with me."

Annie tried not to think of Linda Lee as Nessa's stepmom. Or Nessa's fascination with the prospecting pan and whatever else the box contained.

"What is it, Gary?" Annie asked when they were outside.

"Hold on a second." He opened the SUV's passenger side door for Granny Orla.

"I don't want to leave her sitting there," Annie warned.

"She'll be fine."

Granny Orla was already opening a box of cookies.

"I can't stay long," Annie reminded him. "I have to get up at five."

"It's Nessa."

She should have seen this coming. Gary didn't steal private moments with her except to talk about Nessa or their divorce or Annie's plans for the future.

"She doesn't need a cat. We have two, which we'll get back as soon as we rebuild the inn."

The lines bracketing Gary's mouth deepened. "I'd like you to consider letting her stay with me and Linda Lee more often."

"No." Annie was amazed at her outward calm. Inside, a maelstrom raged. "You are not getting full custody."

"I'm not asking for full custody. Just more frequent custody. Until you're back on your feet."

"Which will be soon. We're on the verge of settling with the insurance company."

"My point exactly. You've got a lot on your plate at the moment. Working. The inn. Nessa. I can make things easier for you."

"Taking Nessa away from me isn't making things easier."

"I'm trying to help."

Annie was hearing that a lot lately. First Sam, now Gary. Granted, she had taken a hard knock, but she was more than capable of pulling herself back up.

"I know you love Nessa—" she began.

"And I only want what's best for her."

Annie tried not to take his remark as an implication that she couldn't provide adequately for their daughter. Still, it felt that way.

"You'd have more room in the apartment," he said. "And she'd have more room at my house. Just think about it."

"I get that you hate the apartment. But Nessa's perfectly happy there."

"Her happiness isn't what's worrying me. It's her safety." He took hold of Annie's arm and drew her away from the SUV and Granny Orla's curious stare. "Let's be honest, your grandmother's becoming very forgetful. And your mother…"

"What about my mother?"

"We both know she's struggling. Emotionally."

Though everything Gary said was true, Annie's defenses soared. "Yes, she has moments when she's down. Who wouldn't in her shoes? But you're not the only one with concerns. I have my own about you."

"Me?"

"What's with the new prospecting equipment? Business in the store is practically at a standstill. Who's to say how long you and Linda Lee will have jobs?"

"It's going to pick up. As soon as Sam's guest ranch opens."

Had Gary just brought up Sam a third time?

"He isn't a miracle worker. It's going to take more than converting the Gold Nugget into a guest ranch to revitalize this town. It's going to take the Sweetheart Inn." Her voice gained conviction. "This is a place where couples come to get married and honeymoon."

"They can do that at the Gold Nugget, too."

Annie switched tactics. "Letting Nessa run around the store while you and Linda Lee are waiting on customers isn't any better day care than my mother can provide."

"We're considering putting her in preschool."

"Preschool?" Annie was aghast. "You decided this without consulting me?"

"I was going to talk to you."

This went beyond anything Gary had done. Just how much influence did his *new* wife have on him?

Fear gave way to terror. "You can't take her. I'll fight you."

"Relax. I'm not taking Nessa from you. This is just preschool we're talking about."

And more frequent custody. If Annie thought she could get away with it, she'd rush back inside the store and grab their daughter. Gary would stop her, however, and the last thing Annie wanted was to make a scene in front of Nessa and Linda Lee.

"I'll be by the usual time to pick up Nessa," she said briskly.

"We're not done talking about this."

"I agree."

"And I'm going to adopt a cat."

"Do whatever you feel you have to." Turning away, she climbed into the SUV and rolled down the window. "Just because Linda Lee hasn't gotten pregnant yet is no reason for her to take my child."

His features hardened. "That's not the reason."

Annie had crossed a line. Which wouldn't help her cause. Gary was relentless when riled.

She and her grandmother left without saying goodbye. At the end of the street, she pulled over, the tremors racking her body too severe for her to continue driving.

"That man is heartless," Granny Orla said, and then called him a name Annie couldn't recall ever having passed her grandmother's lips.

The shock of hearing it eased her tremors.

It didn't eliminate her fear.

"He's just jerking your chain," Granny Orla said. "He's not serious."

Annie would give anything—*everything*—for that to be true.

The pair of young Nubian goats was harder to catch than any fleet-footed calf. Sam took a break, wiping a palm across his sweaty brow. Maybe he should try roping them.

"Thanks." He scowled at Will, who leaned against his truck hood, watching Sam make an idiot of himself. "This is your fault."

The man just shrugged.

"You could help me at least."

"Could. But this is more fun."

"For you."

Will, who seldom showed much emotion, grinned.

He'd delivered the goats thirty minutes ago after calling Sam. A family Will knew was moving, having lost their place in the fire, and wanted to find good homes for their various livestock. Sam thought the goats might come in handy during the gymkhanas and amateur rodeos he was planning for his guests. Plus, the youngsters were bound to enjoy them.

It didn't occur to him when he gave Will the okay that the demon goats would leap from the horse trailer and taunt Sam with the chase of his life.

They abruptly stopped circling the yard to munch on a rosebush. Sam crept up on them, only to have them dart off at the last second. Running in hot pursuit, he lost his footing and nearly fell before righting himself. That earned him a chuckle from Will.

"If you're not careful, I'm going to fire you." Sam braced his hands on his knees, his breathing labored.

"I got a lead on a man selling his roping equipment. He supposedly needs the cash and is ready to talk."

Roping equipment? Another guest-related purchase Sam was considering. "What kind of equipment?"

"A Heel-O-Matic, training dummies, chutes."

Other than lariats, it was everything he'd need. "Fine, you're not fired."

"Didn't think so." Will started off toward the corrals.

"Wait!"

Will kept going.

Just as Sam was cussing the man, Lyndsey emerged from the barn, evidently taking a break from baby-raccoon sitting. Sylvester, the new barn cat, padded after her. He preferred outside to inside and disdained everyone other than Lyndsey.

Sam had insisted they post Cat Found signs around town. As of yet, no one had claimed Sylvester. Singed fur on his back and a starved appearance suggested he had run off during the fire and taken up the life of a stray. Perhaps his owners had already relocated from Sweetheart.

Lyndsey's face lit up at the sight of the Nubians, and she hurried toward them. The pair had stopped to make a snack of the blackberry bushes growing alongside the house.

"Where did the goats come from?"

Rather than run away, they merely lifted their heads and bleated. As if to further humiliate Sam, they stood perfectly still while she knelt beside them and hugged their thin necks.

He muttered under his breath.

"They're so cute. Look at these ears." She stroked the closest one, whose long ears, like its mate's, hung down to frame its funny, yet charming, face. "Are we keeping them?"

Sam came over, and while the goats did cast him the evil eye, they didn't run off. "We are."

Even if he hadn't already agreed to take them, he

doubted he could pry the goats loose from his daughter. Her collection of displaced animals just grew by two new members.

Annie had been the same way, instantly connecting with every creature she encountered, wild or tame.

They hadn't seen each other since the evening of the pony ride and their kiss. Two days. Sam had resisted driving by her apartment on his visit to town that morning. She wouldn't appreciate seeing him anyway, if the way she'd hastily gathered Nessa and departed was any indication.

Kissing her might have been a mistake, but he was very glad he'd done it. At the first sensation of her mouth on his, long-buried feelings shot to the surface. He hadn't been able to shake them since. Nor did he want to.

"Where are we going to keep them?" Lyndsey stood. The moment she took a step forward, the goats followed her like besotted puppy dogs. Figured.

"I think in the empty stall."

The pony had taken up permanent residence in one of the barn's three box stalls. Another was occupied by the half-draft mare from California. Her listlessness and loss of appetite had returned. Then, starting yesterday, she'd begun coughing, and discharge leaked from her nostrils.

Sam had placed a call to Dr. Murry, Sweetheart's only vet, and received a message the man was out of town. He'd yet to decide his next course of action.

"I'll take them." Lyndsey started pulling on the ropes tied around the goats' necks. "What do they eat?"

"We can give them hay and pellets for now. I'll pick up some goat chow on my next trip to the feed store."

The sound of tires crunching on gravel didn't rouse Sam's interest. With the arrival of the construction crew, vehicles of all kinds were constantly coming and going, even on this warm Sunday afternoon.

Then he noticed the town's logo painted on the side of the sedan and went to greet his newest visitor. Though it had been years, he recognized the woman right away.

"Mayor Dempsey. Good to see you." To Sam's surprise, the passenger side door opened, and Granny Orla stepped out. "Granny, what are you doing here?"

"She was walking down the road," Mayor Dempsey said, pumping Sam's hand enthusiastically. "Said she was coming here. Seeing as I was already heading in this direction, I gave her a lift. And called Annie," she continued in a whisper. "Sometimes Granny gets disoriented."

"I know. I gave her a ride home myself last week."

Granny Orla didn't bother saying hello to Sam. She just went directly toward the house.

"Irma's not working today," he hollered after her.

She didn't turn around.

"Should we go after her?" Mayor Dempsey wore a worried frown.

"She'll be all right. I think she likes to wander the place. Brings back memories for her."

"Her affair with the show's star was quite the scandal in the day. Some folks wondered if Fiona wasn't his daughter. Of course, she's not." The mayor gestured dismissively. "Fiona was three or four when *The Forty-Niners* started production. I know because we were in Sunday school together."

Sam tried to imagine Granny Orla as a young, attractive woman. It wasn't hard. She'd probably been quite the looker and, single mother or not, able to catch the eye of a handsome TV actor.

"How long ago did the ranch close to the public?" Sam asked.

"Been three years now. It changed hands several times before then. When old Mrs. Litey retired, that was pretty much the end. The new owners weren't interested in replacing her."

"Whatever happened to her?" Sam's memories of the ranch's curator were fond ones.

"She still lives in town. In a seniors' group home that, luckily, wasn't destroyed by the fire."

"I'd like to visit her."

"You can, but I doubt she'll remember you. She has advanced Alzheimer's."

It was the second-worst news Sam had received since returning to Sweetheart, the first being that Annie's inn had burned down. "That's a shame."

"Indeed." The mayor's glance traveled to the construction vehicles and small army of workers. "My, my, this has become one busy place."

"We're just starting."

"I've been wanting to stop by and tell you how happy we are you're remodeling the ranch. And grateful. You're doing a lot for our little town. Cora Abrams and the Fiersteins have both mentioned using your construction contractor for their renovations. I don't know how or why you're picking up the contractor's profit."

Sam was glad the head baker at the local caterers and the owners of the ice cream shop would be staying. "It's not as much as you think. Chas agreed to lower his profit in exchange for all the business. The slow economy's been hard on construction companies."

"With your help, Sweetheart will be back on its feet before long."

He ignored the remorse eating away at him. He couldn't have single-handedly spared the town, but he should have tried harder. "The ranch is a good investment."

"Well, you could have chosen elsewhere. We're glad you didn't. And glad you came back. You're one of our own, Sam."

"I've often thought about coming back."

Mayor Dempsey checked her watch. "I hate to run, but I'm needed at the bar." Besides heading local government, Hilda Dempsey owned and operated the Paydirt Saloon, an iconic bar and grill that was originally built by the first Dempseys to settle in Sweetheart back in the 1850s.

"Thanks for bringing Granny Orla by," Sam said.

"I didn't want her wandering the roads alone."

Small towns might have their disadvantages. Looking after their own wasn't one of them. Granny Orla would always have someone willing to pick her up and take her home.

Sam and Lyndsey had barely gotten the two goats, Yogi and Boo Boo—clearly he let his daughter watch too many cartoons—into the stall when Annie arrived.

He walked out of the barn at the same moment she slammed the door of her SUV. His breath caught. This was the first time he'd seen her out of uniform. Denim capris showed off her slim legs and curvy hips. A tiny T-shirt hugged her trim waist. Her shiny brunette hair, normally contained by clips or bands for work, hung in bouncy waves around her face.

"Hi." He met up with her halfway to the house. "Your grandmother's inside."

God give him strength. She wore some kind of shiny pink lip gloss. Cherry? Strawberry? A desire to taste it all but consumed him.

"Sorry about this," she said.

"No problem."

He didn't expect her to mention their kiss the other night. Neither would he bring it up and risk scaring her off any sooner than necessary. But it sure was on his mind.

Rather than go inside as he expected, she paused at the front door. "I didn't realize how much work was going on here until I drove in."

"The crew's converting the bunkhouse into three separate guest bedrooms with a shared bathroom. They're scheduled to finish by the end of next week. Then we can start taking reservations."

"So soon?" She sounded impressed but not enthused.

"The architect suggested converting the bunkhouse. We'll use the kitchen in the main house to serve meals until the dining hall is completed. We're also constructing a second bunkhouse and three private cabins."

"Quite an undertaking."

"That's not all. We're enlarging the barn to include an office and clearing land for an arena."

"Arena?"

"A small one. In the meantime, we're using the back pasture. I'm thinking of having a larger cabin constructed for Lyndsey and me. That way, we can open the ranch house back up for tours. There are a lot of fans of the TV show out there."

She nodded silently. "I'll fetch my grandmother."

Sam could have kicked himself. Here Annie was desperately trying to rebuild her family's inn, and he was rambling on and on about the ranch. The one she had wanted to own one day.

"Annie." He reached for her arm.

She kept walking. "We can't stay."

He refused to let her go yet and went after her. "I have a favor to ask."

"Not a good time." Her tone was clipped as she opened the front door.

"I have a sick mare."

That brought her to a halt.

"Is there any chance you can look at her?"

Sam knew he was taking advantage of her soft side where animals were concerned. It didn't stop him. He'd utilize whatever tactics available to him to breach her defenses…

…and didn't let himself think about what he'd find on the other side if he succeeded.

Chapter 7

"Who are these two?" Annie asked.

"Yogi Bear and Boo Boo." Sam shrugged at the names. "Our newest additions, thanks to Will."

"They're cute."

"And a lot of trouble."

"They like me!" Lyndsey glowed.

She was in the stall with the goats, dividing her time equally between them and the kits and leaving very little for Sam.

He missed her. Then again, she was happy caring for the animals. The happiest she'd been in a year and a half. He was either making the best or worst decision of his life.

"They don't like me," he grumped.

"Hmm." Annie gave him a lingering once-over. "What did you do to them?"

"Nothing."

Lyndsey rolled her eyes. "He chased them."

"They were eating the rosebushes and blackberries," Sam protested.

An amused and very appealing glint lit Annie's eyes. "That's reasonable."

Lyndsey came over to stand with Sam and Annie outside the mare's stall.

"Isn't she the draft horse from California?" Annie had offered only mild resistance when Sam had propelled her into the barn.

"Yeah. She was here when Nessa rode the pony." The same evening he and Annie had kissed.

She was remembering, too. Her quick, guilty glance in his direction gave her away.

"Is she doing any better?" She opened the stall door and stepped inside. The mare didn't so much as lift her head.

"I thought at first she hadn't traveled well. Then yesterday, she developed a cough and nasal discharge."

"You called Dr. Murry?"

"He's out of town until Tuesday. Fishing with his sons."

"I'm not sure how much help I can be."

"She's really sick. And seeing as you're here…"

More tugging on Annie's emotional heartstrings. Sam should be ashamed of himself.

"Poor girl," she crooned. "Feeling bad?" She ran her hand along the mare's chest and underneath her shoulder. "You're warm. You have a fever." Next, Annie lifted the mare's head to study her watery eyes and runny nose.

"Could be a simple respiratory virus. Or something

much more serious, like equine herpes or strangles. You really need to have her looked at by a vet."

"I agree. But the next closest large animal clinic is in Lake Tahoe. They're not open on Sundays. I called." Sam leaned against the stall door. "If she's not better by tomorrow, I'll have Will trailer her there. In the meantime, I was hoping there was something you could do."

"Is she eating and drinking?"

He shook his head. "Not at all."

"You might try adding electrolytes to her water," Annie continued. "How much penicillin have you given her?"

"None yet."

"Sam!" She glared at him accusingly. "You know enough about horse care to give penicillin."

"I was heading to the feed store, then the mayor and Granny Orla arrived."

"The feed store doesn't carry equine medications. But Doc Murry keeps a supply at his house, along with Bute paste. That'll help with the fever. I'll call his wife."

"Come with me," Sam said.

"I really should get home."

"Please. I'm not good with needles." That was the truth, and she knew it.

"What about Will? He must have experience."

"I heard his truck pull out a few minutes ago."

"I can't leave my grandmother." Annie frowned.

Sam refused to be deterred. "We'll bring her along."

"I want to come, too," Lyndsey said.

He ruffled her hair. "Wouldn't think of leaving you behind."

"Yay!" The beaming smile she sent him arrowed straight into his heart.

He'd been waiting eighteen long months for that. "What say we stop on the way back for an ice cream cone? To go."

"The ice cream shop burned." Annie's words hung on the air.

How could he have forgotten so quickly? He'd driven by what was left of the shop just the other day, recalling how he'd taken Annie there for sundaes on their first date. Watching her lick chocolate syrup off her spoon, he'd become instantly smitten.

"The I Do Café serves ice cream." It was the only restaurant open for business, other than the Paydirt Saloon.

"Mom's fixing dinner," Annie said.

Sam made one last-ditch effort. "I promise to have you and Granny Orla home in plenty of time."

He thought for sure he'd blown his chance. Annie's brisk nod of agreement came as a surprise. "I'll go with you to Doc Murry's. Not the café, though."

"I want ice cream." Lyndsey tugged on his hand.

"We'll stop at the general store."

Another thoughtless suggestion. Annie's ex-husband managed the General Store and Trading Post.

"Later. After dinner," he amended. "First, we go to Dr. Murry's."

Sam and Annie found Granny Orla in the parlor. She was staring at the framed photographs on the walls, though she must have seen them a hundred times.

She smiled when they neared and pointed to one of the pictures. "I remember when this was taken."

"You were there?" Sam asked.

"I'm in the picture. So is Fiona. We were recruited as extras for the shoot."

Sam scrutinized the photo. Annie did, too.

"Well, lookie there." He smiled when he recognized two figures in the foreground outfitted in prairie clothes.

Annie's features were thoughtful. "You and Mom used to talk about being in the show."

"Those were the days." Granny sighed.

"Why did the producers ever choose Sweetheart for the location?" Sam asked.

"The ranch house. They were looking at historical areas, actual stops along the wagon train routes, to give the show authenticity. The house was already here, though in disrepair."

"Did Mayor Dempsey's family own it?"

"It was one of the few properties they didn't. The owners were actually distant cousins of ours. They all moved away decades ago and were more than happy to sell the place to the show. I can't count the number of times it's changed hands since then."

"I hope this is the last time."

"Me, too." Granny's fingers lightly traced the picture frame. "Lord, he was a handsome man." No doubt she was referring to the star of the show, who figured prominently in the photograph. "He asked me to go with him to Hollywood when the series ended."

"Why didn't you?" Sam asked.

"The inn. I couldn't leave it."

Did Annie realize her answer had been exactly the same when he implored her to go to California with him? It was also the reason why she hadn't attended veterinary school.

What was it about the Sweetheart Inn that chained

the Hennessy women to it, even when it had been wiped off the face of the earth?

"We'd better go," Annie said.

Was she ever not in a hurry to leave?

After informing Chas, the contractor, of their plans, they piled into Sam's truck. During the drive, Annie placed a call to Dr. Murry's wife, who was home and agreed to sell them the needed medicine and syringes from her husband's supply.

This was hardly Sam's first trip to town since arriving in Sweetheart, yet it felt new as he viewed it through Annie's eyes.

Nothing looked the same, even the houses and buildings untouched by the fire. Those with scorched exteriors and sunken roofs saddened him. Vacant ground where a familiar structure had once stood left a gaping hole inside him.

Of the two wedding chapels in Sweetheart, one was gone. The other—Annie's favorite—had survived unscathed but stood empty, padlocks on the door.

There were signs of renewal. Several homes and businesses had begun the repair process, but their revamped appearances only added to the strangeness of the town.

Sam watched Annie as they drove by what remained of the inn. She stared quietly until they'd passed, then returned her attention to the road. The gaping hole inside him grew.

"Four summers volunteering with the Hotshots, and I still don't understand fires," he mused out loud. "Why they destroy one building and leave its neighbor intact. There's no rhyme or reason to it."

With the inn behind them, Annie had visibly relaxed. "I thought you only volunteered two summers."

Another inadvertent slipup. Sam ground his teeth together. To admit he'd led one of the crews battling the fire would require him to reveal his part in the town's demise.

"Well... I..."

"Daddy's a firefighter."

"Was a firefighter," Sam corrected Lyndsey, hoping she'd drop the subject.

No such luck.

"He was here. He told me all about it when he called."

"In Sweetheart?" She turned curious eyes on him.

"Not in town," he hedged. "Nearby."

"How near?"

They turned onto the dirt drive leading to the Murrys' house. Sam parked in front of the garage. No one made a move to get out.

"I joined the Redding California Hotshots last summer. I was having difficulties coping with Trisha's death. The hard physical labor, spending time away from the ranch, gave me a chance to work off my stress."

"I see."

"We were called to the fire on the third day."

"While it was still near Montgomery Canyon? Before it changed direction and headed to Sweetheart?"

He nodded. "We traveled with the fire as it moved across the canyon to Cohea Ridge."

"Why didn't you tell me?"

"I never found the right moment."

"You were there," she repeated, and sat back, appearing to absorb this information.

Sam wished he could read what was behind her

guarded expression. There'd been a time her thoughts and emotions weren't a secret to him.

"That must have been hard for you," Granny Orla said from the backseat. "Watching the town you cared about burn. Knowing the people in it. Knowing us."

Sam met her gaze in the rearview mirror. "You have no idea."

"Well, it's no wonder you avoid talking about it."

Annie said nothing, but Sam didn't think she agreed with her grandmother. She threw open her door and climbed out.

He left the truck running and the air conditioner on. "We won't be long," he told Lyndsey and Granny Orla, then headed toward the house.

Sam had the distinct impression he and Annie weren't done with this conversation.

Mrs. Murry was as affable as her husband. She'd assembled syringes, a bottle of penicillin and a tube of Bute in a brown paper bag for Sam and Annie. After thanking her profusely and promising to call her husband for an update on the mare, Sam returned to the truck with Annie.

Before they reached it, Sam stopped her. "I'm sorry. I should have told you about my crew fighting the fire. You have every right to be angry with me."

"I'm not angry with you. It's not like you started the fire."

He hadn't. But he hadn't stopped it from bearing down on Sweetheart when he had the chance.

"I hate what happened to this town and the forest surrounding it," he said.

"We all hate it."

"But you weren't on the front lines. I watched the

fire consume Sweetheart firsthand. That's why I want to help. You and anyone who wants it. But especially you."

"I don't need help. Yours or anyone's."

"I think you do. You just refuse to admit it."

"I refuse to take your late wife's money." She looked instantly contrite. "Sorry. I shouldn't have snapped at you."

"It's okay." Sam wasn't offended. If anything, he was glad. At least they had gotten to the root of her resistance.

Would she be more willing to accept his help if she learned why his wife had been in that car in the first place and who she was with?

Maybe not. But she might understand what drove him to use the settlement money for good.

The mare stood patiently while Annie administered an injection of penicillin. She was less tolerant when Annie inserted the tube of Bute into her mouth, rolling the gooey paste around on her tongue.

"Easy, girl." She stroked the mare's nose. "It tastes bad but will make you feel a lot better."

Together, she and Sam cleaned the mare's mouth and nose. The nasal discharge was clear, which gave Annie hope that the mare was fighting a simple virus and not something more serious. Still, she wouldn't rest easy until the horse was seen by a vet.

"I'll get the mash." Sam left, returning a short while later with a bucket of grain and bran soaked with water and molasses. The delicacy would hopefully tempt the mare to eat and provide necessary hydration.

Annie didn't expect much, not until the Bute kicked in. "You might also try fresh grass instead of hay."

"I'll have Lyndsey pick some after dinner."

"Try adding a cup of salt to her water."

"Where'd you learn that trick?"

"Trial and error and years of nursing sick animals back to health."

To their relief, the mare ate a few mouthfuls of the mash and drank a small amount of salted water. According to Sam, it was more than she'd taken in the past two days.

"Check on her a couple more times before you go to bed. Watch that her breathing doesn't become labored." Annie brushed off her shirt and capris as she exited the stall. "Where do you think my grandmother took off to this time?"

"She's petting the horses." Lyndsey held both Annie and Sam's hands as they went outside.

He sent her a look as if to say, *Kids.*

Yeah, kids.

Granny Orla was at the corrals. Like Annie and her mother, she had once been an accomplished rider. According to the stories, she and her TV-star lover would ride into the mountains and loll away the afternoons at their secret spot. Sam and Annie had followed suit, finding their own secret place.

What to do about Sam? From the second he'd reentered her life, he'd consumed it.

"Thanks for all your help."

"No problem."

Sam walked Annie to her vehicle while Lyndsey went to fetch Granny Orla. Instead, the two of them got involved doling out the carrots that Will kept handy.

"Can I call you if the mare gets worse?" Sam asked.

"There isn't much more I can do."

He caught her wrist before she could open the door. "I should have told you my Hotshot crew was assigned to the fire."

"Yes, you should have."

"I can see you're upset."

"Not upset exactly." The horses were bunched at the corral railing, vying for a treat. Annie watched them as she gathered her thoughts. "It's hard to explain."

"Try."

"It's like I fell from a high cliff and was critically injured. Then I find out you were there at the top, watching the entire time. You even tried to prevent my fall. But you didn't tell me about it, and I have to wonder why."

"I'd give anything to have stopped the fire from reaching Sweetheart."

There was agony in his voice. Sorrow in his eyes. Pain in his heart, deep as her own. She could feel it.

"Wouldn't we all." She lifted her fingers to his cheek.

Not the smartest move. The next moment, she was enveloped in his embrace.

The kiss, gentle and tender, wasn't entirely unexpected. In all honesty, Annie might have prompted it. She would, she decided, give in for a second or two, then disengage herself. Only that didn't happen. She clung to him, letting his mouth settle possessively on hers.

Pure recklessness. And pure heaven.

This was the kind of careless abandonment that had gotten her into trouble with Sam before, when he was a brash young ranch hand and she the local innkeeper's daughter. She'd let herself get carried away...and she was doing it again.

A soft moan escaped her lips, and when his hand

pressed firmly into the small of her back, she had the sweet sensation of her bones melting.

He increased his hold on her, but it was she who parted his lips. She who sacrificed control without a care.

She'd missed him.

The realization nearly undid her. He'd been her first love. Her greatest love. And she'd never gotten over him—or the hurt and anger at his abrupt departure.

Those thoughts galvanized her and gave her the strength she needed to resist. Bracing her hands on his shoulders, she pushed away.

"I... We can't." Her complete loss of composure embarrassed her.

Why could he alone have that effect on her?

"The whole time I was married to Trisha, I never forgot about you. About us."

"Not the right thing to say." The reminder of his late wife steadied her.

"Annie, I—"

"You were married. And your wife died in a horrible accident. Please don't dishonor her memory or me by bringing her up seconds after we kissed."

"You're right." He stepped away. The warmth of his body lingered. "But it changes nothing. I want to see you."

"See me? Like a date? No way!"

"Why not?"

She glanced at the corral. Thank goodness for small favors. Granny and Lyndsey were still thoroughly engaged with the horses. "I can give you a hundred reasons."

"There's still a powerful attraction between us. Don't deny it."

She wouldn't. Why bother? He had only to recall their kiss. Correction, kisses. Both occurring with their family members a hundred feet away. This one in broad daylight!

"I have to stay focused on rebuilding the inn and supporting my family. I can't let anything interfere."

No matter how tempting, she added silently.

"One date won't interfere."

As if it would stop there. Look at their past history. Look at the past five minutes.

"Gary wants me to give him more custody of Nessa. He'd probably take her full-time if I let him."

"What! Is he crazy?"

"He's very serious. He's mentioned it enough times that I'm losing sleep at night." She despised the catch in her voice.

"Why would he do that? You're a great mom."

"Because of the apartment."

"It's small but nice. I lived in the back of a horse trailer years ago when I first came here."

"The apartment reminds him too much of the one he grew up in in a not-so-nice part of Vegas. He's also concerned about my grandmother and her bouts with confusion. Also my mother."

"Your mother?"

"You saw her at her best the other night."

"What's her worst?"

"She's depressed."

"I'm no expert but that can't be uncommon after a monumental loss. Hell, half the people in Sweetheart are depressed."

"Half the people in Sweetheart aren't responsible for taking care of Nessa while I'm at work."

"Have you considered delaying the rebuilding and using some of the insurance money to get a larger place?"

"I'd do it in an instant if I could. The problem is there's so little decent available housing in town. We were lucky to get the apartment we did."

"Then Gary's being unreasonable."

She put on a brave smile. "I'm counting on him backing off once we start construction on the inn."

"Let me help you."

"Absolutely not. Gary's my problem to deal with."

"With the inn. Talk to my contractor and architect," he insisted. "What have you got to lose?"

Annie carefully debated the pros and cons. Really, she did have little to lose. And possibly a lot to gain.

"All right, but I refuse to let you cover a dime of their fees. I know you've done that for some people in town."

He grinned broadly. "Chas, the owner of the construction company, is here two or three days a week. The architect will drive up to meet with you."

Annie couldn't believe she was agreeing. For a multitude of good reasons, she'd be wise to keep Sam at arm's length. Yet, a slip of paper appeared in her hand a minute later and she knew without a doubt she'd be calling the numbers on it, grateful to Sam for the referrals.

Chapter 8

Twenty-four head of horses now resided at the Gold Nugget Ranch, including the pony and the draft mare, nearly recovered from her bout with equine influenza. Dr. Murry had examined her yesterday and set Sam's concerns to rest.

He needed to thank Annie for her help, except he hadn't seen her for three days. Not since giving her the names and numbers of his architect and construction contractor. A casual inquiry placed to both men confirmed she hadn't called them.

Forcing her to accept his assistance wasn't an option. He'd just have to wait her out. Or figure out another way to break through her defenses. So far, animals in need had worked well, but it wouldn't for much longer. Annie was no dummy.

"That fella's a troublemaker." Will referred to their

one and only mule, a long-eared, ill-tempered, skinny brown beast who gave all mules a bad name.

"Remind me why we're keeping him," Sam said, fighting hard to hide his exertion. Ten straight minutes of attempting to put a halter on the mule had winded him.

Not Will. "Best pack mule in these parts."

"Hmm." Sam debated offering only short trail rides, ones not requiring extra supplies and provisions carried on a mule's back.

He and Will were in the main corral, attempting to move the entire herd to the newly constructed adjacent corral with its large shade covering. The main corral would soon have a similar covering, if Sam and Will could ever empty it.

The mule stood in the center, glowering at them.

"Come on, you worthless sack of bone," Sam called to him. "Cut us both a break." He wiped his hand across his sweaty brow and turned to Will. "How is it you got all those horses to follow the leader when you unloaded them, and now we can't get one stinking mule through the gate?"

"It's a matter of pride."

"Mine?"

"His." Will inclined his head toward the mule.

Sam might have dismissed his employee's notion that the mule possessed human emotions if it hadn't so far refused a bucket of grain, an apple and sugar cubes. All bribes Sam had tried using to coax the mule into the new corral.

"Let's just leave him for a while. He'll be more co-operative once he misses his buddies."

"Don't count on it."

By now, a sizeable crowd had gathered. In fact, construction had come to a complete standstill. Roofers stopped roofing, painters stopped painting and framers stopped framing. Sam thought he noticed money changing hands and bets being placed.

Even Lyndsey and her new little friend—Irma's middle boy, Gus—abandoned walking the goats in order to watch.

Sam grumbled to himself. No mule was going to best him. Not in front of an audience this size.

"Where you going?" Will called after him.

"To get my rope."

Will's affable chuckle didn't inspire confidence.

Twenty minutes later, all the horses including the mule were in the new corral. Sam's victory wasn't without cost. He had rope burns on his palms, a twisted ankle and a seven-inch tear in his favorite shirt. He was also pretty sure he'd dislocated his left shoulder.

All right, he concluded after rotating it, maybe not dislocated. Just wrenched. He'd be useless tomorrow.

The mule looked no worse for wear. He stood calmly among his brethren in the new corral, his tail swishing at flies.

"What's his name?" All this time, Sam hadn't bothered to ask.

"Make Me. It's short for 'Just Try and Make Me.' That seemed kind of long."

He glared at Will. "You wait till now to tell me that?"

"Won twenty dollars."

"You owe me a beer at least. Let's finish up here and you can take me to the Paydirt and settle up."

"Daddy, Daddy! That was cool." Lyndsey and her

pal bounded over. The boy, roughly her age, hadn't left her side since they were introduced earlier that day.

Sam didn't think he had anything to worry about. Yet. Another few years and it might be a different story.

"Yeah, cool." He kneaded his sore shoulder and flexed his twisted ankle. He did not feel cool.

"Gus has been telling me how to take care of the goats."

"You have goats, son?"

"Used to." The boy rolled a pebble back and forth with the toe of his sneaker. "Chickens, too. And a pot-belly pig. That was before my mom lost her job."

"Ever take care of baby raccoons?"

"Naw. Raccoons are varmints." At Lyndsey's gasp of horror, he amended his statement. "'Cept for yours."

She scowled at him.

It looked as if Gus had lost some ground.

Sam felt compelled to help the kid. "Seeing as Gus has experience with animals, maybe he could take care of the goats and cat after we go back home. The kits, too. Until they're old enough to be surrendered to the animal sanctuary."

"I don't want him taking care of the animals. I don't want *anybody* doing it but me." The higher Lyndsey's voice rose, the more her lower lip trembled.

Sam was grateful the construction workers and Will had returned to their jobs. Fewer witnesses.

"Lyndsey, we've talked about this. We can't take the kits home with us."

"Then let's stay here!"

"We can't. School starts in a month."

"I can go to school with Gus."

Stay here? When did she change her mind? From

the very get-go, she hadn't wanted to come to Sweet-heart. Except that was before two abandoned kits, two Nubian goats and an ugly-as-sin barn cat entered her life. Oh, and Gus.

"What about Grandpa?"

"He can move here, too."

Sam was thinking how much his own desire to return to California had waned. Reason, however, prevailed. "We have to go home. Grandpa needs us. There's the fall roundup."

"Porky and Daffy will die without me!"

"I'll take care of them," Gus offered. "Even if they are varmints."

Sam was marginally glad to see he wasn't the only male in the vicinity saying completely the wrong thing.

With an anguished cry, Lyndsey ran into the house. Sam imagined her running up the stairs to her bedroom and slamming the door shut.

Gus sighed. "Women."

Sam didn't think he'd ever be concurring with an eight-year-old.

They found Gus's mother in the kitchen. She confirmed Lyndsey was in her room.

Sam went upstairs and knocked on her closed bedroom door. "Sweetie."

He heard muffled thumping noises from within but no invitation to enter.

"Gus is looking for you."

"I don't want to talk to him. Or you."

Sam hesitated before heading back down the stairs. They'd been through this exact same scenario often since Trisha's death. Lyndsey would sequester herself and refuse to talk to him or anybody until she was ready.

"Irma, you mind keeping an eye on her for me?" Sam asked. "I'm heading into town with Will."

"Not at all."

Gus sat glumly at the long oak table.

"You might as well go outside and play, son."

"I'll wait for her."

He would? Sam wasn't sure how he felt about that.

Behind the barn, Sam discovered Will repairing the same antique buggy that had sat in front of the ranch for decades. Will thought it would be a nice touch for the guests, and Sam agreed.

"You ready to buy me that beer?"

"It's not quitting time yet."

"I need a break. We're taking the rest of the afternoon off."

"You're the boss." Will straightened and deposited the wrench he'd been using into the open toolbox. "Want me to drive?"

"The hell with driving. Let's ride. I haven't seen these mountains from the back of a horse for nine years."

The hills surrounding the Gold Nugget were lush and green, deep in the throes of summer splendor. Birds flitted from one thick Ponderosa Pine bough to another as Sam and Will rode by. Squirrels scampered into hiding. Faces of cows peeked out from behind brush, the grazing stock of some nearby rancher.

Sam relaxed, settling into the rhythmic sway of the horse's easy gait. For a while, he forgot about his troubles and, in this untainted stretch of wilderness, all about the fire.

Then, he and Will crested the next rise. In the valley below lay Sweetheart.

What was left of it.

Strips, some a quarter mile wide and black as coal, crisscrossed the town and continued up the opposing mountain, marking the fire's descent from Cohea Ridge. The place where Sam had been that day, watching in horror and frustration as the wind changed direction.

"Pretty bad, huh?" Will said thoughtfully.

Pretty bad didn't begin to describe it. Fate had dealt this place and its people a terrible blow.

Sam almost turned back around.

Riding through town was equally disheartening. The horses plodded slowly along, giving Sam plenty of opportunity to study the devastation in detail. By the time he and Will reached the saloon, his spirits were low and his determination wavering. He needed more than a beer to erase the images seared in his memory.

The fire had divided countless times as it burned through Sweetheart, attacking some homes and buildings and leaving others to stand alone like tiny islands in a sea of blackness.

So much devastation. Would converting the Gold Nugget into a working guest ranch be enough to revitalize Sweetheart? Doubts crept in and anchored.

Sam and Will tethered their horses to the hitching rail behind the building and went inside. The mayor's bar and grill was the only local watering hole in Sweetheart to survive. Two others had succumbed to the fire, another to a lack of honeymooners and tourists. As a result, the Paydirt was typically crowded most evenings and weekends.

Mayor Dempsey was behind the bar, busily serving drinks with the help of her brother-in-law, who was also on the town council.

Ever since the first Dempseys settled in the area,

one or more of them had continually held positions of prominence and authority. Last election, the tradition continued when the mayor's nephew was elected sheriff.

Annie's family and their inn might have been the heart of Sweetheart, but the Dempsey family was the muscle.

"Welcome, gentlemen." The mayor flashed Sam and Will a broad smile as they approached the bar and placed their orders. "Been a while since we've had a couple of young, handsome cowboys ride up on their horses. Reminds me of the old days."

Sam would have selected a table, but Will sidled over to the last stool at the bar and plunked down, giving Sam the impression this was his employee's regular seat. The stool next to Will was vacant, and Sam took it.

When Will attempted to pay for the beers, the mayor refused him.

"For you, Sam, drinks are on the house. And your hired hand."

"I can't accept that."

"Sure you can. With everything you're doing for this town, the jobs you've given folks, the business your guest ranch will bring in, I wouldn't think of charging you."

As if on cue, a cement truck chugged noisily down the street outside the bar, its hydraulic brakes squealing as it slowed.

"Think the horses are okay?" Sam asked.

Will shrugged, and then nodded. "If they get scared and run off, they won't go far."

"Won't go far" could be all the way back to the Gold Nugget.

"Look at that," the mayor gushed. "Third truck this

hour. Heading to the Abramses' shop to pour their foundation."

Sam was acquainted with the Abramses. They were one of the families who'd taken him up on his offer to assist with their reconstruction costs. He was glad to see work had started.

"If not for you, the Abramses would have moved," the mayor continued. "Now they're staying."

"Hear, hear." A patron sitting down the bar from Sam raised his glass in salute.

The knot twisting Sam's stomach eased slightly.

Not long after, another truck passed, this one bearing the logo of a lumber company from Lake Tahoe. A small cheer went up throughout the saloon and another toast was made to Sam. The mayor declared a round of drinks for the house.

Sam's only regret was that the trucks weren't en route to Annie's inn. Why hadn't she contacted his contractor or the architect?

Maybe he should have *them* call *her*. No, that would be interfering, and Annie wouldn't like it. Any assistance she accepted from him—even something as simple as a referral—had to be on her own terms.

He wasn't convinced rebuilding the inn was the best course of action for her, but if that was what she truly wanted, needed, he'd stand behind her.

Not an hour passed that he didn't think about their kisses and recall the taste of her mouth. The sensation of her going pliant in his arms. The stirrings inside him that she triggered with just a glance or a smile.

It was more than lust or longing. He could admit to himself he hadn't ever really fallen out of love with her, and with a little push, he'd be right back where he was nine years ago.

Where would that leave them? Leave him? Annie didn't appear to be teetering on the edge like he was.

Rousing himself, he drained half his beer. The good thing about keeping company with Will was that the man didn't talk much and appreciated that same quality in others.

At another loud cheer from the patrons, Sam turned sideways to look out the window, expecting to see another truck passing by.

To his surprise and delight, Annie had walked into the saloon. He automatically started to rise as she made her way toward him.

Will also stood and tugged on the brim of his cowboy hat in greeting. "Later," he said to Sam and found a vacant chair farther down the bar.

Sam didn't stop him. He wanted some time alone with Annie and hoped she was here to discuss starting construction on the inn.

Right. He really hoped she was here to see him.

"Hi." Her manner was reserved. "I saw your horses and hoped you might be here."

She recognized his horses? The thought gave Sam a small surge of pleasure. She was paying attention to him.

"Can I buy you a beer?" He gestured to the stool Will had vacated.

"No, thanks. I rarely drink since Nessa was born. Besides, I'm not staying."

She'd hardly finished her sentence when the mayor slid an icy soda in front of her with an "On the house."

Sam made a mental note to leave a sizeable tip before leaving. "Did you need something?" he asked.

"I do." She sat down and took a sip of her soda as if requiring fortification. "Can you come outside with me for a minute?"

"Sure." He motioned to Will that he'd be right back and went with Annie.

She took him to her SUV and opened the rear hatch. Inside the cargo area was a large cardboard shipping box.

"What is it?" Sam peered curiously at the box.

"I found this today. At the base of an aspen tree. We were assisting a team of scientists from the University of Nevada, collecting density readings near Cohea Ridge."

She carefully opened the top of the box, just enough for Sam to see in.

A large bird huddled in the corner and eyed them with insolence and suspicion.

"It's a goshawk," Annie said. "I'm not sure what happened to him, but he's pretty beat-up. Could be he got in a fight with a larger bird of prey over food. The supply of rodents has drastically dwindled. Or, it's possible some other predator tried to make a meal of him."

"That's too bad. He's a beautiful bird."

The hawk sported thick white stripes over each gleaming eye, without a doubt its most prominent feature next to its hooked beak. The wings were tucked close to its body. Unfurled, Sam estimated they would span more than three feet.

"I was hoping you could help."

"With what?"

"Keep him. Rehabilitate him. Until he's ready to

be released back into the wild. I'd do it myself, but my landlord won't allow it. And Lyndsey's so good with animals."

The last thing Sam wanted or needed was another animal for his daughter to foster. She was already too attached to the ones they had. Just look at their earlier blowup over the suggestion that Gus assume responsibility for their brood when they returned to California. And hawks required more specialized care than baby raccoons, goats and a stray cat. He knew that from the times he'd helped Annie with the various birds she'd rescued.

"Annie…"

"Please."

The desperation in her voice turned his resolve to mush. "On one condition."

"Name it," she answered without reservation.

"Come back inside. Finish your soda."

"But the hawk—"

"Will be fine for a little while longer. In fact, he's probably a lot better off and safer in the box than the woods. After dinner, you can meet me at the Gold Nugget. Bring Nessa. Bring your whole family if you want. While Nessa rides the pony, you and I can get this fellow situated."

After a brief hesitation, Annie closed the lid on the box and shut the rear hatch on her SUV. "Thirty minutes. No more."

Not much time. Sam would have to work fast.

Chapter 9

Annie shouldn't have agreed to Sam's request. She should have insisted they go straight to the Gold Nugget. No bringing the family. No pony ride.

Of course, going *straight* there would have been difficult, considering his mode of transportation was horseback. And if she'd refused, he might not have agreed to foster the hawk.

With little choice, she found herself sitting at a table in the Paydirt with him.

Visiting the ranch, conversing with Sam, was becoming a habit. One she didn't seem capable of breaking. One she possibly didn't want to break.

"If you're wondering why I haven't called your architect and contractor yet, I've been busy with work."

"I wasn't wondering."

"Oh." Then why insist they talk?

He appeared far more relaxed than she felt, with his long legs stretched out, his cowboy hat pushed back on his head and one forearm propped casually on the table.

She, on the other hand, couldn't sit still and continuously stirred the ice in her soda with her straw.

"I owe you an explanation," he said.

"For what?"

"Why I didn't tell you about my crew being called to the fire. I wasn't sure what to say, so I said nothing. Not the right thing to do."

"I would have liked to know, yeah." Also that he was returning to Sweetheart and buying the Gold Nugget. If only to prepare herself. "In the end, it doesn't make any difference."

"It actually does. And here's where things get sticky."

"I don't follow."

No longer relaxed, Sam sat up and drained the last of the beer he'd been nursing. After that, he took several seconds to collect himself.

"You remember how the wind suddenly changed direction, sending the fire toward Sweetheart?"

"How could I not? One minute the officials were telling us we were safe. The next, we had two hours to evacuate. Even then, they assured us it was simply a precaution. Ten hours later, the town was a raging inferno."

If Sam gripped his empty beer bottle any tighter, he'd shatter it.

"Are you okay?" she asked.

"No."

He was beginning to alarm her.

"What's wrong?"

His face was flushed and his brow damp. She leaned

forward, tempted to place her palm on his forehead and test for a fever.

"I knew the wind was going to change direction from west to south before it did."

"I don't understand."

"I've been a volunteer Hotshot for a lot of years. It gets to where you have a sixth sense, more accurate than all the scientific equipment and experts put together. I've been right more times than I've been wrong. My gut was working overtime that day, telling me Sweetheart was in danger."

Annie sat slowly back in her chair, Sam's revelation sending a shock wave pulsing through her. "Why didn't you do something?"

"I did. I radioed my commander. Insisted crews be moved from the line we were holding on the west perimeter of the fire to the south perimeter."

"He ignored your warning?"

"Just the opposite. He's worked with me a lot of summers and trusts me. So he relayed my information to Fire Camp."

She could see the outcome in his eyes. "They didn't listen."

"The chief instructed us to hold steady. All the reports and scientific data indicated weather conditions were going to remain stable. The wind would continue blowing in a westerly direction."

"But it didn't."

"No."

The emotion in that single word brought tears to Annie's eyes. Sam was in pain. She was in pain. Her town, her inn, might have been spared.

"Why didn't you disobey orders?" She wasn't criticizing him, only attempting to understand.

"I've asked myself that question a thousand times a day, and the answer comes back the same. I don't know. We're trained to obey orders, and I could have been suspended. Terminated. But that's just an excuse." His voice was hoarse, as if he'd been screaming for hours without rest.

Had it been like that the day of the fire? Had he screamed until his throat was raw?

"Could you have saved Sweetheart? If you disobeyed orders?"

"Not without backup. My crew consisted of nineteen men. There were two other crews in that section. Together, maybe we could have stopped the fire. Slowed it down for sure until reinforcements arrived."

"Only if your crew and the others agreed to disobey orders, too."

"Yeah."

"What were the chances of that?"

"We won't ever know. That's what I have to live with."

"Yes, we do know, Sam. I see the aftermath of that fire every time I look out my window or drive down the street. I also work for the NDF and experience first-hand what that fire did every day on the job. A handful of Hotshots battling a two-mile raging inferno would be like sending a single guy with a garden hose to extinguish a burning building."

"I should have tried harder. Talked to the chief myself instead of leaving it up to my commanding offi—"

"Nobody died."

He looked at her in confusion.

"The fire was the largest and most destructive one

this state has seen in years. The damage to wilderness and property is immeasurable. But nobody died. And there were very few injuries. Most of them minor. Sweetheart was the only town to sustain any damage. It could have been a lot worse. You've seen worse in some of the fires you've fought."

"I have. But those towns weren't places where I'd lived. The residents weren't people I knew and cared about. There wasn't a special woman who once meant the world to me."

She reached for his hand. His large, strong fingers curled instantly around hers. When he applied a slight pressure, she returned it.

"You don't have to beat yourself up with guilt, Sam. We live in the Sierra Nevada. Winds constantly change direction with no warning. It's nature."

"I could have done more."

"You and the other Hotshots gave us enough time to evacuate the entire town. Your warning made those scientists and personnel in charge take a closer look at protocol. Reevaluate it."

"I'm not sure about that."

Maybe he wasn't, but some of the tension drained from him.

"I know you came back to help. Because of guilt. Only the fire isn't your burden to bear, and you're not solely responsible for Sweetheart's recovery."

His smile, though faint, was the first one since they'd come back inside the Paydirt. "I'd still like to try."

Annie suddenly remembered the time. She really should get home. Nessa would be waiting for her, their dinner getting cold. Before the fire, her mother would have been impatiently waiting, too. She'd always been a stickler about how and when her food was served, right down to the china plates and crystal salt-and-pepper shakers.

Now, most of her efforts were centered on making it through the day.

Annie realized that other than seeing Nessa, she had no interest in returning to the apartment. It was a small, dreary and discouraging place. She'd much rather be sitting here with Sam.

"Whatever your motives, people are grateful." She removed her hand from his and resumed stirring her soda. "Can I ask you a personal question?"

"Sure."

"Why are you using the settlement money from your wife's accident to cover the contractor's profit? Shouldn't that money go to Lyndsey? Not that it's any of my business."

"I want some good to come out of Trisha's accident."

"You're spending money on people you hardly know. On a ranch you probably bought strictly for sentimental reasons."

"Spontaneous or not, buying the Gold Nugget was the right decision. I want this town to thrive again. I want to see couples walking hand in hand on their way to the chapel. I want your inn to be the heart of Sweetheart."

Her smile softened. "Is that a hint to call your architect and contractor?"

"Might be."

"I'll do it. Tomorrow. I promise." And not leave the task to her mother. "But what about Lyndsey? It's not fair she lose her share of the money."

Annie had hesitated before speaking. Sam didn't when he responded.

"The settlement was large. Significant. The drunk driver who hit Trisha was well-off and his level of intoxication far exceeded the legal limit. He's currently imprisoned for two felony counts of vehicular manslaughter. Even without the settlement, Lyndsey's well taken care of. My father-in-law intends to leave the ranch to her. Trisha was his only child and Lyndsey's his only grandchild."

Something Sam said stopped Annie. "*Two* counts of manslaughter?"

"Trisha wasn't alone in the car."

"How terrible." Annie released a shuddering sigh. What if Lyndsey had been the other occupant? Imagining it gave her chills. "Her friend's family must be devastated."

"They are. His wife had no idea he was cheating on her with Trisha. Just like I had no idea."

"Cheating!" Poor Sam. What a blow that must have been. "Are you sure they were lovers? They could have been acquaintances or business associates."

Annie had no reason to defend Sam's late wife, but he was obviously suffering, and she longed to ease his grief.

"I'm sure. Trisha and her lover were returning from an afternoon together when they were struck." He resumed choking his empty beer bottle. "She died almost instantly. Massive internal injuries. Her lover lived an hour. Long enough to make a deathbed confession. It damn near killed me. His wife took it worse."

It seemed to Annie as if Sam had taken it pretty bad himself.

She understood his marriage might not have been made in heaven, and she was certainly no one to judge. Not with her track record. His resentment, however, sounded more serious.

"Trisha would have wanted the settlement money to go to Lyndsey and you," she said.

"I won't take a dime of it."

"She had feelings for you."

"I doubt it." He bit out the words. "She rarely thought of anyone besides herself. If she had, she wouldn't have been in that car in the first place."

"I'm so sorry. That must have been…" Annie started to say *unbearable* only to realize how inadequately that described what he must have gone through. "Does Lyndsey know?"

"She doesn't. And I may never tell her. I see no reason to taint the memory of her mother.

Neither did Annie. Not at eight years old. "She may find out when she's older. Family members could talk. There was probably news coverage. If she eventually decides that she needs closure, she may investigate the accident."

"Maybe."

Annie was in no position to advise Sam on how to handle that day if it ever came. She only hoped he'd be ready.

Someday, certainly before *she* was ready, Nessa would inquire about her parents' divorce and what went wrong. Annie prayed she'd say the right thing.

All at once, she wanted to go home and hold her baby in her arms. It didn't seem polite, running off seconds after Sam had revealed such personal and private information.

"If there's anything I can do for you or Lyndsey, don't hesitate to ask."

"Just help find homes for all these critters she's collecting."

"And I've made your problem bigger by foisting a goshawk on you."

"I don't mind."

She didn't think he did. His voice had lost its rough edge. "You're a good man, Sam."

In answer, his gaze traveled her face, long and lingeringly.

Her cheeks warmed under his intense scrutiny, but she didn't look away.

"Can I get you a refill?" The mayor interrupted them, a drink tray balanced on her arm.

Annie glanced around the bar, and her worst fears were confirmed when a half-dozen heads quickly turned away.

"No, thanks." Annie brushed self-consciously at her hair. "People are staring at us," she said after the mayor moved to the next table.

"They've see it before." Sam's grin wasn't the least bit contrite.

"Not recently. And not again. I don't want them or you getting the wrong idea."

"Too late, girl. I've been getting wrong ideas since that first kiss. Actually, since the first day I saw you at the Gold Nugget. Standing at the bottom of the stairs."

She nearly groaned with frustration—and would have if not for Sam's guaranteed amusement.

"I'd better hurry." She scooted back from the table. "I'll be by around seven with Nessa and the hawk. I was thinking we could put him in that old chicken coop next to the barn."

"Will and I will have it cleaned out before you get there. Patch any holes."

He walked her outside to her SUV. His horses weren't the only ones to be tethered behind the Paydirt Saloon, but it had been a while. The familiar scene gave Annie a cozy feeling inside. In this one small way, life was returning to normal.

"I really will call the architect and contractor tomorrow."

"Let me know how that goes."

He propped an arm on the roof of her vehicle, beside her open door, his stance the same pure male one that he'd assumed the other day.

Annie's resistance, never all that strong where Sam was concerned, weakened. Of its own volition, her body swayed toward his.

How many faces were pressed to the bar's windows? How many pairs of eyes were peering at them? She didn't dare look. She didn't really care.

"Better hurry," he murmured lazily, "if Nessa's going to ride that pony. It gets dark by eight."

"Yeah." Annie moved…marginally closer to Sam rather than away, convinced she'd lost her mind. "She'll be really disappointed if we're late."

One minute. Two minutes. What would it hurt? She lifted her face to Sam's.

At the same moment that his head dipped to claim the kiss she offered, a vehicle hauled into the parking lot and came to a tire-squealing stop. Right next to her SUV. Too loud and too close to ignore.

Annie reeled, ready to give the driver a warning.

The van, with the distinctive Dempsey General Store and Trading Post logo painted on the side, was one of a kind.

The door opened, and Gary emerged. He approached Annie and Sam, his gait purposeful and an angry scowl on his face.

Chapter 10

"Gary, what's wrong?" As Annie rushed forward to meet him, she noticed Nessa sat in the van's passenger seat. Not Linda Lee. Her concern spiked to alarm. "Why do you have Nessa?"

"Can we talk?" He fired a decidedly unfriendly glance in Sam's direction. "In private."

Not answering, she tried to skirt him. "Is she all right?"

He restrained her with a hand on her arm. "She's fine. Which is fortunate."

Her heart verged on exploding. Through the window, Nessa appeared safe and secure in her car seat, happily reading a picture book. Seeing her didn't calm Annie.

"What's going on?" she demanded.

"I went to the apartment," Gary explained, pulling her aside. "She'd left her Barbie dolls at my place, and I thought I'd drop them off. When I got there, she answered the door. A three-year-old. Not your mom or grandmother. And the door wasn't locked. With all the construction going on and testing in the mountains, this town is full of strangers."

Guilt and horror instantly consumed Annie. "Where was Mom?"

"Asleep. I went through the apartment and found her in bed."

"I'll talk to her again."

"You don't get it, Annie. Nessa was playing unsupervised. In the kitchen. Where there's a gas stove. And your mom was dead to the world. Took a full minute of shaking to wake her."

The part of Annie's mind clinging to reason argued that sleeping wasn't so terrible. She'd occasionally lie down for a brief rest while her mother or grandmother watched Nessa. Not, however, when she and Nessa were alone. Then, she'd coax Nessa to lie down with her.

"And your grandmother had taken off again. Who knows where? She must have left the front door unlocked." Gary's tone was grim. "Annie, anybody could have walked right in and snatched Nessa. Or, she could have wandered off and gotten into all kinds of trouble. Lost. Hit by a car."

She had no excuse. "Gary, I… It won't happen again."

"I was going to find you, talk to you. See if we couldn't figure out other day care. I get that you have to work, but there must be more reliable resources in town." His concern for Nessa was genuine. "Except here you are, having a drink with your old boyfriend while our daughter's in danger." Another accusatory glance at Sam.

"It was a soda."

"You should have been home. With Nessa. She's your first priority."

He was right. At the very least, she should have called her mother before stopping at the Paydirt. The ringing phone would have woken her up.

But she'd been preoccupied. Talking to Sam. Holding his hand. Gazing into his face. Vying for a kiss.

Oh, God. She was the worst mother ever.

"It won't happen again, Gary. I swear to you." She made another attempt to squeeze past him.

He wouldn't allow it.

"Let me see Nessa!"

"Not yet." Was he angrier about her mother sleeping when she should have been watching Nessa or that Annie was with Sam?

"You have no right to keep me from her."

"I have the right to expect my child is safely supervised when I'm not there. It's also my responsibility to see that she's living in decent housing."

"The apartment's fine."

"It's small and crowded. She doesn't have to live that way. Not when I have plenty of room at my house."

"Sweetheart isn't anything like where you grew up."

His tone softened. "I'm not trying to take her away from you. I only want to provide for her as best I can."

He might not think he was trying to take Nessa away from Annie, but that's sure what it sounded like. "I'm seeing my daughter now," she said sternly.

"I think it's best I take Nessa home with me tonight."

"The hell you are!"

"Stop by after you get off work. We'll make some decisions."

Anger dissolved into pleading. "We have an agreement. Don't use Nessa to punish me."

All at once, Sam's arm stretched out and made contact with Gary's chest. Annie was unaware he'd moved to stand beside her.

"Let Annie see her daughter."

"This is none of your concern, Wyler." Gary didn't budge. "Butt out."

"I'll butt out when Annie tells me to."

She didn't. While Sam and Gary stood arguing, she ducked by them and ran to Gary's van. Hands shaking, she removed Nessa and the Barbie dolls and loaded them into the SUV's rear seat, opening several windows for ventilation. Only then did Sam lower his arm, releasing Gary. Her ex-husband was none too happy.

When Nessa was secure and assured everything was well, that Mommy and Daddy were just talking, Annie returned to the two men and braced herself for Gary's onslaught.

"I'll expect you promptly after work."

"I'll see you Friday when it's your turn with Nessa."

"You either come by tomorrow or my attorney will be in touch. That's a promise. Our daughter deserves better, and she's going to get it."

"Easy now, I've got you."

"Let me go."

Sam held Annie, refusing to release her until her shaking subsided.

"Gary's gone. Everything's fine."

"No, it's not."

The anguish in her voice ripped him in two. "Nothing bad happened, Annie."

"Gary's coming after me for full custody."

"He was mad at me and taking it out on you." Sam stroked her back. "He'll get over it."

"He's threatened before."

"Do you really think he was serious?" That was bothersome. Sam had assumed Gary was simply reacting out of anger or being pressured by his wife. Nice as the woman had been to him, it was obvious she had a grudge against Annie. "You're Nessa's mother. There is no way a judge will grant him full custody just because one time your mom happened to fall asleep and your grandmother left the front door unlocked. Especially when Nessa wasn't hurt."

"He can still make trouble for me," she said unevenly, her glance going to Nessa in the SUV's rear seat. The girl was happily occupied with the dolls Gary had returned. "Between my mom's depression and my grandmother's episodes of confusion, he has a strong case. God, I'd give anything to move."

"Let me ask my real estate agent. She may have some strings she can pull."

"Worth a try, I suppose."

To Sam's disappointment, Annie disengaged herself from his embrace. "I really need to get home. I don't want Gary telling the judge that I stand in front of bars with men while our daughter is forced to wait inside my vehicle." After one step, she paused and pressed a hand to her forehead. "I forgot about the goshawk."

"I'll take care of him."

"How will you get him home? You're riding a horse."

He nodded toward the door of the Paydirt. "I'll catch a lift with someone inside. Will can ride his horse home and lead mine."

"Are you sure?"

"Get a move on and quit worrying."

"I'll stop by tomorrow."

"No rush. Whenever's convenient for you. I learned enough from helping you out with your bird rescues—I can manage to take care of this fellow for a few days without killing him."

"Sam!"

"That was a joke."

She tried to smile, but the attempt failed. "Call me."

"I will. You just concentrate on yourself and your family."

"And on finding alternative day care."

"I have something that might help in the meantime."

"Oh, you're starting a day care center at the ranch now?"

"No, but that's not a bad idea. For the guests."

"Be serious, Sam."

"Okay, I was joking again. A little."

This time a smile broke through. "You've done so much for me already."

Was she including the hug? "If you need help searching for your grandmother, let me know."

"Hopefully, she's at the neighbors' and not the inn ruins."

"Or on her way to the Gold Nugget."

"Right." She opened the driver's side door and asked Nessa, "You hungry, sweetie pie? We'll leave in just a minute. I have to give Mr. Wyler something."

They went to the rear of the vehicle and lifted the hatch.

"I'll have my construction contractor send over an installer tomorrow. When's a good time?"

"Installer for what?" she asked, reaching for the cardboard box and peeking inside. The goshawk hadn't moved.

"A door alarm."

"A what?"

"Individual sensors for doors," Sam answered. "I ordered a few for the ranch. They're like a mini alarm system. When the door's opened, a buzzer sounds. Loud enough to be heard from a hundred feet away. The contractor recommended them to deter guests from going where they shouldn't, like the tool shed or tack room. If your mother were to fall asleep again, the buzzer would wake her."

She paused, hand on the box. "I can't let you do that."

"You can, and you will. For Nessa and your grandmother. And for your peace of mind. You don't need to be worrying about your family all day when you're at work."

"It would show Gary that I'm committed," she said, relenting.

Sam allowed himself a moment's satisfaction. Little by little, he was breaking down her resistance.

"The installer will call your mom and give her a heads-up on his arrival time."

"I insist on paying you." She blinked what might be tears from her eyes.

"Okay, but I'm giving you a smoking deal."

Unable to resist, he reached out and cradled her cheek. She leaned into his palm, covering his hand with hers. They stood like that for several seconds. In some ways, the gesture was more intimate than their recent kisses.

She withdrew slowly. "I wouldn't be surprised if Gary's parked down the road, waiting for me."

Sam remained where he was, holding the box with the goshawk, until her vehicle disappeared behind the bend. Inside the Paydirt, he conferred with Will about the horses and hitched a ride back to the Gold Nugget with Emmett, the ranch's former caretaker. While the old man talked, Sam thought of other ways he could help Annie besides the door alarm.

Something about her day-care comment stuck. Not that he would seriously consider starting one. But Irma frequently brought one or two of her brood with her, and it didn't seem to cause any problems. The opposite was true, if anything. Lyndsey loved having playmates.

There was no reason Fiona couldn't bring Nessa to the ranch, too. And, as long as Fiona was there, she might be willing to pitch in.

Sam needed a guest-relations manager, one with experience. Fiona fit the bill better than anyone else in Sweetheart.

The more he considered offering Annie's mother a job, the more the idea appealed to him. And with Fiona and Nessa at the ranch, Annie might be inclined to stop by more often.

It was, he decided confidently, a win-win for everyone.

Annie sat at the stoplight and replayed the cryptic voice-mail message on her cell phone for a third time. Her mother sounded happy. Like her old self. That might have given Annie comfort if not for the message itself. She'd been concerned enough to leave work an hour early and drive to the Gold Nugget, where her mother was—this part really didn't make sense—employed.

Sam must have invited Nessa out for another pony ride, to make up for the one they'd missed the other day after the run-in with Gary. Annie's mother had merely gotten her words jumbled.

The light turned green and Annie accelerated, unable to shake the concern that had plagued her since she'd checked her messages while on afternoon break.

What could be wrong?

Nothing, she assured herself. Besides, this would give her an opportunity to see the goshawk and rest easy knowing it was being properly cared for.

She passed the inn, what was left of it. She had no choice. This road was the only one leading north out of town and to the ranch.

A hundred yards separated the inn from its closest neighbors on either side. Like the inn, the ice cream shop to the right had been burned to the ground. Luckily, the wedding chapel to the left, with its quaint rose gardens and pine gazebo, had escaped.

Sadly, all the weddings scheduled to take place in the gardens had been cancelled, the couples forced to choose other locations. Annie indulged herself, reminiscing about life before the fire.

Nearly every day, at almost any hour, she could pass by the chapel and catch sight of a ceremony in progress. Many of those couples, young, old and in between, strolled across the adjoining lawns to the inn, where they would begin their honeymoon.

Being a small part of such a big moment had brought joy to Annie, her mother and grandmother. So much, they'd dedicated their lives to it. She wanted that to happen again. To participate in people's happily-everafters. It was the driving force behind her rebuilding her family's legacy.

And silly as it may be, she believed her own happily-ever-after was also tied to rebuilding.

Annie wasn't sure how much longer the chapel owners could hang on. Their minister, a spry and delightful retiree, had moved away last week to live with his daughter in Utah.

On a positive note, she mused as she drove on, to her, Sweetheart was looking less and less like a ghost town. Nearly a third of the damaged homes had been repaired or restored. Another third were under construction, several of those thanks to Sam. The businesses, however, were another story. With no honeymooners and tourists booked, the owners saw no point in hurrying.

The opening of the Gold Nugget might change their minds. Except what would happen to all the wedding businesses if the returning tourists were only interested in the cowboy experience, as Sam put it, and not getting married?

She was half tempted to stop at the inn, check if there were any more treasures to unearth. Definitely not the book Granny Orla had been asking about the other day.

With a start, she realized she hadn't visited the site in nearly two weeks. Not since the day Sam had returned. When had her daily habit stopped, and why hadn't she noticed?

At the next corner, Wanda DeMarco flagged her down. Annie pulled to a stop and lowered the passenger window.

"Hey, Annie." The grade-school teacher grappled with a large plastic crate.

Wanda was both blessed and cursed. Though she'd

lost some of her students when their parents moved, school would start next month, right on schedule. Unfortunately, her home had sustained severe damage, and she'd been forced to move in with a fellow teacher.

"Need a lift somewhere?" Annie asked, leaning across the seat toward the open window.

"I'm fine. This isn't as heavy as it looks. And I'm just going over to the chapel."

"You sure?" The crate did look heavy, and Wanda's ample bosom was heaving with strain.

"Trust me, I need the exercise. Hey, listen, you have some items from the inn you've found, right?"

"A few."

"If you need a place to store them, the Yeungs have opened up the chapel's basement. That's where I'm taking these quilts. My great-great-great-grandmother brought them from Illinois when she and her husband traveled cross-country by wagon train." She hugged the crate closer. "I'm so grateful I got them out before the fire and that I have a place to store them until we rebuild."

"Most everything I've found from the inn is small."

"Well, just in case." Wanda's pudgy face glowed. "There's quite a collection accumulating. I swear, you look around that basement, and it's like seeing the entire history of Sweetheart all in one place. You should drop by."

Annie didn't know if her heart could take it. Too many bittersweet memories. Even so, she said, "Maybe I will. If you're sure I can't give you a lift—"

"Absolutely not. See you later."

"Wait, Wanda. Do you know of anyone offering day care?"

"Not off the top of my head. But you might call the school office. They keep a list of certified day care operators."

"Thanks for the tip."

Annie found herself gawking as she pulled into the ranch. Despite it having been only a few days, the changes were numerous.

The bunkhouse/guest rooms appeared finished, at least from the outside. The new flowerbeds flanking the front steps and the deep green shutters on the windows were a nice touch. The addition to the old barn had been framed, and the workers were starting on the siding and the roof. The exterior walls of an entirely new building had been constructed near the horse corrals. Annie assumed the building would house the tack room Sam had mentioned and possibly an office. The ancient barbed-wire fence surrounding the pasture behind the barn had been removed and replaced with a five-foot sucker rod fence, forming the temporary arena.

A small thrill of excitement coursed through her. It was really happening. Before long, Sam would have a fully functional guest ranch. And people would return to Sweetheart. She could think of nothing more wonderful.

Parking in front of the house next to her mother's sedan, she walked briskly to the front porch, smiling and nodding to the workers she passed. More than one she recognized as locals. Sam probably had no trouble finding extra laborers from the overflowing ranks of Sweetheart's unemployed.

Annie's intention was to locate Irma and ask where she could find her mother and Nessa. She wasn't expecting to discover Nessa and Irma's youngest playing on the parlor floor.

"Mommy, hi!" Nessa shot up and skipped over to Annie, giving her a hug.

"Sweetie pie, where's Grandma?"

Nessa ignored the question. "We're playing animal hospital."

A veritable zoo of stuffed toys was strewn across the hardwood floor, some "patients" swaddled in dish towels, other sporting toilet-paper bandages.

"That's nice. Mommy's going to find Grandma."

In the kitchen, Annie was greeted with a "You're here!" as her mother and Irma emerged from the walk-in pantry, Irma looking tall and ungainly next to petite Fiona.

"Mom, what's going on? I didn't understand your message."

"Sam offered me a job. As guest-relations manager." Her mother stood straighter. "I accepted."

"Wh-when did this happen?"

"Today. He said I could start tomorrow, but I decided to get a jump on things."

"Just like that?" Annie barely noticed Irma depositing her load on the counter.

"I didn't need any time to think about it. The pay is good, the hours reasonable, the benefits generous." She smiled at Irma. "I like the staff."

"Mom, you can't just take a job without talking to me first."

Fiona's smile waned. "I wasn't aware I required your permission."

"What about Nessa? And Granny Orla?" Annie

was thinking she'd need adult day care now as well as child care.

"Sam said they can come here for the meantime."

"You can't do your job and watch them." Her mother could barely maintain their small apartment while supervising the energetic and wily pair. Look what had happened a few days ago when Gary showed up unexpectedly.

"We thought we'd take turns," Irma interjected. "And there's my oldest. Carrie's in charge of the laundry. She can also babysit the kids. Until school starts, anyway."

Annie's head started to swim. "This makes no sense."

"It's only temporary," her mother assured her.

"Nessa and Granny Orla staying here while you work or the job?"

"Annie, we do what we have to. Right now, I need a job and we need the money."

She didn't stop to think how alive and engaged her mother appeared and how much vitality she exuded. Neither did she consider how necessary the extra income was. All she felt was the betrayal, like a spear to her heart.

Her mother had taken a job, made a decision that greatly affected Annie and Nessa and done it without talking to Annie first. Like Gary and the preschool. Did no one think her capable of caring for her child?

Annie glanced around the kitchen. "Where's Sam?"

"Last I knew he was in the barn."

"Keep an eye on Nessa for me. I won't be long."

"Darling, please."

Ignoring her mother, Annie kissed the top of her daughter's head on her way through the parlor, left the house and hastily covered the grounds to the barn in search of Sam. He shouldn't have offered her mother the job without discussing it with her first, and she was going to let him know that in no uncertain terms.

Chapter 11

Sam wasn't where she expected to find him, which was with the raccoon kits. Rather, he, Lyndsey and Irma's son Gus were at the chicken coop beside the barn. The coop holding the goshawk Annie had asked Sam to foster.

The kids crowded around him, watching him repair a hole in the coop door. As she neared, Annie realized Sam was actually instructing Lyndsey and Gus on how to hammer a nail. The two appeared to be taking turns. Cute and charming and typical Sam.

Once again, her anger at him dissipated. Well, not entirely. She was still going to give him a piece of her mind. Just with less vehemence.

Wrapped up in her thoughts, she almost tripped over the stray cat. It crouched on all fours in the high grass, tail twitching as it stared intently at the goshawk. The hawk, perched atop a stripped ponderosa branch inside the coop, was more interested in the humans and their loud banging.

Narrowly avoiding the cat, Annie said, "Sorry to interrupt, but do you have a second?"

"Hi." Sam glanced up. "Tweety Bird and I are glad to see you."

Tweety Bird must be the goshawk, his cartoon name courtesy of Lyndsey.

"It's about my mother."

"Sure. Give me a second." He resumed instructing Gus, pointing out where to place the nail. "That's it, buddy."

Gus struggled, the hammer too heavy for his small hands. Succeeding at last, he grinned broadly.

Sam rubbed the boy's buzz cut. "We'll make a carpenter out of you yet."

Gus gazed up at Sam as if he were king of the world.

Annie could relate. She'd recently stared at Sam with similar adoration.

"What's up?" He left the kids to their own devices and joined her.

Not wanting them to hear, she motioned him a few feet away. "You hired my mother."

His smile dimmed marginally, but the twinkle in his eyes remained. "Guilty as charged."

"Why?"

"I had an opening for a guest-relations manager. She has the experience."

"What about the inn? This morning I retained your architect and spoke to your contractor. We're moving ahead. The architect is starting on the drawings and the contractor's putting together a quote to clear the land."

"Annie, the same goes for your mother and Irma and Lester. They're free to leave as soon as the inn is up and running."

"Lester?" She blinked at him in disbelief. "You hired our maintenance man, too?"

"Didn't I tell you?"

"He's working for Valley Community Church."

"The job was temporary. They let him go last week."

"What! I—I didn't know."

"Being unemployed isn't something a man like Lester brags about."

What was left of Annie's anger deflated, like a sail without wind. Lester was a man of few means but an abundance of pride. Despite a mild mental disability, the result of a fall down an abandoned well as a child, he'd always supported himself. He was good, kind, sweet and loved by all. He was also a decent handyman and had worked for the Hennessys the past twelve years.

Of everyone who'd lost their job when the inn had burned, Annie felt the worst for Lester. Irma at least had her husband, and the others were only part-time or seasonal. Lester was alone.

"I'm glad you hired him. He needs to be working."

"So does your mother."

Sam was right. "I just wish you'd called me first."

"I assumed she'd discussed the job with you."

"This isn't only about her. I depend on her to watch Nessa while I'm at work. If she's going to be bringing Nessa here every day, I have a right to be part of that decision."

"You do. It was thoughtless of me to exclude you."

Annie exhaled slowly, not completely trusting his

sincerity. "Sometimes it seems like you're...undermining me."

"That's not my intention. I swear. I'm just being a friend."

"By offering my mother a job."

"I figured it would motivate Gary to lay off you."

"I'm not sure he'll be any happier with Nessa being underfoot here all day, passed off from one person to the next. I'm not sure I'm happy."

"It's short-term," he reminded her.

She should be relieved. Her mother having a job was a godsend. They'd have extra money to put toward new furnishings for the inn and a larger place to live, if one became available. Her mother would have purpose again, a reason to get out of bed in the mornings and face the day with anticipation rather than despair.

All because of Sam.

Except he'd gone behind her back. Probably because he suspected she'd object. Unless, as he claimed, he was being a friend to her and her entire family.

Was she so focused on herself and the inn that she dismissed the equally important needs of her loved ones? And her mother working did put them one step closer to their goal of rebuilding the inn.

"I'd better go, let Mom know everything's okay. She's worried."

"*Is* everything okay?"

She recalled the last time he'd looked at her with such uncertainty. He'd been twenty-two and leaving for the job in California. In between goodbye kisses, he promised he'd return soon and asked her to wait for him. She'd been twenty-four, deeply in love, desperate to get married and trying her best to put up a brave front.

In one short year, their love unraveled.

Annie had laid the blame on Sam. A bad marriage taught her much of the blame lay with her. Two people were necessary to make a relationship and two to break it.

"Yeah, it's okay," she assured him. "The job's a good fit for Mom. And Nessa will be here only on the days Gary doesn't have her. Next time, however—" she leveled a finger at him "—call me first."

"You got it." Sam grinned. "Before you go, take a look at Tweety Bird."

Annie owed him that much for taking in the hawk.

They went over to the chicken coop. If Tweety Bird was grateful she'd rescued him, he didn't show it and glared at her menacingly.

"Dr. Murry examined him yesterday," Sam said after warning the kids to stay out of the toolbox. "He thinks most of the injuries are superficial."

"Did he have an opinion about what happened?"

"Same as you. Attacked by a larger flying predator."

"Has he taken any food and water yet?" Annie asked.

"Raw sirloin's his favorite. Though he likes chicken, too. I assume he's drinking, though I haven't seen him do it. He keeps to his roost whenever anyone's around. Dr. Murry estimates a week, maybe two, and we can release him. I'm thinking of Grey Rock Point. The fire bypassed most of that area."

"I'd like to be there, if I can."

"Wouldn't think of releasing him without you." Sam glanced over his shoulder at the kids, then at Annie. "I owe you."

"For what?" It seemed to Annie quite the opposite was true.

"Your advice about Lyndsey. She's been lost since Trisha died. The animals, well, they've made a difference. A big one. She's becoming more like her old self every day."

"You did that entirely on your own, Sam."

"Spending the summer in Sweetheart has been good for both of us."

"How long until you leave?" She expected him to say in the next couple weeks, given that school started soon.

"I'm not sure." He shrugged one shoulder. "We may stay awhile longer."

"Stay? Are you serious?"

"Why not? I always figured on going back and forth. Lately, I've been thinking of more forth and less back."

"What about the ranch in California?"

"According to my father-in-law, the foreman's pulling his weight." Sam chuckled. "For all I know, he's after my job."

"And you're not worried?"

"I should be. I stole the last foreman's job." They both sobered at the reminder of nine years ago.

"Doesn't Lyndsey start school soon?"

"I could send her home. She'd probably hate that. For someone who completely resisted coming here, she really likes it. Gus may have something to do with that. I keep reminding myself they're too young for me to worry. They are too young, aren't they?"

The question was directed more to himself than Annie.

"Wouldn't you miss her if you sent her home?"

"Yeah. A lot. Better I enroll her in school here."

"Is the construction not going well?" A delay could be the reason for his sudden change of plans.

"It's going great. We'll be ready for our first guests next week."

"That soon!"

"Well, we have to get some reservations first. Our secretary at the ranch in California hired a website designer and is researching the best places to advertise. Mayor Dempsey also made some suggestions. She thinks we should have a grand-opening weekend. I told her we'd have to wait for the shipment of calves to arrive. The truck's due Monday, and we haven't even started construction on the livestock holding pens."

The mayor was giving Sam suggestions to promote his business? That shouldn't be a surprise. If successful, the Gold Nugget would be a boon to Sweetheart.

"Sounds like everything's coming together."

"Annie." Sam squeezed her arm. "What's really bothering you?"

"Nothing."

"You act like you don't want me to stay."

In truth, she did and she didn't. Sam had the ability to create as much chaos for her as calm. "I'm honestly not sure how I feel."

He moved closer. "Aren't you?"

"There's nothing between us, if that's what you're implying."

"You were never a good liar."

"Just because we shared a couple kisses—"

"Exactly because we shared a couple of kisses."

She shook her head and retreated a step. "We're not the same people we once were. Things have changed."

"I get that you haven't completely forgiven me for leaving you."

"I'm not holding a grudge," she insisted. *Not a big one.*

"You did start seeing Gary before we officially broke up."

The mild accusation annoyed her. "We went to lunch."

"Twice."

She resisted asking him who'd tattled on her. It didn't matter. "I hadn't heard from you in six weeks."

"So you executed plan B."

"It wasn't like that." Only it had been like that. Annie was terrified Sam had dumped her and that she'd wind up the next Hennessy old maid.

Perhaps she was still terrified and that was what held her back. He hadn't cut all his ties to California and could leave again.

"I was working my tail off, trying to get ahead. Saving up enough money for a ring."

"A ring?" The bones in her legs went weak. "Why didn't you tell me?"

"I was going to surprise you with it. Then I heard about Gary. And you were acting distant."

"I was hurt."

"So hurt you married him?"

"After you left. Almost a year after you left." She couldn't help sounding defensive.

"And I got married a mere four months later."

"To a woman who was pregnant with your baby." That was what hurt the most.

"I didn't cheat on you, Annie. I swear. We'd already split up when Trisha and I started dating."

"Barely just split up. You moved on at lightning speed."

"Why did you care? You were already seeing Gary."

"I wasn't seeing him. Not romantically."

"No, you just had him waiting in the wings."

"You make me sound awful when you're the one who deserted me."

"To take a better job. Isn't that what the man's supposed to do? Provide for his wife."

"I didn't need you to provide for me."

"No, you could provide for yourself just fine, thanks to your family's business. I'm the one who needed to make my mark."

Her deepest, darkest fear tumbled out. "I thought you were running away. That you didn't love me anymore."

"I thought the same thing when I heard about Gary."

The revelations, rather than bring them together, hung in the air like a poisonous cloud.

"Hey, Daddy." Lyndsey and Gus scampered over. "We're going to feed the kits and the goats."

Annie swallowed her reply to Sam. She wouldn't argue in front of the kids. She wouldn't argue any more with Sam, either.

"Thanks again for giving Mom a job," she said stiffly. "I'll see you later."

"I'd like to continue this conversation."

Another man wanting to "continue the conversation." She'd had her fill of them. "What would that accomplish other than reopening old wounds?"

She had just started toward the house when a car pulled into the driveway. Annie didn't recognize it, but then there were a lot of vehicles coming and going at the ranch.

The man waited at the walkway for her, and then asked, "Ms. Hennessy?"

"Yes?"

Her heart momentarily stalled. Had Gary made good

on his threat about revisiting their child custody agreement? Was this a process server? He was carrying a manila envelope. Why had she answered yes when he asked her name?

"Good to meet you." The man extended his hand. "I'm Dermitt Wilson."

The architect!

Relief flooded her. "Nice to meet you." She gripped his hand. Possibly too hard. "What are you doing here?"

"A last-minute meeting with Sam. I was hoping to find you and kill two birds with one stone." He handed her the manila envelope. "That contains preliminary artist renderings of the inn. I thought you might want a look before I finalize them and start drawing the plans."

Artist renderings. The architect's vision of the new inn, based on her description.

"Already?"

"I worked all morning. Your story inspired me."

Excitement coursed through Annie as she opened the envelope and drew out the heavy sheets of paper.

She couldn't believe her eyes. This wasn't the Sweetheart Inn. It was even more beautiful.

"What do you think?"

Sam studied the cabin floor plan the architect had given him. The design was simple and functional, yet attractive. He could easily envision his guests staying there and being comfortable.

"I like it."

"Good. See anything that needs changing?"

He pointed to the bathroom. "This looks a little small."

"I can enlarge it, but I'll have to reduce the size of the closet."

"Do it. Most women I know would appreciate a larger bathroom. And the closets only need to hold a week's worth of clothes."

Sam and Dermitt Wilson stood in an empty field at the Gold Nugget, each holding one end of the plans for the guest cabins. Dermitt, who usually wore nice slacks and a button-down shirt, had chosen jeans and athletic shoes for his second visit to the ranch in three days.

"How many cabins did you say you're going to build?" he asked.

"Six to start with." Sam had already hired the surveyor and the engineer. They were scheduled to begin work tomorrow. "Six more next spring if things take off."

"Do those six include your personal one?"

"No." Sam flipped to the next sheet, on which were the electrical and plumbing specifications for the guest cabins. He didn't pretend to understand them. "I still need to decide where to build."

"The hill over there is a good possibility."

Sam's gaze followed Dermitt's. The hill was separate from the guest cabins but not too far. Perfect for the three-bedroom deluxe cabin he was planning for him and Lyndsey.

Or should he change it to four bedrooms? Just in case.

In case Annie changed her mind about there being anything between them? According to their heated exchange earlier in the week, that was pretty unlikely. Especially when they hadn't spoken since then.

Better to stick with three bedrooms. For now.

The rumbling of a truck and stock trailer had Sam and the architect looking away from the hill and toward the ranch house. Will was walking out from the barn to greet the oversize rig.

"Appears my calves are arriving ahead of schedule," Sam said.

Fortunately they'd recently finished constructing the livestock holding pens.

Dermitt rolled up the plans into a tube and secured them with a rubber band. "I'll revise these to include a bigger bathroom and drop off a new set on Monday."

"Hate for you to make another trip up here just to deliver plans."

"No problem. I'll already be here. I have a meeting with Annie Hennessy to review the preliminary drawings for the inn."

He'd told Sam the other day how much Annie had liked his initial rendering, a smaller and more affordable version of the original inn.

The two men strode across the empty field, Sam in a hurry and Dermitt keeping up. At the house, they parted. Sam caught up with Will at the livestock pens. The driver was backing up to the gate Will held open.

"Need any help?" Sam asked over the loud chorus of bawling calves and idling diesel engine.

"You're welcome to watch."

If Will was half as good with calves as horses, all Sam would be doing was watching.

With the ramp lowered, the calves, eighteen in all, spilled from the trailer in a small stampede. They were a variety of longhorns and jerseys, their coats ranging from black to red to light brown. Finding the water trough, the calves immediately slaked their thirst and then investigated the feeders.

Will shut the gate behind the last one while Sam signed the bill of lading the driver presented him. The truck and empty trailer no sooner pulled forward than Sam and Will rested their forearms and boot soles on the pen railing and studied Sam's latest purchase.

"You order the dewormer and vaccinations yet?" Will asked.

"They're in the supply room."

"Tan one looks kind of puny."

Sam agreed. "Maybe we should put him by himself for a while. Till he grows some."

Will merely nodded.

"You set a time with that buddy of yours yet?"

They discussed Will's acquaintance with the used roping equipment for sale until Sam's cell phone rang. His pulse spiked at the name and number on the display screen.

"Hey, Annie. How's it go—"

"Sam, sorry to bother you." She sounded rushed and anxious.

"No problem. What's up?"

"I'm trying to find my mother. Is she there?"

"She went to the warehouse store in Reno for supplies."

"Shoot. She must be out of range. Every time I call it goes straight to voice mail."

"Is something wrong?"

"No. Yes, but I'll take care of it."

"Are you sure?"

"I am." After a pause, she blurted, "Actually, I'm not sure. I hate to impose."

"Tell me."

"Wanda DeMarco called me. She's one of the grade-school teachers. Granny's at the inn. I have no idea how she got there. Wanda tried to give her a ride home, but Granny refused and became agitated when Wanda started insisting. She actually ordered Wanda off the place. I'm worried. It's not safe for Granny there alone."

Sam didn't hesitate. "I'll leave right now."

"Are you sure? I can be there in an hour. If you could just check on her…"

"I'll call you from the inn."

"It seems I'm always thanking you," Annie admitted.

"I'm here anytime you need me."

They disconnected. Will waved Sam away when he started to explain the situation.

"I've got this covered, boss."

"See you later." Sam had no doubts the puny calf would be moved to a different pen and the entire herd dewormed and vaccinated by the time he got home.

Irma assured him she'd watch Lyndsey. Not that he could have pried his daughter away from Gus.

Fifteen minutes later Sam arrived at the inn and parked. He'd witnessed the ruins up close before, but the devastation rocked him anew. This wasn't some random home or building. It was a place where he'd spent endless hours for two years of his life with people he cared about.

Some of those hours in Annie's bed, making sweet love to her.

It was also a place that might have been spared had he disobeyed orders the day of the fire.

"Granny Orla," he called out, the heavy weight pressing on the inside of his chest making it difficult to breathe. Reaching the entrance to the inn, he called her name again.

Had she left between the time Annie phoned him and he arrived?

"In here," came a faint response.

He found Granny in what was once a sitting room off the lobby, on her hands and knees, digging through rubble.

"Be careful. You'll hurt yourself."

"I'm fine. Don't you worry." She was filthy from head to toes.

"Let me help you." He knelt beside her. "What are you looking for?"

"My book. It used to be on a shelf in this room."

All that remained was one exterior wall, the entire surface scorched black, and the floor, three feet deep in places with debris.

"I don't think it's here, Granny." He laid a gentle hand on her shoulder.

She sat back on her calves, the movement stiff as if her joints ached—or her heart had become too weighted with grief for her small body to carry.

"I'm not crazy."

"I know that."

"You look at me like Annie does. The same worry on your face."

"We care about you." Sam's voice had grown thick. He was responsible for this, too. Granny Orla had always been sharp as a tack.

"It's easier sometimes," she said softly, "not to face the real world. Sort of a mental vacation."

"I understand."

"I imagine you do." She looked at him directly without a trace of confusion. "Must have been hard losing your wife. A lot of guilt. A lot of regrets."

"More than you can imagine." Sam suffered a fresh wave of both.

"I always felt terrible about you and Annie. You both went off and married the first person you stumbled across."

Stumbled across. An interesting way to describe the start of his and Trisha's relationship. She'd certainly put herself in Sam's path, the second he'd returned to California after breaking up with Annie.

"I don't regret my marriage."

"Course you don't. You'd be a fool if you did. That's a beautiful little girl you have."

"As is your great-granddaughter."

"She's a dickens, all right. I think she takes after me."

"No doubt about it. A Hennessy through and through."

"I hope she's smarter than the rest of us." Granny Orla rolled something around in her hand.

Until the movement caught Sam's eye, he hadn't noticed. "You're all pretty smart as far as I'm concerned."

"Not when it comes to men. You've heard the rumors. Probably scared you silly when you were younger."

"I did want to marry Annie."

"Eventually. But you weren't ready, and she was in an all-fired hurry. Makes for a bad combination." Granny sighed. "She was bound and determined to escape the Hennessy curse. Problem was, she didn't have the whole story. Her father no more abandoned Fiona than her grandfather abandoned me."

"What happened?"

"We refused to go with them. They wanted us with a powerful passion, make no mistake. And us them.

But we couldn't leave Sweetheart. It was the same with Annie when you asked her to go with you to California."

"I did more than ask."

"She couldn't tear herself away. Not her fault. She inherited that same awful stubborn streak from me that her mother did."

"The thing is, we could have returned in a couple of years, once I'd saved up some money and gotten ahead in my job."

"She was impatient. And worried."

"That you and Fiona couldn't run the inn by yourselves?"

"Heavens, no." Granny Orla's smile was that of a young woman. "That she loved you more than the inn."

"I doubt that." His stomach tightened. "There isn't much Annie puts ahead of the inn."

Granny opened her hand, revealing a tiny blackened jewelry case. One corner had been rubbed clean, revealing the silver finish underneath.

In spite of its ravaged condition, Sam immediately recognized the case, and his chest constricted. It had once contained a heart-shaped pendant with an opal mounted in the center. He'd given the necklace to Annie for her twentieth-fourth birthday. Less than three months before he'd left.

"She kept this on her dresser always," Granny said, placing the case in Sam's hands. "Even after she married Gary. Don't think she told him where it and the pendant came from, but I'm sure he suspected."

"I can't take this. It belongs to Annie."

"I thought maybe you'd want to give it to her. She's accumulating quite a collection of things from the inn."

Sam balanced the case in his palm and carefully

opened the lid. It was empty, the velvet lining having been incinerated.

"The necklace was lost in the fire," he said. Emotions, raw and powerful, overtook him. He cleared his throat.

"Oh, it wasn't lost." Granny Orla's eyes lit up. "Annie has it. One of the first things she grabbed when we got the notice to evacuate."

Sam closed the lid on the case and folded his fingers protectively around it. Annie still had the necklace he'd given her.

No way could he leave Sweetheart now.

Chapter 12

Annie raced back to town the instant she could cut loose from work, dreading what she might find. Her grandmother was at the ruins of the inn again. With Fiona working, no one was home to watch Granny Orla or hear the new door alarm screeching.

Was Annie's life ever going to return to normal?

Not for a while, but tiny pinpoints of light had recently appeared at the end of the tunnel.

Gary hadn't backed down completely about revisiting their custody agreement. He had agreed, however, to give Annie a little more time when she told him about her mother's new job and being on the wait list for a three-bedroom house to rent—one with a small backyard for Nessa. If all went well, they could move the following month.

Though her mother still had her moments—didn't

they all?—she was much improved and left for work with a spring in her step. Annie had every faith that when construction started on the inn, Fiona would be her old self.

There were also the drawings for the inn, which the architect had promised would be done later this week. She couldn't wait. At least ten times a day Annie pulled out the renderings.

It was their old inn, but different. More functional with a nod to the modern while still maintaining the country charm of the original. Less square footage but designed for easy future additions. Most important, it could be built within their budget if they held off on replacing some of the original antiques.

She and her mother had settled with the insurance company earlier that week and were expecting a check in the mail any day. Annie was relieved. Signing the agreement had worked a sort of magic, allowing her to move forward emotionally.

She had to acknowledge Sam's part in her turn-around. Without a doubt the architect's *very reasonable* retainer and the construction contractor's *enormously fair* bid to clear the land were his doing. He'd done so much for her already, including rescuing her grand-mother today.

Annie hated admitting it, but for once she was glad Gary had Nessa for the day. At least Annie didn't have to worry about her daughter as well as her grandmother.

She would have to do something about Granny Orla and soon, Annie just didn't know what. There were no doctors in Sweetheart specializing in geriatric med-icine. No professional grief counselors or organized support groups. Only so much assistance available on the internet.

Several victims of the fire did meet regularly to talk and share and give each other strength. Annie had tried once to coerce her mother and grandmother into attending a meeting with her. The attempt was met with resistance. Maybe she should try again.

Several pieces of the yellow caution tape surrounding the inn had come loose from the metal posts and were fluttering in the summer breeze like party streamers. Annie didn't concern herself with refastening them. The construction contractor would remove the tape and posts in order to erect temporary fencing around the property.

Granny Orla and Sam were standing beside his truck, chatting amiably, when she pulled into the lot beside them. All that concern for nothing, Annie thought. Her grandmother looked fine.

Sam looked...mouthwatering. There were no other words. His jeans hugged his lean hips, his short-sleeved Western shirt stretched taut across his broad shoulders, his Stetson was pulled forward at a rakish angle.

Without thinking, she reached a hand up to the opening of her uniform shirt and felt for the necklace he'd given her. Lately, she'd been wearing it more often. If only she'd remembered to grab the silver jewelry case the necklace had come in during the evacuation.

"Granny," she scolded the second she got out of the SUV. "You can't just leave the apartment without telling anyone. And how in the world did you get here?"

"I walked." Granny's small chest puffed out. "And you're not the boss of me, young lady."

Not the boss of her? Where had her grandmother picked up that phrase?

"If you wanted to come here, you should have waited until I got off work."

"Like you'd have brought me."

Probably true.

"Why didn't you let Wanda give you a ride home?"

"Her car's always a mess."

Annie resisted expelling a tired sigh. "That's no reason."

"If I let Wanda give me a ride home, then this handsome man wouldn't have shown up to keep me company." Granny slipped her arm through Sam's.

Annie didn't know whether to laugh or cry. She turned to Sam. "You have an admirer."

"It goes both ways. We had a real nice talk before you got here."

"Oh?" Annie didn't like the sound of that and strove for nonchalance. "What did you two talk about?"

"Your collection of things salvaged from the fire."

Whew! That wasn't such a dangerous topic. "I saw Wanda the other day. She told me people have been storing some of their more valuable recovered possessions in the basement at the chapel next door. Especially those with historic significance. Apparently, there's quite an assortment."

"I'd like to see what's there. I bet a lot of people would." Sam sought her gaze and held it. "I'd like to see what you have."

"Nothing much." She laughed—a little too nervously. "A candlestick, a key, a padlock. I wish I could find more. They'll start clearing the lot soon. When the soil tests are complete." She forced herself to look at the ruins. "I should probably come back on my day off and go through this mess one last time."

"I'll help you."

"Me, too," Granny Orla added. "And Fiona. We'll make it a family outing."

Annie noticed that *Sam* noticed Granny had included him as part of the family. Was her grandmother having another episode?

She didn't think so. Granny had always adored Sam and had probably hoped he'd be her grandson-in-law one day.

He held out his hand toward Annie. "In the meantime, you can add this to your collection."

She stared at the jewelry case, everything inside her going still. "When did you find that?"

"Granny Orla did. Today."

"I can't believe it. I thought I'd lost this forever."

"Maybe there's a reason Granny found it when she did." He waited for her to take the case.

She did, cupping it in her palms. "Thank you." The case felt warm. Sam's heat, she realized. Now seeping into her.

Tears filled her eyes as another piece of her former life was returned to her.

"Amazing something that small and delicate could come through the fire intact," he said. "Well, almost intact. The velvet lining was burned away. But there was bound to be some damage."

"I suppose." She traced the intricate scroll pattern on the lid with her fingertip as she'd done countless times, always thinking of Sam when she did.

He watched her. "With some cleaning and a little repair, it'll be as good as new."

He was likening them and their relationship to the jewelry case. Did that mean he thought they had survived their painful pasts, superficially damaged but intact underneath, enough to forge a new relationship?

Even if she did want a relationship with Sam, it wasn't what she needed. Not until the new inn was built and they'd moved to the new house. Her family and their welfare had to come first.

"I don't know about the good-as-new part," she said. "It's going to take a lot of cleaning and polishing."

"I'm good at cleaning and polishing."

Resisting the pull of his blue eyes was impossible. Against her will, she was drawn into their depths.

He had her, and his half smile told her he was well aware of it, too. If she could, she'd grab hold of her shirtfront and shake some sense into herself. Instead, she murmured, "We'll see."

"I'll buy the silver cleaner."

"I have some already."

"Then we're good to go."

Shivers traveled up her spine.

This couldn't be happening. She blinked in an effort to clear her head. Sam wasn't going to divert her from her plans. Not again.

"Wonderful idea!" Granny Orla beamed. "Come to breakfast on Saturday. After you finish cleaning the jewelry case, we'll all come here."

"I accept," Sam said before Annie could protest, his smile widening.

She could put up a fight but chose not to. It was only breakfast after all. And cleaning the jewelry case.

"We can look for my book."

The spell Sam had cast promptly broke and reality returned. "Granny, I don't think your book is here."

"Won't know for sure unless we scour the place."

"All right," she relented. "Saturday it is."

Granny preened with satisfaction.

Humoring her, Annie asked, "What's so important about this book anyway?"

"How else can I remember what the inn was like before the fire?"

"We'll never forget the inn." She squeezed her grandmother's shoulders.

"None of us will," Sam agreed.

"My memory's not what it used to be. Having something tangible to hold on to will make remembering easier. The new inn won't be the same."

"True. But it'll be nice." Annie had shown her family the artist rendering. She assumed Granny had loved it, too.

"Won't be the same," she repeated to herself, and straightened her spine. "Which is why I've decided to retire."

Granny Orla's announcement wasn't entirely a surprise. She'd frequently kidded about retiring. This time, however, she spoke with a ring of conviction that left no doubt. Annie's hopes of running the newly rebuilt Sweetheart Inn with all three Hennessy women working side by side were soundly dashed.

Sam nudged the large buckskin into a lope, and they circled the makeshift arena at an easy pace. The horse, Will had called him Cholula, responded well to Sam's commands. Obedient and strong, but with a touch of spirit and a mind of his own. Exactly the kind of horse Sam liked to ride.

Reining Cholula to a stop at the fence where Will stood, he said, "Tell your buddy I'll take him."

"Already did."

"You were that sure?"

As always, Will's casual shrug spoke volumes. He had Sam pegged and had matched him with a horse he was confident Sam would like.

"Did you also negotiate the price on my behalf?"

"Talked him down as far as he'll go."

Sam nodded approvingly at the amount Will cited. "Let's keep him in the barn until the new stalls are finished next week."

"Luiz is already laying down fresh sawdust."

Will was quickly becoming indispensable. Good thing. Sam needed reliable staff to cover for him during his visits to California.

His father-in-law had taken the news of Sam's decision to make Sweetheart his home base better than expected. He'd made only two requests during their hour-long phone conversation the previous night: that Sam allow Lyndsey lengthy visits during summer vacations and holidays and that he return home for a few weeks to wrap up any loose ends and walk the new foreman through preparations for the fall cattle roundup.

It wasn't too much to ask, and Sam readily agreed. His one problem was what to do about Lyndsey and school, which started soon. He'd debated his options long into the night when he should have been sleeping.

Lyndsey would have to come home with him, there was no other choice. Her grandfather would want to see her and she him. But a few weeks was a lot of school to miss.

If she returned to Sweetheart early, who would she stay with? Irma had enough of her own children to worry about. Annie didn't have the room. Sam wasn't comfortable leaving Lyndsey with anyone else.

He didn't want to think about the raccoon kits. They'd have to be surrendered to the wildlife refuge before he and Lyndsey left, and she'd be heartsick.

He decided to call his father-in-law back tonight. If they could arrange for a tutor in California and home-school Lyndsey during their visit, she could resume public school here in Sweetheart when they returned and not have to work so hard catching up.

With one problem potentially settled, Sam dismounted, his test drive with Cholula at a satisfactory end.

"Have you ridden the west ridge yet?" he asked Will on their walk to the barn.

"Yesterday afternoon."

"And?"

"First mile's clear."

"But the next ten miles aren't."

Will's nod confirmed Sam had come to the correct conclusion.

"How long to get the job done?"

"A week. With enough men and the right equipment."

An expensive undertaking. Also a necessary one if Sam wanted safe and navigable trails for his guests to ride.

"What about the terrain?"

Will became even more quiet than usual. "Folks won't be raving about the view anymore."

Not about its beauty, anyway. "Is the north side any better?"

"I'll ride out there tomorrow."

They continued their discussion inside the barn while Sam unsaddled Cholula and settled him in the stall next to the pony. The big gelding made himself right at home, apparently liking Sam and their future prospects together as much as Sam did.

On their way to the cattle pens, Sam's and Will's attention was drawn to an official-looking SUV pulling onto the ranch. Sam caught the county sheriff's logo on the driver's side door just as it opened and a uniformed man stepped out. Mayor Dempsey accompanied him.

Sam grinned as he strode forward to meet the law-enforcement official. "I thought the citizens in these parts were smarter than to elect you sheriff."

"I'm surprised you had the nerve to show your face here after all these years," Cliff Dempsey answered, just as good-naturedly.

They shook hands, Sam noting the strength in the other man's grip. He and Cliff had been acquaintances when he lived here before. Cliff had worked part-time at the Paydirt for his aunt while Sam had been a ranch hand. Then, Sam had left for California and Cliff enrolled in the Vegas Police Academy.

Sam hadn't seen Cliff since his arrival in Sweetheart. When he asked, he'd been told Cliff was in Ohio, helping his cousin and her children return home after a messy divorce.

Apparently, he was back on the job, for he produced his citation book from his back pocket.

"Did I commit a violation?" Sam asked as Cliff produced his citation book from his back pocket.

"Not you. Your construction contractor. Is he here?"

"At the corrals. We're building new stalls. Can I ask what he's done?"

"Illegally parked his trucks in town."

"Hmm. Don't suppose you could cut him some slack. It's for a good cause."

"I have. Up till now. But Miranda Staley's sworn if I don't do something, she'll file a complaint against me. And given that the election's next year..."

"I get it. Do your job." Sam decided not to argue, and simply reimburse the contractor the cost of the ticket. Also warn him to avoid parking in front of Miranda Staley's house.

"Can't really blame her," the mayor added. "She has five residents in her elder-care group home. Getting them in and out and around is challenging enough without having to navigate fully loaded construction vehicles."

The mayor waited with Sam while Cliff sought out the construction contractor and performed his duty.

"This place looks fantastic." Her smile reflected the admiration in her voice. "How soon until you open?"

"I was going to stop by the Paydirt on my next trip to town and deliver the good news. We've got our first reservations. Three, actually."

"Oh, my God! That's wonderful." She threw herself at Sam, surprising him and nearly knocking him off his feet. "When do they arrive? And are they getting married?"

"'Fraid not." He peeled her gently away. "The first guests will be here mid-August."

"That's less than two weeks away!"

"They understand we're still remodeling, but they

don't care. They're husband and wife wildlife photographers. On assignment to take pictures of the animals and their habitats post-fire for some nature magazine. The other two reservations are for families. Their kids want to learn team roping."

"We don't have much time."

"For what?"

"A grand opening."

"The ranch? I'm not sure—"

"The whole town." She gestured wildly. "We'll call it a reopening."

"Mayor Dempsey, with all due respect, I don't think three reservations are enough to warrant a grand opening."

Her features fell, then immediately lifted. "But you'll have more. This is only the beginning."

"The beginning of what?" Annie asked.

Sam had been so preoccupied, he'd missed her arrival, not that he was expecting her. She must have parked at the house and stopped to check on her mother and daughter first. Whatever the reason, he was always glad to see her.

He'd spent half the day with her on Saturday at the inn ruins. Fiona and Granny Orla, too. It might have been the company. Or the difficult and emotional task of sifting through a ton of debris with very little to show for it. Possibly Granny's nonstop talk of retirement. But there had been no special moments between him and Annie. Not like when he'd given her the jewelry case.

"We have our first reservations," he said, studying her face and gauging her reaction.

She didn't reveal much. "That's great. Congratulations."

"I was saying to Sam," Mayor Dempsey injected,

"that we should have a grand reopening. For the entire town. We can promote the event, use it to entice even more tourists." She gasped excitedly, her hand flying to her chest. "I know, we could run a contest. The first couple to marry in Sweetheart after the fire can have a free week's stay at the Gold Nugget."

"Seems a little premature," Annie said.

Sam didn't think he'd ever witnessed a flatter smile. "I agree. We only have three rooms available."

"But there's the RV Resort," the mayor continued. "That place was hardly touched in the fire. Well, except for two of the cabins. They're gone. But four cabins are left and all those RV parking spots. And the Mountain-side Motel. They have twenty rooms."

"I'm sure it'll be very successful."

Mayor Dempsey was too caught up in her idea to notice Annie's forced enthusiasm.

Not Sam. His goal was always to help the town and bring back the tourists. He just hated that they wouldn't be staying at the Sweetheart Inn. Annie must hate it, too.

Cliff returned, his citation book stuffed in his back pocket. His aunt immediately launched into the news about Sam's reservations and the town's grand reopening.

"I'm going to take a peek at the kits," Annie told Sam, excusing herself. "Is Lyndsey in the barn?"

"She's with the kits or the goats or the hawk. Just look for Gus. Wherever he is, you'll find Lyndsey."

After Annie left, he escorted Cliff and his aunt to their vehicle. The two men made plans to meet up for a beer before Sam's trip to California. He had just seen the mayor and sheriff off when the contractor strolled over from the horse stalls, waving the citation.

"I'll take care of that," Sam assured him.

"No worries. My fault. We're working on the house next door to Ms. Staley. I should have verified with her before blocking her driveway."

Sam liked the construction contractor. A few years older than Sam, Chas had an easygoing demeanor that was the complete opposite of his nose-to-the-grindstone work ethic.

"Is there a problem?" Sam asked.

"I noticed Annie Hennessy arrived. We have a meeting."

That explained her unannounced appearance. "She's in the barn with my daughter."

They found Annie by the kits' cage. Alone. Lyndsey and Gus must be elsewhere.

She was sitting on the floor, Porky cradled to her chest, and furiously wiping at her eyes with the hem of her shirt.

Sam felt the blow like a kick to his stomach. He'd hoped he was through with making Annie cry.

Chapter 13

"You're here." Annie returned Porky to the cage and stood, greeting Sam and the construction contractor. "That didn't take long. The mayor must have been in a hurry."

"You know how she gets." Sam's tone was apologetic.

"I didn't see Lyndsey or Gus." She hadn't looked, either. Glad to find the barn empty, she'd let the unexpected tears fall.

The Gold Nugget Ranch was hosting its first guests. A dream that had once been hers. Now, it belonged to Sam.

She was glad for him. Glad for the town. Mayor Dempsey was right in suggesting there be a celebration.

Annie was also jealous. Her envy reached every fiber of her being. The Sweetheart Inn should be the reason people flocked to town.

Adding salt to the wound, the ranch was where her

mother was now employed, along with the Hennessys' former housekeeper and maintenance man. The place where her daughter spent many a day under her grand-mother's care while Annie was at work.

More and more, her life was revolving around the Gold Nugget. She should be grateful, and she was. That didn't lessen her anguish, however.

"Nice to see you again, Chas." She mustered a smile for the contractor, hoping he hadn't noticed anything amiss when he came into the barn.

"A pleasure, Annie."

She avoided looking at Sam. His concerned expression would break down her hard-won resolve.

"I was wondering, could Chas and I use your kitchen table to go over the drawings? The one at the apartment is too tiny."

"Of course." Sam nodded to both Annie and Chas. "I'll leave you to your business. The back door to the house is open."

"Would you..." Annie decided she was certifiably crazy but asked anyway. "Would you mind joining us?"

His brows rose. "You sure?"

"I could use another opinion, and you have far more experience when it comes to construction than me."

"I wouldn't say that, but I'd be happy to sit in."

Fiona, Irma and all the kids, including Lyndsey and Gus, made themselves scarce, cleaning or playing in other rooms. Chas unrolled the drawings and laid them out on the large oak kitchen table while Sam and Annie took seats across from each other.

Her mood instantly improved. In fact, it soared. "Wow!"

The floor plans were on top: basement, ground floor

and second story. She loved, loved, loved the design. Spacious, yet efficient. Chas pointed out the areas where even more money could be saved. Replacing some of those antiques might actually be possible.

"It's perfect," she exclaimed when Chas was done explaining the supplemental pages.

"I glad you like it." He grinned at her praise.

"What's our next step?"

"Keep the drawings. Go over them for a few days or a week. Something may occur to you, a change you want to make. In the meantime, we clear the lot."

"How soon can we start?"

"As soon as the soil tests are completed. Here's a proposal from the engineering company."

Annie glanced at the document. "What will the tests show?" She wondered how different residential testing was from the ones she'd been running in the field over the last several weeks.

"General condition of the soil. Rate of erosion. How stable it is. How much contamination."

"Contamination?"

"The inn was old, constructed long before modern building codes were in place. There could have been lead-based paint and treated wood. Any number of things. When a house or building burns, those toxins seep into the soil."

"And if the soil's contaminated?"

"We treat it."

"What does that involve?"

He made the process of removing the soil, treating it and then replacing it once it was decontaminated sound simple.

Annie suspected the opposite was true and remained skeptical. "That sounds expensive."

"I won't lie, Annie. It isn't cheap."

"How much?" She braced herself. What had started out so well was going rapidly downhill.

Sam reached across the table and put a hand on her arm. "You've come this far. You can't rebuild without clearing the land, and you can't do that without having the tests. Might as well get them over with."

"Just so you know," Chas said, "the tests we've done on other properties in town have shown normal or low levels of toxicity. Unless your inn was constructed with vastly different materials, it should have the same results."

Both men sat watching her, waiting for her to decide. She clicked the pen over and over.

Sam was right. If she didn't consent to the tests, the inn would definitely never be rebuilt.

"Where do I sign?"

Chas pointed to the engineer's proposal. Her fingers trembled only briefly before she scrawled her signature across the bottom line.

"Here you go."

He placed the proposal inside his portfolio. "We'll get started right away."

"Thank you." Annie felt fresh tears prick her eyes. These ones were of joy. She'd taken another step to regaining her old life and finding her happily-ever-after.

She escorted Chas to the back door. Sam was about to leave with him—Chas had asked him to inspect the foundations for the new guest cabins that had been poured earlier—but Annie stopped him.

"Do you have a minute?"

"Sure."

Sam had always been the impetuous one, though Annie was eager to follow his lead and usually glad she did.

Today, she took the initiative.

The moment the door was closed behind Chas, she reached for Sam and pulled his head down to meet her hungry lips.

His stupor didn't last. Within seconds, he had her pinned against the door.

"What was that for?" he asked when they paused long enough to catch their breath.

She arched into him. "Does it matter?"

"Hell, no," he said, and resumed kissing her with a passion that left no doubt as to his desire for her—or hers for him.

"Are you sure Tweety Bird will be okay?"

"He'll be fine, honey."

Early Saturday morning, and Sam was taking the goshawk into the mountains to release him. Lyndsey and Gus were along for the ride. They sat in the rear seat. Annie rode up front with him, brightening his mood.

Tweety Bird was in the truck bed, closed inside a spare dog crate Annie had procured. He wasn't in a good mood. But he would be soon.

"What if he gets hurt again?" Lyndsey asked.

"He won't."

"You can't promise that."

Annie shot him a you-should-know-better look.

"You're right," he admitted. "I can't."

Lyndsey had been pestering Sam nonstop since Dr.

Murry pronounced Tweety Bird healed and ready for reintroduction into the wild. She was convinced the hawk would meet with misfortune again.

"Tweety Bird is used to living in the mountains," Annie told her. "He's not happy in a chicken coop."

"But we take care of him. We give him raw hamburger."

"He misses flying. He misses hunting for his food. He misses other goshawks. He misses his home." Her demeanor gentled. "Sometimes, wild animals are so miserable in captivity that they let themselves waste away and die. You wouldn't want that."

Sam glimpsed his daughter in the rearview mirror. Her small chin trembled.

Dammit. Maybe he should stop the truck and give her the reassurance she longed for. His poor daughter dreaded loss of any kind, the reminder of her mother's passing too terrible to bear.

He had just started tapping the brake when Gus reached over and gripped Lyndsey's shoulder. "You can't keep Tweety Bird forever. You gotta be tougher."

"Okay." She sniffed, and then nodded. The next instant, the two of them were sharing the pair of earbuds and listening to Lyndsey's MP3 player.

Sam quietly fumed. That was it? One micro pep talk from Gus and Lyndsey was fine. He glanced at Annie. The corners of her mouth quirked with suppressed amusement.

He cut his eyes to the rear seat and muttered in a low voice, "Should I be jealous?"

She laughed then, warm and rich enough to cause a familiar stirring inside him. "You're her dad. No one will ever replace you."

"Right." He wasn't reassured. Gus had wormed his way into a place in Lyndsey's heart Sam thought belonged exclusively to him.

"You can't keep Lyndsey forever," she said, echoing Gus. "You gotta be tougher."

"But she's only eight. Surely I have a few more years."

"They'll go quickly."

"That's what I'm afraid of."

"Me, too."

They shared a look, a slight brushing of their fingers across the seat. It wasn't their first that day. Or even their first that week. Something had changed recently. Sam recalled the exact moment. It was when Annie had kissed him in the kitchen after her meeting with the contractor. She'd finally let down her defenses.

Thank God.

"I swear I won't let Lyndsey lead Nessa astray." He squeezed Annie's fingers again just to reassure himself they were wrapped in his.

"Nessa's a spitfire. I'm more afraid of her leading Lyndsey astray."

The road gently curved as they climbed the mountain to Grey Rock Point, the place Sam had chosen to release Tweety Bird. The peaks, lush and green, rose up from the ground as if only recently born of the earth, their vibrant color brilliant against a clear blue sky.

If Sam stared at the pristine peaks long enough, he could almost imagine that the fire never happened. With a turn of his head, the illusion was lost. The valley lay below, a scarred wasteland.

Guilt widened the hole in his gut. Would he ever get over it?

A short time later they reached Grey Rock Point and began searching for a place to pull safely off the road and park. When he lowered the tailgate, Tweety Bird greeted him by beating his newly healed wings against the inside of the dog crate.

Sam pulled the crate forward, then donned the thick leather gloves Dr. Murry had recommended he wear for protection against the hawk's sharp talons. "He must know what's about to happen."

Lyndsey tried to peer inside the crate. "I wanna help."

"Careful, honey." Sam eased her back. "We don't know how's he's going to act. He might try to bite you."

Dr. Murry had recommended placing a hood on Tweety Bird. Sam tried his best to find one, but there were no bird hoods in Sweetheart. Annie helped with the release by cracking open the crate door while Sam reached in and grabbed Tweety Bird the way the vet had shown him, taking care not to reinjure him.

The hawk squawked and pecked at Sam's hands— and might have done serious damage if not for the gloves.

Sweat formed on Sam's brow. Getting the hawk out of the crate was definitely harder than getting him in. The instant Tweety Bird sensed the outdoors, he started struggling. Sam barely held on. Then, he couldn't anymore.

The release was far less spectacular than those he'd seen on nature documentaries. He nearly dropped Tweety Bird and was swatted in the face several times with a flapping wing before the hawk managed a clumsy liftoff.

Tweety Bird hung suspended in front of them for several endless moments, gathering the wind beneath his wings. Inch by inch, he rose straight up until he hovered ten feet above their heads.

"Awesome," Gus said.

Well stated, thought Sam, shielding his eyes from the glare of the sun.

All at once, Tweety Bird caught an air stream and rode it higher. Before flying away toward the peaks, he executed two perfect circles.

"Look! He's saying goodbye," Sam said, waving his arm.

"He's saying thank-you." Lyndsey's voice wobbled. "He did want to be free."

Sam knelt and wrapped his daughter in his arms. She returned his hug with all the strength in her small body.

"I love you, Daddy," she whispered.

"Love you, too."

Sam felt a sudden bump.

Gus had wrapped an arm around him and Lyndsey both. "Group hug." Did the kid have to insinuate himself everywhere?

Gus motioned to Annie. "What are you waiting for?"

She bent down and joined them, her arm sliding over Sam's shoulders. All right. He supposed the kid did have his uses.

The mood was considerably more jovial on the drive home.

"Daddy," Lyndsey asked, "when can we visit the wildlife refuge?"

His daughter was ready to give up the kits, too? This was real progress.

"Whenever Annie can take us." He cast her a glance.

"Maybe next weekend. Nessa would probably like to see it, too."

Lyndsey and Gus promptly began making plans.

"You miss Nessa?"

At Sam's question, Annie became quiet. "It's not so hard during the week when Gary has her. I have work to keep me busy. The weekends are tougher."

"Is he still bringing up the custody agreement?"

"Not lately. If the rental house doesn't come through, however, that could change."

"Call me if you get stuck."

"I can fight my own battles, Sam."

"I know you can. But you don't have to."

Her reply was a noncommittal sound. But then, a minute later, she reached across the seat for his hand.

Sam hoped Gus wasn't getting any ideas from watching them and checked the rearview mirror. The boy was wisely keeping his mitts to himself.

When they stopped to drop off Gus at his family's mobile home, Irma made an unexpected offer.

"The day's young. Why don't I watch Lyndsey and you two go for lunch or something?"

Or something?

Sam turned to Annie. "I'm game if you are. Unless you have other plans."

"I don't," Annie answered.

His pulse quickened. "Hungry?"

"Not yet. I was thinking…"

Sam was thinking, too. Probably not the same thing as Annie. "What's that?"

"I haven't been horseback riding in ages."

Riding. Okay. That was doable. "Are you sure?" he asked Irma. "Lyndsey can be a handful."

"What's one more?" Irma shooed them away. "Have fun."

After wrangling a hug and kiss from Lyndsey, Sam left with Annie for the ranch. When he aimed the truck in the direction of the barn, Annie stopped him.

"Actually, if it's all right with you, instead of riding I'd like a tour of the house."

"You've already seen it."

"Not the upstairs. Not the new furniture." She paused. "Not your bedroom."

Sam hit the brakes, harder than he intended. Gravel shot out from beneath the tires.

"Whoa, cowboy," she joked.

He turned toward her, resting his arm on the steering wheel. "Sorry. When you said you wanted to see the upstairs, I immediately..." He faced forward. "Never mind."

"Tell me."

"I'm a guy. You mention anything to do with upstairs and bedrooms, and I get ideas."

"What kind of ideas?"

"Ones that involve you and me and the shades drawn."

"Mmm." She nodded as if deliberating a weighty matter. "Well, can I still see the upstairs?"

"Sure." He turned off the engine and hopped out, capping his overactive imagination.

Annie went ahead of him up the walkway to the porch, where he unlocked the front door. He had only just closed the door behind them when Annie spoke from the bottom of the stairs, her voice low and seductive enough to turn a man's blood to fire.

"Just so you know, when I mentioned seeing the bedroom, I was having ideas, too. About you and me and the shades drawn."

Sam gulped. Then he crossed the room to her and didn't stop until they were toe-to-toe, eyes locked.

Extending her arm, she opened her hand and let her purse drop to the hardwood floor. The thud went straight to his pounding heart.

"Annie." He had to be sure. "This isn't a game for me."

"Me, either." Her chest rose and fell sharply, drawing his attention to the V opening of her shirt and the necklace he'd given her. It rested above a hint of cleavage that had enticed him all morning.

"I want you, make no mistake." He was desperate to touch her. Dying to touch her. Yet, he waited. "I have from my first day here when I saw you standing in this very spot."

"What's stopping you?" She lifted her mouth, everything about her going soft in an unspoken invitation.

His body responded with a will of its own, awakening after a long and dreary dormancy.

"I need to know. Why now? What's changed? I've chased you from day one, and you've resisted me at every step."

She averted her gaze, her expression endearingly shy.

He did touch her then. One finger. Under her chin. And tilted her face toward him. "Tell me."

"Tweety Bird."

"The hawk?"

"When you released him, it was as if something inside me was released, too. I realized I can't let the past rule me anymore."

Sam kissed her then, pulling her into his arms and

aligning the entire length of her body with his. She responded with a needy moan that turned him instantly hard.

Upstairs. To his bedroom.

He was distracted the next second when his hands found the hem of her shirt and slipped beneath it. Her skin was warm. No, hot. He fitted his palms to her ribs, and then covered her breasts. She rewarded him with a languid sigh of contentment, her nails digging into the flesh of his shoulders.

She inhaled sharply when he abandoned her mouth to taste her neck. "Show me the new bedroom furniture."

Another minute, and he'd have made love to her on the stairs. "My pleasure."

Hand in hand, they climbed upstairs. At the top, he lifted her into his arms, only to set her down at the doorway to his room. She would have to take the last steps on her own.

"Nice." She smiled approvingly. "How's the mattress?"

"Better than the sagging, creaking sack of rags that used to be in here."

"Good." The look she sent him was utterly devilish. "Show me what I've been missing the last nine years." Yanking her shirt over her head, she entered the room and crossed to the bed. There, she unsnapped her jeans and shimmied out of them. "Care to join me?"

Sam didn't need to be asked twice. He was not only going to show her what she'd been missing the past nine years, he intended to give her a preview of what lay in store for them the rest of their lives.

Chapter 14

Annie had let Sam make love to her.

No, not let him. She'd *initiated* it. In broad daylight. At the Gold Nugget. What had she been thinking?

Only that it was *so* worth it.

She stretched luxuriously across the mussed bed-sheets, her limbs still humming from the delicious sensations he'd evoked in her. She and Sam may be guilty of a ton of mistakes, but this wasn't one of them.

"Hey."

At the sound of his voice, she rolled slowly over and greeted him with a lazy smile. "Hey to you, too."

He walked across the room and set two glasses of ice water on the nightstand. "Miss me?"

Oh, yes.

"Wait." She stopped him before he slid into bed with her. "I want to look at you."

Sam had spent several long minutes taking in her naked form earlier. Annie wanted her turn.

He was gorgeous. Broader and more muscled than he'd been as a young man. The dark patch of chest hair was thicker. She'd tested its density by sifting her fingers through the springy curls. His hands, though calloused, were gentle when they'd explored her intimate places and capable of bringing her intense pleasure.

He was also a more patient lover, savoring the journey rather than rushing to its conclusion. She appreciated that last change the most.

He studied her as she gazed her fill, and his body hardened in response, letting her know they weren't done. Annie was all ready for round two. Just not yet.

"Come here." She opened her arms.

Sam must have sensed her desire for closeness and not sex. He lay beside her and wrapped her in his embrace.

"When are you going back to California?" she murmured into his neck.

"What? How did you—"

"Lyndsey told me. She's excited."

"You're not mad?" He brushed her hair with his lips.

"It's a visit. And you have to go, your father-in-law needs you." Unlike the last time, Annie wasn't worried. He was coming back. She knew it and didn't stop to question him.

"Come with me."

"I…" She shut her mouth, considering her options before answering.

Was there any reason she couldn't go? Her refusal the last time had been their undoing.

"For a long weekend, maybe. If I can get the day off work."

"Bring Nessa."

"She'd probably love to see a real live cattle ranch."

Annie sighed and wriggled closer to him. Like that, simple as pie. If they had made these kinds of compromises nine years ago, they might never have broken up.

No purpose in playing the what-if game. They were here now, together. *Very* together.

Soon, construction would begin on the inn. Annie would move her family to more spacious living accommodations. One that allowed pets. And there was Sam.

The pinpoints of light at the end of the tunnel had grown into spotlights.

"You hungry?" Sam asked. "I could make lunch. Throw some sandwiches together."

"Mmm. Tempting." She reached between them and took hold of his erection, which instantly swelled. "More tempting."

He groaned. "You're distracting me."

"That's my plan."

"It's working." He pressed her into the mattress, covering her entire length with his body.

His mouth came down on hers, and she lifted her hips to meet him. Like that, they were lost in each other, unaware of the world around them.

So much for lunch.

Afterward, Annie drifted off, the most content she'd been since before the fire. Sam must have fallen asleep, too, for at the sound of a loud banging on the front door, he suddenly jerked and then sprang out of bed.

"It's Mayor Dempsey's car," he said from the window, and quickly snatched his clothes off the floor.

"You could ignore her." Annie pushed up onto one elbow.

"When has the mayor ever given up easily? She'll drive over to the construction site and find Chas. He knows we're in here."

The knock came again. Louder this time.

"You're probably right."

"Wait here." Fully—and hastily—dressed, Sam gave Annie a quick kiss and hurried downstairs.

She abandoned trying to nap after five minutes. Dressing and freshening up in the bathroom, she debated what to do next. It wasn't as if she and Sam had anything to hide. No reason for her to remain secluded upstairs.

Even so, she took the stairs slowly and quietly, wincing each time a step creaked. At the bottom, she noticed Sam had picked up her purse from the floor and hung it on the banister. Voices, Sam's and the mayor's, drifted through the house from the kitchen. They were discussing reservations—Sam had received several more apparently. He hadn't mentioned that to Annie. The mayor was obviously excited and telling him about her ideas for the grand reopening celebration.

"I was thinking, the couple who wins the contest would be guests of the entire town. They'd stay here, get married in the Yeungs' wedding chapel, and we'd host a reception at the Paydirt. All free of charge."

"It sounds great."

"If all goes well, the couple would bring along their family and friends. And the publicity will generate more tourists. I have connections all over the state. TV stations, newspapers, professional organizations. I'll get them to spread the word."

"Count me in."

"I knew you'd say that," the mayor gushed. "Sam, you're the best thing to happen to this town in years. Decades."

"I wouldn't go that far." There was an odd quality to Sam's voice.

Annie wondered if he was thinking of the fire and the orders he didn't disobey. She continued toward the kitchen, only to halt at the mayor's next words.

"I'd go that far and more. The Gold Nugget is the new heart of Sweetheart."

What was Mayor Dempsey saying? Annie's family's inn had always held that honor. And would again.

Pain, razor-sharp, sliced through her.

"Mayor, it isn't," Sam insisted.

"Don't be so modest."

Spinning on her heels, Annie raced back upstairs to the bedroom.

Sam found her perched on the end of the mattress ten minutes later, staring into space. The distant sound of a car engine let her know the mayor was leaving.

"I didn't think she'd ever stop talking." He sat beside Annie. "Though some of her ideas are actually good."

"I heard." She lacked the courage to look him in the face.

"You did?"

"I came downstairs and overheard part of your conversation. I wasn't eavedropping."

"Why didn't you join us?"

Finally, she met his gaze. "She called the ranch the new heart of Sweetheart."

Sam let out a long breath. "She did do that."

"Apparently she's unaware construction on the inn is starting soon."

"You know how the mayor is." He took her hand in his and rested both on her knee. "She was in politician mode. Rallying the troops. She wasn't thinking about what she was saying."

"Or, it's what she believes."

"Annie girl. Please. Don't let her upset you. It's not worth it. You'll rebuild the inn, and it'll be full of guests. Six months at the most. Not everyone who comes to Sweetheart will want to stay at a working cattle ranch."

He was right. But the mayor's slight still stung like a betrayal. Another deserter on a growing list of deserters.

"Instead of letting her get to you—" Sam released her hand to cup her cheek "—prove her wrong. When construction's done, she'll be coming to you, begging you to include the inn in her latest promotion scheme."

She would, too. The design was wonderful.

"I'm being childish," Annie confessed.

"No, you're not." He kissed her, a light brush of his lips across hers. "And, truthfully, I should have defended you more. I got derailed by her excitement. She has that effect on people."

"The contest is a good idea. For you, for the town, for everyone."

He kissed her again. By the third one, Annie was mostly over her hurt. She had only herself and her family to worry about. Mayor Dempsey had the entire population of Sweetheart, and she would do what was best for them.

Besides, Sam had a point. The Hennessys' turn to

reign over Sweetheart would come again. Annie would count the days.

"How 'bout I buy you that lunch before I take you home?" he asked.

"Anyplace but the Paydirt. Yes, I'm being petty."

"Who cares if you are?"

She laughed then, her mood mostly restored.

Rather than dine out, they decided on making sandwiches. Annie fixed a quick salad to round out the meal. Chopping lettuce and tomatoes and setting the table went slow with Sam constantly interrupting her for a kiss or a squeeze from behind.

They were chatting over the last bites when her cell phone rang, the chime carrying from the parlor.

"Do you mind?" She was already rising from the table. "It could be Gary. Nessa was fighting the sniffles when he picked her up yesterday."

"Don't worry about it."

The call had gone to voice mail by the time she fished her phone from her purse. She read the number as she returned to the kitchen, her brow knit in confusion.

"Everything okay?" Sam asked. He was carting the empty dishes and plates to the sink.

"It's the architect. Why would he be calling me on a Saturday?"

"He's in town today. At least, he was earlier. Consulting with a new client."

Annie listened to his message. "He says to give him a call when I have a minute."

"Go ahead. I'll finish the dishes."

Annie hit Redial, an unexplained anxiety squeezing her middle. She had no reason to assume the worst, yet she did.

The architect picked up almost immediately. "Hi, Annie. Hope I didn't interrupt your day off."

"Not at all." She pulled out a chair and slid into it. "What's up?"

"I have the soil test results. The firm emailed me a copy late yesterday. I apologize, I've been so busy I didn't check my account until now."

"How do they look?"

"Is there a chance we can get together today?"

His tone put her even more on edge. "What's wrong?"

"It might be better if we discussed this in person."

"Please." Her fingers tightened on the phone. She was aware Sam had come over to stand by her. "I have to know."

"The results aren't good. There are high levels of contamination. The soil can be treated, but it'll be expensive and time-consuming."

"How much?"

"Hard to say for certain without getting a quote from the engineer."

"Give me a rough estimate."

The amount he stated was more than a third of the entire insurance settlement.

"I can deliver a hard copy of the report when we meet."

She barely heard the rest of what he said. It was lost in the thick fog that had come from nowhere to swallow her.

"There are government grants you can apply for," Sam said.

"We've already looked into those. It's a paperwork nightmare and takes forever. Plus, there's no guarantee."

"Might be worth it." He glanced over at Annie.

She stared listlessly out the passenger side window of his truck, avoiding him. She'd avoided him since the architect delivered the devastating news about the soil test results.

Déjà vu.

She'd been like this before, withdrawing into herself. The first had been the night he told her he was taking a job in California. The second, when they broke up for good a year later. He wasn't sure he could handle a third time.

At some point, Annie had to trust him completely. Trust them. If she didn't, their chances of making it were slim.

"Let me pay for the soil treatment."

Indignation flashed in her eyes. "I won't take your money."

His *late wife's* money, as she'd pointed out. "I wouldn't expect you to. Consider it a loan."

"No."

"You can pay me interest."

"I'll figure this out on my own."

"That's just it. You don't have to. We can be in this together if you let me."

"It's not together if you're pulling all the weight."

He turned onto her street and parked in front of her apartment. Annie bailed out of his truck. So did Sam. He followed her inside even though no invitation was issued.

"I didn't mean to insult you," he said.

"You didn't."

She threw her things down on the coffee table and gave a huge sigh of exasperation. Or, was it despair?

The apartment was empty, and Sam was glad for small favors. Annie would talk more openly if they were alone.

He took out his cell phone and called Irma, asking if Lyndsey could stay a little longer. Annie watched him during the entire conversation, not hiding her misery.

"I know the results weren't what you expected," he said, disconnecting from Irma.

"You think?" She folded her arms protectively across her middle.

She might have turned her back to him but he went over and placed a hand on her shoulder.

"We can figure this out. It's going to take a little longer, sure, and a little more money. But, it's not impossible."

"Why does everything come down to money?" She pulled away from him and flung herself onto the sofa, covering her face with her hands. "I hate wallowing in self-pity."

"You have a right to wallow." He sat down beside her. "Let me help."

"Stop saying that," she snapped. "You can't fix everything by whipping out your checkbook."

Silence hung between them. Lingered.

"Not everything." Reining in his impatience, Sam broke the lull. "But I can make this right. What's the difference between borrowing money from me and from a bank?"

"I don't sleep with the bank."

"Wow." Stunned by her insensitivity, he sat back, telling himself her remark was a product of her frustration and disappointment and not a stab at him. "I didn't make the offer because we're lovers. I made it because we're friends. Because I care."

She scrubbed her cheeks. "I do appreciate it even if I sound ungrateful."

"Then take it."

"I can't."

"The money's not Trisha's. It's mine."

"Try and understand." She shook her head. "I've lost so much these last few months. I'm hanging on by a thread, and that thread is mighty fragile some days. You, on the other hand, have it all. As if you're scooping up everything I've lost. My dream of owning the Gold Nugget. My mother. Our former employees." Her posture sagged. "The Hennessys' place in the community. Imagine how that makes me feel."

"Imagine how I feel. All I've done is try to help you, and your response every single time is to throw it back at me. As if my offer's worthless. I don't deserve that."

"You don't." She grimaced and pressed her palm to her chest. "I'm hurting, Sam, and I'm afraid I won't ever stop."

"Mayor Dempsey shouldn't have said that about the ranch."

"But she did, and it's true. You're practically single-handedly bringing this town back from the brink of extinction." She straightened, though it wasn't with determination. "Sometimes I think the universe is trying to send me a message. I shouldn't rebuild the inn."

"If you won't borrow the money from me, then let me cosign a bank loan with you."

"Why do you want to help me so badly?"

"I told you. To put the settlement money to good use."

"You can't buy off guilt, Sam."

Another stab, this one a direct hit in the heart. "Is that what you think I'm doing?"

"Kind of, yeah."

He tensed. "I didn't cause the fire. And even if I'd disobeyed orders, I couldn't have prevented it from ravaging Sweetheart. Not alone or even with my crew. You helped me realize that."

"I wasn't talking about the fire."

"Leaving you when I did, then. Okay, I could have done a better job delivering the news about taking the job in California. Called more frequently. Returned for visits."

"That, too." Her look implied he'd yet to hit the nail on the head.

"Trisha."

"Let's face it. You and I, we weren't the best of spouses. We married for reasons other than a deep and abiding love, which should be the only one. You feel responsible for Trisha's death. It's obvious when you talk about her. Her death and Lyndsey losing her mother. And I feel responsible for my failed marriage."

"I have guilt. Who wouldn't? Had I been a better husband, a more devoted husband, a more attentive husband, she wouldn't have strayed. Not been in that car when the drunk driver plowed into her at thirty miles over the speed limit." Sam hadn't realized how loud his voice had risen until it echoed back at him from the walls.

"It's noble of you to spend the settlement money on others," she said. "And generous."

"But not noble if I spend it on you. Then it's…something else. A payoff for services rendered."

"I'm probably too independent for my own good."

Sam's temper snapped. "I'm so tired of hearing you say that. You, your mother and your grandmother wave your independence like some banner of glory when what you really do is use it as an excuse not to get close to the men who love you."

"That isn't true."

"No? Look at all three of you. Love has to be on your terms or not at all."

She shot to her feet. "If you're trying to convince me to take the loan, you're doing a terrible job."

"I've done everything, bent over backward for you. Hell, put you before my own daughter and father-in-law, the best friend I have. It's still not enough. For God's sake, Annie, what more do I have to do to prove myself? Until you stop punishing me for leaving you?"

Shock widened her eyes. "I'm not punishing you."

"Sure seems like it."

She hugged herself, and in that instant, she looked as young as her own daughter. "I'm scared, Sam. How do I know you won't leave again?"

"Lyndsey loves it here. I'm not taking her away."

"And you?"

"I love it here, too, Annie."

If she read between the lines, she gave no indication. "You're returning to California."

"For a month at the most."

"You could change your mind. You've done it before."

Anger surged inside him. He removed his hat and threw it on the coffee table next to Annie's things. "I'm at my wit's end. I don't know what to do. I admit it, I screwed up when we were younger. But you have to quit holding it against me."

"And you have to quit holding my one mistake against me. I lost faith in you, and I did start seeing Gary while we were technically together." ·

He shoved his fingers through his hair, taking a moment to compose himself. "I understand you're going through a rough patch. Been there, done that."

"Losing everything is a lot more than a rough patch."

"Which is why I've tried to help."

"Sometimes it feels like your offers are just your way of placating me."

"What?" That was the furthest thing from his mind.

"You don't think I should rebuild the inn. I can tell."

"I think you should reconsider, yes. Especially in light of the soil contamination. Especially when you don't have to rebuild."

"I do have to rebuild. For my family. You know that. They're *all* I think about. I've made every sacrifice for them."

Sam couldn't believe they'd gone from making incredible love just two hours ago to an all-out blowup. Yet, they had.

"At least you still have your family," he said. "Given the choice, I'd have sacrificed my home and job for Trisha any day. For Lyndsey's sake."

"This isn't a game of comparing who's lost the most or who's the most miserable."

"You're right. That was low of me."

"We need to stop squabbling and act like adults." She rubbed her cheeks and sighed heavily. "What if we've rushed into this…you and me…too quickly?"

"Are you saying you want to take a step back?"

"I'm saying, instead of Nessa and I flying out to California, maybe we should use the time you're away to reevaluate. You might decide to stay there after all and be a long-distance owner of the Gold Nugget."

"What do you want?"

She didn't answer right away. When she did, she was probably the most honest she'd been since they started arguing.

"What if I never get my old life back? What then?"

"The new one might be better."

"I have so little left. I can't take that chance right now."

Was *he* so little?

"You're pushing me away again, and I'm tired of it, Annie."

"I might be doing that. And not to play the comparing game again, but your loss is older than mine and your recovery time longer. I'm still grieving and I'm not ready for you to come in here and rescue me like some knight in shining armor. I've got to heal on my own."

Annie didn't want him. Not in her corner. Not in her life.

"Guess I'm wasting my time here." He rose and grabbed his hat. Yes, he was acting surly by walking out. Still, he couldn't stop himself. "I have to pick up Lyndsey. I'll see you later. Let me know if you need anything either before I leave or while I'm gone. But we both know you won't ask."

"Sam." She reached for him. "Earlier today, it was the most incredible day I've had in…years, I guess."

She waited till now to tell him?

"Goodbye." He didn't look back as he left the apartment. If he had, she'd see how completely her rejection devastated him.

Annie wasn't the only one who'd had the most incredible day in years.

For Sam, it was also one of the worst.

Chapter 15

Annie dropped to the ground amid the rubble that had once been her home, her life, her security.

Her first love.

Sobs racked her entire body. At last. She'd staved them off for months, refusing to yield even when the fire officials delivered the news that the inn was gone. Especially then. Hard as it was, she'd maintained control. For her family, for her friends in town and for herself.

Now, tears fell freely into the hands that covered her face. An outpouring of pain, for which there seemed no end.

Was she being *too* independent, as Sam had accused during their fight? So much so that she pushed people away? Sabotaged any chance she and Sam—she and anyone—had for a relationship?

Oh, God. She was.

With her grandmother's bouts of confusion, her mother's depression and her daughter being completely dependent, Annie had seen no other alternative than to bear the entire weight of their misfortune alone.

And she hadn't forsaken that burden for anything. Including a future with Sam.

One week. A decade-long week. Without even a single glimpse of him. What if she'd accepted his offer to loan her the money for the soil treatment instead of refusing?

She'd be here now, rejoicing. Preparing to move into a new place. Not falling apart.

Annie didn't lose everything in the fire. But she had now.

Not lost. Thrown away.

According to her mother, Sam and Lyndsey were departing for California in a matter of days. He'd return but Fiona said it would be without Lyndsey. Sam was making his home base in California instead of Sweetheart.

History was repeating itself, all right. Annie had pretty much guaranteed that. Fresh tears fell.

She didn't try to stop them. This crying jag was long overdue. Eventually, however, it subsided. Only because she ran out of energy. Wiping her eyes, she realized she was kneeling in one of the few bare patches the engineering company had left behind after the soil tests.

Contamination. Due to toxins. The hardwood floors her grandmother had commissioned to be built and the chemicals used to treat them would be responsible. Plus asbestos in the basement and attic. With a building as old as the inn, there could be countless other culprits, like lead paint and fertilizer in the storage shed.

She covered her face with her hands. What now? She had no choice but to hire Chas's construction company to clear the land. The debris couldn't be left to rot indefinitely. It was a health hazard as well as unsightly. And guests staying at the Gold Nugget...

The reminder of Sam's success launched a fresh wave of misery. She was happy for him. Happy for the town. Happy for the people he'd employed, including her mother.

Annie had kept her family fed, clothed and sheltered. But it was her mother who'd enabled them to improve their standard of living. Thanks entirely to Sam.

Really, Annie was happy. Even though anyone stumbling across her at this moment would think differently.

"Hello! Annie?"

"Over here." She quickly used the hem of her uniform shirt to blot her cheeks, then finger combed her hair.

"There you are." Granny Orla poked her head through the opening that had once been the inn's front door. "Are you all right? You look awful."

"I'm fine."

"Have another run-in with Gary?"

"Not at all."

"Must be Sam then."

"Why do you automatically assume it's Sam?" She hadn't mentioned anything to her family, preferring to avoid their questions.

"I've seen that look on your face before."

"What are you doing here?" Annie removed her sunglasses from her shirt pocket and donned them. "And who brought you, by the way?"

Her first visit to the inn in two weeks, and she'd been interrupted by her grandmother. What were the odds?

A hundred percent, apparently.

"I came to look for my book."

Oh, that again. Granny's fixation with her phantom book was growing old. Annie wasn't in the mood today. "Where's Mom?"

"At home with Nessa."

"She didn't bring you?"

"Heavens, no. She's fixing dinner. A real dinner. Pot roast. Been nice having her take an interest in cooking again. Fiona's a culinary genius. Don't know where she got it. Certainly not from me. Maybe her father. Though that man never fried an egg or toasted a piece of bread that I ever saw. But, Lord, he was a handsome devil."

Her grandmother was rambling again.

"Granny, don't tell me you walked here."

"Certainly not. Irma's daughter gave me a lift."

"Carrie only has her learner's permit. Was Irma in the car, too?"

"Irma's at the chapel. Helping Wanda with sorting through all the things they've collected. Have you been there lately? The basement is crammed to the ceiling in some places."

Annie refused to be sidetracked. "Granny, Irma's daughter can't drive without a licensed adult in the car with her."

"I'm a licensed adult."

"You haven't driven for five years."

"I don't think that matters."

There was no reasoning with her. "Come on, let's go."

"Not till I find my book." She started across what had been the lobby, picking her way carefully and with surprising agility for a woman her age.

"Fine. I'll help." With no other option, Annie accompanied her grandmother. "Where's the last place you remember seeing it?"

That ought to be a trick question.

Only her grandmother didn't hesitate. "On a shelf in the sitting room."

Their private rooms had been on the first floor. Fiona's was off the kitchen. Granny Orla had used a small room near the downstairs bathroom. The sitting room was adjacent to that. Annie started out, the mountains of debris not hindering her in the least. She instinctively knew the layout of the inn.

"This is where the sitting room was."

Nothing recognizable of it remained. Any furnishing or contents were buried beneath tons of wreckage from the second story and the roof.

"Oh, dear."

Annie spun at the sounds of distress coming from her grandmother. The older woman was trembling. Her hands covered her mouth, and her eyes were red and moist.

She went to her grandmother, who looked to have shrunk in the past few minutes, and rubbed her back, praying she wouldn't drift off into confusion. If she wasn't already halfway there.

"Don't worry yourself," she assured Annie. "I'm fine."

"If your book's here, there's no way we can find it."

"We certainly can't find it if we don't look."

Annie resigned herself to digging through the muck and mess. For a little while.

"Let me get my gloves and a shovel from the SUV. I don't want you touching anything while I'm gone. You hear me, Granny?"

"I'm not deaf."

Granny, of course, went right ahead with her search,

touching everything. When Annie returned, she found her grandmother bent over, attempting to lift a heavy plank and, Annie was convinced, give herself a heart attack.

"Wait. Let me do that."

Granny ignored Annie, demonstrating that the Hennessy stubborn gene had originated with her.

Annie forcibly removed the plank from Granny's hands, lifted it and shoved it aside. The plank fell with a mighty thud, shooting clouds of black ash into the air.

Granny gasped, and then coughed. Annie covered her nose with her arm. If only she'd brought face masks. They worked for twenty minutes, discovering an old watch, completely useless, various TV components and an antique oil-lamp base that was in reasonably decent condition.

"I'm tired, Granny, and it's getting late." Annie leaned on the shovel for support. Every bare inch of her skin was coated in grim. "Let's call it a day."

"What's this?" Granny Orla knelt, lifted the end of what looked like part of a metal shelving unit and reached underneath.

"Granny, stop. You'll hurt yourself."

"I think I found it!"

Impossible. "Trust me, nothing made of paper and cardboard could survive this." She gestured with her hand.

"Help me," Granny implored.

Annie seized the shelving unit. After this, they were out of here. Even if she had to drag her grandmother kicking and screaming. She was too physically and emotionally exhausted to continue.

If only Nessa wasn't with her father this weekend. Annie craved the special comfort her daughter provided.

"Lord Almighty," Granny exclaimed, tugging on a bulky object. "It's my book."

She couldn't have found it. Annie heaved the shelving unit aside, which made a terrible clatter when it fell. Then she went over to her grandmother—who did indeed hold a large square object.

Annie removed her sunglasses and stared, unblinking. Granny let out a wistful sigh and cradled the book to her bosom.

No, not a book. A photo album. And it appeared intact! How could that be?

Slowly, Annie lowered herself onto the ground beside her grandmother, a strange sensation coursing through her.

"What's in it?"

"Our history."

Granny cracked open the cover on the photo album. Charred flakes fell like snow. Though the outside was badly burned, by some miracle, the inside had sustained little damage.

Memories returned. Annie vaguely recalled seeing this album when she was a child but not since. She'd all but forgotten its existence.

Not her grandmother.

Granny Orla turned page after page. A few of the photographs were scorched. Others merely discolored and their corners curled. Some were almost like new. Could the metal shelving unit have protected the album from the flames? It didn't seem possible.

Yet, here was the proof.

The pictures told the story of the inn, and with it, the Hennessy women. The first ones, over fifty years old and in black and white, were of the wooded lot before construction started. Someone, Annie assumed her grandmother, had taken photos of the inn during each stage. It grew from a plain cement foundation to the building she'd lived in most of her life.

There were pictures of Annie's mother as a child with Granny Orla. Pictures of Annie as a child with her mother. Men Annie didn't recognize.

"Who's that?" she asked, her throat scratchy.

"Your grandfather." Granny Orla gazed at the brown-edged photograph with tenderness. "I told you he was a handsome devil."

Had she loved him? Annie always assumed her grandmother's affections belonged to the star of *The Forty-Niners*.

"Why did he leave?"

"Why do they all leave? We drive them away."

"Mom told me my dad didn't want to settle down. That, according to him, he had to be free."

"He was a wanderer. Like your grandfather."

"Like Sam, too." Annie hadn't noticed the similarities before.

"Sam isn't anything like them. I've yet to meet a more devoted family man."

"Now maybe."

"Always. You were just three steps ahead of him and unwilling to wait."

Granny Orla's words hit home. "I'm not sure I've changed."

"We all change, sweetie. And we have to move on. Can't stay in one place forever."

She handed over the photo album. As Annie's fingers made contact with the cover, a chill ran up her spine, and she was once again overcome with amazement.

"I'll carry it to the SUV for you."

"No." Granny covered Annie's hands with hers. "I want you to keep it."

"Granny!"

"I know you'll take good care of it."

"But it's yours."

Granny shook her head. "You're trying so hard to rebuild the inn. Sacrificing so much. More than you should. More than you need to. Have you ever asked yourself what's driving you?"

"The inn is our legacy. It's been in our family for fifty years. I want to pass it on to Nessa."

"Annie, this is your legacy." She squeezed the album. "The Hennessy spirit. We are strong women. We are fighters. We make fulfilling and wonderful lives for ourselves despite all odds. Nessa will, too."

"I suppose I could have the photographs restored and framed."

"I hope you will. But isn't there more you can do with them?"

Another chill ran up her spine. She'd been so focused on rebuilding the inn, she'd missed out on what was really important.

"Maybe. Yes, there is more I can do." She stood and reached out a hand to her grandmother. "Let's go."

"Where?"

The universe had been sending Annie a message. She was finally listening.

"To the chapel."

Annie's first inclination was to chew out Irma for letting her daughter drive Granny to the inn. But the moment they entered the chapel basement, her mind emptied…

…and her heart filled.

Besides Irma and her daughter, Mayor Dempsey was there, along with Wanda and the school principal.

"Can you believe this?" The mayor's gaze traveled the room.

"No." Annie walked a narrow makeshift aisle, the photo album resting in the crook of one arm. "Where did it all come from?"

"Most of it was either saved by the owners or pulled from wreckage. They had nowhere else to store it so they brought it here."

There wasn't a single piece of junk in the place. Each item, from the rooster weather vane that had sat atop the Millers' house and the Welcome to Sweetheart, Nevada sign posted at the town limits, stirred a fond memory.

"I have pictures," she stammered. "Of the inn. Some of them are really old."

"How lucky you saved them."

"We didn't." Annie held the album out for the mayor's inspection.

"We found them," Granny Orla supplied. "Just now. In the ruins."

Mayor Dempsey frowned in puzzlement. "How is that possible?"

"I don't know." Annie nudged open the cover. "Look for yourself."

The mayor wasn't the only one impressed. Everyone crowded close.

"Amazing!"

"Incredible."

There were more gasps of surprise with each turning of the page.

"A metal shelving unit apparently fell on top of the album. It must have shielded it. Granny..." Annie stopped. "How did you know?"

"I had a hunch." She winked. "I'm not as confused as everyone thinks I am." She certainly wasn't acting disoriented anymore.

"What are you going to do with all this stuff?" Annie left the album with the mayor as she perused the room. She let her fingers graze the front of a circular saw blade the size of a tire, wary of its deadly teeth. The saw blade had hung on the wall in the Lumberjack Diner, a reminder of the days when ponderosa pines were harvested to build homes. The Gold Nugget Ranch. Her family's inn. The diner had contained many artifacts from the town's early days. All gone.

No, not all. In addition to the saw blade, Annie recognized an old anvil and a sledgehammer. Pieces of history, reminders of what the town had been like before it was crippled. They deserved to be preserved.

The chills that had started at the inn grew stronger.

"Problem is, we can't keep everything here," Wanda said, looking to the school principal for confirmation. "The Yeungs need the space, what with the tourists starting to return."

"Is there anywhere else you can use for storage?"

Wanda shook her head sadly. "You know what a premium available space is in Sweetheart. It's a shame, too. For some, these items are all that's left of their home or business."

Like Granny's photo album and the other small treasures Annie had recovered from the inn ruins.

"If there was only some way to preserve everything for posterity," Annie mused. "Where everyone could view them."

"Don't forget the pictures." The mayor closed the album and returned it to Granny. "I have dozens of the town, going back every bit as far as these and further. I even have a tintype of my great-great-great-grandfather. He was one of the original settlers in Sweetheart."

"There's the photographs at Sam's ranch, too," Irma added. "Of *The Forty-Niners* show."

Interesting how the Gold Nugget had become Sam's ranch. He was now an integral part of the town, and he probably didn't realize it. If he did, would he change his mind and move here permanently?

"We need a place," the mayor reflected. "A central location."

"What if we convert one of the old empty buildings into a museum of sorts." *The Sweetheart Museum,* Annie thought.

The Sweetheart Memorial!

An homage to the town before the fire. Surely, there were many, many more antiques and artifacts people had saved or salvaged. Things they'd be willing to donate in exchange for safekeeping.

"Why not?" Her question was met with a roomful of blank stares.

"Where would we locate an old building?" the mayor asked.

"Annie." Granny Orla came closer. "What's going through that head of yours?"

She smiled at her grandmother. "The inn."

"Display all this at the new inn?"

"No. Build the memorial on the site of the inn." She quickly calculated the numbers in her head.

After covering the cost of the soil treatment, there would be enough money left over from the insurance company to construct a simple structure. Perhaps reminiscent of the original inn. Glass cases could be designed for the more fragile pieces, like clothing and china. Wooden stands for the hardier ones.

The more her idea took hold, the more her excitement mounted. Words tumbled out in a rush as she tried to explain.

"My God, Annie," Mayor Dempsey said when she was done. "What a marvelous undertaking."

"But would tourists really care about our history and what the town was like before the fire?" the principal asked.

"It wouldn't be for the tourists," Annie insisted. "Not entirely. It would be for us. So our children could learn about their heritage and what their parents went through. Why we fought tooth and nail to save this town."

Granny Orla gripped Annie's hand firmly in hers. "Are you sure? You've had your heart set on rebuilding the inn."

She couldn't explain it. She only knew that constructing a memorial on the former site of the inn was the right course.

"I'm sure, Granny. But it's really up to you. The deed's in your name."

"I can't think of a better or more fitting use for that land."

Granny Orla's eyes weren't the only damp ones in the room. Even Irma's daughter was a little emotional.

The group stayed and brainstormed for another half

hour, until well after dark. It was agreed they'd form a committee, headed by the mayor, and individuals were recommended for recruitment. Annie and her family would be in charge of the construction, and the memorial would be dedicated to the Hennessys. Mayor Dempsey wouldn't hear of anything else.

When Annie and Granny Orla left, they took the album with them. They would have the photographs restored as best as possible and framed. In the meantime, Annie wanted to show the album to Nessa.

She was too young to understand its importance. Someday, however, she would. And she'd carry on the Hennessy legacy, like her mother, grandmother and great-grandmother before her.

Chapter 16

Sam was still in Sweetheart. Eight days since he'd last seen Annie. Since their blowup.

Why hadn't he left for California yet? The fall cattle roundup was scheduled to start next week, and he'd promised his father-in-law.

Easy. He didn't want to go without seeing Annie.

Running out of excuses and unable to keep stalling, he'd instructed Irma on what to pack. He and Lyndsey had visited the wildlife refuge the day before and surrendered the raccoon kits. His poor, sweet daughter had cried the entire way there and the entire way back. And he feared the worst was yet to come.

As much as she loved her grandfather, she didn't want to leave Sweetheart. Not forever. The prospect of future visits didn't lessen her misery.

Sam stood on the front porch, watching Gus and

his younger siblings play a game of tag. Lyndsey sat off to the side, distancing herself. Par for the course. Between the kits and moving soon, she'd been moping round the clock.

Beyond them, in front of the barn, Will led a group of five guests on the ranch's first official trail ride, the horses walking nose to tail. Their destination: observing the sunset from Potato Hill.

Sam indulged in a moment of self-satisfaction. His goal of owning a working guest ranch had become a reality. Reservations weren't exactly pouring in, only a handful each week. That would change soon.

The heart of Sweetheart.

He'd never imagined stealing that title from Annie and her family. Never wanted it. When he objected, the mayor persevered. Promotion was well underway for the free wedding and reception and advance interest was exceeding expectations. Annie had to be hurting.

He'd heard from Irma who'd heard from Fiona that Annie was burying herself in her work. Just like when the inn had burned. Her family was worried. Sam, too. He'd talk to her if he thought it might help, but he doubted she'd take his call.

Was that the only reason he hadn't checked on her? Hell, no.

Avoidance was a tactic he'd relied heavily on after Trisha died. A tactic the grief counselor warned him against.

"Hey, kids," Sam called, interrupting their play. "Time for evening chores. Who wants to help?"

"Me, me!" It was Gus, not Lyndsey, who answered.

Sam strolled over to her. "What's wrong, honey?"

"Where's Annie?"

"Probably at work. Why?"

"Why didn't she come with us to the wildlife refuge? She said she would.

"She's busy."

"She hasn't been here for days." Lyndsey's voice was ripe with accusation. "You and she had a fight."

"Who told you?"

Her glance went straight to Gus. Sam glowered at him.

The boy wasn't intimidated. "My mom blabbed. Ms. Hennessy figured it out."

Fiona.

Sam groaned. "Let's talk about this later, okay?"

Lyndsey acted as if she hadn't heard him. "It's not fair. She was my friend, too. And you messed it up. Now we're leaving, and I won't ever see her again."

Oh, boy. He hadn't seen this coming. "I'm sure Annie will visit if you ask her."

"No, she won't. She's mad at you."

"She's not mad." Not exactly.

Gus shook his head disgustedly.

Sam refused to defend himself to a pair of eight-year-olds.

"How could you?" Lyndsey demanded, her fists clenched at her sides.

What he heard was, *How could you make another mistake? Drive another important person away? Wreck my life?*

"It's complicated, honey. And hard to explain."

"You don't have to explain it to me. You just need to make up with her. Tell her you're sorry. So we don't have to move back to California."

"We're not moving because Annie and I had a fight. Your grandpa needs me for the fall roundup—"

Lyndsey stormed off to the barn, Gus and his siblings hot on her heels.

Sam remained, rooted in place. Could he make up with Annie? Did he want to? He certainly didn't like the way they'd left things.

An empty lumber truck drove past the house and down the drive, having unloaded its shipment. With the cement foundations on the new cabins poured, framing had started. Before long, two months at most, Sam and Lyndsey could reside in their deluxe cabin. For a visit.

Or longer. Lyndsey did love it here. Sam, too.

But Annie might not want him living in Sweetheart full-time. A town this size, bumping into each other was inevitable.

Maybe he should hunt down Chas at the construction site and pump him for information. Soil treatment at the inn had started. Sam noticed the equipment and temporary fencing that morning when he'd driven past en route to the general store. Annie was finally rebuilding the inn. Without his help.

He'd just decided to walk over to the new cabins when Irma opened the front door and beckoned him inside, delight showing on her plain face. A welcome change after Lyndsey's constant sour expression.

"Come see what I found," Irma said before he'd reached the porch.

She scurried ahead of him, across the parlor and up the stairs, taking him to the tiny third bedroom that wasn't being used. A tattered cardboard box lay in the middle of the empty floor.

"I was cleaning in here, haven't given it a thorough top to bottom yet, when I found this on the closet shelf, shoved clear in the back."

"What's in it?" He lifted one of the flaps.

"Film reels. From the show."

Glimpsing the contents, Sam knelt beside the box, his heart beating faster.

Irma bent at the waist and braced her hands on her knees. "I took a quick peek, then came running to fetch you."

He was almost afraid to pick up the fragile, dust-covered film reels for fear they'd break. Curiosity overruled caution, and he removed the top one. It felt sturdier than it looked.

"They must have been in there all along. Forty years or more," Irma continued. "Aren't those pictures underneath?"

There were indeed photographs. Black-and-whites. A hundred at least. Sam dug carefully beneath the reels and extracted two. They featured the show's main cast members, including Granny Orla's lover, wearing street clothes. They were lounging in front of the ranch house, having a laugh, their handsome faces split by generous smiles.

"I wonder what's on the reels?" Irma's hushed voice echoed in the empty room.

"Outtakes, maybe. Unused footage."

"Must be worth a fortune."

"I doubt it. Probably worth no more than sentimental value. If the film is even viewable."

Sam considered the benefits of having it restored. Once they reopened the house for tours, visitors might enjoy watching the old footage on a closed-circuit TV. And the photographs could be added to the ones already hanging on the walls. Unless…

He flipped over one of the pictures. No name, no copyright stamp. Would that be a problem? Could they legally display the photos or show the film without permission?

"I'm going to have our secretary in California do some investigating. Try and locate anyone involved in the production of *The Forty-Niners*." Another task to complete when he returned.

"Isn't that Granny Orla?" Irma exclaimed.

"You're right."

Sam extracted the photo Irma was pointing at. The glowingly happy young woman could be none other than Annie's grandmother. She was wrapped in the arms of the TV star. The grainy quality and weathered finish of the photo didn't diminish the fact they were head over heels in love.

"Whatever happened to him?" Sam mused aloud.

"His wife took ill right after the series wrapped up. Breast cancer, they say. Terminal. He went home to Hollywood to be with her."

"I didn't realize he was married."

"It wasn't a secret. Not really. Supposedly he and his wife had an ~~arrangement~~. They were both stars and married because it benefitted their careers. After she passed, he came back and begged Granny Orla to marry him. She said no."

"Why? Was she afraid of a scandal?"

"Like that would have bothered Granny." Irma harrumphed. "She didn't want to leave Sweetheart. You know how those Hennessy women are. Married to the inn." She abruptly slapped a hand over her mouth. "Sorry about that, Sam. No offense."

"None taken. From what I've heard, men who love the Hennessy women don't tend to stick around long."

"It's the curse."

"Do you really believe that nonsense?"

"Must be some reason none of them has married their true love."

Break it. Break the curse.

Sam suddenly wanted that more than his next breath. But Annie would have to want to break the curse, too.

"Have you heard about the Sweetheart Memorial?" Irma asked, straightening.

"The what?" Sam rose, balancing the box of film reels in his arms.

"I wondered if Annie mentioned it to you. She's building a memorial to the town. On her family's land."

Sam almost dropped the box. "What about the inn?"

"They decided not to rebuild."

"Not rebuild?" How could that be? The inn meant the world to Annie.

He needed to see her. Right away. Hammer some sense into her. If she'd even agree to see him.

Irma waited for him at the top of the stairs. "They already have a huge collection for the memorial. At the chapel. You should see it. Mayor Dempsey's formed a committee. If you don't want all those pictures and film reels, I'm sure the committee would."

"Is Annie by chance on the committee?"

"Course. She's in charge of construction."

And the committee might want the film reels.

"You know, Irma, that's a really great suggestion." Sam felt better than he had in eight days. "Remind me to give you a raise."

"Won't hear me object." She practically danced down the stairs ahead of him. "I'll take the box for you. I'm stopping by the chapel on the way home. Me and Carrie are both helping out. Annie will be by later, too."

Irma's suggestion was getting better by the minute.

"Not necessary. I'll do it and meet you there."

In the kitchen, Sam checked the time. Annie would be off work soon.

"If you don't need me anymore," Irma said, "I'll grab my kids and head home."

"They're in the barn. I'll go with you."

Sam stopped first at his truck and loaded the box. In the barn, Irma collected her children, leaving Sam and Lyndsey alone. She was cleaning out the goats' stall. Sylvester the cat observed from atop a grain barrel.

Sam liked having all the animals around. The only one missing was a dog.

There were plenty of dogs at the ranch in California. They could bring one back with them—if they were to settle here for good.

"Hey, there."

Lyndsey continued to ignore him. She might only be a child but she could hold a grudge with the best of them.

"I thought maybe you'd like to take a trip with me."

"Where?" she asked grumpily without looking up.

"To the Sweetheart Memorial. To see Annie." He grabbed the empty kits' cage, which leaned against the wall. "And return this."

That got her attention. And the smile he'd been waiting for.

Sam was smiling pretty wide himself.

"Sam! Hello." Pleasure resounded in Mayor Dempsey's voice.

Startled, Annie dropped the polishing cloth she'd been using. As of yesterday, she might have resented Sam's unexpected appearance in the chapel basement. Instead, a jolt of anticipation raced through her, reminding her of the day he'd returned to Sweetheart.

Of the first time they'd met.

Finding the photo album and deciding to use the insurance settlement for a memorial had changed her perspective. About a lot of things.

She loved Sam. Had always loved him. Marriage to Gary changed nothing. Neither had losing the inn or Sam buying the Gold Nugget.

Annie was like all the Hennessy women, utterly and completely devoted to one man. For her grandmother, it had been the TV star. For her mother, it was Annie's father.

She rose and set aside the leather horse collar she'd been cleaning. What was Sam doing here anyway? And he'd brought Lyndsey with him.

The girl ran over to Annie, only to stop short a few feet in front of her.

"Are you mad at me, too?" she asked in a small voice.

"Why would you ever think that?" Annie opened her arms.

Lyndsey flew into them. "Can I call you when I'm in California?"

"As often as you want."

"We brought some stuff for the memorial."

"Oh?" Annie hadn't noticed Sam holding a cardboard box. She'd seen only him.

Their gazes connected, and she tried to gauge what lay behind his. He revealed little. Funny, she was usually the guarded one.

"Can I look around?" Lyndsey asked.

"Sure, just be careful and don't touch anything without permission."

"Come along, dear." Granny took charge of Lyndsey.

Which left Annie with no barriers between her and Sam. He continued to stare at her to the point where Annie became self-conscious.

"If I were you," Granny whispered loudly from across two crowded tables, "I wouldn't let that man get away for a third time."

A peek at Sam confirmed he'd heard. Annie's cheeks flamed at his amused smile. This was absolutely the last time she was taking her grandmother anywhere.

The mayor beckoned her over. "Annie, you have to see what Sam brought. You, too, Granny."

"Hurry," her grandmother encouraged when Annie dawdled.

"Yeah, hurry," Lyndsey echoed.

Annie meandered over, her calm exterior hiding the bundle of nerves that had become her stomach. When she would have stood next to the mayor, Granny squeezed by, leaving Annie no choice but to occupy the vacant space beside Sam.

She became intensely aware of his proximity. The fresh outdoor scent that clung to him, more intoxicating than any cologne. The warmth radiating off his skin. The pull of attraction impossible to resist.

No longer unreadable, his expression reflected a longing that her rapidly beating heart answered.

"This is simply incredible." The mayor had her head buried inside the box and was gushing over its contents. "What do you suppose is on these?" She came up for air, a wheel-shaped object clutched in her hands.

Annie was no expert, but she guessed it to be a reel of film. The other committee members had started to gather around as well.

"It's from *The Forty-Niners,*" Sam said. "Or, so we think."

"I found the box in the back of a closet shelf." Irma brushed her fingers along the side of the box, leaving lines in the thick dust.

"This is quite a discovery." The mayor handled the reel of film as if it were a priceless artifact.

"There are some photographs, too." Sam reached into the box for one. "You may want this." He passed the picture to Granny.

She gasped softly. "My word! Can't believe I was ever that young."

Annie studied the photo, mesmerized. The closest she'd seen her grandmother in love was when she reminisced about those days. Here it was in black-and-white.

What Annie would give to experience a love like that. Experience it again. With Sam.

Only he was leaving. In a matter of days, according to her mother.

He might delay his departure if she asked him.

Finding out would put Annie at risk. If she was mistaken, she'd be in for another loss. One she might not recover from. Annie stepped back.

"Can I have this?" Granny Orla asked Sam.

"You should go through the box. Take as many as you want."

"What about the film reels?" The mayor had yet to relinquish the one she held.

"I'm hoping to have them restored and transferred to a more durable media. And if there's no copyright issue, I'll show the film to tourists at the ranch. Same with the photographs. Add a few to the ones already hanging in the parlor. The rest..." He paused and didn't continue until Annie looked at him. "The rest are for the memorial."

The distance she'd placed between them magically narrowed. When he next spoke, they were inches apart.

"What you're doing," he said, "donating your land and the insurance money for the memorial, it's pretty wonderful. And very brave."

"I'm glad to do it."

"Won't you miss the inn?"

"Working for the NDF isn't so bad. At least I don't have to deal with cranky guests all day long."

"You're making a huge sacrifice. Your family, too."

"Fiona likes working at the ranch," Granny Orla interjected. "So don't you be laying her off anytime soon."

"No fear of that. Who else would run the place for me? Unless you're willing to come out of retirement."

She dismissed him with a wave. "Not much of that. Though I might be talked into volunteering at the memorial now and then. Being old does have its advantages. Aren't many folks who know more of the town's history than me."

"What about giving tours at the ranch house?" Sam asked. "When we reopen it to the public. Like Mrs. Litey used to."

"I'm not up to a full-time job. These joints of mine give me too much grief."

"However many hours you want. I'm flexible."

"I'd like that." Joy spread across her face. "I've had my fill of cranky guests, too."

"I can't vouch for the tourists who will visit the ranch," Sam said.

"If they're fans of the show, we'll get along fine."

"I want to help give tours," Lyndsey piped up.

"You can be my assistant." Granny put an affectionate arm around the girl. "When you visit."

"Daddy, can't we stay longer? Please."

"Maybe. I need to talk to Annie first." If only they weren't surrounded by people.

"You've done so much for me and my family," she said. "I'm running out of ways to say thank-you."

His mouth curved up at the corners in a sexy grin. "I can think of one or two."

So could she. "We could talk, I suppose."

"That, too." He lowered his head.

"Wait!" She placed her hands flat on his chest.

"Why? No one's watching."

She looked over in time to see Granny Orla ushering everyone up the basement stairs. She and Sam were alone.

When he pulled her into his arms and kissed her hungrily, she gladly and freely let go of her remaining doubts and insecurities. Whatever challenges lay ahead, they would conquer them together.

"I thought I'd lost you," he said, dragging his mouth away from hers.

"Me, too."

Another kiss, this one stealing her breath. "I swear to you, Annie Hennessy, I won't disappoint you." He kept her tucked inside the circle of his arms. "I'm here for the long haul."

"If not, I'd have to chase after you to California."

"You'd do that?"

"I'm here for the long haul, too." She pressed closer to him.

"Your mom and Granny Orla are happy in the apartment. Why don't you keep it for them?"

"But we found a bigger place."

He rested his chin on the top of her head. "I want you and Nessa to live with me at the Gold Nugget."

"Sam…"

"Think about it, at least. There's plenty of room. More when the cabin's built. You've always wanted the ranch. Now you can have it. And me."

She cupped his cheek with her hand. "I wouldn't move there just for the ranch."

"God, I hope not."

"It's a big decision."

"Let me sweeten the pot." He took her hand and turned it palm up, then kissed the sensitive center. "Marry me, Annie Hennessy."

"Sam!"

"Today. Tomorrow. As soon as possible. The mayor can perform the ceremony."

"We can't get married on the spot."

"Sure we can. This is Sweetheart, Nevada. A place where people have married on the spot for generations."

She laughed. A giddy, light-headed sort of laugh. "You're crazy, you know."

"I've wanted to marry you from the moment I saw you riding that bike on Cohea Ridge."

She didn't think her feelings for Sam could grow. But they did, filling every corner of her heart.

"Let's not waste any more time," he said. "I want to be a family. You, me, Lyndsey and Nessa. Maybe one more. I wouldn't mind a boy."

"Slow down! Let's not get too far ahead of ourselves."

"You don't want more children?"

She softened. "There's nothing I'd like more than to have a child with you. But we have a guest ranch to build."

"The best working guest ranch in the entire western United States," Sam boasted.

Well, he deserved to boast.

"We'll pass it on to our children," she said. "Along with the memorial."

"Deal. There won't be just one heart of Sweetheart, there'll be two. Yours and mine."

"You drive a hard bargain."

"Say yes, Annie. I'll make you happy, I swear."

"I do like the menagerie you've collected. Especially the goats."

"I hate the goats."

"I know."

Taking his hand, she led him up the stairs and outside. The same crowd from below greeted them.

"Well?" Granny Orla demanded, hands on her hips. "Are you ready to make an honest woman out of my granddaughter?"

"Yeah." Lyndsey mimicked the older woman.

"Past ready," Sam assured them. "But she's dragging her feet."

"What's wrong with you, girl? Have you lost your marbles?"

Annie made them wait a few seconds longer before wrapping her arms around Sam's waist. "Yes, I'll marry you. Of course I will."

She lost track of the hugs and congratulations after that. Except for Lyndsey's. Hers was the most poignant.

"I always wanted a little sister," she said.

Annie melted on the spot.

Mayor Dempsey offered to host the reception, free of charge. More offers followed, for catering, flowers and decorations.

"When's the happy occasion?" the mayor asked.

"Soon, I hope."

Sam wasn't the only anxious one. The others were equally eager for the first wedding since the fire.

"Fine, fine." With an exaggerated groan, Annie caved to the pressure. "Three weeks from Saturday."

"Three weeks?" Sam's grin collapsed.

"After the cattle roundup. You have to go back for that."

"We'll get married first. Then I'll leave."

"Sam!"

"For crying out loud," Granny Orla grumbled. "Put the poor man out of his misery."

"Two weeks from Saturday then."

"This Saturday," Sam insisted. "And you and Nessa fly back with Lyndsey and me for the roundup."

Before Annie quite knew what was happening, her wedding date was decided.

Sam pulled Irma aside. "Can you give Granny a ride home and watch Lyndsey for a while?"

"Take your time. No hurrying on my account."

Granny kissed Sam soundly on the cheek before leaving with Irma. "Welcome to the family, son."

Sam immediately steered Annie to his truck.

"Where are we going?"

"To celebrate. At the ranch."

Instead of taking her inside the house, they headed to the barn and up to the loft.

There, atop a pile of fresh, sweet-smelling hay, they reminisced about the past, planned for the future and made incredible love.

Well after dark, Sam returned Annie home so they could break the news to her mother and Nessa. At the door to the apartment, he stopped her in order to pluck a few stray stalks of hay from her hair and apparently missed a few.

Fiona noticed and commented. Annie was too happy to care.

Epilogue

Annie stood at the top of the stairs, one hand resting on the banister, the other clutching a bouquet of fresh-picked wildflowers. At the bottom of the stairs, her grandmother waited, smiling brilliantly. She was there to walk Annie down the aisle.

The aisle, such as it was, consisted of the short distance across the parlor, between two dozen white folding chairs. Her and Sam's closest friends and family occupied the chairs. Later, during the reception at the Paydirt Saloon, half the town was expected to show up.

It seemed fitting, marrying Sam—the love of her life—here, at the Gold Nugget. A place important to them both. A place they'd always loved. Where their future and those of their children stretched ahead of them.

Hard to imagine, seven weeks ago, that she and Sam had met again on these very stairs, only then he had stood at the top and she at the bottom. So much had happened in that incredibly short time. And, yet, they were where they should be: at the end of a journey that had started eleven years earlier.

Annie descended the stairs. Stepping daintily from the last step, she linked arms with her grandmother.

"Nervous?"

"No. This is one of the best days of my life."

"That's my girl." Granny Orla patted Annie's hand. "You look stunning."

"Thank you."

The dress had been loaned to her by the school principal's wife. Mayor Dempsey was officiating the ceremony. The decorations were courtesy of the Sweetheart Memorial committee members. Lyndsey's and Nessa's frilly flower girl dresses had been sewn in record time by Linda Lee. *Linda Lee,* not Gary's new wife.

Having finally found her own happy ending, Annie wished nothing but the best for her ex. He deserved more than she'd ever been able to give him.

Everyone stood as she entered the parlor, their faces beaming. Annie had invited the head of the wildlife refuge where Daffy Duck and Porky Pig resided, the pair now fat, healthy raccoon cubs. Lyndsey would be volunteering there once or twice a month with Gus. She'd recently proclaimed she wanted to be a veterinarian when she grew up. Living Annie's dream.

Annie had no problem with that. She was too content living her own dream.

Speaking of which...

The girls, adorable in their dresses with matching wildflower bouquets, stood beside Annie's mother, who served as her maid of honor. Sam's parents had flown in for the wedding, along with his brother, the best man. Also at the wedding was Lyndsey's grandfather.

Annie thought it must be difficult for him to watch his former son-in-law marry another woman. It was quite a testament to their friendship and the man's character.

She'd liked him instantly and, after noticing the interested and frequent glances between him and her mother, invited him back for a visit in the very near future.

Her gaze wandered to the makeshift altar near the large picture window. At the sight of Sam in his dress Western suit and polished black boots, her mind emptied of all save him. He was that same young man she'd first glimpsed on horseback, only incredibly more handsome.

Handing off her bouquet to her grandmother, she clasped hands with him.

To her shock and surprise, he hauled her against him and kissed her senseless.

The room let out a collective gasp, then erupted in whoops and hollers.

"Hey," the mayor protested with feigned irritation when the noise died down. "You have to wait till the I-pronounce-you-man-and-wife part before kissing your bride."

Sam looked longingly and lovingly into Annie's eyes. "I couldn't."

The mayor answered with a sparkle in her voice. "Considering how long it's taken the two of you to get here, I guess we can let you slide."

Sam kissed Annie again when the ceremony was over. Sweeping her up into his arms, he carried her over the threshold—not inside but outside. Onto the porch. There, he set her on her feet and enveloped her in the most exquisite of embraces.

"I love you, Mrs. Wyler."

Mrs. Wyler. That had a nice ring to it. "I love you, too."

"We're going to have an amazing life together."

She rose on tiptoes and pressed her lips to his, pouring all the love she'd felt for him into that single moment.

Annie would always miss her family's inn. But together she and Sam would build something even greater and of more importance. For the town, for their family and most especially for themselves.

* * * * *

SPECIAL EXCERPT FROM

HHARLEQUIN
SPECIAL EDITION

*Harrison McCord was sure he was the rightful owner
of the Dawson Family Ranch. And delivering Daisy
Dawson's baby on the side of the road was a mere
diversion. Still, when Daisy found out his intentions,
instead of pushing him away, she invited him in, figuring
he'd start to see her in a whole new light. But what if
she started seeing him that way, as well?*

*Read on for a sneak preview of the next
book in Melissa Senate's
Dawson Family Ranch miniseries,*
Wyoming Special Delivery.

Daisy went over to the bassinet and lifted out Tony,
cradling him against her. "Of course. There's lots
more video, but another time. The footage of what the
ranch looked like before Noah started rebuilding to the
day I helped put up the grand reopening banner—it's
amazing."

Harrison wasn't sure he wanted to see any of that. No,
he knew he didn't. This was all too much. "Well, I'll be
in touch about that tour."

*That's it. Keep it nice and impersonal. "Be in touch"
was a sure distance maker.*

She eyed him and lifted her chin. "Oh—I almost
forgot! I have a favor to ask, Harrison."

Gulp. How was he supposed to emotionally distance
himself by doing her a favor?

She smiled that dazzling smile. The one that drew him like nothing else could. "If you're not busy around five o'clock or so, I'd love your help in putting together the rocking cradle my brother Rex ordered for Tony. It arrived yesterday, and I tried to put it together, but it has directions a mile long that I can't make heads or tails of. Don't tell my brother Axcl I said this—he's a wizard at GPS, maps and terrain—but give him instructions and he holds the paper upside down."

Ah. This was almost a relief. He'd put together the cradle alone. No chitchat. No old family movies. Just him, a set of instructions and five thousand various pieces of cradle. "I'm actually pretty handy. Sure, I can help you."

"Perfect," she said. "See you at fiveish."

A few minutes later, as he stood on the porch watching her walk back up the path, he had a feeling he was at a serious disadvantage in this deal.

Because the farther away she got, the more he wanted to chase after her and just keep talking. Which sent off serious warning bells. That Harrison might actually more than just like Daisy Dawson already—and it was only day one of the deal.

Don't miss
Wyoming Special Delivery *by Melissa Senate,*
available April 2020 wherever
Harlequin Special Edition books and ebooks are sold.

Harlequin.com

SPECIAL EXCERPT FROM

LOVE INSPIRED SUSPENSE
INSPIRATIONAL ROMANCE

A murder that closely resembles a cold case from twenty years ago puts Brooklyn, New York, on edge. Can the K-9 Unit track down the killer or killers?

Read on for a sneak preview of
Copycat Killer *by Laura Scott,*
the first book in the exciting new
True Blue K-9 Unit: Brooklyn series,
available April 2020 from Love Inspired Suspense.

Willow Emery approached her brother and sister-in-law's two-story home in Brooklyn, New York, with a deep sense of foreboding. The white paint on the front door of the yellow-brick building was cracked and peeling, the windows covered with grime. She swallowed hard, hating that her three-year-old niece, Lucy, lived in such deplorable conditions.

Steeling her resolve, she straightened her shoulders. This time, she wouldn't be dissuaded so easily. Her older brother, Alex, and his wife, Debra, had to agree that Lucy deserved better.

Squeak. Squeak. The rusty gate moving in the breeze caused a chill to ripple through her. Why was it open? She hurried forward and her stomach knotted when she found the front door hanging ajar. The tiny hairs on the back of her neck lifted in alarm and a shiver ran down her spine.

Something was wrong. Very wrong.

Thunk. The loud sound startled her. Was that a door closing? Or something worse? Her heart pounded in her chest and her mouth went dry. Following her gut instincts, Willow quickly pushed the front door open and crossed the threshold. Bile rose in her throat as she strained to listen. "Alex? Lucy?"

There was no answer, only the echo of soft hiccuping sobs.

"Lucy!" Reaching the living room, she stumbled to an abrupt halt, her feet seemingly glued to the floor. Lucy was kneeling near her mother, crying. Alex and Debra were lying facedown, unmoving and not breathing, blood seeping out from beneath them.

Were those bullet holes between their shoulder blades? *No! Alex!* A wave of nausea had her placing a hand over her stomach.

Remembering the thud gave her pause. She glanced furtively over her shoulder toward the single bedroom on the main floor. The door was closed. What if the gunman was still here? Waiting? Hiding?

Don't miss
Copycat Killer *by Laura Scott,*
available April 2020 wherever
Love Inspired Suspense books and ebooks are sold.

LoveInspired.com

LISEXP0320

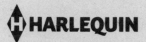

HARLEQUIN

Heartfelt or suspenseful, inspiring or passionate, Harlequin has your happily-ever-after.

With new books published every month, you are sure to find the satisfying escape you know you deserve.

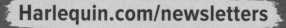
HNEWS2020